'*Out of Breath* is a dream of a n
deeply felt and thrilling, with
The exotic cast of characters, the diving, the atmosphere of
freedom and the thrum of impending disaster … I genuinely
could not put it down. It will appeal to anyone who loves
intelligent character-led suspense. I both tore through the
pages, desperate to find out what happens, and languished
in the story, never wanting it to end. Wonderful.'

—Anna Downes, internationally bestselling
author of *The Safe Place*

'*Out of Breath* is an atmospheric, perfectly paced and
emotionally gripping novel. Through Jo's story we are taken
to the remote coastal region of Australia, a place bursting
with contrasts of darkness and light, earth and water. With
great skill, Snoekstra conjures the startling landscapes and
inner turmoils of her characters: the deep ocean diving and
burning sun act as potent metaphors for those who hope to
escape their dark and troubled pasts, only to find that they
can only ever rise again to the surface.'

—Katherine Brabon, Vogel Award winning author of
The Memory Artist and *The Shut Ins*

'I read this book quickly, and felt close to the protagonist, Jo,
from the very first page. She is a complex, bruised, lovable
character, and I wanted to see where she was going, and what
she was running towards. *Out of Breath* is so readable because
it's so believable, despite the unthinkable twists and turns.
Snoekstra has managed to create an atmosphere that stands
the hairs and feels as close as skin, without taking us beyond

what we understand and know. This book is about human nature, in all its manifestations, and it paints something scary and stark and hopeful.'

—Laura McPhee-Browne, Glenda Adams
Award winning author of *Cherry Beach*

'*Out of Breath* is a pacy, layered thriller with a troubled and traumatised woman at its heart. Gorgeous writing. Sinister, smart and totally riveting.'

—Laura Elvery, Fair Australian Prize winning
author of *Ordinary Matter*

'Snoekstra's excellent debut stands out in the crowded psychological suspense field with smart, subtle red herrings and plenty of dark and violent secrets.'

—*Library Journal* (starred review)
on *Only Daughter*

'In Anna Snoekstra's dark and edgy debut, a young woman slips easily into the life of a girl missing eleven years, only to discover the grisly truth behind the disappearance … Truly distinctive and tautly told, *Only Daughter* welcomes a thrilling new voice in crime fiction.'

—Mary Kubica, *New York Times* bestselling
author of *The Good Girl*

'*Only Daughter* is a dark meditation on the secrets we keep about our families and about ourselves. Twisty, slippery, and full of surprises, this web of lies will ensnare you and keep you riveted until you've turned the final page.'

—Lisa Unger, *New York Times* bestselling
author of *Ink and Bone*

'Unreliable narrator thrillers are practically a subgenre of their own, and there are two unreliable narrators here as well as a wickedly twisted and fast-paced plot that leaves numerous questions unanswered … readers who enjoy a creepy thriller that will keep them guessing will be unable to put this down.'

—*Booklist* (starred review) on *Only Daughter*

'*Little Secrets* is both twisty and twisted, a portrait of the ugly secrets simmering in a dying town. Snoekstra writes an original tale that is mysterious and dark but also touching and true.'

—Janelle Brown, *New York Times* bestselling author of *Watch Me Disappear*

'A smart and compulsive psychological thriller. I couldn't put it down!'

—Graeme Simsion, *New York Times* bestselling author of *The Rosie Project*, on *Little Secrets*

'A story of high school grudges and revenge wrapped up as a crime thriller, Snoekstra's latest will appeal to fans of *The Trap* and *Gone Girl*.'

—*Books + Publishing* on *The Spite Game*

'*The Spite Game* is a clever, gripping tale of the demons that we carry throughout our lives, and the damage they can cause if we fail to let them go.'

—*Better Reading*

Photo by Samantha Iliov

Anna Snoekstra is the author of *Only Daughter, Little Secrets* and *The Spite Game*. Her novels have been published in over twenty countries and sixteen languages. She has written for *The Guardian, Meanjin, The Griffith Review, Lindsay, LitHub* and *The Saturday Paper*. Her first audio drama, *This Isn't Happening*, is out with Audible in late 2022.

Also by Anna Snoekstra

Only Daughter
Little Secrets
Mercy Point
The Spite Game

OUT OF
BREATH

ANNA SNOEKSTRA

First Published 2022
First Australian Paperback Edition 2022
ISBN 9781867231646

OUT OF BREATH
© 2022 by Anna Snoekstra
Australian Copyright 2022
New Zealand Copyright 2022

Published by
HQ Fiction
An imprint of Harlequin Enterprises (Australia) Pty Limited (ABN 47 001 180 918), a subsidiary of HarperCollins Publishers Australia Pty Limited (ABN 36 009 913 517)
Level 13, 201 Elizabeth St
SYDNEY NSW 2000
AUSTRALIA

® and TM (apart from those relating to FSC®) are trademarks of Harlequin Enterprises (Australia) Pty Limited or its corporate affiliates. Trademarks indicated with ® are registered in Australia, New Zealand and in other countries.

A catalogue record for this book is available from the National Library of Australia www.librariesaustralia.nla.gov.au

Printed and bound in Australia by McPherson's Printing Group

For the magnificent Phoebe Baker

PART ONE

CHAPTER 1

SYDNEY, SEPTEMBER 2018

Sydney looks nothing like the places where Jo grew up. The first few years of her life in the village of St Ives shone in pastels: mint green and warm cream and the iced aquamarine of the bay. Then Chesterfield, the colours washed out and muddied. London could be captured in monochrome; even the water of the Thames looked more grey than blue for most of the year.

There's something about the quality of light in Australia that's different to anywhere else. Jo can't place why exactly, but it makes colours more saturated.

The bus pulls in for a stop and Jo is crammed further into the window as more passengers get on. It's a hot day, the air on board soupy with body heat. Sweat itches her face and her t-shirt sticks to her back. A woman with a baby presses up next to her. Jo grins at the infant, who hides its eyes under the edge of the carrier.

They turn a corner, and this is it, this is the reason Jo loves catching the bus even though it stinks of BO. She watches Sydney Harbour stretch out, postcard perfect. All silvers and blues and stark whites. The baby peeks around the carrier again, smiling this time. She pulls a face at it and it giggles and everything feels so right. She's finished a long shift at the café and now she's on her way to her second job and she's exhausted but still, she is filled up. She's going to make this life work. This is going to be her place, her home, for keeps.

Jo presses the stop button and weaves her way through elbows and backpacks, steps out onto the street right in front of the pub where she hosts her trivia nights.

*

Jo sits on a stool at the edge of the bar, checking the trivia results from the first round. She goes down the list with her red pen, marking ticks or crosses next to each line and tallying the results.

'Beer?' the bartender asks her over the taps.

'Just a soda water.'

'Course.'

She likes pubs in Australia much more than the ones back home. In England, the pubs felt closer, darker. They were always too warm with their cranking heaters and open fireplaces. The pubs here have high ceilings, cement floors. They keep the doors open because the air outside is balmy and the sun doesn't set until eight pm.

The bartender gives her the soda water, a wedge of lime straddling the rim of the glass.

'Cheers.' Jo holds the papers under her arm and slides off the stool. She likes to see the different groups who turn up to her trivia nights. She speculates at what binds each team. Sitting by the window is a couple who come every week. They usually score last, since they are only two compared to the teams of six or seven, but it doesn't seem to bother them. They put their heads together, whisper answers to one another, laugh private laughs. She gives them their sheet and they thank her.

There is another regular group who sits at the long table in the centre of the room. Work colleagues, Jo assumes. Their team name is *Jane's got the number* and every time she reads it out they laugh.

'We're winning, right?' one of the guys asks as she approaches. His t-shirt is a dark red, bringing out the pink in his nose, the freckles on his hands. It had taken Jo a while to get used to people's skin in Australia. Even for the average person, it is more weathered, it tells more of a story. It's the sun, bringing everything to the surface.

'You'll see,' she says. They are, by a mile. She hands them their sheet and they crowd over it. All except one woman, who doesn't check to see how they scored. She's wearing bright lipstick and seems uncomfortable. Her shoulders are stiff. Jo didn't see her here last week. There is often someone like this in a group, someone who knew none of the answers and felt more and more like an idiot as the game progressed. Round by round, Jo would see their eyes glaze over as their focus turned inward.

Now, she smiles at the woman over the heads of the others. The woman seems surprised and smiles back in a pained sort of way.

Jo passes out the rest of the sheets. Up close, she can see the group near the door are related. The same green eyes, some lined with wrinkles, smile at her as she drops the sheet. The table in the corner all have beards. The group in their early twenties on the far wall have tattoos that are so new they look like they've been drawn on their smooth forearms and thighs with felt-tip markers.

She has one sheet left in her hands. It's for Eric's team, but their seats are empty. Their dinner plates haven't been cleared yet, massacres of tomato sauce on porcelain under scrunched-up napkins. She leaves their sheet in the centre of the table. Goes to find them outside.

The dimming evening air is cool enough to wake her up a little. She stopped taking her sleeping pills a few weeks ago and her insomnia is back. It's not as torturous this time. She used to lay awake with her uncertainty spinning the room. Now, lying next to Eric, she thinks about their future. It grounds her.

His group is sitting at a wooden table in the beer garden, smoking. Ashwan, Alice, Briena and Eric. They fit together too, in a way that isn't as easy to identify. It's something in the confidence of their laughs, the way they gesticulate with their cigarettes. The concavity of their shoulders from too long hunching over academic journals.

On their first date, Eric had first told her that his PhD was on the commodity culture of cult television. She'd thought he was joking. He'd been offended when she'd laughed.

'You need to put rice on it,' Eric is saying to Ashwan, who shares his office space at the university.

'Nah, don't do that, it gets under your keyboard. Then every time you hit a key it crunches. It's awful.'

'Didn't you use quinoa or something that time?'

'Nah, bulgur wheat. Stupid.'

'I already dried it anyway, and it's working.'

Eric puts an arm around Jo as she slots in next to him. 'How'd you dry it?'

'Just with a fucking towel.'

They laugh at that. Then Briena takes the sheet from Jo, but doesn't bother checking how they did. Briena is her only real friend here in Sydney. When Jo realised she wasn't going to make rent just from her trivia nights, Briena got her a job at the café where she works. Briena dropped out of her Arts PhD in her first year and now she's putting herself through law school making coffee.

'Eric, can you please convince Jo not to go to Broome? She has no clue what she's in for.'

Jo laughs. It's endearing how close anger and kindness are for Briena.

'I can't convince her to do anything she doesn't want to do.'

That's not true. And anyway, Jo no longer has any intention of going to Broome. She can't.

Alice blows out her smoke, smiles. 'I went on a road trip around there, I don't know, six years ago. With Lauren when we first started going out.'

'That's a way to break the ice,' Eric says. He holds his cigarette out, away from the group. Its smoke dissolves into the greying sky. There is an elegance to the bend of his wrist.

'What was it like?' Jo asks.

'So beautiful.'

Jo knows that, she's googled it. Red dirt, huge blue skies. It didn't look like anywhere she'd been before.

'Yeah, but it's isolated, right?' Briena says. 'And there's some absolute creeps out there.'

Alice thinks about it. Fiddles with her bottom lip, running a finger along it like she's remembering a kiss. 'So we were driving around in a four-wheel drive, you know, camping along the way. It was always fine, really nice, but this one night we were at a campground and there wasn't anyone else. It was kind of cool, like we were the only people in the world. The sky was so big, huge, like you wouldn't believe. But then this guy showed up in his car. People are usually so friendly out there. But he, I don't know, the energy just changed. He didn't come say hi or anything. He stayed in his car, parked far away in the shadows of a tree. All night he didn't come out, just sat in his car. We suddenly felt so aware of ourselves, you know? Two women by ourselves. We hadn't felt that before then. We left as soon as it got light.'

'Creepy,' Briena says.

Alice raises her eyebrows. 'Was probably nothing.'

'I'd guess he was hiding out from the cops or something.' Briena holds Jo's eye, face serious. 'That's why people go out there you know—to disappear.' She grins at Eric. 'You guys should get married. A visa wedding would be so much fun. Then she wouldn't have to go.'

Jo tries to feel Eric's reaction next to her. Did he stiffen? Did he pull away at all? They are meant to be talking about this later tonight.

'It could just be a party,' Briena insists.

'Are you proposing to my girlfriend for me?'

'She's awesome, why wouldn't you want to?'

'I'm right here,' Jo says.

'Why are you going so far out?' Ashwan asks.

'I don't want to go so far. I don't want to go at all, you don't need to convince me.' She looks pointedly at Briena, then back to Ashwan. 'It was the only place that agreed to take me.'

A 'cultural exchange' they call it, but she knows it's about cheap labour. Still, eighty-eight days wasn't that long. Eighty-eight days and she'd come back and her life would return to normal, or at least that was what the plan had been. When she'd first started applying, she'd been excited. A new adventure, a whole new experience. She'd see the other side of Australia. The Australia with farmers and kangaroos, not skyscrapers and arseholes in suits.

But everything is different now.

'Isn't there some place you can do it that's a bit closer? I mean, the Kimberley is, what, two flights away? Eight hours?' Ashwan asks.

'The ones that were closer were mostly hostels. If you stay there they find you work, apparently. But I don't want to stay in a hostel for three months with a bunch of English people.'

'Jo isn't very patriotic,' Eric says, his arm still around her, fingers fiddling with the ends of her hair.

'I guess I'm not. I was on a bus with a group of them on the weekend. God, they were horrible. All drunk.' She laughs, remembering the lads with shaved heads and dumb laughs, the pitchy screams of the drunk girls with crap fake tans. She had felt mortified on their behalf. It was like she was back in England.

'You know what I heard one of them say? This girl, prissiest girl you'd ever seen, she screams, "I was so shocked I could feel me stomach falling out of me arsehole." I mean, bloody hell. Way to give the English a bad name.'

'You call people like that chavs, right?' Eric asks.

Jo stiffens. 'I hate it when people use that word.'

'Chavs?'

'It's classist.'

Eric pulls his arm away. 'Nah, I don't know,' he says, 'it's like saying bogans here.'

'That's classist too.'

'You can have rich bogans.'

'Yeah, but the fact you have to qualify it with "rich" says it all. Like they've got new money, but they are still low class.'

Eric shakes his head. 'You don't get it.'

He likes to say that. They've been together eight months now and she is getting to know all his habits, the little tells that let her know when he is irritated, upset, nervous. She is about to reply when her stomach buckles. She takes a breath, has a sip of soda water, feels the bubbles shimmer down her throat.

'Where are you from in England, anyway?' Alice asks. 'For some reason I always just think everyone from England is from London.'

'I was born in St Ives, actually. It's kind of an English coastal holiday town. Then I went to live with my dad in Chester-field when I was seven, which is in the East Midlands—' she laughs, '—and definitely not a tourist town.'

She hopes they won't ask why she went to live with her dad. She is feeling too sick to lie well.

'But you did live in London,' Eric interjects before anyone gets the chance. He likes to tell people she's a painter, rather than the truth, which was that she is a failed painter. An art school dropout. She hasn't picked up a brush in over a year and she is glad of it.

'Yeah. I studied in London for a bit before I moved here. Anyway, next round is starting in five.'

'Are we losing?' Ashwan asks, looking over Briena's shoulder at their sheet.

She stands, grabs her glass. 'It's the fun of playing that counts, right?'

*

With the microphone in her hand, Jo finds it easy to control the room. She's halfway through the last round. Everyone's heads are bent over their papers, whispering answers at one another. She's done the music round, and everyone sang along to everything from Blink-182 to Marilyn Monroe. She loves that she has this power, to unify not only teams but to bring a whole room of strangers together, create a feeling of joy from their shared experiences. Now it's the general knowledge round.

'The southern hemisphere is: A, ten per cent land and ninety per cent ocean. B, twenty per cent land and eighty per cent ocean. C, thirty per cent land and seventy per cent ocean. Or D, forty per cent land and sixty per cent ocean.'

Over at *Jane's got the number* she can hear them hissing at each other.

'I have no idea. Do you know?'

'It's a stupid question.'

'I think it's twenty.' It's the woman speaking, the one with the bright lipstick who had seemed on the outer earlier.

'Are you sure? I don't know if trivia is your strong suit, to be honest.'

'I swear I read it somewhere,' she says. 'Maybe I'm wrong.'

The woman sits back, looks away. Jo catches her eye and says into the microphone, 'Trust your instincts,' then smiles.

The woman sits up again. 'It's twenty, I'm sure.' The glaze has gone from her eyes. She's in it now, bent forward, whispering.

Jo moves away to read the next question. Her stomach jabs again. She grits her teeth. 'Alright, let's make this a power round.'

*

Jo holds the edge of the sink. Her head is spinning, her stomach writhing. She takes a breath, slow, in and out. She hears someone come in. Briena. She straightens, attempts a smile at her, expects Briena to walk past into a stall, but she comes up to her.

'You've seen this, right?' Briena pulls up something on her phone, hands it over.

Jo's hands are trembling. She pushes her hip into the sink, tries to steady herself.

It's an article in *The Guardian*. Jo has already seen it. She turns the screen off. She doesn't want to see that photograph—the dark-eyed woman with her dark-eyed daughter, smiling in a suburban driveway. Larissa and Nika Makos. Larissa had left her husband, was driving across the top end of Australia to her parents' house. She and her daughter had been missing for two months now. The woman, the little girl and the silver Honda, gobbled up by all that red dirt and nothingness.

'I know you think I'm being pushy, but it's like *Wolf Creek*. Seriously, you have no idea.'

Jo wants to scream that she doesn't want to go, tell Briena to stop making it worse. Instead she says, 'They were hours away from where I'm going.'

'Yeah, but hours are nothing. It's a fucking desert. What if your farmer is the one who did it?'

'What? And they're buried underneath the mango farm?'

Briena leans against the sink. 'Possible.'

'You've been listening to too many true crime podcasts.'

'I know. I can't even walk my dog any more without getting freaked out.'

Jo gives Briena her phone. 'You don't need to worry about me.'

Briena eyes her. 'You okay?'

'Yeah.'

'You look exhausted.'

'I haven't been sleeping.'

'I thought you had pills for that?'

'Yeah, but I'm taking a break from them. I'm okay, honestly.'

'You always say that, even when you're not.'

'Do I?'

'Yeah. Plus, you aren't drinking.'

'So?'

'Are you down or something?'

'You're talking as though I'm a pisshead.'

'Well ...' Briena is grinning. Then she stretches her back out, cricks her neck. 'Whatever. If you're fine, you're fine. I mean, I'm pretty bloody tired too. The café all day, that woman who kept bringing her coffee back for you to make it hotter. How many times did you remake that bloody latte?'

'I'm pregnant.'

Jo claps a hand to her mouth. She hadn't meant to say it. The words had just tumbled out. She laughs. It's a little hysterical.

Briena gapes. 'Really? Or are you fucking with me?'

'I am. Not fucking with you. The other.'

'And … it's good? You're happy?'

Jo just nods. It isn't like she planned this, so it has surprised her how happy she is. All night she watches headlights from the cars on the street below slide along their bedroom wall and imagines this new firm future. A little family unit. She and Eric and their child. It would be a different life, a solid one, full of sacrifices and love and warmth. It feels like everything that she's experienced before—failing art school, her crap relationship with her tutor in London, the decision to come to Australia—all of it had a point. All of it led her here, to creating this child, to starting her real life.

Briena's eyes glint. She rubs them, smudging her brown eyeshadow. 'Okay. God. What did Eric say?'

'I haven't told him yet,' Jo says, 'but I will. We're going to talk tonight. I tried talking to him last night, but he had that presentation to do this morning and he said he was too distracted.'

Briena rests a light hand on her shoulder. 'How do you think he'll react?'

'I mean, it's not that crazy. The kids I went to high school with are basically grandparents now.' It's an exaggeration, but not by much. 'I'm twenty-seven. He's thirty. It's not like we're teenagers, although I know I still dress like one.' She looks at her band t-shirt, her black jeans.

Briena puts an arm around her. 'I don't think you dress like a teenager.'

*

On the drive home, Eric is quiet. Jo is driving, she often does even though it's his car because he can never help but have one drink too many. They stop at the intersection, the tail lights of the van in front of them washing Eric's face with a cold red. She's playing Olympia through the speakers, an Australian musician she's just discovered. The volume is low, but the sweet sound of the singer's voice fills the car. She sees it again, that family unit, Jo and Eric and their child. Walking to the bus stop together, slotting into each other's days, piling up on the couch at night.

'I wish you hadn't said that thing about being classist.'

She turns to him. He's still facing straight ahead at the back of the van in front of them. 'What? The thing about chavs?'

'You made it seem like I was a snob.'

'Did I?'

'Yeah. It was kind of embarrassing.'

'Oh. I don't think you're a snob, that's not what I was try-ing to say.'

He doesn't respond. The light turns green. She glances at him as she drives, trying to get a read on how annoyed he is.

'Sorry,' she says, although she doesn't mean it. She just doesn't want things to be tense later, when they are finally going to talk.

'It's fine. The whole night was kind of weird.'

'Weird how?'

'I don't know, all that stuff about a visa wedding. It was awkward.'

'It was just a passing comment.'

'Yeah, but then Briena laid into me again later on. It was so ridiculous.'

Her hands are sweaty on the wheel. She grips it tighter. 'I thought we would talk about this when we got home?'

'Yeah, we will.'

Silence again. She should wait until they get back. Sit down and tell him the situation. Talk about it when they are actually looking at each other.

'I mean, why is that so ridiculous, though?'

'What?' He laughs, but it's not his real laugh. 'Getting married? For a visa?'

'It's kind of romantic.'

'Come on,' he says, 'romance is bullshit. You always say that.'

'Yeah. Roses and candles and this idea of a woman being swept off her feet. That's bullshit. But I think getting married because you can't bear to be apart for three months, just saying "fuck it" and doing it, there's something kind of beautiful in that.'

'Really? I mean, marriage is an archaic institution, one that was used to capture women, to use them as property—'

'I know that. It's not what I mean.'

'I hate when you cut me off.'

She takes a breath; her stomach is twisting again. She thinks of them walking, their kid swinging between them, giggling.

'I just don't see how it could ever be romantic,' he continues. 'It seems pretty crazy to me that you, as a feminist, could think that way. And what? You want me to save you? A man to save you from going and having your own individual experience?'

'So, I would go have my individual experience and you would stay here and have your individual experience? Is that what you want?'

'Yes,' he says, 'exactly.' He takes her hand from the gear shift, holds it to his mouth, kisses it. 'And then when you get back we'll see where we are.'

He's so self-assured, so complete in his belief that he knows what the stakes are.

She keeps her eyes on the road. 'But we aren't individuals any more,' she says, 'or at least I'm not.'

'What do you mean?'

'I'm not just me. I'm pregnant.'

CHAPTER 2

'You've been in there ages, are you sick again?'

'I'm fine.'

Jo tries to breathe through the clenching of her throat. She dips a cloth in the water and rests it on her forehead. The warmth soaks through her eyelids. It's been almost three weeks since she told Eric she was pregnant and their relationship has shifted. His family have opened up to her, his mother calling her to talk about cribs and nappy bags and good muslin wraps, his dad texting photographs of Eric as a child, his older sister bringing over boxes of ginger tea she swears saved her during her own morning sickness, his younger sister emailing her links to white lace dresses with a bit of room around the waist.

'Are you pissed off with me? For not coming today?'

Eric is on the other side of the bathroom door. She can hear him standing there, waiting for a response. She wants him to go away.

'I don't know why you booked it for Wednesday,' he continues. 'You know I meet with my supervisor on Wednesdays.'

Things have been shifting with Eric too. When she first met him, on a Tinder date, she had almost decided that she wasn't interested. And then he'd started talking about his PhD and she'd seen the other side of him. He was dedicated, even though his thesis sounded entirely pointless. But it mattered to him. Eric had whole-hearted conviction in what he believed in and Jo admired that. Since she'd told him about her pregnancy, that conviction had started translating to her, to them. Part of him was unsure, she wasn't stupid. But he'd booked an infant first aid course. He'd started making a list of wedding venues, even though she told him the registry office would do. He told her if they were going to do it, he wanted to do it properly.

'I'm not pissed off,' she says, 'it's fine.'

'It doesn't seem like it's fine. If you're annoyed it's better that we talk it out.'

'Can you just give me a minute?'

Today was their first scan. Jo had lain on a bed while a woman with cold hands rubbed gel on her stomach. The woman had dimmed the lights to see the screen better. There had been something magical about it, being in that little darkened room, waiting. Jo watched as the woman stared into the black-and-white shadows on the screen, sliding the wand across Jo's almost flat belly. A furrow had appeared between the woman's brows.

'Don't forget my parents are coming this weekend,' Eric says through the door. 'All the way from Ballarat just to meet you in person.'

'I know.'

'So if you're pissed off I'd prefer we worked it out now. It'll be embarrassing if there's tension between us at the dinner. My mum's really intuitive. She'll notice.'

'I'm not pissed off. Promise.'

The woman had put down the wand, excused herself, said she'd be back in a moment. But she was gone a long time. When she did come back, she turned on the light.

'I already ate with Ashwan,' Eric says, 'but I can order you something if you want?'

'No, I'm okay.'

'Okay.' He moves away from the door. She hears the squeak of him pulling out a chair at the kitchen bench.

The water trickles from the flannel down her cheek, splashes into the bath. It's like he's here, her boy, the little chestnut inside her, splashing in the water. But when she imagines him, she sees that he is not some dreamed-up son. He is Jamie, her baby brother. Giggling the way he used to in their baths together. Propped up in a corner, hair an oil slick. She'd lay on her belly in the bubbles, a palm stretched up from the back of her head. *A shark*, she'd cry, pulling at his chubby ankles and he'd shriek his laughter.

Her stomach puckers. She shouldn't think of him. Of either of them. They're both gone now.

She gets out. Slips on her pyjamas. She has to tell Eric. Get it over with.

In the kitchen, he is sitting at the kitchen bench. He's on his laptop, writing, with his headphones on. She can hear the music from here. Eric loves to write with jazz turned up almost deafeningly loud. He says it's the only way to free his inhibitions. He doesn't turn around, so she doesn't interrupt him

She's hungry but she's not allowed to eat. Or drink either. No food or water for twelve hours beforehand, that's what they'd said. She always imagined losing a child would start with a sudden stream of crimson down her thigh. But there's been no blood, not even one drop. The doctor told her that, based on the size, she lost the baby over a week ago. She said that sometimes it goes this way, the body holds on to the pregnancy, even when the little flicker inside has gone out. She told Jo they could wait and see if her body expelled the remnants of the pregnancy on its own or she could have the tissue removed surgically and get it over with.

Jo gets into bed, but knows she won't sleep. The devastation is within reach, but she doesn't allow herself to feel it. Not yet. She needs to get through tomorrow first. She'll let herself feel it once she gets through tomorrow. She races through trivia in her head. Every time she thinks of tiny toes, of chubby thighs, of sweet, soft cheeks, she pulls away and makes herself name the great lakes of Canada, the winners of the Best Actress Oscar over the last twenty years. When she imagines a little hand clasping hers and her throat starts to close again, she forces herself to recite the periodic table of elements.

*

Her mouth is like sandpaper when she walks into the operating theatre in a shower cap, cotton gown and paper booties. She tries not to look at the stirrups at the end of the bed.

'Hi, Josephine,' the doctor says. A man this time.

'Hi.'

'So what do you do then?' he asks.

'Erm.' She sits on the bed, then lays on her back. Immediately, gloved hands are on her. Strapping on a heart monitor, placing a sheet over her legs. 'I work in a café and I do trivia,' she says, 'as in, I host it.'

'Great.' He grins at her from between the stirrups. 'We don't usually get interesting jobs like that.'

'Thanks.'

'So you're like a trivia queen, are you? What do you call them, a quizmaster?' the anaesthetist asks, an older woman.

'Yeah, sort of. I mean, not really.' There is a huge needle in the woman's hand.

'I've got one for you,' the doctor says, 'how many pints of blood are in the human body?'

She searches through her memory, but nothing comes. A nurse puts a mask on her face.

'You're climbing a mountain,' the nurse says, 'it's a warm day.'

'Sorry?' Jo's voice sounds muffled through the mask. The anaesthetist is now flicking the veins at the crook of her elbow.

'It's a warm day,' the nurse continues, 'you can feel the heat on your back.'

Jo's heart is beating quicker. She can't breathe with the mask on her face and she doesn't know how many pints of blood are in the human body and she has no idea what the nurse is talking about.

'Just relax,' the nurse says, 'imagine the mountain.'

'Oh,' she says, 'oh, I get it. Sorry.'

She tries to breathe deeply so that the nurse won't be offended, then she feels a sharp prick. She turns to see the anaesthetist insert a long needle into her skin.

'Feel the heat on your back,' the nurse says. All Jo can feel is a cold jangling moving up her arm. Then nothing.

*

Briena picks her up from the hospital in an Uber. Jo struggles to sit up straight in the car. The anaesthetic is still thick, clogging her thoughts.

'Busy day?' Briena asks the driver.

'Been on since five,' he says.

'Wow,' Briena says. The rest of the drive is silent. Every so often, Jo catches his eye in the rear-vision mirror.

When they arrive, Briena walks up the stairs with her to the apartment. 'Is Eric here?' she asks.

'No,' Jo says, unlocking the apartment door. Briena comes in after her, carrying Jo's bag. Jo sits on the couch, too tired to stand. Briena hovers near the door, holding Jo's bag in front of her so awkwardly it is sort of funny.

'It's okay,' Jo says from the couch, 'you can go. I should probably go to bed.'

'Are you sure you're okay?'

Jo nods. 'Just tired. Thanks so much for picking me up.'

'It's okay.'

'Seriously. I know I should have just told him last night. It was too much.'

Briena nods. 'Are you upset? You know, with ... it seems like you've taken it pretty well.'

Jo tries to swallow. 'I think my body was trying to tell me I'm too self-involved to have a kid.'

'God, you're so bloody harsh.' Briena puts the bag down, relaxing.

'But I'm right, aren't I?'

Briena surveys her, then smiles. 'Yeah, probably. At least now you're free to go and get murdered in the Kimberley.'

Jo tries to smile, but it stings. Briena doesn't seem to think there's even a chance Eric will want to get married. They could try again. It could still happen.

'Okay, well, if you're sure.' Briena comes and kisses her on the cheek, squeezes her shoulder. 'I do have an absolutely huge essay due this Friday.'

Jo just sits on the couch for a while after Briena leaves, staring at the television even though it isn't on. Sunlight shines through the branches of the tree outside, creating a pattern on the grey screen. Every so often a breeze comes through and the pattern sways a little. She tells herself to get up again and again until eventually her body goes along with it. The bedroom is dark, the blinds are closed. She is so tired she probably will be able to sleep, but she can't risk it, not now. The rattle of the temazepam pills against the plastic is enough to calm her before she even opens the cap.

She dreams that same dream. It's recurred in her sleeping mind for as long as she can remember. She is in the bay of St Ives, dog paddling by the boat. Her mother stands on deck staring into a camera. Seaweed slicks against Jo's ankle, trying to grip, trying to pull her under.

She wakes to the sound of Eric's alarm. She rolls over, her spit thick.

'You creeped the hell out of me last night,' Eric says, voice sleep groggy. 'I didn't think you were even home, because none of the lights were on. Then I saw you were in bed, even though it was only eight pm.'

'Sorry.'

'Are you still not feeling well?'

She knows she has to meet his eye when she says it.

'I'm sorry,' she says, 'we lost it. We lost our baby.'

And there it is, written right across his face just like Briena must have known it would be. Relief.

*

Her next weekly trivia night rolls around. Usually, she'd have it all worked out way ahead of time. She'd have written out the questions, decided on the music round, printed out the sheets. But every time she thinks about it, about standing in front of all those people, her heart starts beating so fast she wants to puke.

'Are you still doing tonight?' Briena asks as they close the café.

'Of course,' Jo says. 'I'm going to finish the questions off now. A bit last minute, but hopefully no one notices.'

She walks home with her music on loud until she finds that she has stopped walking. She is sitting next to a tree in the small scrap of park next to her apartment block. It hadn't been a conscious choice to sit, but she finds she can't stand. She watches people walk past, their dogs sniffing at her ankles, and she tries to smile, but it is watery and strange and the people jerk their dogs away. Jo turns her music off and the silence is like an exhale. She can't do the trivia night. Everyone will come: the *Jane's got the number* team, the nice couple who hold hands under the table. She will have to stand in front of them and be funny and wry. She can't do it.

Eric has told her his parents aren't coming to meet her. He hasn't said he doesn't want to marry her any more, not yet, but she knows he will.

These last few days, all she can think about is escape. Going somewhere no one knows her. She's been thinking about the mango farm again. The work would be hard, but it would be an adventure. She would be in it with the other pickers, they'd have nights and weekends to go exploring, to get to know each other. Her weak body would toughen, callus, become strong. It would be an entirely different life. It isn't like she has much of a choice. If Eric calls off the engagement—and he will, she knows he will—then her choice is farm work or going back to England. There's not a choice. She doesn't ever plan to go back to England. But it's nicer to think of it this way. A new adventure. An escape. Something she is choosing.

With slipping fingers, she googles how many pints of blood are in the human body. Nine. She thought there'd be more. She emails the farmer and asks if there is any chance there's a space free at the mango farm.

CHAPTER 3

The hotel in Perth would once have been opulent. Now it is falling apart. The garish red and orange carpet is stained. The black buttons on the elevators are cracked. If Eric were here he'd say, *This place has major Stephen King vibes.* But he isn't.

As soon as the email had come from the farmer saying there would be a spot opening for her in a week, she had packed her backpack. The conversation with Eric didn't last long. He was smiling at the end of it, said it was for the best this way. Jo hadn't realised she'd made him feel so trapped.

She'd gone straight to the airport, booked a hotel on last-minute.com.

She finds a certain rhythm while she waits in Perth. She wakes early and rides down to the lobby for the buffet breakfast. The dining room is only half full, with men and women in suits eating alone. She's out of place, with her band t-shirts and mop hair and claggy eyes. She opens a newspaper in front of her, a prop, and gorges herself. Pancakes first, with strawberries and honey. Thick-cut toast with peanut butter melting down the edges. Roast potatoes, creamy scrambled eggs. She brings pastries to her table, wraps them in her cloth napkin and hides them in her jacket pocket. The waiter sees her do it one morning. She catches his eye and stares at him until he turns away. She can't afford both the hotel and dinner.

Bloated and aching, she heads to her room. The television goes straight on. She sticks to talk shows. Graham Norton sipping white wine and laughing, Jimmy Fallon and his dumb little games, Dr Phil's holy judgement. Or crime shows, the violence so pointless it makes her feel emptier. When her muscles are stiff and aching from the bed she turns the television off and forces herself to get up. To pull on her swimsuit, drying on the shower rail, and take the lift to the pool level. She does lap after lap until her body is weightless. Then, before the sky even dims, the rattle of the pills against the white plastic bottle, her reward for making it through another day. She shakes out two onto her palm, double the dose so she won't even dream. She doesn't want her subconscious to take her to the bay of St Ives again, she can't deal with that now. She swallows the pills without water and sleeps for fifteen hours of delicious disappearance.

On the last day, she packs her bag, checks out and goes to the airport. She turns her phone on while she waits for her plane and texts Briena, Alice, anyone else who'd been worried after her no-show at trivia: *Everything is fine, just needed some time, no need to worry, all good now, excited for the trip, finally going to get that tan, finally going to get fit, I'll be in touch, I'll send a postcard, I'll call if I have reception, everything is fine.*

She sets her phone on aeroplane mode when the flight starts to board. She's never been on a plane so small, only one seat on each side of the aisle. She clips her seatbelt, plugs her earphones in and turns her music on, watching the city as they lift off.

*

The air is different. It's the first thing Jo notices when she steps off the tiny plane onto the tarmac at Broome airport. The heat here is tropical. It sticks to her skin, makes her clothes feel damp before she has even started to sweat. Jo pulls her bag onto her shoulder and walks over to the terminal. If you could call it that. It looks more like a shed.

She weaves through the passengers waiting for their luggage to the exit on the other side. Bus 239, Denny the farmer had told her in his email. Get off at Langrange—it'd take two hours or so—and he'd pick her up and drive her to the farm. He'd used no commas or full stops.

She doesn't need to search far to see the bus station. It's right there on the other side of the road. A group of tourists stand by red benches under a small shelter with a noticeboard. A bus pulls in, 'Pearl Town Explorer' adorned on its side in holiday hues of clear blue and yellow.

Jo puts on her sunglasses. The glare bouncing off the road makes the asphalt shine. The last of the tourists get on the bus and it pulls away. She goes to sit on an empty bench, but the metal sears through her jeans. It's been baking all day in the heat. She stands up, ventures under the covered section of the shelter, though the shade doesn't offer much relief.

The community noticeboard is scarred cork and faded posters. That photo of the woman and her child, Larissa and Nika, grinning above their heights and weights and last known sightings and the make and model of their silver car. Their poster is the newest on the board, its blacks stark. She knows that photograph from the paper and Briena's phone. Jo inspects the other posters. A used washing machine for sale. A young Korean man, last seen three months ago. A cleaner, three-hour special. Two Italian women, a reward for any information on their whereabouts. A missing French Canadian guy.

Jo steps backwards. The noticeboard is covered in missing persons posters. Some are crinkled from rain, many faded to a blur. The faces are young, between twenty and thirty, and international. People she might know, smiling from photographs that could have been Instagram profile pictures. Except for what's written above each one. Missing. Missing. Last Seen. Missing. She imagines Briena's reaction. She'd be horrified and excited, take photos on her phone, post them on her true crime groups on Facebook. Theories would ding in seconds.

Jo turns away, back to the road. She can feel the eyes from the posters on the back of her neck.

Her bus arrives about twenty minutes later, long enough for her to sweat through her t-shirt and empty her bottle of water. Just when she's considering rushing back into the airport to refill it, the white shape lugs around the corner. Its brakes squeal as it pulls in.

The driver is wearing the shortest shorts she's ever seen. He's in his fifties, belly fusing with the steering wheel and socks pulled to his knees.

'Langrange, thanks,' she says.

'You a Brit?'

This surprises her. She'd only said two words. 'Is it that obvious?'

'Knew you weren't Chinese. Took a punt you weren't a Frog or a Swede. Three dollars forty.'

Jo takes out her wallet and places two two-dollar coins on the tray. He sweeps them away and flicks a switch next to the wheel. The bus doors close. He doesn't offer her change. She walks up the aisle as they swing onto the road. There is barely anyone else on the bus: a middle-aged white woman, her skin leathery-tanned, with a little girl fidgeting on the seat next to her, a First Nations man in a cowboy hat further on, who smiles at Jo as she passes. She smiles back, slides into a seat towards the rear.

The little girl sits up and stares at Jo. She turns away, the girl's soft pink cheeks unbearable to look at. As she zips the coin section of her wallet she notices a folded-up receipt inside. She takes it out, unfolds it. On one side is a list of coffee orders in shorthand: *FW—skinny, LB—2sug, Cap T/A.* On the other side is a scrawled list of names. Mostly boys' names but a few girls' names as well. Ben, Bailey, Jessie, Charlie, Jamie. Her eyes stick on that one—Jamie.

She scrunches the list into a little ball and slips it into a gap in the seat, where the fabric seam has ripped. She pushes it into the foam stuffing with one finger, as far as it will go, then zips up her wallet and puts it in her backpack.

The town of Broome is more beautiful than she'd expected. In her mind, Australian small towns were dusty places, with lorries and kangaroos and local pubs. She'd watched *McLeod's Daughters* as a kid, eating toast for dinner in her dad's sunless house in Chesterfield. She'd loved the horseback-riding sisters, the tough love they shared and the hard, dirty droving they did together, squinting in the sun.

The bus passes pearl shops with grand facades, Japanese day spas with white frangipani trees out front. The town centre is filled with rows of pale yellow buildings with pointed corrugated iron roofs, like the airport. Palm trees are everywhere. The prickling excitement returns. The last few weeks fade. This is going to be amazing, a whole different life, something she'd never imagined she'd do.

Within ten minutes, the buildings are gone. After another five, so are the houses.

They turn a corner and she sucks in a breath. They have come out along a cliff looking onto the ocean. It's bright, no shadow at all. It would be impossible to paint. So much brightness, without dark to balance it out. The colours are pure, no mixing required, straight from the tube. The ocean is Ultramarine, the cliffs Burnt Sienna.

She sees a group of people bobbing in the water. She leans closer to the window, her nose tapping the glass. They are young, her own age, and naked. The women's bare breasts jiggle with their laughs, and they splash sea water over their faces. They are so free and happy. One of them, a man, slicks his hair back with wet hands. The gesture is enough for Jo to feel her breath catch. His shoulders are thick, broad, his chest dark with hair

In unison, the people put their fingers to their noses and dive under the surface. The water reseals over them. Thirty seconds. Forty. The ocean is clear and empty, the sunshine glittering from it. Jo cranes her neck to look back around as the bus speeds away. She wants to see the man again, but he doesn't reappear.

The guilt appears before she has time to remember she has no reason to feel bad looking at another guy. She and Eric are no longer together. That life, the family, the baby, is done. There's no point thinking about it.

She tries to swallow the memories down to the place where her other lives live. The versions of herself she doesn't like to remember. She imagines the most recent one, her London self—the girl with the two-pound Margaret Olley postcard from the Australian Still Lifes exhibition tacked to her tarnished mirror, the girl with the seven hopeful condoms in her top drawer, the girl with constant dirty tissues on her bedside table because her bedroom walls were full of black mould. She imagines London Josie taking Sydney Jo by the hand and pulling her into the dark.

CHAPTER 4

LONDON, 2016

Richard watched Josie set their drinks on the table and slide into the booth across from him.

'So I think I'm going to leave,' she said as she settled into the seat.

'Leave Slade?' Richard asked. He tried to keep his face neutral.

'Definitely.'

He took a sip from his lager, gave himself a moment to process. They were at the pub they often went to. A crummy place not far from Josie's flat. Three tube stops away from Slade School of Fine Art, so he never worried too much about them being seen. Still, he always made sure they took one of the quiet booths away from the windows. It used to be sexy, all the cloak and dagger.

'You don't need to leave, I don't want to make you feel like—'

'It's not that.'

'No, listen, I never wanted to put you in a position where you had to pick between us and—'

'I'm not picking, I'm failing,' she said.

He already knew this but he tried to look surprised. She brushed a finger down the condensation on her pint glass, got that distant expression that used to drive him crazy. He'd wanted to understand it, see what went on inside her head. It had been two years. He still didn't know. Now it just frustrated him.

'Do you remember when we first came here,' he asked, 'and you ordered a snakebite and black?'

She looked at him, laughed, and that distance was gone.

'Oh god. Yeah. Please never tell anyone that, alright? I think I thought it was really punk rock or something.'

'Josie Ainsley, you are very punk rock.'

She shook her head.

Back then, when this thing between them had first started, she'd been so unsure of herself. Had that thick Midlands accent. Wore black. Came back with her drink, lager and cider with a shot of blackcurrant to make it black. Only Goths drank that. It had made her seem so young, made the whole notion of it—dating one of his students—feel like a terrible idea. It had also made him reach under the table and put his hand on her thigh.

But that was all over now.

'I think I was trying to impress you,' she said.

'So tell me, is there anything I can do that might make you change your mind? Maybe I can talk Geoffrey out of a complete fail.'

He would do it for her, half-heartedly at least. He was happy she was leaving; it was what he'd hoped she'd wanted to meet him to discuss. That was the ideal situation. Their relationship couldn't continue while she was a student and he a teacher, that was clear when he'd had to mark her pastel work, but if she weren't, things could be different. They could try again. He liked this thing between them, missed her body. The way she was so unknowable. How little he needed to do to get his end away.

'No,' she said. 'I'm done. I can't bear to be told to think more figuratively ever again.'

He shrugged. 'You're just a different kind of artist.'

'That too. I don't want to have to be told that my art is out of style, or that if I'd been born a few hundred years ago, I'd be famous.'

'Who said that?'

'Mary.'

He nodded. Glad she was as sick of the conversation as he was. She'd spoken about it so many times, that crease between her eyebrows, her navy-coloured quilt wrapped around her. That horrible damp room of hers, so small it was like the walls were closing in and smelling faintly of curry from the takeaway joint below. It didn't matter when they were shagging. God, he couldn't think of anything else when they were shagging. It had surprised him, that first time. He'd thought she would be meek. Nervous. That every piece of her clothing would be a hard prize to remove. But it wasn't like that at all. She was happy with it hard and fast. Gripped her legs together so she was gloriously tight, told him to pull her hair. After a while, she hadn't wanted to do it like that. But by then it was all he wanted.

Afterwards it was different. She'd want to talk about school, about the course, and he wanted to be the kind of guy who'd stay and listen. He had tried to tell her that she should try other things, see what happened if she were less literal. She'd hated when he'd said that. Turns out if a girl loves painting the way light falls on a glass bowl of plums then that's what she loves.

He'd listen until he was tired, then he'd kiss her forehead and turn over. One night, near the end, he'd woken hours later. The room was filled with the silvery blue light of her phone.

'What are you doing?' He'd turned to her, squinting. 'What're you looking at?'

'Oh,' she said, not bothered that she'd woken him, 'just reading about the Civil War.'

'What?' he'd asked. 'Why?'

'I was doing a quiz. Realised I didn't know much about it.' She was wide awake, the phone screen reflecting in her eyes.

'It's the middle of the bloody night.'

'Oh,' she said. 'Oh, yeah. Sorry.'

She'd turned the phone screen off and he'd closed his eyes, tried to go back to sleep. But he could feel her next to him, prone. Alert.

'Anyway,' she was saying now, staring into her beer, 'that's not what I meant.'

'About leaving?'

'Yeah. I think I want to leave London. Maybe even leave England.'

'What?' His hand almost shot out, grabbed for her knee.

'Not straight away.' She was back to drawing lines in her condensation, a picket fence around her pint glass. 'I'd have to save up a bit more.'

He opened his mouth, closed it again. Then he said, 'But why?' and he sounded so much like a teenage girl being dumped that he winced.

'There's nothing for me here, you know? I'm flunking out, which should bother me, but art school has completely killed my love of painting anyway. My flat is shit. My flatmate has a new boyfriend and won't stop bonking him at all hours. You and me are done.'

Done. He didn't like that. He would have preferred she use 'broken up'. 'Done' sounded so final. Like she wasn't here to try to get him back at all.

'But you have friends!'

'Yeah. Sort of. Art school friends. I don't think they'll translate to real life.'

She was right. Her friends were so consumed by their art school identities, so concerned with being ironic, with things being meta, with their practice. She'd never fitted in with them to begin with. It was part of the reason he'd first noticed her. The way she seemed to exist on the outside of things.

He was just about to say it. To say *What about us?* Or *This could be a new beginning,* or *This wasn't part of the plan.* She was wearing her distant expression. Her gaze over his shoulder. That unknowable quality of hers. Maybe she was wondering about him, hoping he would save her from this. Maybe this was her attempt at an ultimatum.

He reached for her hand but she laughed. He pulled back.

'I've seen this one before,' she said, eyes still over his shoulder.

This time it wasn't that distance of hers. She was just distracted by the television behind him. They were playing a quiz show, *The Chase.*

'Have they got a new host?' he asked. It didn't look like Bradley Walsh.

'This is the Australian one,' she said. 'I like it better.'

'Watching afternoon telly rather than going to class?'

She didn't bite. 'They're so funny, Australians. Their accents make me feel happier for some reason.'

'I bet the questions are easier on the Australian one.'

She gave him a courtesy laugh, eyes on the screen, 'Not really. I'm quite good at it, you know. Used to watch them all the time when I was a kid.'

'Really?' he asked, not that he cared.

'It was basically the only time me and my dad would spend time together. He'd come downstairs for *Midsomer Murders* once a week, but for *Countdown* every night. He loved trying to guess the answers—we'd both call them out if we knew them. I always thought he was smarter than the contestants. It was a novelty to begin with. I didn't even have a telly when I lived with my mum.'

Richard examined her properly now. Not once, in all the time they'd been together, during the late-night phone calls, the pillow talks, had she brought up her mother.

'I went to a quiz night the other night, you know, pub trivia. God, it was crap. I think I could do way better.'

'So, wait, is that your plan? Quit art school? Move away somewhere and … what? Be a trivia host?'

He wanted to reach for her hand again, tell her that he was sorry. That he'd open himself to her for real this time, that it would be different. Now that they didn't have to hide it, they could be a real couple. He knew when he did she'd grip it tight, she'd tell him that was all she needed to hear.

'I know this one,' she said.

He turned back to the screen. The grinning host was asking how many breeds of snake there were in Australia. He shivered.

'One seventy, I think,' she said. 'Yes, one hundred and seventy.'

He took her hand. 'Josie,' he said. 'Come on. You can't leave London. Be serious.'

'Richard,' she said, meeting his eyes finally. 'I'm completely serious.'

She slid her hand away. She was already somewhere else.

CHAPTER 5

LANGRANGE, 2018

The Great Northern Highway has been going on forever. Behind them and ahead of them is identical. The same grey road, the same orange dirt, the same thin tangle of scrub. The sun is setting, low and huge, casting a red glow over everything. The bus begins to slow and pulls over. There is a stop, but there's nothing around. It's just a white pole and a dirty sign with the numbers 239. The doors open.

'Langrange,' the driver calls.

Jo sits forward. This can't be it. This isn't a town. This isn't anything.

'Langrange,' he repeats, louder now.

She pulls her bag onto her shoulder, walks down the aisle.

'Say g'day to Denny for me.'

She turns on the step. 'Erm. How'd you know I'm going to Denny's farm?'

The driver laughs, a barren sound. 'You ain't got many options round here.'

Jo steps onto the orange dirt and the bus drives away. She watches until it becomes the size of a bean and disappears into the oblivion of the horizon. Everything looks on fire in this light. Even her skin has been cast red, like she's pressing her fingers to a torch.

Inch by inch, the huge orb of sun sinks, the light turns from red to grey and the farmer doesn't come. She sets her backpack onto the dirt, fishes out the folded-up email, reads the lines she already knows back to herself. She's followed his instructions. She's where she's meant to be.

No cars drive past. Not a bus, not a lorry, nothing. There is a tree not far away, but it's not like any tree she's seen before. Its trunk is huge, shaped like a bottle of whiskey. Its branches come out the top, thin and spindly like Eric's arms, reaching with broken elbows towards the sky. There's nothing else around but this tree.

The final sliver of red glow disappears under the horizon. She watches as it happens. It's dark, so dark, and it will get darker. There's not even streetlights out here. She pulls out her phone, thinks about taking a photo. Posting it with: *Stuck out here with just this nightmare tree for company.*

But it's too dark to take a photo. Plus, she sees, she has no service.

Another ten minutes pass and she's panicking. She crosses the huge road to the other side, skimming her eyes down the timetable. Only five buses go towards Broome each day. They have all left. She crosses the road again, back to her side, as though it will make any difference. She could walk back, or sleep here. If she's going to walk, she should start now. Instead she holds her phone in the air. Spins around. Her lit-up screen is some kind of solace. She turns it off and then straight back on again. Still no signal. It's no use. But she tries again. She holds down the button, slides to turn it off, waits for it to go blank and unresponsive in her hand, then switches it on. Nothing.

Then, in the very distance, she sees something: two tiny pinpricks in the grey sky. Headlights.

And music. At first it's so faint she thinks she's imagining it. A tune she knows. It's Britney Spears. She remembers the song, 'Toxic'. She'd loved the spangled bodysuit, the orange hair. She was at the age when it wasn't cool to like Britney, but everyone did. She had even heard her father humming along under his breath when the song played on the radio in one of their quiet car rides.

As the twin lights grow, the song gets louder. A white lorry. It pulls in beside her. The music is turned down. She pulls the door open. The guy inside looks out at her. He's around fifty, wearing a flannelette shirt. What's left of his hair is fluffy and unkempt, and his bulbous nose is pockmarked.

'Denny?' she asks.

The man inside doesn't cut the engine. 'C'mon. Chuck your bag in the back.'

She throws her bag into the lorry's tray and slides into the passenger seat, pulls the door shut. Denny stares at her for a second, his eyes the palest of blues. She turns away, turns back. He's still staring.

'Thanks for coming to get me, I was starting to worry.'

'All good,' he says, eyes returning to the road. He doesn't notice her intentional passive aggression, or doesn't care. He swings the wheel, does a U-turn in the middle of the road and turns back the way he came. 'Didya have far to come?' he asks.

'Yeah. I've never been to this part of Australia before.'

He turns to her again. Now the inner light is off she can barely see him. There is only the glow of the headlights reflecting off the road.

'You from England?'

She freezes. She'd told him in her email she was English. Sick, heady panic pulses through her. She should have made sure before she got in the car. He might not be Denny. He could be anyone.

'Yes,' she says. 'It was on the resume I sent you, and in the email.' She watches his reaction. But it's too dark to see if there's a change.

'Are you looking at my scar?' he asks.

'What?'

'You were looking at my scar, weren't ya? It's all good, I know it's a beauty.' He rubs a hand over his forearm and now she does look. Even in the dark she can see it, a thick white line curving to his elbow, the dots from the stitches visible too. 'Take a guess how I got it, go on.'

'I don't know,' she says, her voice high.

She looks around. Their surroundings are shades of black. The ground a pure black, velveteen. The sky the darkest of greys. They speed past more nightmare trees, their broken arms silhouetted, only micro shades of difference from the sky.

Britney keeps singing.

She'll test him. See if it's the real Denny. 'So, erm, how many other workers have you got at the moment?'

'Go on. Plenty of ways to get scarred round here. You're not going to guess?'

'No,' she says.

'Alright, alright, I'll tell ya then. It was 'bout four or five years ago. I was minding my own business, on the dunny actually, if you must know.'

She eyes the door handle. He hasn't locked it. She could jump out. The speedometer needle is hovering over 100. She'd hurt herself at this speed, break some bones maybe, but she could run. Sprint out into the shades of black.

'So I'm sitting there when I hear this hissing sound. This real loud hissing sound. And I'm thinking fuck—'scuse my language—I'm thinking fuck, the tractor's blown its head gasket. So I get up, quick as I can, and—'

'Are we far?' she asks.

'Huh?'

She's interrupted him. She doesn't care. 'How far are we?'

'Get car sick?'

'No. I was just wondering.'

'Not far. So I get up, throw open the door and rush out. And d'ya know what was standing right next to me? Biggest bloody bird you'd ever see. A cassowary, them with the blue heads and black bodies, you know? Taller than me! He hissed at me again and I was thinking, ah, shit, I'm done for. Then his foot comes up, they got a hooked claw there, you know? Bigger than your face. So he swings it down and I throw out my arm and he gets me, hooks his claw right in, it hits bone. Blood everywhere. But he can't get it out, you know? Because it's hit the bone. So I twist my arm round, and he loses his footing and falls right over, clumsy fucker, and the weight of him pulls his claw right out. I run to the house. Would have been funny if it weren't for all the blood.'

He glances at her, then starts laughing, a deep throaty laugh. She grips the door handle. He swings the wheel onto a dirt driveway and she hears her bag slide across the metal tray behind them. They are on his property now. Her hand tightens on the door handle. She could pull it open, jump out now that they've slowed a bit.

'So where you from, Yorkshire?'

'Chesterfield.'

He's still staring at her, not looking at the road at all. 'Sound like you're from Yorkshire. What do you call them, tykes? I've got a chink, a schmeisser and a paddy here already. Not great workers, but they try, and that's all that matters. I always tell them that, long as I know you're trying that's all I care about.'

She exhales. It is Denny.

'Great,' she says.

'If you ain't trying, though, that's what annoys me. Some people I get up here, they think it's a holiday. I tell them, you want me signing you for those days, you have to earn it, you know? I ain't some resort. I give accommodation for less than budget, I throw your food in, because where else you going to go?' He turns back to the road, begins to slow.

The farm spreads out around them. Fenced-off fields. She can't see any animals.

And then, in the light from the headlights, mango trees. Rows and rows of them. Hunched over from the weight of their fruit. She could laugh with relief.

'Now, you guys work hard, I'll leave you alone, okay? Tyson can be a little shit, I know that, but just ignore him and he'll get bored.'

'Who's Tyson?'

'My boy.'

The farmhouse is ahead. It would be white in the sunshine, but in this light it's a ghost. But Denny pulls in by the mango plants. He turns the ignition off and the shades of grey turn black. Britney's voice is gone.

'Grab ya bag.'

She unclips her seatbelt and even that sound is loud. She gets out and lifts her backpack from the tray and follows him.

He pulls something metal out of his pocket and she takes a step back. But it's a torch. He clicks it on.

'Now, I've told them to have the bunk ready for you, alright, I told them that this morning so they've had plenty of time.'

The torch lights circles of the plants and then, up ahead, a shed. Denny's footfalls are loud; she follows close to him. She can hear him breathing.

Reaching the shed, he pulls the tin door open. It scrapes against the cement floor. He shines the torch inside. Bunk beds are set up on each side, three of them occupied. As he shines the torch over the forms, they cover their heads with their arms. There are clothes and bags stuffed everywhere. In the corner is a small porcelain sink overflowing with deodorants and cleansers and toothbrushes.

'Alright, so, great,' Denny says. 'I'll see you in the morning then, bright and early.'

He closes the door behind him, leaving her in the complete blackness. She waits for one of the others to speak. No one does. She stumbles her way towards the empty bed. She needs to wee, but she doesn't want these people's first impression of her to be the sound of her pissing in the dark.

With her hands held out blindly in front of her, she touches steel. The bunk. She slides her hands along it. Feels the edge, then the rounded rungs of the ladder. She bends into the empty bottom bunk. She climbs onto the mattress, drops her bag onto the floor as quietly as she can, though she knows they must be awake, pulls off her shoes, socks and jeans and slides under the sheet.

The moment Jo stops moving, the room fills with total black silence again.

Then, hovering in the dark, a man's voice with a thick German accent. 'What was the story?'

'Sorry?' she asks.

'Denny's story about his scar. I got a bull shark attack. Sorcha got a crocodile, Yan got a python.'

She can't help but smile. 'Cassowary,' she says.

A snort of laughter. 'They don't even have those around here. He's getting creative.'

She's about to reply, but she's cut off.

'Shut up, El, would you?' A girl's voice, Irish. 'It's the middle of the fecking night.'

'Sorry,' he says. 'Goodnight.'

'Goodnight,' Jo replies. And the shed returns to silence.

PART TWO

CHAPTER 6

THE FARM, OCTOBER 2018

It is black inside the shed when the alarm clock goes off. Not the fake trill an iPhone makes, but a real alarm clock.

'Bloody hell,' comes the girl's voice from last night, her Irish accent thick.

Jo listens to the shuffle of people getting up. She's been awake most of the night, thinking of the plastic bottle of pills in her bag, but not wanting to take it out. The idea of being unconscious in this strange new place is scarier than the hours of darkness. She's kept herself rigid, ready to jump, ignoring her swollen bladder. When she did sleep for an hour or two it had been twisting dreams of fear and cars, her dad behind the wheel, trying not to look at her.

Someone goes to the door and pulls it open to the dimmest glow of dawn.

'Better wake, new girl,' another female voice says in a throaty monotone. Her accent is harder for Jo to place.

A hint of Cantonese or Mandarin blended with TV American.

'I'm awake.' Jo sits up, her head pounding. 'Hi. I'm Jo.'

Now, in the light, she can see them. A guy putting on socks, a girl by the door, the light illuminating her green hair, and another pulling on some clothes on a top bunk.

The guy is the only one to smile, glancing up as he ties the laces of his boots. 'I'm Elias. That is Sorcha and Yan.'

He is the one who was talking to her last night. Tall and German, with long glossy hair in a bun. The other two don't acknowledge her. She pulls on her clothes under the sheet and stands, brushing her fingers through her hair. She needs to seem normal, not like someone who has spent the last four days alone in a hotel having a breakdown. She wants to be liked.

She goes to the bathroom, the toilet seat cracked, and pisses. The crack pinches her bum. She jumps as a loud bang comes from the wall behind her. Then another further down. And another.

'Come on! Come on! Come on!' The screaming voice of a kid.

She pulls up her jeans, rushes out. 'What the hell?'

'It's Tyson. Denny's kid,' one of the girls, Yan, says from across the room. 'His idea of a wake-up call.'

Jo goes to the entrance. A boy of about twelve is riding an old silver bike around the shed. He has a stick in his hand and he is banging and scraping it on the walls. He comes to a stop in front of her, feet brushing onto the dirt.

'You the new one?' His cheeks are freckled but his skin is buttery smooth. His hair looks home cut.

'Yes,' she tells him.

He wrinkles his nose. 'I liked the other one. She was way hotter.'

*

Despite the gloves Jo wears, the shears dig into the web of skin between her thumb and forefinger. She tries to move fast, but with softness. The mango's skin is fragile; easy to bruise. Over the morning she's found a rhythm. She holds the fruit with one hand, cuts the stalk with the shears and places it into the jute sack she wears around her neck while her shears are already finding their way to the next. Elias follows her. He has shears with long handles, taking the high fruit while she focuses on the low-hanging ones. He waits for her when she moves slowly, doesn't make a big deal of it.

On the other side of the row are Sorcha and Yan. Sorcha does the high branches. In the light, Jo sees that she's blonde and strong looking, the kind of girl Jo could imagine being a real estate agent or working in HR in the real world. On the low fruit is Yan from Hong Kong, who seems to be utterly uninterested in Jo. Her pastel green–dyed hair has started to grow out, and she has a septum piercing. Together, they're intimidating.

When Yan passes her, emptying her sack into the tray, Jo can hear music coming from her headphones. Loud and fast punk or metal, the kind of music Jo likes.

'What are you listening to?' she asks.

Yan pulls an earbud out. 'What?'

'Oh, erm, I was wondering what you're listening to.'

'CharmCharmChu. I doubt you would know them.'

'No, are they—' But Yan has already replaced her earbud. Jo notices that she's using a Discman rather than her phone or iPod. Jo hasn't seen one of those since she was in primary school.

'Blondie!' Denny stands on the hill staring at them, his arms folded over his chest.

'Eejit,' Sorcha mutters, closing her shears.

'Hungry?' he yells.

Sorcha turns to him, all smiles. 'Sure. Time to play wifey,' she says, and walks up the hill to the house. The rest of them resume picking, so Jo does too. She reaches for the next mango too firmly and it snaps off from the stalk, spitting out sap, a little eruption of thin cream. It's hot against her wrist, slips into her glove. She flicks it off.

*

They eat their lunch between the rows. Sandwiches. White bread smeared with butter and thick-cut tomatoes. Usually this wouldn't seem appetising, but now it's decadent. The tomatoes are sweet and tart and bursting with juice. Jo eats, feeling the sugar of the bread charge her muscles. She scratches the back of her hand, flexes her fingers, rolls her ankles.

Last night had been awful, but in the daylight things don't seem so bad. The sleeping arrangement isn't ideal, but maybe it doesn't matter if they are outdoors most of the time. The sky is huge and open. Rows of mango trees stretch out in all directions. Sorcha and Yan lie side by side with their heads between the plants, the only shaded place. Elias sits across from Jo, his skinny legs folded in front of him, writing on a notepad. She needs to talk to him, seem normal.

'Do you keep a diary?' she asks, scratching at her hand again.

He looks up, smiles. 'No. I'm making a letter. There's no mobile coverage here, you've probably noticed. So I write to my girlfriend.'

She's always found the German accent slightly adorable. 'That's nice. So old fashioned.'

'It is more fun than I would have thought.'

'So she's Australian?'

'Yes. Emma. She is in Melbourne. I met her when she was travelling in Berlin.' His face has lit up just saying his girlfriend's name.

'You miss her?'

'I do. I am going to try to use the payphone this weekend.'

She scratches her hand again. It's burning. 'Denny won't let us use his?'

He is about to answer when his eyes go to her hand. 'Shit,' he says.

She follows his gaze to where she's been scratching. The back of her hand has turned red. Pinprick blisters are forming all the way up her wrist.

'Oh god,' she says, 'is that, what? Sunburn?'

'No, the mangoes.'

Sorcha sits up from her spot, glares over at her hand and groans, 'Great.' She gets to her feet and runs towards the buckets of mangoes.

'Come on.' Elias puts out his hands and pulls Jo up. She follows him along the row of mangoes, away from Sorcha.

'What is it?' She's freaked out now. Her hand is burning.

'Mango rash. The sap, it burns and some people's skin have the stronger reaction than others.'

He stops at the tap where the sprinkler system is attached. He takes the orange plastic attachment off and turns the water on. 'Just rinse it. You'll be fine.'

She rinses her hand. The cold water is soothing.

Sorcha comes storming up to them, holding Jo's bag of mangoes. 'Move.'

Jo moves out of the way and Sorcha delicately washes the mangoes. The creamy white sap is all over them. Some have browning blotches on their skin already.

'These ones are ruined. I'm not taking the blame.'

'I'm sorry, I didn't know,' Jo says, but Sorcha ignores her.

'It's no big deal, Sorc,' Elias says, taking the stained mangoes himself.

'Yes, it is,' Sorcha says, then marches off with the mangoes pressed to her body, wet patches darkening her t-shirt.

Jo puts her hand back under the running tap, using the excuse to turn away so that Elias won't see her face. Sorcha's tone has stung. 'The sap stains the mangoes too?' she asks him.

'It happens all the time. It is just that if half a crate is ruined, Denny will take it from our time. He'll only mark us off for half a day rather than a full one.'

'Really?' she says, rubbing her thumb gingerly over her burn. Elias shrugs. Jo pulls her glove out of her back pocket and runs water into it too. There's probably sap on the inside. It fills up, the fingers straightening. Her throat unclenches a little.

'Sorcha seems like she's got an issue with me,' she says.

'It's not you.'

She looks at Elias from her half-squat next to the tap. He might mean it's because she's English. She's felt it before, that animosity from the Irish. But it's usually a lot subtler.

Elias is gazing towards the house. The sunlight is on him, gleaming off his blond eyelashes, making him squint.

'It is just, okay … so, the rest of us started since last week. And there was another girl, Juliana. She was cool. Denny knew you were coming too, so he would use it as a threat for us. Every day he would be saying if we didn't pick enough, we would be replaced, if we were not polite enough to him, we would be replaced.'

'I didn't know that.' No wonder they hate her. 'So in the end it was Juliana?'

'She complained about the pay slips. Denny has them in the house. He says that he will give them to us when we are finished. But Juliana said that was illegal, he is meant to give them to us at the end of each week. Otherwise, how will we know how much we are being signed off for? If he's not making them correctly we will not even know until the end.'

'She got fired? For that?'

'She said she was going to go talk to him about it yesterday, but she didn't return. When we got back to the shed all her stuff was gone. He did not even let us say goodbye.'

'But that's complete crap. Surely that's not legal?'

A tiny white dog shoots towards them. It jumps on her, yapping. She straightens. She likes dogs, but this dirty little thing looks mean.

'I guess break is over,' Elias says.

'Slackers!' Tyson rides up on his bike. 'Caught you!'

The dog nips at Jo's heels.

'Who's this, then?' She pats the dog on the head. It growls at her, its snout wrinkling, its tiny white teeth bared.

'That's Bryce,' Tyson says, eyeing her.

'Well, Bryce is very cute. I'm Jo.'

'You're a slack bitch,' Tyson replies.

'Right.' She turns to Elias. 'We should get back to it.'

*

Her hand burns more and more as the day wears on. Her thighs begin to throb from squatting for the lower branches. Denny has turned Britney on. The hours repeat, it gets hotter, sweat drips down her back. Flies keep landing on her face, and she tries to wave them off without pausing, continually brushing her cheek against her shoulder. Her head spins from exhaustion. Tonight, she'll take two pills.

A green lorry, old, with peeling paint, comes up the long drive. The others don't pay it any attention, but when Jo hears the click of the door opening, she turns. A young man gets out, dark hair, broad shoulders. Her hand stills around a mango. It's the guy she saw yesterday, she's sure of it, the guy who had disappeared into the ocean. She'd never seen him come back up.

'Who's that?' she asks Elias.

He glances over. 'Gabe.'

Gabe. He spends five minutes inside, then he's out, walking towards the van. Denny doesn't follow. Gabe looks at them. She puts her hand up, a wave. He catches her eye, smiles but doesn't wave back, just climbs into the lorry and drives away.

*

When the picking day is done, Yan sets up a campfire out the front of the shed. Exhausted, Jo lies on her bunk watching her through the open door.

'Why is she making a fire?' she asks. 'It's still pretty hot.'

'For the light,' Elias says from the bunk above her.

She sits up. Looks around. She hadn't noticed it before, but of course he's right. There isn't a light on the ceiling. There isn't a light, because there isn't any electricity in the shed. There's a small bathroom with a toilet and shower, where Sorcha is now, washing off the sweat from the day. There's a sink on the wall of the main room. So there's water at least, but not electricity.

Within half an hour, the shed begins to darken. The three of them sit around the fire. Jo lies on the bunk, alone in the space for the first time. She takes stock. A pale green towel hangs from Yan's bottom bunk. She can see headphones twisting out from under her pillow. On the bunk above, Sorcha has a pink silk pillowslip, a few scrunched-up tissues tucked down the edge of the mattress.

Jo waits as long as she can, then she gets out of the bunk. Part of her doesn't want to join them. It would be desperate. Like she is pandering for them to like her when, aside from Elias, they seem to have already decided that they don't. But she can't spend all evening lying in the dark alone.

Outside, Elias has resumed writing on his notepad. Sorcha and Yan are talking quietly to one another. Jo sits in the dry grass, watching the flickers of flame dance. Now that the temperature is starting to drop, the fire isn't so bad. She rubs at her hand, the blisters now angry and burning. She wonders if it's too early to take a pill. Maybe they won't even notice. It's dark, and her first day. They might just think she's tired. And she is.

'I can't keep watching you do that.'

Sorcha is staring at her from across the fire.

'What?'

'Your hand. You're making it worse.'

Sorcha goes into the shed. Rummages through one of her bags. 'Can't see a bloody thing,' she mutters. 'Here it is.' She comes out with some cream and sits next to Jo. 'Let's see.'

Jo puts out her hand. Sorcha takes it softly in hers and inspects it, then dollops a bit of cream on the red rash. At first it is so cold it makes Jo try to pull her hand away but Sorcha grips on.

'Don't be a baby,' Sorcha says, rubbing the cream in more. Soon the cream starts to soothe the burning.

'That's way better.'

'It's just cortisol.'

She watches Sorcha's fingers, sees how scratched and chapped her hands are. The webbing between the forefinger and thumb on one hand is scabbed.

'Thanks.'

'It's alright.' Then Sorcha meets her eyes for the first time since she arrived. The light flickers on her skin, the heat making her cheeks rosy.

'I'm sorry about your friend. I didn't realise I'd be replacing someone by coming here.'

'We weren't really friends. I only knew her a week.'

'Still. If I'd known, I would have found somewhere else.' Sorcha turns away.

'But I didn't know,' Jo goes on.

Not far away, a screeching.

Jo peers into the dark. 'What was that?'

Another screech, and then the sound of something heavy landing in one of the mango trees.

'Fruit bats,' Sorcha says, screwing the top on her cream.

'But wait for it,' Elias adds.

More and more screeches and thwacks of fruit bats landing in the trees. There must be fifty of them at least.

'Wow,' Jo says.

Elias holds a finger up. *Wait.*

Another scream, this one human and male. She jumps. In the house, Denny is screaming at the bats. She hears the slaps of their wings as they fly away. Then, 'Yeah, that's right! Fuck off!'

The screen door slams shut, then everything is back to silence.

'So how many farms have you been on so far?' Yan asks, as though nothing has just happened.

'This is my first.'

'You are lucky,' Elias says, 'the last place I was at, I was staying at a hostel which organised the work. I went all the way to Mildura and they kept putting me off. Saying the work would come tomorrow, then the next day. By the end I stayed there since a whole month, but I'd only worked ten days. I owed the hostel five hundred dollars and they wouldn't give my passport back until I paid it. Five hundred for this disgusting roach-infested shared room and I still had seventy-eight days to do. My skin was covered in bed bug bites. This is much better than that.'

'Exactly,' Sorcha says. 'Denny's alright. I mean ... he's thick as shite and only half as handy, but he's alright.'

Yan snorts a laugh.

'He doesn't bother you when you go and make lunch?' Jo asks.

'Apart from the *Farmer Wants a Wife* audition?'

'What?'

Sorcha laughs. 'He's fine. Doesn't touch me. I tell you, some of my friends haven't been so lucky. Although I had a dream run for my last one, a dairy farm. The lady there said we were like her grandchildren, she was such a champ. The work only lasted three weeks, of course.'

Elias goes back to his notepad. Sorcha puts the cream in her pocket and sits with Yan. They start their own conversation, quiet voices and small smiles. Jo stands.

'I might have an early night.'

'Do what you want,' Sorcha says.

She'll take two, just for tonight, then she'll go back to one a night. She needs to make them last, she's not sure where the closest pharmacy would be from here and she went through too many at the hotel. But for tonight, as a treat, she'll have two.

She dreams of St Ives again.

She is in the ocean next to the boat, dog paddling. Her mum is on the deck, her face twisting as she adjusts the focus on the lens, Jamie on her chest. Why is she in the water by herself? Why is her mother not looking at her? She wants to go home by the shop and get a packet of Hobnobs. She yells out but splashes, screams.

Jo wakes, groggy and blinking. That sick guilt in her gut that she always gets from that dream. The light under the door is grey. A new day will be beginning soon.

CHAPTER 7

After a week in the fields, Jo's body changes. Stooped back, cricked neck, bent knees, clawed hands. A metamorphosis into some kind of human–bird hybrid shaped by picking mango after mango after mango. The sun beats against her shoulders, sweat drenches her long-sleeved shirt. Britney Spears plays on.

She wakes bleary and numb and the day goes on like that, as though she's still asleep. Bryce, the little dog, shadows her, yapping and pulling on her socks with his teeth. Tyson rides around them in circles, singing along to the music, loudly and out of tune. While the work makes her body hurt, it blunts her mind. By the time her monotonous shift is over, her brain feels bleached. Then there are only a few hours to get through until the sweet snip-clicks of the cap of her temazepam bottle.

Sunday is break day. She wakes cringing, expecting to hear the clanks of Tyson beating the walls with a stick. No sound comes. There's a thin line of white coming from underneath the door. Daylight.

The others wake. Elias goes to the house, and Yan and Sorcha sit on Yan's bunk playing cards.

'How far are the shops from here?' she asks them.

Sorcha laughs. 'You'd have to go with Denny.'

'I can't walk?'

Yan looks at her like she's a complete idiot. 'It would take you hours.'

'Oh,' she says. She had taken her last two pills last night. She'd been banking on getting more today.

'You need something?' Yan asks. 'If you write it down and give it to Denny with some cash he might get it for you.'

'I wrote down tampons last week,' Sorcha says. 'The state of him when he read it. Face like a smacked arse.'

'I need to go with him though, I need a script filled from the pharmacy so they'll want to see my ID.'

'No pharmacy at Langrange. You'd have to go into Broome for that, I'd say. No buses on a Sunday.'

It's so definitive. She should have checked before she double dosed. She should have gotten more before she left.

'Is it something serious?' Yan asks.

'Oh, erm … no. I guess it's fine.'

She sits on her bed. It stinks of sweat and drugged sleep. She needs to get out, do something.

'I'm going to go for a walk, do you want to come?' she asks.

'No,' Sorcha says, 'we went for a long walk last Sunday and got lost.'

'And you got sunburnt,' Yan says.

'What do you expect? Dublin never gets over twelve degrees.'

Yan looks to Jo. 'She didn't even bring sunscreen.'

'Do you think Elias would want to?' she asks. It would be nice to walk with Elias. She could ask him questions, quieten her mind by listening to him.

'Probably not for a few hours,' Sorcha tells her. 'I think he's hoping to go along with Denny to use the phone booth in Langrange. He hasn't gotten a letter from his girlfriend since he got here, you know. I think he's worried that he's being ghosted.'

'Can't he just use Denny's phone?'

Now they both stare at her like she's an idiot.

Jo turns away, slips on her denim shorts and pulls a sports bra on under the t-shirt she slept in. She puts her sunglasses and her blue baseball cap on and smothers herself in sunscreen and insect repellent, slips a bottle of water and some biscuits into her backpack, then walks out into the sun. She'll go and find the ocean. If she finds it, maybe she'll stop dreaming of it. She'll put her aching feet in that perfect shade of Ultramarine Deep and it will cure her.

It takes her twenty minutes to even get to the edge of Denny's property. It's unbelievable that one such unremarkable man could own so much land. The fields are endless. She walks down his dirt driveway and it seems to go on and on. Behind her, she hears the sound of yipping. Bryce. She quickens her pace. The last thing she wants to deal with today is either Bryce or Tyson. But soon the yipping is louder and she feels the familiar tug on her sock.

'Go away,' she hisses. Bryce growls at her. She flicks her foot, pulling the cotton out of his mouth. She continues, but Bryce follows, yipping. She kneels in front of him and points a finger in his face.

'Go home.' She tries to get her voice low and threatening. Bryce just growls at her again.

Eventually she reaches the main road, Bryce a few paces behind her. He's stopped barking and so she hopes if she ignores him he'll get bored and go back. She steps off Denny's driveway onto the road. Left or right. It doesn't matter. She doesn't even have a watch. The whole day is hers.

It's strange to walk for so long without distraction. Her phone was down to ten per cent battery on her second day, so she turned it off. There was no electricity to charge it. She has no music. No podcasts. Just the crunch of one foot in front of the other. The faint trill of a bird in the distance.

The sky is clear, not one puff of cloud. She knows the colour, it's a few shades from International Klein Blue. She'd learnt about it at art school. Created by Yves Klein, a French guy in the 1940s who became obsessed with capturing a very specific shade of blue. Both deep and bright at once, like this sky. He'd created his own pigment, then spent the rest of his life painting only with that colour. She wonders what he would think of this place, where colours are so pure.

A rumble begins, heavy and deep. Over her shoulder, the sun flashes from the windscreen of a lorry. She walks off the road, watches it approach, hears the deep rumble in the earth, in her teeth. Bryce barks, but the sound is drowned out by the road train. It blazes past. She's a few metres from the road, but the loose gravel and dust showers her.

She coughs, the dust in her throat. She wants to yell after the lorry, shake her fist at him and swear. Her breathing quickens. She has to find a way to get to a pharmacy. She can't do this work on no sleep, she can't be awake in that hot shed all night thinking about Eric's expression of relief, remembering that even the baby wanted to escape her. After eighty-two more nights she'd go mad from it.

Bryce barks again.

'What?' she yells at him.

He's on the other side of the road, sniffing at what looks like a miniature graveyard. She crosses over to get a better look. The mounds of misshapen rock are bigger than they'd appeared from a distance. About ten centimetres around their base but almost a metre high. There's more than fifty of them, spaced out haphazardly. They're orange, like the dirt around them. She gets closer to the one Bryce is barking at. The rock is dimpled, like cottage cheese covered in dirt. There's a hum coming from it, the growl of a thousand insects. She steps away, itchy, and keeps walking.

She hears the sound of another engine and flinches. But this one is a small lorry, not a road train. She pulls her sunglasses away from her eyes to squint down the road.

It's the green lorry. In the driver's seat is the guy she had seen in the water, the guy who'd come to visit Denny. Gabe. Another car is tailing him, a silver sedan, the sun winking from its bonnet.

Jo backs away from the road, not wanting the dust and bits of loose gravel to blow into her face again. But the lorry slows and pulls off onto the shoulder on the other side of the road. The window winds down and she hears the faint sound of soft folk music playing.

'Hey,' the guy says, smiling at her, 'you're one of Denny's pickers, right?'

'Yes.' She crosses over, goes to his window. 'I'm Jo.'

'I thought so.'

The sedan pulls in behind him. There's a woman in the driver's seat. She's middle-aged, pale skinned with soft features.

'That's Ally.' He juts a thumb out behind him. 'And I'm Gabe.'

From a distance, she'd presumed he was Australian. But now she can hear an accent.

'American?' she asks.

'Guilty. New York. But I live here now. English?'

'Yeah.' She leans in closer to the lorry. He grins at her. He has the faintest crinkles around his eyes. She hadn't seen them from a distance. The sun lights them up, defines them, and makes his eyes shine. Behind him the woman is watching out the window.

'How's it going?' Gabe says. 'He has you guys working so hard.'

She leans forward. 'I'd kill for a beer.'

His eyes slide to her feet. 'Is this a friend of yours?' he asks.

She's confused for a moment, then hears growling. She looks down. Bryce is baring his teeth.

'Can't get rid of him.'

'I think he likes you.'

'No. He just likes the taste of my ankles.' She leans closer, her elbows on the edge of the window, the metal hot against her skin. 'You should see them, covered in cuts.'

He laughs. 'You want to show me your ankles? We only just met.'

A strange blush creeps over her. She knows he was kidding, but nonetheless her cheeks heat.

The woman unwinds her window, looks out at Jo.

'Where are you going all by yourself? Do you need a lift somewhere?' She's Australian, her accent syrupy warm.

Jo smiles at her. 'Just out for a wander. See what I can see.' She's in no rush to get back to the farm, no matter how hot it is. Better to have distraction.

The woman holds her gaze. She has beautiful eyes, caramel like her voice. 'Be careful,' she calls.

'I'm fine. I have a bodyguard.'

Bryce growls again, hackles raised.

Gabe smiles, touches her forearm with the tips of his fingers. 'It was nice to meet you, J.'

They drive off. She can feel the place where he touched her, his hand so gentle. Bryce runs after the lorry, yipping at the exhaust fumes. Good. She turns away. Hopefully he'll follow Gabe back toward Denny's.

As she walks, the heat recedes from her cheeks. She wonders what he's doing, how an American found his way to these deserted roads. Who were those people in the ocean with him that day? Who was that woman? His mother perhaps, she had a motherly sort of feeling about her. The kind of soft, round woman who would give amazing hugs.

Bryce comes running back to her, still yapping. He bites her squarely on the ankle and she swears under her breath.

Instead of continuing down the endless road, she sets off into the scrub in the direction she hoped was the coast.

Soon she's walking through grass, trying to avoid the prickly thistles, and remembering every terrifying piece of trivia she's learnt about Australia and snakes: How many species of snake are there in Australia? One hundred and seventy. How many of them are poisonous? One hundred.

The scrub thickens. She pushes through spindly trees, just taller than her with thin trunks and sharp leafless branches.

Up ahead is one of the trees she'd seen on the day she'd arrived. Elias had told her they were called boabs. He showed her a postcard he'd gotten from the store, intending to send it with his most recent letter to his girlfriend. 'Do you think she will find this funny?' he had asked.

On the front was a boab tree, its hollowed-out centre fitted with a toilet. On the back was a little description of the tree. How the really old ones would hollow themselves out naturally as they grew.

'Definitely,' she'd said, although she had no idea.

She approaches the tree, its shape just as strange up close, spindly branches and wide, bottle-like trunk. It's huge; if she tried to hug it her arms wouldn't span half its girth. Its trunk is a pale dove grey, smooth to the touch. There is a slit in its side and, when she walks around to it, she sees an opening to its hollow centre. Pressing her face to it, she tries to see inside, but it's too dark. It smells damp and cold and earthy.

Bryce trips past her legs and goes inside the darkness of the tree centre, sniffling the ground. For a moment it's like he's stopped existing, but then she hears a bark and he comes back. He sits and scratches behind his ear.

The deeper she walks, the thicker the scrub becomes. And wetter, with more greenery. She listens for the ocean, but hears only her own footfalls, Bryce's occasional yip, the echo of a bird's cry. She should stop soon, eat her biscuits and have some water.

The smell reaches her first. That hideous sweet smell of something rotting. She stops and looks around for a dead animal.

The earth has turned from orange dirt to mud. She must be close. Pushing deeper into some spindly trees she can hear, faintly, the sound of lapping water. But it isn't the ocean that appears before her after five sweaty minutes of fighting through the trees, it's a swamp. The trees have created a canopy overhead blocking out the sky, letting the light fall in speckles. It's cooler in here, though the smell is worse. The roots of the trees are visible, standing on short stilts above the pool of Oxide Green water. It's beautiful. Her fingers twitch with the urge to sketch it, to trace the spindly branches, the twisting roots. She hasn't felt that in a long time.

She walks on, Bryce behind her, for another ten minutes or so. She's sure that the ocean must be on the other side of the swamp, but the trees just get thicker. This is probably the only water she's going to reach today. Sitting on the top of the drier-looking roots, she pulls out her bottle and gulps the tepid water. She takes a breath, inhaling the damp air. Bryce barks at her again. She tries to ignore it, but the high pitch of his yelping is starting to get into her ears. She takes out her crackers, wishing she had something more substantial to eat. They're salty and dry.

'Do you want one?' she asks Bryce, holding a cracker out. His little black eyes flick to it and his pink tongue emerges. He licks his lips. She drops it on the ground in front of him and he bends his head to eat. He looks cute for a second, his rounded white head leant over like that. She strokes him behind his ear. He snarls. His head snaps up and he bites her hand, quick and hard. She yanks it back. Her hand is bleeding, three small cuts under her thumb. Bryce goes back to the cracker. She can hear it breaking between his teeth. The sound is loud. Or at least it seems loud. Everything around her has turned quiet. The sounds of insects, the murmur of birds. She's sure she had heard them before. Now, everything is muted.

She puts her water bottle in her bag and gets up. She swings her way through the space, holding onto the branches, using them as leverage as she steadies each foot on the mud. Each of her movements sound loud. She focuses on the mess of roots underneath her, some of them clogged with algae. She doesn't want to fall into that stinking water.

Bryce yips again, but it's different this time, higher. It cuts off abruptly. She hears a splash from behind her. A snap.

'Bryce?'

He doesn't come. She turns back, walking the way she came.

'Bryce?'

Back where she left him she notices the water is swirling. Half the cracker is on the shore. But there's no way he would have fallen in and not come back up. He must be off chasing something.

She tries to focus on studying this amazing place, on mentally taking photos, but her hands are sweating. Her heart is beating. Everything is too silent.

She looks over her shoulder. A bubble surfaces. Then pops.

'Bryce?' It comes out as a whisper.

Silence.

She moves quicker, trying to go back, away from the mangroves. Then she stops. She can hear her own blood, the thwacking drumbeat of her heart. There's a lizard on the bank. A huge lizard, probably half the length of her own body. Maybe even longer. It isn't moving. It has no face, no legs. Her mother used to have a handbag like this. Jo would run her little fingers across it, letting them bounce over the bumpy, fake, green skin.

The lizard twitches. Then slides into the water. It isn't a lizard. It's a tail.

She pushes off, grabs branches, her sweaty fingers slippery, tries to not make a sound. But her stumbles are amplified. She turns back. The water ripples.

Her foot lands hard on some algae-covered roots. They give way. Her foot splashes into the water. She grabs tight to the branches, her skin burning as they slip through her hands. She scrambles, gets a proper hold and pulls her sodden foot out.

She throws her weight forward, doesn't look back. It's right behind her. She knows it's right behind her. Her wet shoe slides on the roots as she runs. She holds her weight on the branches, jangle-panic in her muscles.

The trees are getting thicker. She's close. She pushes on. The earth is there, ahead. Muddy, but there. She reaches it, her one wet foot slipping, her shoe full of water. As soon as her feet are on stable ground she runs, forearms up to protect her face. Then she's out, on the other side of the trees, but she keeps going, keeps running.

Only then does she turn back. She's not sure what she expects to see. The crocodile slithering out after her? But there is nothing. Just the mangrove trees.

She keeps running, wet shoe squelching, not sure if she's even heading in the right direction, her breath escaping in ragged puffs. She slows for a while, jogging, then starts running again. The landscape stretches out around her. Spindly trees that all look the same. She can't see the road. She might not even be on the right side of the mangroves. It's so hot her shoe is drying; she starts to feel the throb of her palms. Her hands are scraped red raw.

A soft rumble. A car. The road. Thank god. She follows the sound, runs towards it.

She breaks out onto loose gravel, falls to her knees. She stands. There it is in the distance, Gabe's green lorry, driving away from her. She stands, raises her arms in the air and jumps up. 'Hey!' she yells.

He's too far away, there's no way he will hear. But she sees the car slow, brake. Then, a three-point turn in the middle of the road and the lorry is coming towards her.

She leans down, hands on knees, trying to get her breath back. A drip of sweat beads onto her nose and drops onto the road in front of her.

The lorry pulls in. The squeak of old brakes and car doors opening.

'Hey, you okay? Everything alright?' Gabe's voice.

A hand warm on her back, she looks up, expecting it to be Gabe. But it's not. It's Ally, standing by her, contemplating her with genuine concern.

'What happened, baby?' she whispers. Gabe is behind her, watching.

Jo straightens, still breathless but embarrassed. 'Back there,' she says, looking behind her, 'a crocodile. I think. I was in this swamp, and there were ripples, and—'

She stops. Gabe looks around her.

'Where's your bodyguard?' he asks.

She puts a hand over her mouth, doesn't know what to say.

'Come on,' Ally says. 'Gabe, you drive. Me and J here are going to ride in the back.'

'Jo,' she says, but lets herself be led towards the lorry. She looks around for the silver sedan Ally was driving before, but it's gone. When they reach the tray, Gabe's arm wraps around her and lifts her onto the metal. She turns to him, but he's already holding a hand out to Ally, who is pulling herself up as well.

She hasn't felt tenderness in a long while. Now, Ally is stroking her hands across her skin. Checking her legs, her muddy knees, inspecting the scratches on her arms, her raw palms. The engine starts and they jerk a little as the lorry pulls out.

'You're okay,' Ally concludes, still holding her hands. 'I think you've just had a shock.'

'I never thought I'd actually see one of those things in the wild.'

Ally smiles at her, pats her hands. 'Honey, those mangroves are infested with crocs. Did you not know that? That's where they live. Some are twelve feet long.'

Jo wraps her arms around her knees. 'Shit.' She starts shaking. Full-body trembles. 'But I mean, Bryce was just there and then he wasn't. Don't they have to, I don't know, death roll or something? Isn't that what they do?'

'No need with small prey. They're quick. But there's no point thinking about that.'

Ally shifts around to her side of the lorry, wraps an arm around Jo's shoulders.

'Thank you,' Jo whispers, 'you're being so kind even though I'm a complete stranger.'

'What else can you depend on but the kindness of strangers?'

Jo laughs, but she isn't sure if the woman is joking.

They sit in silence for a while, Ally's arm around her. Jo's back is sweating where their skin is touching, but she doesn't move. Her heart slows, her breathing evens, she stops shaking.

The car jolts around a corner. She straightens. They are on Denny's driveway. Tyson will want to know where Bryce is.

'What am I going to do about the dog?' she says to Ally. 'I mean, Tyson is just a kid, he's going to be so upset.'

'I don't know, honey,' Ally says, 'that's up to you. Maybe sleep on it? It's getting late.'

Gabe comes around and holds out his arm. Jo takes it and jumps onto the lawn.

'I got you these,' he says, holding a six-pack of beer. 'We went past the shop before. I was on my way to drop them off here when we spotted you.'

'Wow,' Jo says, 'that's really nice. Thank you.'

Ally is standing next to her. 'Look after yourself, alright?'

'I will.'

They get into the lorry and drive away. Ally leans out of the window to wave. Wherever they were going, Jo wishes she was going with them, not back to the shed alone.

*

Later, around the fire, warm beer in hand, she tries hard to breathe deeply. She is okay. She's safe. She's going to find a way to get her prescription. Everything is going to be fine.

'You know there's a place in Broome that actually makes beer out of mangoes?' Yan holds the bottle in front of her, inspects the liquid. The light of the fire throws the amber colour across one side of her face.

'Is that possible?' Jo asks.

'Ferment anything and you will get alcohol,' Elias says, taking a sip. 'Ah, fuck me. I love beer.'

Sorcha bursts out in laughter. 'You know, I don't think I've ever heard you swear, El.'

'Guys, I'm German. It's in my blood.'

'Beer is in your blood?' Yan asks, giggling. Sorcha puts her arm around her and their temples touch for a moment.

'Did you get onto your girlfriend?' Jo asks Elias.

'No,' he says, the smile flickering away. 'And you? How was your walk?'

Sorcha eyes the dirt on her knees. 'Look at the state of you. Did you trip, did you?'

Jo tries to smile, tries not to picture that lone air bubble popping on the surface of the green water.

'It was great. Nice to see some stuff and meet Gabe,' she says. She'd considered telling them about Bryce, but she doesn't trust them, not really. If they tell Denny, she might get fired and she needs her pay slip, otherwise this past week would have been for nothing. Plus, surely it would be nicer for Tyson to believe Bryce ran away.

Jo takes another sip of her beer, tries to let the alcohol relax her, slow her heart. 'So what's Gabe's deal anyway?' she asks. 'He doesn't look much like a farmer.'

Sorcha laughs. 'He's not. I dunno. I was actually thinking, do you think he might be one of those radge Rossack nutters?'

Yan sips her beer. 'Maybe.'

'Rossack?' Jo asks. 'What is that?'

'It's like … I don't know,' Sorcha says. 'I heard stories about it from the other farm I was on.'

'So have I,' Yan says. 'Someone said they had built a little town behind a waterfall. That they want to live together, they don't want to get involved in the outside world. It sounds made up to me.'

'Yeah,' Sorcha says, 'someone told me there is a woman there who says she can heal people.'

'I heard that too.'

Jo thinks of Ally. She could imagine Ally having that effect on people. She'd made Jo feel so much better.

'No,' Elias says, 'it is just a group of people who decided to camp out, long term.'

'Sounds a bit creepy though, doesn't it?' Sorcha says. 'Being so isolated without proper technology or anything. This is different, it's kind of cool because we know it's only short term. But I wouldn't want this to be my whole life. Going through life without my iPhone? And no telly? Jesus, feck that.'

Jo looks around at the darkness. The fields she can't see stretch out around them. She turns to Sorcha, who is now fiddling with the label of her beer. She's digging a dirty fingernail underneath the gum of the sticker, trying to pull it neatly from the glass.

'So, why does Gabe come by here?'

Sorcha looks into her empty bottle. 'They go into Denny's study. I don't know. Denny's paying him for something. I see the money laid out on his desk sometimes. Before Gabe arrives.'

'Drugs?' Jo asks.

Sorcha gets up. 'Probably.' She grabs the two remaining beers, gives one to Elias and sits next to Yan with the other one. 'We can share,' she says to her.

Jo waits, and eventually Sorcha meets her eye over the fire.

*

That night in the complete blackness of the shed, Jo opens her eyes and closes them again. Above her would be the wooden slats under Elias's mattress, if she could see them.

A place that cuts itself off from the rest of the world. She knew Yan had meant it as a negative, but it sounded almost idyllic. A community of people like Gabe and Ally. Kind people who look out for each other. She never thanked them properly.

She wonders again if Ally is Gabe's mother. She'd be a good mother. *What happened, baby?* Ally had said and Jo can see a little girl with dirty hair and downcast eyes. Herself, back when she was Josephine. A time she doesn't want to think about. But she can see Ally hugging little Josephine, helping her up from the dark, and she realises she's not thinking, she's starting to slip into dream. Somehow, miraculously, she's falling asleep.

CHAPTER 8

ENGLAND, 1999

When his home phone rang, Sam was watching *Midsomer Murders*. He always watched it when he got home from work. He never used to, crime was not his thing, but he'd caught the end of an episode after tea last week and now he was hooked. These were nice murders, no blood and gore. Polite murders.

Detective Chief Inspector Tom Barnaby was making his way down a country lane. Sam knew this would be the scene where it was all explained, where the unlikely villain spilled the beans. Barnaby had just been speaking to his wife, who always cracked the case, although she never knew it. Now Barnaby knew who the murderer was, though Sam had no idea. If Sam had been a rude man he'd have let the telephone ring out. But he wasn't rude so he got up and answered it, one eye on the telly.

He didn't recognise the voice of the man on the other end of the phone. He was official sounding, government, maybe from the council. Though his accent was southern English, posh. Barnaby knocked on the door of a little house and the nice old lady answered. Of course, Sam should have guessed. It was often the nice old lady.

'... regarding the custody of your daughter,' said the voice on the phone.

Sam stopped listening to the telly. *Your daughter.* He hadn't heard anyone say those words before.

'I'm sorry?' Sam said.

'Your daughter, Josephine. We need you to collect her.'

*

It was a six-hour drive from Chesterfield, the old market town where Sam was born and raised, to the seaside village of St Ives. Sam woke before light and only stopped for a quick piss and a coffee at the services off the M5. He spent the drive trying hard not to think what she'd look like. If she might look like him.

It'd been a one-night stand. He'd never had a one-night stand before or in the years since. He'd taken his mother to St Ives in the last years of her life, thinking that a seaside holiday might do her good. His mother hadn't liked it. It was cold the whole time. She was dead nesh, his mother, her bones always aching.

It was hard, spending all this time cooped up with his mum. He loved her, course he did, but he was quick to anger with her. All those years when she'd been sorting herself, when she'd sent him off to Beechwood Home. Those years were hard to forget when you were sharing a five-by-eight twin room.

When she was asleep he'd go out walking. Down by the beach usually, he liked watching the boats. When it started full plothering he made his way to the Sloop Inn, had a pint of lager at the bar. The dim lights, the crackling fire, the smell of history. He'd enjoyed it there. He'd enjoyed the girl behind the bar too: Charlotte. She was smiley with him and he liked the way she jutted her hip to close the fridge door when her hands were full. She told him about her photos, how she was saving up to buy her mate Tony's old boat so she could go out on the water to take them. It was just the lager, probably, and being somewhere different. He wasn't that type of bloke.

She'd called him a few months on. She didn't want anything. Just thought he should know. She'd called again when it was born. A girl, she told him. She'd sent him a picture, which he'd kept. He'd never showed it to anyone, but he'd kept it and looked at it every now and then. The soft pink blanket. Them tiny fingers clutching round it.

When he arrived, Josephine was sitting on a grey chair in the hallway.

'Alright, love?' he said, his heart hammering like you wouldn't believe.

Josephine didn't look up. She kept on staring at her skinny knees. She was skinny all over. Too skinny, he thought.

When he was in the office they told him all that had happened. He couldn't believe it at first. Charlotte had been all warmth and laughter. But he hadn't known her long, he supposed. And Josephine … she was young. Hopefully she wouldn't remember what had happened when she was grown. It would be a lot to carry with her if she did.

'But Charlotte could want to see her some?' Sam had said. 'When she's herself again, she could want her.'

'If that's the case she will have to file. Go through the courts.'

The paperwork took longer than he'd thought. But then, once it was done, that was it. The girl was his to take home.

'C'mon, love,' he told her, 'let's get going. Don't want be driving in the dark.'

Josephine pushed off the bench and followed behind him. He wondered if she was disappointed. If she'd had some fairytale notion of her father, imagined him some young handsome prince, not a middle-aged plasterer with greying hair.

He opened the door for her and she sat in the passenger seat without question. The social worker must have explained it all to her already. He put her pink backpack in the back. It was light. A kid should have more than this. Surely there was more she'd need than this?

'Do your seatbelt then,' he told her when he got in. He saw her fingers were trembling as she clipped it in. She still had them tiny hands.

'You need stop anywhere on the way, love?' he asked.

Josephine shook her head, a swish of dirty hair. This crumpled little broken bird in his car was his to look after now. His responsibility. His daughter. He'd have to cook meals with vegetables in them. Drop her off at school. He couldn't watch his new show. Polite murders or not, it wouldn't be appropriate.

'Allreet,' he said, and they were off.

*

Rain speckled on the windscreen, a car horn blasted, but the girl didn't look up. She was playing with a beaded bracelet. Not real jewellery. Plastic. Little shiny beads in the shapes of cats' heads.

'You like cats then?' he asked.

For a while there was only silence—was she a mute? They hadn't said she was a mute at the office—then she peeked up at him. She was a dead ringer for Charlotte, that was for sure. But there was something of him too, around the mouth. He turned back to the road.

'Do you have a cat?' she asked, dead quiet so he could only just hear her.

'No.'

'Oh.'

His belly was twisting. They'd need to stop soon. She looked like she could use a feed as well. Her big eyes bore into the side of his face. And he saw she wasn't being mardy, staring at her knees like that. She wasn't sulking. She was looking at him now like he was some monster, a kidnapper. She was scared of him.

'My mum had two,' he said. 'Persians. Beautiful animals. She'd bath 'em every week, and when visitors came she'd dust 'em with talcum powder so they were extra white.' He laughed. 'Every time someone stroked 'em powder would fly off.'

She was still looking at him.

'Dead now, though.'

It was a long drive. Longer than on the way there. They stopped at a rest stop with a Wimpy's. He bought them both a sausage and egg muffin, got himself another coffee. He shouldn't've had that second coffee. His heart was beating too fast and he didn't want to get back on the motorway. He saw the other kids with their families, all with their little kids' meal sets. He hadn't even thought of that. His eyes hadn't even flicked to the kids' board. He watched her eat—head down, bony elbows jutting out—and did the math in his head. Two more years of primary school. Then six of high school. There was a school around the corner from his house. That relieved him a bit, the fact he could even think of that school so close to home. He'd noticed the road, parents piling up waiting for their kids, not the school. But still. Josephine could go there. She could walk in fact, it was only ten minutes away.

He wasn't a social man. Not at all. There were folks he smiled to, folks to nod hello to, to chat to at the shop. His real friends he'd made online, on Facebook to begin with. They were there when he wanted them, behind the computer screen, but they didn't expect much, just his words when he felt in the mood to give them. And he was happy with that, happy with his lot. He didn't need nothing more.

Once they got to Chesterfield, his shoulders dropped. His jaw unclenched. It would be alright. Not everything would have to change.

'What's that?'

It was the first time Josephine had spoken since the cats. She was pointing through the windscreen, at the spire. It was crooked, twisted around at a strange angle.

He chuckled. 'People used to say it was kicked over by the devil.'

He saw her face.

'No, love. They put iron on untreated wood. Warped when the rain came.'

She was staring at it, mouth slightly open. To her, it might be scary, that warped gothic spike. To him it just meant he was home.

*

When they pulled into his drive, it was close to dark. He took her pink bag from the back and led her up the stairs to her room. It was lucky that he'd had a spare. It wasn't much for a kid. A single bed, a side table with a lamp, a clock on the wall. They'd have to get a desk for her homework. He'd look in the traders in the morning.

He checked the clock. His show would have started, the first of the nice murders committed. She was looking around at the room. Must be knackered from it all. He was.

'I'll let you get settled,' he said. 'Shout out if you need something, okay?'

All night he didn't hear a peep from her.

Later, when he made his way to bed, he peered in. She was in bed, lights off, but she was awake. Her eyes big and shining. It scared him more than anything, them haunted, needing eyes.

''Night,' he said, and closed her door tight.

CHAPTER 9

THE FARM, 2018

Jo's finger joints crunch with each clip of the shears. She stops for the third time and rubs her hands. There's a rustle from the row behind her. She's going to get yelled at. She's slowing everyone down.

'Swapsies?' Sorcha asks.

Jo turns. 'Huh?'

'Let's swap. You do the high branches. It uses different muscles.' She hands Jo the shears with the long handles and basket. Jo gives her the small ones.

'Thanks.'

'My arms are hurting from reaching up.'

Jo crosses over to the other side of the row, next to Yan, who pulls one of her earbuds out.

'I think we're going to be in the packing shed in a couple of days,' Yan tells her.

'Is that better?'

'Yeah. It's out of the sun.'

Jo holds the rubber grips at the bottoms of the long handles of the shears. They are a clever invention. A black plastic basket is attached under the blades. She positions the open shears over the stem and the basket cups the bottom of the mango. She squeezes, and the mango drops into the basket. The action uses the muscles in the backs of her arms, needs more grunt from her shoulders.

She slept until dawn. A full seven hours. She can't remember the last time she was able to do that. Natural sleep is so different to drugged sleep. She's less muzzy, less numb. Her head is clearer. She doesn't know what's caused it. The hard work maybe? The fresh air? She knows it was probably a one-off, she can't count on it happening again. She needs to find a way to get to Broome, get some more pills.

'Bryce!'

They've been hearing it all day. Tyson searching for the dog.

He rides closer. 'Where the fuck is Bryce?'

'Jesus, we told you,' Sorcha says. 'We don't know.'

He skids to a stop, points at Jo. 'You took him.'

'No,' she says, staring at the pink tip of his finger.

'You did. I saw him following you. He likes you.'

'He always bit me.'

'That's because he knows you're a bitch.'

'That's enough. I know you're upset, but you can't talk to people like that.'

'Where is he? Where'd you put him?'

'Jesus, kid, would you ever feck off?' Sorcha yells.

Tyson glares at her then he kicks off with his bike and rides away, calling for Bryce.

Jo takes a shaky breath, and resumes picking. She notices Yan hasn't put her earbud back in. 'What was your place before this like?' she asks. 'You said you'd already done half, right?'

Yan stares at the mango in front of her but doesn't pluck it. 'It was bad,' she says. She snaps with her shears and doesn't continue.

Jo turns away. It seems that is all she is going to get. She keeps going. Snipping the mangoes off so they fall into the basket, then putting them into her jute sack. The bag is weighing on her shoulder by the time Yan continues.

'The farmer's name was Tom,' she says. 'It was a bigger farm than this. There were eight of us, nine for a while. We were camping on the grounds. I hated it at first, but I got used to it pretty fast. At least it was free. We all camped except for this one guy who stayed at the house, Xiu, although I didn't know his name. I'd only see him through the windows, cleaning and cooking for everyone. Tom said he was too weak to do farm work, so he had him doing the housework instead. Xiu was probably only nineteen or twenty and he was petite.

'Xiu never left the house. Even at dinner, when Tom would come and sit at the table and eat with us, Xiu would be inside. I'd caught his eye through the window once and something hadn't seemed right. He'd just stared at me, his eyes so haunted. I wanted to ask Tom about him, but I was worried. Tom was moody. He'd flown off the handle at this guy once because he'd asked for more break times. Made him leave. Tom talked about Thailand sometimes when he'd been drinking, about the ladyboys, how you could never even tell. It was like he was bragging. The other workers would just laugh along. No one wanted to say anything. Or maybe they really did think it was funny. I don't know. This girl told me that she'd seen Tom watching porn on his phone while we worked. He hadn't even tried to hide what he was doing.

'Anyway. One time I saw Xiu come out of the house. He was hanging up laundry. I waited until Tom was doing something in the packing shed and I raced up there. I asked him if he was okay. The way he looked up close scared me. He barely spoke English; he couldn't understand me. So I asked him again in Cantonese.'

Yan stops picking. She takes a breath. 'He said, "你可唔可以幫我?" Do you know what that means? It means "Will you help me?" We left right then, the wet laundry in the basket. We grabbed our stuff and walked the four kilometres to town, hoping Tom wouldn't notice too quickly and follow us. I asked Xiu what had happened, but he didn't say anything else. We went to the cops and you know what? They didn't even seem surprised. I think that kind of thing had happened before.'

'That's awful.'

Yan shrugs, but her hands shake a little as she puts the shears on the ground. She walks away, down the line of mangoes.

Jo turns to Elias and Sorcha.

'I haven't heard that before,' Elias says.

Sorcha puts her shears down and hurries to catch up with Yan. She clutches her elbow and Yan stops. The air is too still for their voices to carry. Yan crosses her arms. Sorcha leans in and kisses Yan on each temple, pulls her in close.

The Britney Spears stops. They look up the hill to the house. Denny is standing there, staring at Yan and Sorcha. Then he turns and goes inside.

*

Josephine is under the surface of the water, eyes squinted, trying to go deeper. She wants to reach the bottom of the bay, gather sand into her fist. She wants her mum to see she's not there. She wants to get her mum to look at her, not Jamie.

The water is rolling and swelling. She's dizzy. She pushes deeper. Her skull thrums.

The sound of metal scraping against concrete wakes Jo. No grogginess. No delay. Natural sleep is a thin and flighty thing, it doesn't hold her under like temazepam. She rises straight up from her sleep, right into fear. She feels the others wake as well. Their four breaths held in unison.

There's a shuffle, rubber shoes against concrete. Someone is coming into their shed. She opens her eyes but it makes no difference. It's too dark to see. The figure has moved closer to her, towards the end of her bed. She can't see him but she can feel him. The presence radiates heat.

'Denny?' she asks the dark.

The metal door scrapes against the concrete and clanks into place. The dark shape, the silent presence breathing extra air from their windowless room, he is gone.

No one says anything and she thinks that maybe this is a collective dream, that maybe they'll all go back to sleep and no one will mention it in the morning. Like a nightmare you forget the moment you open your eyes. But then she feels something else.

Something cold moving against her leg.

It is a twitching muscle against the curve of her calf. She screams, high pitched and piercing. It hurts even her own ears.

'What?' Elias calls. 'What is it?'

She pulls back, throws the covers off her. Clambers to the head of the bed.

'Torch, torch, torch!' Sorcha yells. 'Where is it?'

A light shines onto Jo and she is blinded for a second, then it sweeps over the covers.

'What happened?' Yan asks.

'There's something!' she yells. She knows it makes no sense.

They watch the light wash over her bed again. And then, movement. A long, thin shape making the white sheet buckle and shift around its form.

'Snake!' Sorcha screams. 'It's a fecking snake!'

Then, from behind the tin wall, a boy's laughter.

They look at each other. Faces shadowy in the reflected light from her sheet. Yan looks so tired.

'That little shit.' Jo pulls her boots on, hopping on the spot, no socks. 'That's it. That's enough.'

She pulls the door open, the metal screams. It is dark, but the moon is bright and low.

There he is, around the side. Tyson, an empty sack in his hand. He's smiling, a mean smile, but it slips off his face when he sees her expression.

He runs. She chases.

It's been three nights of solid natural sleep now. The temazepam is out of her system. She's clearer. The fog has lifted. Now, the anger burns. It makes her run faster. It's overwhelming, blinding. He darts around the fence and she races after him. Her bare feet slip in her boots, the backs rub.

She's gaining on him and he keeps looking back. The empty sack in his hand slapping in the air. She's almost caught up, he's in grabbing distance. She wrenches the top of his arm, but he yanks it away.

'Go away! Fuck off!' he screams.

She launches at him, whacks onto his back, tackles him to the ground. They fall heavily. Her elbow thuds against the earth. His shoulder smacks into hers. But she doesn't pause, clambers onto him, pinning him to the ground with her knee.

'Say you're sorry!' she yells.

'Get off!'

'No,' she pants, 'say sorry.'

His breath comes in heaves against her. His ribcage is fragile under her knee. Like she could crack it.

'I'm not sorry!'

'You put a snake in my bed, you little psycho.'

'Just a tree snake. It's not poisonous!'

'It doesn't matter!'

'Yeah, well, you killed Bryce,' he says. His face crumples. He squeezes his eyes shut as tight as they'll go. 'You killed him. I know you did!'

She almost yells something back, but the anger is already draining away. Her head is starting to spin.

'I'm going to get off you, okay? But don't run away.'

'Just get off!' He's sniffling now, trying not to cry.

She moves her weight off him, sits on her bum on the ground, puffed. She expects him to jump up and run away, but he doesn't. He sits up slowly, covers his face with his hands.

'I'm sorry about Bryce.'

'So he is dead?'

She nods.

In the moonlight his pale face is blue. If she were to paint him she would mix a dab of Cerulean in the grey. She would use specks of white for where the light reflects from the tears hovering on the rims of his eyes. But now, she pretends not to see them.

'Do you want me to tell you what happened?'

'Yes,' he whispers.

So she tells him. The truth. The walk, the mangroves. The snap she'd heard, the swirling water.

Tyson doesn't look at her as she talks. He stares at the ground, balls his fists. When she finishes he doesn't say anything for a while and it's almost peaceful, sitting there with this kid. The sun hasn't risen yet, but the sky is starting to lighten.

She puts a hand on his shoulder and he doesn't flinch away. The opposite—he turns towards her.

'So he was a hero? He was barking because he was trying to tell you not to go in there.'

She swallows. 'Sort of.'

'If he hadn't died, those crocs would have gotten you for sure.'

She thinks about it. He could be right. 'I guess he was warning me.'

'You're an idiot,' he says.

She drops her hand from his back.

'What kind of idiot goes into a swamp like that? You're pretty lucky he was with you.'

She pulls her knees into her chest, wraps her arms around them. 'I suppose I was.'

Tyson stands. 'See ya,' he says. Then, 'Sorry.'

She sits in the grass for a few seconds, listening to the crunch of his footfalls receding towards the house. She stands as well and heads back to the shed. Getting closer, she can hear yells and see torchlight flashing from out the door, beams dissolving into dim grey.

'Did you get it?'

'Oh my god, oh my god, oh my god.'

'Get it!'

'Just kill it!' Sorcha is saying. 'Stomp on its head.'

'Where is it?' Jo asks, peering in through the door.

'Under your bunk, in with your bags and stuff,' Yan tells her. She and Sorcha are on Sorcha's bunk.

'I feel sort of bad for it.' Elias is on his own bunk, blanket wrapped around him like it can protect him.

'Okay, if you feel so bad, why don't you come and take it outside?' Jo asks him, staring into the black space under her bed.

'I'm fine up here,' he says.

Jo doesn't want that thing there, in with her stuff. The idea of it touching her clothes makes her shiver.

'Okay.' She thinks through the options. 'Erm … okay. Wait, I have an idea. Come down to the bottom bunks.'

'No,' Yan says.

'Should we just go back to sleep then?'

Sorcha and Yan look at each other, then climb down to the bottom bunk. Jo runs over to hers. Elias comes down the ladder, the blanket wrapped around him.

'Okay, I read that vibrations scare them, alright?' she says. 'So let's all jump up and down. Ready?'

They don't seem ready.

'One, two, three—jump!'

They jump on their bunks, clapping their hands. From beneath her bunk, the snake slides into the centre of the room. It's huge, at least a metre, and an impossibly bright pale green. The way it moves, that flexing and shifting of one long muscle. Jo can feel its wrongness in the back of her throat.

Sorcha shrieks. The snake stops, then rises and turns to her. It rears back, ready to strike. Sorcha's lip quivers. Then something flies across the room from next to Jo. A pillow. It whacks the snake, flipping it onto its back. It lashes its tail to right itself and slides straight out the door and into the night.

Yan jumps down after it, slams the door shut, the metal giving a clipped-off screech. They look at the pillow in the centre of the room.

'A pillow?' Jo says, turning to Elias.

He shrugs.

Jo looks at Yan and Sorcha, and then they are laughing.

'What?' Elias says.

Sorcha's laugh is manic. 'I seriously almost peed myself, I did. I'm not even kidding with you!'

The strange thing is, once the laughter dries up, once their torches are turned off and they slip under their sheets, Jo falls back to sleep. Even with the memory of that cold muscle against her leg, with the night air still in her hair, barely five minutes pass until she is pulled under.

CHAPTER 10

There is almost a camaraderie between them as they start work the next morning. Like they have been united by facing the snake. Sorcha and Yan are yawning, as though interrupted sleep is a huge deal.

For once, they talk as they pick. Yan doesn't have her headphones in and Elias is not somewhere else in his mind and Sorcha is being pleasant. They talk about shows they've seen recently and films they loved as kids and somehow end up discussing *The Matrix*.

'What I want to know,' Sorcha says, 'is whether there are dogs hooked up to the matrix as well? As in, are there little doggy pods with dog VR going on.'

'No,' Jo says. 'The dogs would have died in the climate apocalypse. All the animals would have died.'

'Was it a climate apocalypse?' Elias says. 'Wasn't it human versus robot and the robots won?'

'No, the humans destroyed the sky,' Yan says. 'So it's sort of a climate apocalypse. But I think they would have dogs and big mammals hooked up to the matrix. Why not?'

'Why would they bother?' Jo asks.

'Well, it's about conducting power, right? They're using them as batteries. A husky would probably give about as much power as a person.'

'So you think just big animals? Surely they wouldn't have cat pods.'

'But isn't it about payback?' Sorcha asks.

'They're robots,' Yan says. 'I don't think they are doing things for revenge.'

'Pom!' Denny calls.

They stop talking. They hadn't even noticed him watching them.

'Come do lunch!'

They turn away from the plants, towards Jo. Food is Sorcha's job.

Denny walks back inside, the screen door slapping shut behind him.

Sorcha hisses, 'Go on, or we won't eat. He's fine.'

Jo puts her shears on the grass. She peels her gloves off and places them one on top of the other next to the shears. She turns to Elias, but he turns away and lifts his shears to the plants.

It takes her almost five minutes to walk to the end of the row of mangoes, then up the slight incline to the house. She opens the screen door and the white front door.

She's not sure what she was expecting, some kind of lair perhaps. Dirty carpet and piles of newspapers. But it isn't like that. The floors are tiled beige, some of them cracked, and the windows are covered in gauze curtains. And there is air conditioning. It's icy cool. She stops, feels its tingle on her skin.

'Stuff's in here.'

She follows Denny's voice down a hallway. He is sitting at a small circular table in the kitchen. It's a messy room, filled with clutter. In another room she can hear the quiet sound of a man's voice, tinny, like it's coming from computer speakers.

'Bread's there, vegies and spreads are in the fridge. Cheese too if you want that.'

'Thanks,' Jo says to him. He looks back at her with those pale blue eyes of his. She turns away, goes over to the fridge. Takes out what she needs. She knows she's moving stiffly as she pulls out the chopping board and knife.

'How long has that being going on for?'

'What?' she asks, though she knows what he means. She knows the reason she is here now instead of Sorcha.

He just stares at her. 'Didn't take her as a lez.'

She bangs the knife down on the counter, turns back to him.

'Don't look at me like that,' he says before she can speak. 'I voted yes for gay marriage. Each to their own is what I say. It's just that …' He averts his eyes, then slides his chair back. 'Well, good for them,' he says. 'Let me know if you can't find anything.' He leaves the room.

She begins preparing the sandwiches. One for her, one for Sorcha, one for Yan, one for Elias, one for Denny and one for Tyson. She counts each slice with a finger through the plastic wrap. Twelve slices of bread, almost the whole loaf. She wonders if he'd fancied Sorcha. If that's what he'd been about to say. Maybe he was hurt, after seeing her with Yan yesterday.

The tinny male voice drifts into the kitchen. It's from a computer, she's pretty sure, a video about dinosaurs.

'... it's called the Albertosaurus because it lived in Alberta province in Canada. Although it looked similar to the Tyrannosaurus, its skeletons were often found in groups. It was a pack animal. Can anyone name any other dinosaurs that lived in packs?'

A torrent of children's voices comes through the speaker, all at once.

'Tillie!'

'Damo!'

'Amy!'

And on top of them Tyson is yelling, 'Tyson! Tyson!'

'Okay, what do you think, Tillie?'

Tyson groans.

'Um,' comes a girl's voice, 'I think ... um ... Terrydactous?'

'Pterodactyl. Good try, but they aren't known to have been pack animals. Can anyone think of another answer?'

'Tyson!'

'Okay, Tyson, give it a go.'

Jo hesitates, the knife quivering atop the slippery tomato flesh.

'Um. Oh, hang on, wait, I know it. The cool little evil ones. Velociraptor!'

'Yes, you're exactly right, well done!'

'Thanks, Mr Banari.'

'Alright, everyone, that's the end of our lesson for now. Speak to you all again on Wednesday. And make sure to ask your parents about the cluster muster.'

There's a beep, a shuffle, footsteps into another room.

'Dad? Can I watch TV now?'

'Sounded like you were doing really well. You've been studying?'

'Yeah, I said I was.'

Tyson comes into the kitchen. When he sees Jo, he smiles.

'Here,' she says, holding out a sandwich on a plate to him.

'Thanks.' He lingers, watching her cut another sandwich and put it onto a plate.

'You want to watch TV with me?' he asks.

'I can't. Got to get back to work.'

'Whatever,' he says, already walking away.

She heads to the doorway on the other side of the hallway, where Tyson had come from. Inside, the room is filled with clutter. It's hot and the air is stuffy. Each wall is lined with shelves and filling cabinets piled high with folders and paper. Denny sits behind the desk, the computer screen bright in the dim room.

She knocks with one knuckle on the open door. 'Shall I just set it down in here?'

'Oh.' He peers up at her. 'Yeah, thanks.'

She steps inside the room and places the plate on the far edge of the desk.

Denny looks at the sandwich. 'You've cut it into four. That's nice.'

She'd done Denny's and Tyson's the same, hadn't thought about it. But now Denny is smiling at her like she's made a gesture.

'Hope my boy didn't bother you, he gets bored sometimes. Doesn't get much time with young people.'

She goes to walk out.

'He got close to one of the workers a few years back,' Denny continues, 'broke his little heart when she left. I told him not to get attached, but he didn't listen, of course.'

'You must get a lot of people through here,' she says.

'Yeah. Never the same face two years in a row. It's rough, you know? Workers flaking out at the last minute every single year. Or I'll train them, teach them how to use the machines, and then the next day they say their mum is sick or their grandma is dead. Every year, someone's grandma seems to die.'

'That's why you don't want us to have our pay slips? So we won't run off after a week?'

'Smart girl. Got to have some sort of insurance, you know? Otherwise I'll spend the whole season training and never pick a piece of goddamn fruit. You lot are not so bad. Last year they worked so slow they were barely even moving, but still they complained it was slave labour.'

'I hear what you're saying,' she's being careful, 'but it's so hot out there and it's really, really hard work.'

He laughs. 'Course it is. What do you expect? You're on a farm. This isn't the city, with the cushy office jobs where people think they're working themselves to the bone if they sit in front of a computer for eight hours in a climate-controlled office.'

'I guess,' she says, wrapping her arms around herself. The smell in here. Sweat and dirt and men's deodorant.

'Farms are hard work. You wanted to see Australia? This is the real Australia, not that Sydney bullshit.'

She wants to argue the notion of a farm being the *real Australia*, but instead she fakes a smile. 'Okay.'

'Tell you what, though, you ever want a break from the heat, you're welcome to come up here, okay? I'm sure Tyson would like it.'

'Thanks,' she says. 'Well, I should bring the others their lunch.'

'Oh,' he says, like he'd forgotten why she was there. 'Yeah, yeah, go on then.'

She piles the rest of the sandwiches up, not rushing any more. She's in no hurry to be back out in the sun. She can hear the television from the lounge room. It's *The Chase*. She recognises the theme music as it comes back from a commercial. She lingers by the screen door, holding the tower of sandwiches in front of her.

'Who is the highest selling Australian artist of all time?' asks the host.

She heads for the door. 'Kylie Minogue,' she says. Easy.

Tyson grins at her. 'You reckon?'

She shrugs and goes out into the heat.

*

Sunday cartoons are different in Australia. When she was a kid, Jo loved *William's Wish Wellingtons* and *The Poddington Peas*. The Australian cartoons are drier, the humour broad. Her favourite is a new show called *Bluey*, about a family of cattle dogs who stand on their hind legs and get into mischief. Tyson keeps groaning and saying it's for kids, but he's the one holding the remote.

'You know, we used to have a dog like that when I was little,' Tyson tells her now. 'Her name was Chooks. She lived until she was eighteen. She was Dad's dog to begin with. He cried when she died.'

'That's sad,' she tells him.

He shrugs and changes the channel to a violent anime show with a plot too complicated for her to keep track of.

Denny walks past to the front door. He takes in the two of them, slumping into each end of the couch. He grins at Jo, then looks to Tyson.

'Half an hour, alright, then homework.'

'What? The footy will be on.'

'Then you should have finished yesterday. One more hour, right, Jo?'

She nods. 'I'll do lunch then too.'

'Fine,' Tyson says, but when Denny turns to walk out of the house he rolls his eyes.

Over the last week, Jo has been spending more time at the farmhouse. The days are steadily getting hotter, and the relief of the air conditioner is hard to refuse. But it's more than that. Denny invites her, he wants her to be there. Tyson too. He seems happy when she's around. She loves the domesticity of their house. Making food, watching television. She'd started by just dawdling when she made lunch. Now it's her day off and after she woke from her new deep sleep, she came straight here.

'What's your homework?' she asks Tyson now.

'Comprehension,' he says. 'I have to read this thing about rocks and shit but if I write the answer the same as in the book, Dad says it's copying. It's so annoying.'

'Sucks,' she says.

After the show finishes she looks at him. He groans again and turns the television off.

She pushes herself up and goes to the kitchen. She passes Denny's room, his bed unmade. On one bedside table, Denny's, is a half-drunk glass of water, an alarm clock, some scrunched-up tissues. On the other is a romance novel. On the cover a man clutches a woman to his chest. Even from the doorway she can see the dust covering the book.

She doesn't know where Denny's wife is, just that she's been gone a while. She finds traces of her around the house. A rusted bobby-pin caught between two kitchen tiles. A mouldy bottle of geranium-scented conditioner on the shower rack. Even the bread bin in the kitchen is covered in painted roses, not something she can imagine Denny buying.

Jo takes the bread from it, starts dividing it. She enjoys preparing food for everyone. It makes her feel maternal, creating the sustenance that keeps the farm operating. Filling everyone's stomachs, keeping them working.

She makes Denny's sandwich first, takes it out to him in the sorting shed. He's working on the conveyer belt motor, his sleeves rolled past his elbows.

He straightens when he sees her. 'You got my boy working?'

'Tried to.'

'He'll do it if you tell him. He likes you. Nice for him to have someone around who's a little younger. Years can be long out here. When you all head off, it's just the two of us.'

His pale blue eyes stare at her. She can feel his loneliness. Eight months of just him and Tyson alone on this property. She can't even imagine.

He holds up his dirty, greased-up hands. 'Do you mind leaving that sanga in my office? I'll get to it once I've washed up.'

'No problem.' She turns and walks out into the heat, the sun bouncing off the white ceramic plate into her face.

Denny's study is dim, as always, the only light source the computer. She places the plate in the middle of the desk, then hesitates. By the computer is a stack of paper, the top one marked *Pay Slip*.

She shouldn't snoop. He's trusted her to be in his space. But, then again, the pay slips are theirs. If he's not filling them out correctly, all this could be for nothing. She stands still, the split loyalties making her freeze. Her own self-interest wins. She'll just take a peek.

It feels wrong to go around to his side of the desk. Her eyes flick over the document so fast the first time she doesn't even read it. She's listening for sounds. But there's just the TV, which Tyson must have turned back on. She takes a breath, inspects it more carefully. The name on the slip is 'Sorcha Helen Robertson'. The numbers don't make sense at first. They aren't hours they've worked but, it seems, the number of crates they have picked. She puts the paper down and opens the manila folder underneath it. She flicks through the slips. She finds her own for last week. It's the same. No hours, just the amounts of crates.

She opens the top drawer.

She's not even sure what she's searching for, but now she's started snooping she may as well continue. There is a letter inside. It has Elias's name on. Underneath is more mail. Post-cards. Some of them for Sorcha and Yan, some for names that she doesn't recognise. She hears a sound from the lounge room and closes the drawer. The movement makes something roll loose on the desk. A white bead travels across the table, taps against the papers, then rolls away a little more. She grabs it before it falls on the floor. It's a pearl. Surely a fake, though it shines like it's real. She puts it in the drawer.

Jo expects she'll walk out of the study straight into Denny. But no one's there. She passes Tyson again, sitting on the couch now, his feet on top of his homework.

Grabbing the stack of sandwiches from the kitchen, she gives him one and raises an eyebrow at him. He groans and turns the TV off again.

She walks out of the house, the screen door slapping shut behind her.

Sorcha and Yan are sitting by the ashes of last night's fire.

'Oh, amazing.' Sorcha's voice is dripping with sarcasm. 'The farmer's wife has come to check on her bodachs.'

'What's a bodach?' Yan asks.

Jo wants to swear at her, she's getting sick of Sorcha's crap. Instead she says, 'Just listen, alright?'

Elias comes out of the shed as Jo talks, telling them what she found.

'I knew I must have missed a letter,' he says when she's finished, 'I haven't heard from her since I got here.'

'Yes, the mail is creepy,' Sorcha says, 'but I'm more troubled about the fact he's writing just the piece rate on our pay slips.'

'I know,' Jo says. 'It didn't look right to me.'

Yan pulls her feet onto the chair, perches her chin on one knee. 'What will happen if he gets the pay slip wrong?'

'The government would make him do it again, right?' Jo looks at them. Then, seeing their faces, 'God, you're going to tell me some horrible story, aren't you?'

Sorcha squints at her. 'My friend did the farm work but had to go home because the paperwork wasn't right. I'm not being thick with you—if he's doing it wrong this all might be pointless.'

They look at each other.

'If we had wifi we could look it up,' Jo says.

Elias crosses his arms over his chest. 'Do any of you know someone we can ask?'

'Yeah,' Jo says. 'But I'll have to figure out a way to call Sydney.'

CHAPTER 11

Jo is sweating by the time she arrives at the shops. Everything is moist. Her fringe is sticking to her forehead.

The shops don't amount to much, just a post office and a petrol station. It's the phone booth she's interested in. She pushes the bike onto the kerb and leans it against the booth. When she asked Tyson if she could borrow it she was sure he'd say no. But he'd surveyed her and said, 'You might be too heavy. If you break it then you have to buy me a new one. A BMX.'

'Are you sure?'

And he'd glanced towards the sorting shed then turned back to her. 'I want ten dollars. And,' he pushed his lined exercise book over to her, 'you have to explain why I'm doing this wrong.'

She sat with him in the air-conditioning for the next half-hour. Again, there was that tug as they sat on the floor with his books on the coffee table. It was nice, helping him with his homework.

Now, she grabs the bag of coins and mobile phone out of her bag. She turns it on. The Apple logo glows over the black background. Without reception, the thing is basically an electric torch and address book. Still, she's lucky she turned it off when she did. She has eight per cent battery.

Stuck on the glass of the phone booth is a missing poster. It's for the woman who drove through here with her daughter. The photocopied image is almost faded to nothing now, Jo can only see the outline of their faces, their eyes, the ghostly shape behind them of their silver car.

Jo feeds the coins into the phone. Seven dollars in silver and gold. She opens her phonebook on her iPhone and finds Briena's number. She keys it in, crosses her fingers, hoping like hell that Briena isn't at work. Isn't in class.

'Hello?' Briena sounds tired, like she'd been asleep.

'Briena! Hi! It's me,' she says, 'Jo.'

'Jo? Holy shit! So you haven't been murdered yet?'

'No, not yet.'

Briena laughs. 'How are you? Are you alright?'

'I'm fine.'

'You kind of just disappeared. I was worried about you. You know, mentally.'

'I know. Sorry,' she says. 'But it's awesome here. So beautiful and the people are great.'

'Really? And the farm is okay?'

'It's great,' Jo says, staring out at the huge empty road behind her, 'but there's this one thing. I thought it would be good to get some advice. You know, legal advice.'

'Oh, I see, so you didn't just want to ask me how my life was going?'

'No,' Jo says, 'just legal advice.'

Briena laughs. 'God! You know, I actually miss you. Okay, shoot.'

'So in order to get our new visa we need to supply evidence of the work, right? Apparently we need to send pay slips. But I saw our pay slips yesterday and the farmer isn't actually writing the hours we're working each week. He's writing the number of crates we are filling.'

She hears a shuffle, then typing.

'There's no internet here, so I can't check. And you know, I find all that stuff pretty confusing anyway.'

'Yeah,' Briena says, 'you shouldn't have to do all that work for nothing.' Jo hears more typing. Then, 'Alright, I'm looking at it now.'

Jo stares at the screen of the payphone while she waits, watching her funds tick away.

'You know, it seems like it's fine. It looks like it's not uncommon. They know how many crates are average in each industry so they figure it out.'

'Really? God, that's such a relief.'

'Anything else you wanted to know?'

'Legally?' Jo asks.

'He's fine,' Briena answers.

'I didn't ask.'

'You didn't need to. He's fine. Same as normal.'

Jo feels a little short of breath. She doesn't want to think of him. She doesn't want to think of him being same as normal.

'It might be nice for you to call him, though? I'm sure he'd appreciate it.'

'I've got to go. I've only got twenty cents left for this call. Thanks so much for your help.'

'No problem. I'll send you my bill.'

When Jo hangs up she takes a breath. She sits on the kerb, opens the photo album on her phone. She knows this is masochistic. She isn't sure why she's doing it, but she keeps going. It's like she's gorging herself. Eric, one eyebrow raised, looking up from his laptop. Briena laughing from behind the coffee machine. Screenshots of trivia questions. Eric squatting to pat a dog on the street, smiling, the collar of his denim jacket up. The further back she goes, the warmer people's clothing is, the darker the sky is behind them. She doesn't feel any fondness for the pictures of Eric. The more she studies them, the more his face seems smug, the more his expressions irritate her. She keeps flicking until it's just tourist photos. Sydney Harbour Bridge. The Opera House. A nice sunset. And then her own tired face, a selfie she'd taken, looking at the camera in triumph, despite the shadows under her eyes. Her first day in Australia. She'd made it. She tries to swipe further back, but there is nowhere to go. It's the first picture on the roll.

The phone runs out of battery, turns off in Jo's hand. She looks up. The vast landscape around her seems to shimmer. The last few weeks feel unreal, like a strange dream she's had, and her life in Sydney is her real life. She stands, shakes her head, trying to ground herself.

Righting the bicycle, she squeezes her fingers into the rubber grips on the handlebars to stop them from shaking. Then she gets back onto it, bouncing off the kerb onto the road. She needs to get back. Back to where she can sleep and she doesn't have to think. Her knees tap against her fists. Her breath comes in gasps. She tries to regulate her breathing, even it out, but the further she goes the more her lungs burn. Each inhale scorches her throat. Behind her, the sound of an engine and her shoulders clench expecting another storm of tiny rocks and dust. But the car slows. She turns. It's the green lorry. Gabe.

Jo skids to a stop and puts her feet on the road. Her breath comes in hot gasps. She tries to regulate it, rubbing the sweat from her face with her sleeve.

Gabe leans out of the car window. 'Hey, J,' he says, 'want a lift? We can throw the bike in the back.'

'Yeah,' she says, still puffing, 'that would be amazing.'

She gets off the bike, stumbling a little as the toe of her boot catches on the crossbar, and Gabe jumps out of the car. She wheels it towards him. He's wearing a grey shirt, the sleeves pushed over his elbows. The cotton is so worn it's almost see-through. She remembers the way he'd looked from the bus, the dark hair on his chest.

'That bike is a bit small for you.' He's smiling at her.

'It's Tyson's.'

He picks it up easily and she grabs the back wheel, twisting it round so the bike lays horizontal in the tray. She sees a metal bucket with a lid clipped on.

The seats of the lorry are green fabric, ripped so she can see the yellow foam poking out. She gets in and pulls the door shut behind her. Her head already feels better. It's the first time she's been in shade for hours. The part of her hair prickles—it must be sunburnt. Her skin is itchy and damp. She brushes down her fringe again.

'Want some water?' he asks. There's a bottle in the cup holder between them. 'I don't have cooties, I swear.'

She wouldn't mind catching his cooties.

'Thanks,' she says, and takes a gulp. It's tepid but she doesn't care.

He starts the ignition. 'You know, I feel like I should offer you some mints too. I'm like your Uber driver.'

'I think this place could use an Uber service. Although you'd need reception for that.'

He laughs. She can smell his sweat. He smells like seawater and musk.

'Thanks for everything the other day. Ally too. You were ... well, you were both really nice.'

'I guess I'm a really nice guy.'

'You know only arseholes say that, right?' she says.

He mocks horror. 'Oh no. Maybe I'm an asshole then. If I say that does it mean I'm actually a nice guy?'

'No, it still means you're an arsehole.'

He laughs. 'You Brits, I can barely tell when you're joking.'

She raises an eyebrow at him. She never thought much about her nationality when she was in England, now it's her defining characteristic.

'You were joking, right? Buy a girl a beer, she calls you an asshole.'

'You wouldn't get that in the US?' she asks, intentionally also defining him by his nationality.

'I'm from New York. Girls call you far worse things there.'

She tries to imagine it. This guy in a city like that. 'If you're from New York how did you end up here? In the literal middle of nowhere?'

'I could ask you the same thing.'

'You could, but I'm only here for another—' she thinks about it, '—seventy-two days. Depending on how long harvest lasts.'

'Still. Australia is very far away from England.'

'Exactly why I picked it.'

He presses play on the car stereo. Music starts and it's nice, but she worries that maybe he put it on because he doesn't want to talk to her. Or that she was being too rude.

The glare of the sun is starting to make her eyes water. She pulls the sun visor down and is surprised to see her own reflection. A square mirror glued onto the back of the visor. She stares at herself. Her skin has changed. There are freckles on her neck that weren't there before.

'So did you tell them what happened?' His face is serious.

'Only Tyson. He's okay now, but it was bad. That dog was a little shit, but he was Tyson's only friend, I think.'

'Poor kid.'

'It must be hard, you know? All that time out there, just the two of them in all that space. I can't really imagine it.'

'They're very isolated.'

'You don't know any puppies for sale or anything? I know nothing can replace Bryce but I want to do something.'

'No puppies, no, but ...' He taps his hands on the sides of the steering wheel, glances at her, then back to the road. 'How long have you got? Denny expecting you back?'

'I could be gone all night before he noticed.' She laughs, then realises it's true.

'Up for a drive? I have an idea for Tyson.'

'Sure, alright.' She stares out the window so he can't see her face.

Gabe passes Denny's farm and keeps going down the road. It's beginning to get dark. She wants to ask if it was him she saw in the ocean with those bare-breasted women. She's sure it was, but the question feels like a strange one.

'So, are you New York born and bred? Or were you chasing a dream?'

He smiles. 'I'm from DuBois. You know it?'

'No.'

'No, I wouldn't have thought so. It's northwest of Pittsburgh. The most famous it has ever been was when Tina Fey made some joke that you could get a Subway sandwich from the gas station.'

'Is it pretty? Small American towns seem idyllic. But maybe that's just in the movies.'

He chuckles. 'I don't think they shoot many movies in DuBois.'

'So what was the dream?'

'What?'

'The dream you chased to New York.'

'It's funny, isn't it? How when you are a kid you have to have a dream. You have to have an end to "when I grow up" and it can't be working at Walmart.'

'True.'

'What about you? What did you want to do when you grew up?'

'An artist in London.' She groans. 'That turned to be loads less fun than I thought.'

'An artist. I can see that.'

'And you?'

'A writer.'

'Oh, I see. So you came here to write the next great American novel. Although, I guess a great American novel can't be set in Australia.'

He laughs. 'No, probably not. Anyway, I didn't want to be that kind of writer.'

He turns on the indicator, though there are no other cars around, and they drive along a dirt driveway. Fields of cows watch them from either side of the lorry.

They pull up in front of a white house. It isn't too different from Denny's.

'Should I stay in the car?' she asks.

'Why would you?'

She doesn't know, so she gets out and follows him to the house. She finds herself falling a step behind him and catches up. Something about living in that shed, all the mind-numbing work, she's started feeling more like an animal than a person.

Gabe knocks on the door. 'Mick?' he calls.

'Round back,' comes a voice from the side of the house.

A farmer, young, with red hair and covered in orange freckles, is working on the engine of a tractor. He's wearing a blue singlet and shorts, and Jo stares at his shoulders. He has freckles on top of freckles.

'Hey, mate,' Gabe says, and they clap hands and pull each other into a sort of bro-ish half-hug. 'How's things?'

'Good, mate, good,' Mick says.

'This is J,' Gabe says, looking at her. 'Jo.'

'Hi,' she says, but the guy barely registers her.

'I was wondering if you still had the kid?' Gabe asks.

'Yeah, mate, you want her? I was going to sell her.'

'Kid?' Jo asks.

'I can make it up to you next time if we can take her today,' Gabe says.

'Yeah, that's no problem,' Mick replies. 'I'll go get her.'

Mick hops down from the tractor, wipes his hands on an old shirt and wanders into the house.

'What's going on?' Jo asks.

'I thought you wanted a pet for Tyson?'

Through the window of the farm house, they can see the farmer holding a baby goat.

'Bloody hell,' she whispers. 'I thought you were talking about kidnapping or something.'

'No. Only goatnapping.'

'Do you think Denny will mind, though? What if he gets pissed off?'

'We'll say it's my idea. He won't get annoyed with me.'

'But what if Tyson doesn't look after it?'

'You have a lot of worries, don't you?' He puts a hand on the top of her head. She would normally find this condescending, but the heat of his hand, the way his palm fits over her head. It's nice.

'Here you go,' Mick says, 'you saved her from being some rich cunt's cutlet.'

He hands her the tiny goat. Jo grabs it, presses it against her chest. It scrambles against her, makes a bleating sound so she puts it on the ground, kneels next to it, strokes its back. Its coat is springy and wiry. It has soft little ears and a pink nose. It looks at her, trembling.

'You have to feed her with this.' Mick tosses Gabe a baby's bottle. 'Milk every couple of hours.'

'Why isn't she with her mum?' Jo asks.

'Didn't want her. Kept kicking her in the head. It happens sometimes.'

*

Back in the lorry, Jo holds the little goat close to her chest as they drive.

'How is it going with Denny?' Gabe asks, turning onto the main road. 'I don't think it's right, the way he treats you guys. You shouldn't be living out in that hot tin shed.'

'Oh, you get used to the shed. I quite like the shed now. Feels like home.'

He surveys her, then returns his eyes to the road.

'It's fine,' she says. 'I've been sleeping well since I've arrived. It must be the hard work or something, I don't know.'

'Do you usually not sleep well?'

'I go through patches of it, long patches. Got myself diagnosed once. Chronic insomniac, they said. But between the hard work and the sleep, I barely have a chance to think, so I like it.'

'You don't want to think?'

'Well, you know.'

'No, what do you mean?'

He's pushing her. It's not going to work. She'll change the subject, talk about something lighter.

'Something happened before I left,' she says instead. 'I'm still a bit all over the place.'

'What happened?'

'Oh, it's intense. And no big deal.'

'People are always minimising things that happen to them. It doesn't have to be a big deal to be important. Just acknowledging that something happened doesn't mean you are asking for sympathy, or asking for anything. It's just being honest.'

He stops talking, like he's expecting her to respond. She decides that she'll let the silence hang between them until he feels awkward and changes the subject.

'I had a miscarriage.' It just comes out.

'That's not a small thing.'

'No, it's fine. Probably a blessing. I broke up with the guy right after, plus I had to come here, so I don't know how that would have worked.'

'But you wanted it?' he asks.

She doesn't say anything. She is trying so hard to hold in the tears. Her throat burns. She rests her palm against the little goat's side. Its ribs expand with its breath.

'You know, Ally is really good with that stuff. She helps people get through things.'

'I'd ask her to cure my insomnia, but I think picking mangoes seems to have done the trick.' Her voice sounds weird, throaty. He either doesn't notice or pretends not to.

'How did picking mangoes cure your insomnia?'

'The hard work, I guess. I'm too exhausted to not sleep.'

'That's great. So you started sleeping once you arrived? I always thought insomnia was more psychological rather than physical.'

She thinks back. 'No, actually. It was after I saw you that day with the crocodile. Maybe it was the near-death experience that did it.'

'It was probably Ally.'

'What? Just by touching me?'

'It's more than that ... it's her presence. It's healing.'

Jo wants to scoff. 'You're talking about her like she's some kind of shaman or something.'

'I don't know about that. But I do know she's helped everyone where I live.'

'Where do you live? Rossack?'

He eyes flick to her. 'How'd you know?'

'Sorcha and Yan were talking about it. They say there are rumours.'

'I know there are.' There's a strange expression on his face, but it slides away too fast for her to understand it.

'So where is Rossack?'

'Remember where I bumped in to you on the road? When we first met?'

'Oh yeah, near those strange orange rocks, right?'

'Yeah, the termite mounds. It's … dead west, from there. Although you'd have to walk across a waterfall to get there.'

'How did you end up there? All the way from the States?'

'People find their way there if they need it. I needed it.'

She raises her eyebrows at him, but he keeps his gaze on the road.

'I saw you,' she says, 'in the ocean. On the day I arrived.'

He doesn't say anything, but she can see the corners of his lips twitching. Like he's going to smile.

'I saw you go under the water, but I didn't see you coming up.'

He doesn't reply to that either.

'So?' she asks.

'So … what? Is that a question?'

'Yes! Was it you?'

'Yeah. We'd been in the car all morning, we couldn't resist going into the water.'

'To cool off?'

'Something like that.'

'The people you were with, are they, erm … part of your group, or whatever?'

'Yes.'

'You're not being very forthcoming.'

'I know.'

'So how do you become part of this group?'

He shrugs.

'Oh, come on. I won't tell.'

'I told you, people find us if they need us. That's what I did. It's not like we're sticking up posters in town or anything. But somehow we manage to collect people who don't fit into the world.'

'Sorcha and them were talking about it. They made it sound creepy.'

He looks over at her now. 'I think you'd have to be a certain kind of person to really get it. We all got sick of being told how to live. I know I did, I got sick of living in a concrete box I couldn't afford. Everyone I knew was always lonely and always thought they were the only one who felt it. Everyone had problems with anxiety and depression.'

She nods. 'Is that what it was like in New York?'

He bites at the inside of his cheek. 'Everyone was always so tired.'

'But your life isn't like that now?'

'God, no, not at all. No, it's ...' His brow furrows, golden light comes through the window behind him. 'All the bullshit is stripped away. Everything is shared, you know? We are all in it together. It's so much more natural.'

'So you're trying to create a socialist utopia?'

He laughs. 'Socialist utopia. I like that.'

'But in real terms, how does that work? Is it like a farm or something?'

'Not really.'

'Kind of sounds like a commune.'

He keeps his eyes on the road.

'Are you being intentionally cagey?' she asks.

'Yes,' he says. 'So, how are you enjoying Britney Spears?'

She shakes her head, but lets him have it. If he doesn't want to talk about it, she can't force him.

'Yeah, what is it with all the Britney? Honestly, is it some kind of weird torture technique or something?'

'I think he just likes it.'

'You know, there's all these theories going around that Britney is basically imprisoned by her dad, and she's using her Instagram to send out messages. There's a podcast about it.'

He thinks about that, eyes on the road. 'I guess it's possible. I don't know. Podcasts and Instagram and all that seem pretty alien to me now. I don't think I've even looked at a screen in a year.'

'Do you miss it?' she asks, thinking of the photo binge and then trying to push the images out of her head.

'Nope. I feel like it's a stand-in for something else, you know? If you have people around you, and you feel connected and there is always something important to do, you don't need screens.'

'Yeah, maybe,' she says.

'What's your plan for after this? Harvest must be almost over.'

'Yeah, we've got packing after this. I think we've only got a couple of weeks or so left.' She'll need to find another farm after that. She hasn't even thought about it. How is she meant to even find one without any internet?

'That's a pity.'

'What do you mean?'

'I'll be heading back after this, to Rossack. I've finished my rounds with the farmers.'

'When will you be back?'

'Not for a while. A month maybe, or longer.'

They turn into Denny's driveway.

'So I won't see you?'

'No, I guess not.'

She doesn't want to get out of the car. He drives to the house and pulls in. She assumes that he'll keep the motor running, expect her to jump out. But he turns off the car and gets out himself.

'Gabe!'

Through her side mirror she watches Tyson run to Gabe. He stops short, like he is suddenly aware of coming off too eager.

'Hey, man,' Gabe says. 'How're you doing?'

'I'm okay. Is that my bike?'

She pulls the door open, adjusts the little goat in her arms.

'Yeah, man,' Gabe says, 'nice of you to lend it.'

Jo comes around to the back, watches as Gabe pulls the bike onto the ground, holds the two handlebars in front of himself. It looks comically small in front of him.

Tyson stares at her, squinting in the glare of the sun. 'Why've you got that?' he asks.

'She's for you,' she says, kneeling and dropping the animal onto its feet. It's unsteady for a moment, wavering a little on the spot.

'To eat?' Tyson asks, looking between them and the little goat.

'Nah,' Gabe says, 'nah, man, don't you know they make the best pets? They're just as loyal as dogs.'

Tyson seems doubtful, but he steps towards the goat.

'Her mum left her,' Jo said, 'so she needs someone to take care of her. We thought you'd do a good job.' She hands him the bottle.

'This is because of Bryce, isn't it? Because he died for you being a stupid idiot?'

She glances at Gabe, then back to Tyson. 'Yeah.'

Tyson kicks a bit of dirt, then walks into the house. She looks at Gabe, disappointed. 'You might have to take it. I can't really have it in the shed.' Although she wants to. She'd love to have that thing, to have it sleeping against her again.

'Yeah, that's fine,' Gabe says. He bends to scoop up the goat. But Tyson is bounding out of the house. He's holding a collar and lead in his hand.

'Bryce didn't need this, but I reckon she looks pretty stupid, so she probably will.' He touches the little goat on its head. The goat bleats and Tyson laughs, delight in his eyes. He fastens the collar loosely around the goat's neck. 'Maybe I could look after her for a couple of days,' he says, 'if Dad doesn't mind.'

'I'll talk to him,' Gabe says. 'I need to go in for a sec, anyway.' He opens the bucket to grab something, but secures the lid again before she has a chance to see what it is.

'Okay,' Tyson says. He walks back to the house, pulling the goat along with him.

'Thanks,' she says to Gabe before he goes. 'Today was … I don't know. It was nice.'

He grins at her, then leans in and pulls her towards him. She presses her cheek against his chest. His arms wrap around her for just one squeeze. The smell of his sweat makes her swallow.

'You're welcome,' he says.

She wants to ask what exactly his rounds are for, tell him that she doesn't want to say goodbye, but he's already moving away from her.

'Okay, bye.'

He smiles over his shoulder.

She doesn't rush to the shed. She wraps her arms around herself as she walks. She wants to hold onto the day for a few minutes. Her throat is tight, and the memories of Sydney are too close to the surface, but there's a pleasant humming in her chest as well.

The walk to the shed isn't a long one, but she knows there will be so many questions. She makes the walk last, noticing everything she passes. The uneven mounds of earth beneath her feet. The tiny ripple of breeze that travels from one mango plant to the next. The huge sky doming around her, like she's in a bizarre snow globe where it's always summer and nothing falls from the sky. She keeps her arms wrapped around herself.

The sound of Gabe's ignition starting carries. He revs the engine and the tyres crunch on the dirt drive. She hears him circle around the clearing in front of the house, then start towards her. She is walking a few metres from the drive, on the grass, but she decides not to turn back. Looking over, to wave or smile, is too exposing. She keeps her shoulders straight. His lorry passes her. But then it stops, idling. She keeps walking, expecting him to stick a hand out to wave or call *see ya later*, sounding cheery and American. But he doesn't.

She can see him through the open driver's window, eyes set forward. She approaches, but he doesn't turn to her.

'Hi,' she says. 'You okay?'

She grips the edge of his window, her fingers curling over the rubber seal. He turns to her. There's something different about his face now. A nakedness to it. There's a crease between his eyebrows. His expression is pained. His eyes meet hers and there's something in the way he takes her in. He wants her too.

She leans into the car, on the tiptoes of her boots, and places one hand on his shoulder. The worn-out cotton is soft under her palm. She kisses him gently, on the very corner of his mouth. His stubble is rough against the her lips. His hand comes around the back of her head, slips into her hair, and his mouth finds hers, open and wet and needing. She kisses him until she is breathless, and is unable to stop herself grinning when she leans away. He's smiling too, the vulnerability gone from his face.

She stands back and brushes a hand through her hair.

He shrugs. 'Bye, J.'

'Bye.'

And then he turns to the road and resumes driving.

CHAPTER 12

Jo thought she'd dream of Gabe that night. Dream of their kiss, of his fingers in her hair. Maybe it was her cockiness, her expectation that sleep was hers again. She'd got into bed still smiling. Feeling good. The sleepiness was there; she could feel it. The tiredness a rising tide, ready to pull her under. But then, just the way it used to, it didn't grow. It receded. The sleepiness slipping away from her until it was gone completely. And it was her and her own mind and hours and hours of nothing in the hot dark shed to think and remember and try not to think and try not to remember.

Now it is day three without sleep. Jo wraps the leftovers and puts them in the fridge. She shifts the gauze curtains of the kitchen window and peeks out. The sun makes her raw eyes ache. Denny is outside, talking to the lorry driver while the others load the mango crates. The lorry driver has one foot on the wheel of the car and he is pushing back and forth into it as they talk, stretching his calf. Elias turns towards the house as he walks to the sorting shed, brushing his hands on his shorts, his expression expectant.

If she weren't so tired, her heart might be beating fast as she walks into Denny's study. She opens that top drawer, the one she'd seen them in before. They are still there, a rubber band wrapped around envelopes and postcards. She sorts through them, takes out the right ones and puts back the others with names she doesn't know, previous workers who must have thought no one was writing to them. Hopefully Denny isn't keeping track of them. She's betting on him not noticing the difference.

She tucks the mail down the back of her jeans and pulls her shirt over. As she walks, there is a quiet crumple of paper.

When she returns into the sorting shed, Elias meets her eye from the conveyer belt. She winks at him. She's never been much of a winker before, but now in her fatigue-drunk state, it seems hilarious to wink. Elias grins at her and she sees the way his hands quicken as the mangoes fly past him.

When Denny passes he smiles at her. That soft smile. She shouldn't have gone to his house those times, given him the wrong idea. She'd thought this place had cured her. Something to do with the physical labour, or the air. But now she's had time to think. Endless black hours to think, and she's realised that she was wrong. She'd slept that first time after she'd first met Gabe and Ally. It had worn off. Gabe had said Ally could fix people and he was right. She had felt it when Ally wrapped her arms around her. She had felt that this woman had some kind of heal-ing quality, but she'd dismissed it, been too cynical to let herself believe it. She'd got everything wrong. Because it was never the farm that had made her able to sleep, of course it wasn't. It was Ally.

*

When they get back to the shed none of them can wait. The excitement is contagious, even through her sleep-fog, even though she knows there'll be no letter for her. It's like Christmas and she is Santa. She pulls the mail from her jeans.

The name on the first envelope is Elias's, in cursive handwriting. 'First up we have a love letter.'

Elias grins at her and she passes it over.

'Is it?' Yan asks.

Elias rips it open, pulls out three pages of lined paper covered in black pen scrawls. He goes up onto his bed, flops back to read while there is still some light coming in from outside.

The next is for Yan.

'My parents, maybe.' Yan flips the envelope over to read the back. 'Yeah, my mum. Probably just full of questions about when I'm coming home.'

She's smiling, though, and places the envelope gently on her lap. Jo pulls the next letter from the pile, another for Elias, which she passes to him. The next is for Sorcha, the handwriting a little jagged.

'Probably my parents too,' Sorcha says, but when she sees the handwriting, her face changes. She flips it over and sees the name on the back, then rips the letter open. She says nothing for a few seconds, her eyes scanning each line.

She breathes out in relief. 'Oh, thank feck. It's Juliana.'

'Really?' Yan moves in closer, reads over Sorcha's shoulder. Even Elias stops reading, watches on from his bunk.

'She's fine,' Sorcha says, 'pissed off with Denny. She says …' She keeps reading. 'She says that he fired her as soon as she asked about the pay slips and told her she had to leave straight away. Then he dropped her off at that bus stop, harping on and on the whole time that he was going out of his way even doing that. She had to wait an hour and a half for the bus and then she had nowhere to go in Broome. Apparently she got a hostel for a few days, then found some work in Kununurra.'

'That's a relief,' Elias says, already going back to the pages in front of him.

Sorcha's eyes keep scanning, then she grins and passes the letter over to Yan.

'Were you worried?' Jo asks.

Yan keeps her eyes on the letter. 'People go missing around here sometimes. It was worrying the way she was just …'

'Gone,' Sorcha finishes.

'No wonder Denny didn't want us to have that one,' Yan says. 'I'm surprised he didn't open it himself.'

Jo winces, hoping he didn't keep stock of what mail was in the drawer. She'd left the ones with names she didn't recognise. If he does keep track, he'll know she's been going through his desk.

'Anything left?' Sorcha asked.

The rest are postcards, held together by another elastic band. Jo flicks through the first couple: all for Sorcha.

She gives the lot to her.

Sorcha grins when she sees them. 'Here we go, these are from my parents. Last time I talked to them they were planning on a coastal road trip.' She begins flicking through them. 'Liverpool, Swansea … god, I can't believe Swansea even has postcards! Who'd want to even admit they went there?' She keeps going. 'Cardiff, St Ives, Plymouth. I've actually always wanted to visit Plymouth.'

Jo's mouth goes dry. She tries to swallow. She saw it, only for a flash, but she can tell.

'Is it okay … erm, can I have a quick look at the St Ives one?'

Sorcha looks at her, hearing the difference in her tone. 'Sure.' She passes the postcard over.

Jo takes it, looks at the image again. The bracken rooftops, the silken bay. She flips it over, skims past the flowery handwriting, to the tiny printed text in the corner: *Summer at St Ives, by Charlotte Ainsley*. Her mother.

Jo hands the postcard back. 'Cool, thanks.' She stands and leaves them to their letters. 'I'll get the fire going.'

Outside, the light is fading, though the heat still shimmers in the air. She goes over to the pile of timber, tears some of the smaller branches off with her hands. She picks up one of the big logs and puts it on the chopping block, its cut side facing upwards, grainy and flesh coloured. She grabs the axe, marks her place on the edge of the log, then throws it over her head and whacks it down. The log snaps open. She does it again and the log breaks in two with a thud. She's sweating already.

Picking up one piece at a time, she lugs them over to the fire pit. Splinters gnash at her fingers. She throws the log in, but sits, doesn't light it. She squeezes the bridge of her nose with her fingers. The lack of sleep is making her face puffy and sore. Her eyelids are swollen; she rubs them, trying to convince her claggy eyes to moisten.

Sorcha and Yan come out, followed by Elias, the letter in his hand.

'I think it's too hot for a fire,' Jo says. Even last night they'd been sweating sitting around it.

'It's too far into wet season,' Yan says, 'the temperature isn't going to drop at night so much any more. We might get a few epic storms before we leave if we're lucky.'

Jo nods, too tired to figure out if Yan is being sarcastic or not. The sun hovers at the horizon.

'Sucks you didn't get any mail,' Yan says.

'It's fine.'

She can feel Sorcha looking at her, wanting to ask more. She saves her the bother. 'I used to live in St Ives. That picture brought back weird memories, that's all.'

'Ah, okay,' Sorcha says. 'Your family moved on, did they?'

'No,' she says, 'just me. I used to live there with my mum and my brother. Then I moved to the East Midlands, to Chesterfield, with my dad when I was seven.'

'Chesterfield is pretty shit, right?' Sorcha says.

Jo laughs. 'Yeah, it was. That's why I'm here, as far away as I can possibly get.'

Yan and Sorcha laugh, smiling at her as though they like her.

'So what's your brother up to now?' Yan asks.

'Jamie,' Jo says. She considers for a second, then, 'He's at university. He loves it, having the time of his life.' She's not sure why she's lying, but it feels so good to say it. 'Anyway,' she goes on before they ask her more questions, 'how did your parents' road trip go? Was Wales as crap as everyone says it is?'

'No, they loved it actually.'

'I've heard Cardiff is nice. I had an aunt who went on holiday there once,' Elias says, looking up from his letter.

The sun slips down a little further, the sky turning grey. All Jo wants is to climb into bed, to pass out. But she knows that she'll just lie there, feeling worse. Thinking about all the things she doesn't want to think about.

'So, what are you all going to do when you finish your days?' she asks.

Elias grins. 'Emma and I are going to move in together. At the end of the year we'll apply for de facto permanent residency.'

'That's great,' she says.

Yan and Sorcha glance at each other, then Yan says, 'Me and Sorcha are thinking of travelling more. We're going to get a campervan and work our way down through Western Australia. Maybe get work in a bar or a café along the way. What about you?'

'I guess go back to Sydney,' she says. But there's nothing waiting for her there. The only friends she had were Eric's first. She doubts the café will rehire her since she skipped out on her last few shifts.

She's working so hard to push through the days, but for what?

The sun slips under the horizon, and they sit in darkness.

*

In bed that night, the image from the postcard is waiting on the backs of her eyelids. The water of the bay lugs and pulsates, glinting in the dim sun. The boats dipping and shifting on its surface. Their colourful sails catching the wind.

She tries to force her mind to picture something else, but the boats keep coming back. The bay. She's not even asleep, but it's all she can see.

*

The whack of the stick against metal in the morning is softer now. No longer the crash that made her surface from her dreams too quickly, making her head spin.

Still, Sorcha yells, 'Jesus, kid!'

Jo is happy to get out of bed. She sits, takes a breath, then stands and goes to the bathroom. Brushing her teeth, she stares into the sink.

The four of them walk to the sorting shed. The sun creeps above the horizon, shining golden light onto Sorcha's and Yan's hair as they walk ahead of her. They talk quietly to one another, she can't hear what they're saying, and then Sorcha laughs and elbows Yan in the ribs. 'You suck,' she says.

Beside her, Elias is staring at the ground.

'As of today, I'll only have thirty days left,' he says, 'only one month until I'm with Emma.'

'Do you think you'll miss any of this?'

'I don't know.' He takes a breath. 'Maybe the clean air, you know? And the silence. I grew up in Kreuzberg on a busy street. I loved it but there was so much going on. Even at four in the morning, there would be people walking around. Coming home from bars or getting döners or shift workers on their way to work. Me and my friends would sometimes go and drink in this parking lot on the top of an office building. It was dirty and not very nice, but from up there it would be quiet. You would be above all the people and the noise and the U-Bahn. You could see the horizon.'

He looks at the sky, squinting. She looks too, but it makes little droplets sparkle in front of her eyes. They don't shrink away entirely until she reaches the sorting shed.

It was a relief to be in there, after those long days out in the sun. But the work is even more repetitive. The air is frigid. It smells of cement. She knows that by the end of the day it will be a hot house, the sun baking the steel roof above them.

The mangoes they have picked are waiting for them in tall stacks of crates. Their green cheeks have been yellowing. In the sorting shed, the job is to de-stem the mangoes as well as separate the fruit that has been too bruised or scratched by the edges of their shears. Every tiny tap, every little scrape, is magnified in the mango's flesh, creating glaring brown evidence.

The machine is old, its parts rasp and hum. There is a frame along the top fitted with jets that spray a tepid soapy solution over the mangoes as they pass underneath on a conveyer belt. The solution neutralises the mango sap. It sprays over their hands as they snap the stalks from each piece of fruit as it passes. At the end of the belt is another crate to catch the fruit.

Jo ties on her apron as the machine gasps to life. She wonders what Gabe is up to. She's been doing this most days since they started in the shed. Thinking about Gabe is a safe place for her mind. Lately, she's been imagining what would have happened if, instead of kissing him, she'd gone around to the passenger side and gotten into his car. He would have taken her with him to Rossack. She would have gone to this utopian-sounding place. Ally would be there, and she'd be happy to see Jo. She'd wrap her arms around her again, give her that steadying touch. Make her sleep somehow like she'd done before. If Jo was in Rossack now, she'd be a different person. Bright and high from natural sleep.

Her hands move fast, snapping a stem off, letting go, snapping a stem off, letting go, snapping a stem off and letting go. She removes a mango with a battered side, puts it in the crate to her left with its imperfect kin.

Elias catches her eye across the belt. 'I'm already thinking about lunch,' he says, pushing his hair out of his eyes with the back of his wrist.

She snaps a stem off, lets go, snaps a stem off, lets go.

Gabe had said that people find Rossack themselves. So perhaps he wouldn't have taken her there. Maybe it was some sort of test, to make sure the people who lived there were committed, that it wasn't just some holiday.

More and more mangoes have brown scorch marks on them. The sun has been too hot for them. When Denny comes to check on them he surveys the burnt fruit.

'Shit,' he says, 'twice as many as last year.'

He goes back to the house, shoulders tight with worry.

She snaps a stem off, lets go, snaps a stem off, lets go. Snap, let go. Snap. Snap. Snap.

The people in the ocean had seemed so happy. She remembers the way the women had flung their hair from their eyes, she imagines the beads of water sliding down their bare breasts. She's never been that uninhibited.

They'd dived back under, fingers pinching nostrils, and the ocean had sealed over them. It was amazing how it could do that, close over like someone was never there. The bay of St Ives is back, the lapping water, the undulation of the boat.

Snap. Let go. Snap. Let go.

Her eyes unfocus. Four nights without real sleep. She's starting to find it hard to tell the difference between her spinning thoughts and when she actually dips below consciousness. She can almost feel the tide now, feel the sway of exhaustion.

'Missed one,' Elias says to her. He leans forward with his long arms, reaches towards the mango that has passed her, its stem sticking up like a mast. Then he freezes.

'Verdammt! Verdammt!' The end of one tendril of his hair has fed into the conveyer belt. 'Schalte es aus!'

He moves with the belt, his hands on his hair trying to yank it free.

Sorcha screams, 'Get Denny! Turn the fecking machine off!'

Jo jumps back, looking to the machine, searching for some sort of switch, for a button to turn it off, but there isn't one.

Elias screams. It's high, horrible. Jo puts her hands over her mouth, can only watch. It happens in a split second. His hair is pulled tight and his head slams flat against the machine. It's not his hair that rips. It is his skin. Two inches of his scalp is lifted off the bone, above his ear. She can see his skull for a moment, before the blood wells over it. The piece of scalp rips away. Elias falls backwards. His hair and skin continues down the conveyer belt.

CHAPTER 13

Jamie grins at her, his soft baby cheek pressed into her mother's wool coat. He's in the carrier, strapped to her mum's chest, but he keeps peeking at her. She makes a face at him, wrinkling her brow and crossing her eyes, trying to make him cry.

'I want to go to the shop!'

She's asleep, Jo knows that. She's finally managed to fall asleep.

The sailboat bobs in front of her. She presses her hand against it. Her mother is on deck. Won't look at her. She has pulled away from the camera and is gazing at the sky. The clouds are turning steely; the morning light is dimming fast.

The water rolls, dizzying. Jo wants to wake up. She doesn't want this.

The metal door screeches against the cement. A torch lights up the shed. It passes over her, spotlights her eyelids so they glow pink. She covers her face with the blanket.

'Now I've told them to have the bunk ready for you, alright, I told them that this morning. There you go. Top bunk.'

'Okay, cool, thanks.'

'Alright, see you in the morning then. Bright and early.'

The torch light goes out. The door scrapes shut. She hears movement.

'Hi?' comes the male voice. It has a Nordic-sounding accent. Jo doesn't reply, the others don't either. Another light comes on, bluish, the light from a phone. She hears a shuffle and her bed creaks as he goes up the ladder to the bunk above her.

Jo closes her eyes. If there was any doubt left in her mind, it's gone now.

*

In the morning, they walk to the sorting shed. Jo has her backpack on, and neither Sorcha nor Yan asks why. No one speaks much to the new guy. He makes an effort, trying to crack jokes and ask questions. Talking about how hot it is already, about how Denny had been late, about how he told him that he'd got this great big scar from a boxing match with a kangaroo. Jo feels bad for him. Sort of. It's hard to feel much of anything now. Eight nights with only the thinnest whispers of sleep. She manages no more than a few words and some diluted smiles.

In the shed, Jo watches as they pull on the elbow-length gloves, the rubber so new she can smell it. They slip on their hair nets, making sure not a strand is loose, and tie on the aprons. Jo goes over to the washed and de-stemmed mangoes, the ones packed tight in crates waiting for the lorry to come and collect them to take them to supermarkets and hotel chains. She takes five, the ones with the fullest cheeks, the most perfect, and puts them into her backpack.

'What are you doing?' Sorcha asks. Her gloved hands on her hips.

All three of them are watching her. She pulls the drawstring of her bag. There's a little room left at the top.

'Going,' she says. 'I'm going to go get the bus. Get out of here.'

She won't tell them the truth. They'll try to stop her.

'What? Why?' the new guy asks.

But she ignores him and instead looks at Yan, who says, 'The pay slips. He won't give them to you. Especially not if you take those.'

Jo doesn't have an answer for that.

'Are you going to get him to drive you to the stop?' Sorcha asks. 'It's a long walk.'

'Yeah, probably. I just need to get out of here.'

Her eyes wander to the dark stain on the concrete floor.

'There's no way he'll give you the slips,' Sorcha says. 'If you go now, it's going to be a headache trying to get them long distance.'

But Yan just gives a tiny smile, the faintest tug of her lips. 'If you want to go, go.'

Back at the shed, Jo fills her water bottle. Then she takes Elias's from the bundle of his stuff that is under the bed and fills that too. She wraps hair ties tight around the bottles' necks and attaches one to either side of her pack. She's pulled out all her clothes to make way for the mangoes. She's selective with what she puts back in. Some underwear. Her wallet and passport. Her dead phone. She tries to fit in the sunscreen, but there isn't room, so she lathers herself with it. Rubbing it thick and white down her legs and arms. The back of her neck, her cheeks and fingers and her lower back where her t-shirt and shorts gape when she bends over.

She pulls on the straps of the bag, wriggles her shoulders. It's heavy. The water bottles sway. But the heaviness is good, the closer she gets, the lighter it will become.

She walks into the sun. She isn't afraid.

*

When she reaches the termite mounds, she turns off the road. She weaves between the strange alien-like rises. The sun is rising so she walks towards it. Dead west. That's what he had said. She heads straight into the spear grass.

As the sun rises above her, the air ahead begins to shimmer. She lets herself sip from the water, but doesn't pause. She keeps her footfalls even, her breathing controlled. It's a game. She waits until her mouth is dry and then waits a little longer. Then she pulls off one of the bottles from where they sway on her backpack and takes a mouthful of liquid, not breaking her stride. Then the game starts over and it is the other bottle's turn. It isn't long before her pack doesn't feel so heavy.

She can see small orange hills ahead through the desert shimmer. Getting closer, she sees they aren't hills, they are rocks. Large orange boulders. She rubs her hands on her shorts, they're sweaty already, then begins the climb. She alternates between walking and pulling herself along, crab-like. Her sweat has prickled through the sunscreen, made her skin feel syrupy. But it's good to use her whole body, to pump blood into her legs. She jumps down on the other side. The scrub is thicker now.

*

Jo and Sorcha had half carried Elias to Denny's lorry. He had a towel wrapped around his head, which was already black against the wound. Jo had never seen a face so pale. His eyelids had turned translucent. His body was covered in a slick hot sweat. He was making guttural noises, German words she didn't know.

'Shh,' she kept saying, 'it's going to be okay. You're going to be fine. Almost there.'

Denny ran out from the house, shouting to Tyson over his shoulder, 'If they call again say we are on our way, tell them to be ready.' He saw them, the blackened towel, and started swearing under his breath. Jo looked back at the house, where Tyson was standing by the screen door, watching.

Denny bumped her out of the way and took Elias tightly under the arm.

'Ready?' he said to Sorcha. She nodded and they hoisted him onto the tray of the lorry.

'You're alright mate, you're fine.' Then to Sorcha, 'Hold onto him tight.'

Sorcha jumped into the tray and sat next to Elias and Denny went around to the driver's door.

'Wait!' Yan called, running from the sorting shed. 'Hang on!'

She sprinted the last few metres, holding something out in her hand. Sorcha leant down and grabbed it from her. It was wrapped in a jute sack. There was no blood soaking through, but still Jo cast her eyes away.

Denny started the lorry and they sped down the drive. Sorcha held onto the edge with one hand and had her other on Elias's shoulder. Jo and Yan watched until they turned onto the main road and disappeared.

In the quiet days that followed, Jo could still hear Elias's scream in the silence. The days were getting hotter and hotter. She would lie on her foam mattress, a sponge of sweat, and plead with her body to sleep. Make deals. Anything, so she wouldn't have to remember that scream. A few times, she'd dip into unconsciousness, hear his scream but see a woman with dark hair and thick blood pouring down her face instead, and she'd be awake again after a moment, gasping, guilt twisting in her gut.

*

The sun has begun its descent now. Out in the wilderness, she sits with her back against a tree. Faint tremors run through her hands as she breaks the skin of a mango open with her thumbs. She dips in with her teeth, ripping and sucking at the flesh inside.

Once there is nothing left but skin and stone, she looks at the sky again. The sun has set further. She sucks on the inside of her cheek. It tastes sweet.

The sun is so bright it bleaches out the blue of the sky, turns more and more orange as it sets. But the angle is wrong. With sticky hands, she forages through the undergrowth, finds a straight stick. Bits of bark and dirt and dry grass glue to her hands. Digging into the earth in a patch of sunlight, she buries the stick's end so it stands up straight. If she'd been walking dead west, the stick's shadow should point back directly the way she'd come. It doesn't. The shadow hangs to the left. While the sun was bearing down on top of her, she'd veered off course.

Her blood jangles. That elation, that freedom of possibility, of becoming unstuck, it's slipping away. She claws at it, tries to keep it. She keeps walking until it is so dark she can no longer see her feet. The sounds of crickets have gotten so loud she can't hear her footfalls either. She tells herself she's almost there, that one night out here won't kill her.

Still, she can't help but think of it. A question she'd had on the first pub trivia night she'd ever hosted: How long can the human body go without water? Three days.

He'd said dead west, although you'd have to go over a waterfall. Once she hits the waterfall she'll know she's almost there. It can't be that far; he wouldn't have given her directions if it was really that far.

And then, from behind her, a shift. A definite crunch in the black. The crickets seem to quieten.

*

The day after the accident Jo, Sorcha and Yan didn't leave the shed. The door was shut against the sun, the tin steadily heating up.

Yan and Sorcha were on the top bunk across from her. Yan laying down, her feet on Sorcha's lap, who sat with her back against the wall. Jo sat in her own bed, wearing her underwear and a singlet, the sheet wrapped around her legs. They didn't talk to her and Jo knew why. It was her fault. She missed the mango, Elias leant over to get one of hers. She has caused this.

'It's happened before, you know,' Yan said, breaking the silence that had lasted hours.

Jo turned to her. The heat made everything sluggish, like she was moving through water.

'A couple of years ago. Some massive fruit farm, one of the big ones, they had workers lying under the conveyer belt, cleaning it as it went around. I guess it cost money to stop production in order to clean it. This girl, it was worse for her. Took her full scalp, from the back of her neck to her eyebrows.'

Jo swallowed. 'Was she okay?'

'Dunno.'

'What about the farm?' Sorcha asked.

'I think they had to pay a fine.'

They went back to silence. Jo fiddled with a stray thread that was pulling from the sheet. She tugged at it and it made the sheet crimp. She went through her geography questions in her mind, seeing if she could remember which country had the most natural lakes and the name of the river that ran through Baghdad. It got hotter. It was her fault. She had caused this. She couldn't remember the name of the river.

After a while, they heard the crunch of footsteps outside. A knock on the shed door. No one had ever knocked on that door before. They looked at one another.

'Yeah?' Sorcha said.

The door screeched open and they heard Denny muttering, 'Another thing to fucking fix,' under his breath. He squinted in at them. Wrinkled his nose. Maybe it smelt.

If she had painted it, the bunk beds would be greys and browns. Yan, Sorcha and herself in murky shadow. Denny would be standing in a white rectangle, his skin cast yellow, the tips of his hair bleached out. It would look strange, the contrast too dramatic, unreal.

He shifted his weight between his feet. 'So I just talked to the doctor, they said he's awake now.'

He looked at them. They looked at him.

'They said that they've called his girl in Melbourne and she's flying in. His family too, maybe.'

Jo breathed.

'And his head?' Yan asked.

Denny squinted, trying to see her in the dark. 'Yeah, well, they said all this stuff about nerves and blood flow. Think they took a crack at sticking it back on.' He swallowed. 'You guys did good. Real good, in the circumstances. And … yeah. It was rough. A real rough one. But you did good.'

Jo turned to Sorcha and Yan, but her eyes had adjusted to the light outside and she couldn't see their faces. Just the vague outlines of them.

'Anyway. We'll start again tomorrow. Let's get those days sorted for you, all ticked off. How long have you got left?'

'Twelve,' Sorcha said.

'Nine,' Yan said.

Jo didn't say anything. She couldn't remember the number.

'No good sitting around doing nothing while the fruit turns. Let's just get you sorted. We'll count today and yesterday as full days. And, yeah, so …' He looked at his house, then back to them. 'Yeah.'

He didn't look at her, didn't ask her to come to the house, to come see Tyson and enjoy the air conditioning, and she was glad. He closed the door and she could hear him swearing under his breath again as it stuck. She lay on her bed, the sheets sticking to her.

After a while she said, 'What is the only sea without any coasts?'

'Huh?' asked Sorcha.

'It's a trivia question. What is the only sea without any coasts?'

'We don't know, Jo,' Yan said. They went back to silence.

Later, Sorcha lay next to Yan and they began talking quietly. Jo got up and went outside. The sun was setting and the sky had turned hot pink. She'd had swimmers that colour as a kid, she remembered, a one-piece with a frill around the chest that she'd loved. The colour of it, the amplified femininity, just the feel of the fabric stretching over her body had made her happy.

She heard a sound and turned to see Tyson in the distance. She watched him through the mango trees. He was running, the goat galloping along next to him. Then he stopped and held out a palm and the goat stopped too and sat, then he started running again and the goat ran too.

Jo remembered what Gabe said. About how things didn't have to always feel so stuck. Things could be beautiful; she just had to grab hold of them. Make choices herself rather than letting things happen.

She wrapped her arms around herself and watched Tyson and the goat play. He'd be okay without her.

CHAPTER 14

The realisation comes slowly.

She's walking into the umber dawn. Everything rich orange. The sun, the dirt, the sky. She couldn't paint this; it wouldn't make sense. The eye needs other tones, a point of contrast, in order to understand an image.

She eats a mango as she walks, digging her dirty fingers into the skin, her teeth scraping against the seed. She thinks about the sour taste, thinks about the orange colour. Anything except the lightness of her backpack or the angle of the sun. But it's right there in front of her. The sun rising ahead.

She's veered off course in the dark.

She's lost in this never-ending flatness. Because of course there is contrast in this image. It is her. The lone figure that doesn't belong, and its shadow pointing the wrong way.

She squats, digs a small hole and buries the mango seed. Then begins walking into her shadow.

Her dry mouth has turned the mango's juice to sweet clag, but she doesn't touch for the swaying bottles. Only a precious inch of sloshing water in each one.

It must have happened during the night, when she'd zigzagged through the trees in the broiling dark. She'd heard it, following her. The slip of its low body against the dirt. The snap of its jaw. She'd heard it. Better to be out here, in the flat nothing, where there was nowhere for it to hide.

She pushes on.

Three brolgas fly above her in formation.

This must be part of the test. He wouldn't have given her directions if it were impossible to reach. She has to believe.

Before she left Sydney, she'd added some facts about the Kimberley into her trivia nights. The Kimberley is A, the size of California. B, three times the size of England. Or C, bigger than Germany. All of the answers were correct. She'd thought it was clever.

She had written that question on the balcony of the apartment she'd shared with Eric. She would leave Eric sprawled on his stomach in their dark room and make herself muesli, a plunger of coffee. Sunrise used to be the one thing she liked about sleeplessness. That magic moment when the ghost moon disappeared, when the light changed from silver to gold.

One morning, not long after she'd first moved in, she had sat out there, the glow from her phone going from bright to dim as she looked up facts. She'd heard a warble, then the beat of wings and a slap. A huge bird perched on the balcony railing. It was black and white, like a magpie. But apart from that it didn't look much like the magpies back home. It was twice the size, for one. And its tail feathers became a sharp point, unlike the fanned tails of English magpies. It cocked its head to look at her with red eyes.

She took some of the seeds from her muesli, stood carefully and scattered them on the railing. The bird eyed her.

'Go on. It's okay.'

It looked at the seeds, then at her. Cocked its head again.

There was a sharp laugh from the kitchen. The bird flew away.

'Where you trying to feed it your cereal?' Eric asked.

'No, well, erm … seeds.'

He laughed again, coming to lean next to the glass sliding door. He was shirtless, wearing just his cotton boxers, rubbing his eyes. 'Magpies don't eat seeds here.'

'Well, then, what do they eat?'

'Meat,' he said, and grinned. 'And don't get too close to them. They're vicious. Territorial. They'll peck your eyes out.'

She keeps walking. The sun beats down. She just has to keep heading west. She'll make it. She has to believe.

*

It starts with a spark, the glint of a silver tooth. A desert mirage behind the thickening scrub to the right of her. A waterhole. Her parched mind's imagining. It glitters as she approaches. A dare. It's asking her to come close, to kneel, to fill her mouth with water. To drink.

It's there, she's sure. Not a mirage at all. She can hear frogs. She can smell the damp. It must be there, under the surface, waiting for her to lean down. She stares, unsure, aware of the light bottles. There may not be water again.

The sun-sparkles get into her eyes, fire flies, as she tries to see. Then—there. A twitch. She's sure. She knew it. A ripple in the water. The pucker of a scaled snout. She runs. It's time to hide. She heads away from the flatness into the thickening scrub. She needs a space. A cavern. Somewhere small and snug where it won't find her.

She pushes into some bushes, spindling branches snipping at her. One of her drink bottles gets stuck and she wrenches it free, pushes on, fast as she can, until the cuts start to hurt. She's breathless, the air oven-hot. She curls herself away from the spindles, rests her head on her sweaty knees. It won't find her in here, she's safe away from water. She needs to breathe. She pulls her legs in close. She just needs to rest a moment. Then she'll keep going.

She's in the rolling water, back in her dream. Black hair wraps around her wrist, tries to pull her under. The woman is screaming, but no sound is coming out. Her dark hair dribbles wet. Blood drips from her forehead. It's getting in her eyes. She turns into Elias, black blood down his face, then back into the woman. It was her fault. Jo's fault. Josephine's fault. The screaming again. Then the boom of a gunshot.

Jo wakes. Her hands are crawling with black ants, attracted by her sticky skin. She scrambles to her knees, waves her hands. Brushes them against each other. The ants bite, tiny scissor mouths, but eventually she gets them all off. She pushes out of the spindly bushes. Nothing around her but trees. She must have dreamed the gunshot, although her heart is racing. And she's sure—*sure*—that she can hear its echo. A real sound echoes.

Maybe she's been wrong. Maybe she was wrong about who has been following her. Not a croc, after all, but worse.

The trees start to blacken, their thin trunks burnt looking. There must have been a wildfire. The black Gothic against the red soil. She comes to a clearing covered in clumps of yellow spinifex. Three cranes are picking through the scrub. She wonders if they are the same birds she saw in the sky earlier, flying through the orange. Their long white necks are elegant, with bright red on the tops of their heads. She can hear another bird too, a loud echoing call. A hawk maybe.

She stops to take a sip of water. Just a sip. Her throat is too dry, sandpaper. As dry as it was that morning stepping into the hospital room with paper booties, casting her eyes away from the stirrups at the end of the bed. No water for twelve hours. Has it been twelve hours since she'd last drunk anything?

There—she spots the bird that's calling. It's in a tree. A huge kite, tawny brown but with black down its back and under its wings. Its head swivels around. Eyes her.

The crack of a gunshot. Jo chokes on her water. The kite flies off, the cranes too. She fumbles to screw the lid back on the bottle, attach it to her bag, and then she is running. She's not sure which angle the shot came from, the echo was huge, but she needs to get away from it.

He's out there with her. Denny. He's followed her into the night. Kept back, slithered on his belly. He's been waiting, aiming from a distance like a sniper, waiting to take his shot.

The water bottles thwack against each other as she runs.

She tries to keep going west. She has to stay west. It's not long before she's puffed out, the air already brutally hot, but she has to keep going.

Something silver through the trees. A fence, she realises. A fence that's blocking her way west.

She slows as she reaches it, looks around for him. Denny, out here in the land he knows better than her. Angry. She covers her face with her sticky hands. Her skin hurts, the sun is too hot. She can't keep going west if the fence is there.

She turns around again. She can't see him, but she can smell him. Or something he's killed. The smell of raw meat. A coppery blood smell.

There is a track in front of the fence, a bumpy dirt road, and the tyre marks of a four-wheel drive. She steps closer. The smell is stronger. On the other side of the fence are rows upon rows of what looks like raw steak. At least twenty pieces, cut up and laid out across the ground.

She takes a step away then jogs left along the fence. She needs to get around it, she could jump over it even, but she doesn't want to go near those hunks of meat.

Up ahead there is something on the fence. Beige bits of material hanging from the wire. She slows. Not sure whether to turn back, run in the opposite direction. She keeps going, getting closer to the hanging shapes.

She stops, lurch-grip in her stomach. They're dogs. Dingoes maybe. Hanging from the fence by their ankles.

'The billy's on.'

She whirls around. There's a four-wheel drive and a man off the track in the scrub. He's boiling a cooking pot and smiling at her from beneath a moustache. His skin is the colour of ham. She's never seen a man so sun-weathered. He wears a hi-vis orange shirt, so worn and sun-faded that it's almost yellow. Behind him, leaning against his ute, is a long black rifle.

CHAPTER 15

'On a bushwalk?' the man says. 'Be careful round here, mate. You on your own?'

Jo gapes at him, staring at her reflection in his shiny wraparound sunglasses.

'I'm makin' peppermint,' he says. 'I used to have coffee but wife reckons it's bad for my health.'

'Are those dogs dead?' she asks.

'Nah, they're sleepin',' he says, then laughs, a deep throaty sound. 'Killin' Jimbo's calfs, poor darls. Found five dead yesterday.'

'Is that your meat up there?' she asks, pointing.

'Bait,' he says, then pours her a mug and holds it out. She looks around, walks over. Takes it.

'You right, mate?' he says once she is closer.

'Yes.'

'You campin' or somethin'? Bit far out for a bushwalk.'

'I was at the waterfall,' she says lamely.

'Waterfall? What, you mean Bell Gorge?'

'Yes,' she says, nodding.

'Right.'

She takes another sip of the tea. It's burning hot, scalds her tongue. He takes a gulp of his, smacks his lips.

'Erm … I was actually with a tour group.'

'Righto.'

'And I, erm … I think I took the wrong path. Can you point me in the right direction to get back there?'

'To Bell Gorge?'

'Yes.'

He stands up, laughing again. 'You fuckin' Brits,' he says and tips the rest of his tea into the scrub. 'I'll take ya, alright? But gotta pick up the wife on the way.'

'You'll take me to the waterfall?'

'Yeah.' He starts packing the stove away.

She looks around. Can't hear anything. 'What about the erm … the dogs? You'll just leave them?'

'Nah, mate, need your help throwing them in the back.'

'Sorry?'

He laughs, bent back, one hand on his belly. 'Your face.' He straightens. 'Me and the wife will be back for 'em.'

He grabs the gun and puts it between the seats.

She doesn't move, watching him as he steps up and slides into the car. He's got thin legs, a barrel chest.

'Comin'?' he asks.

She gets into the passenger seat, slaps the door closed, pulls her seatbelt on. He turns on the radio and the car fills with some 1980s Australian rock band that she can't place. He swings the wheel and she notices he has tattoos on his knuckles. The ink is so blurred she can't make out what they spell.

'You really wandered off all this way?' he asks.

'Yes,' she says, 'it's not that far though, is it?'

He whistles under his breath.

'So, erm,' she says, 'is your wife at your house?'

'Huh?'

'Are we going past your house? To pick up your wife?'

He laughs again, shakes his head. 'No goin' home for me for at least another week, mate. I'm out at Waterbank. 'Nother week out here at least, I reckon. There's some real buggers, I tell ya. They're gettin' smarter.'

'Okay,' she says. He's blasting the air conditioning and it's like ice. Her skin shivers. Her brain is too big, too hot, inside her skull.

They drive for fifteen minutes, stuttering along the dirt track.

'Used to be a creek bed through here, you know, that's what we're drivin' on,' the guy says, his eyes must flick to her, she can't tell behind his sunglasses. 'Looks like you've had some sun there, mate.'

'Yes,' she says, 'I did put cream on, but—'

He pulls in with a jerk, winds down his window and calls out, 'Oi, fuckhead!'

A shock of orange is coming around the bend. It's Denny. She knows its Denny. Waiting.

But it's not. Not a woman either, but a man. Heavier than Ham-face next to her. This one is closer to the colour of roast beef, with a bald head covered in white spots, his hi-vis shirt almost new. He's wearing sunglasses, polarised ones that flash blue. A metal trap dangles from his hand. He has a rifle on his shoulder.

'Fuckin' catch has gone again,' he says, flinging the trap into the back. He comes round and pulls open Jo's door, then steps back, surprised. 'Oh, fuck. Sorry.' He looks at Ham, then pushes the door shut and gets into the back.

'Found meself a tourist,' Ham says. 'Somehow lost her group by Bell Gorge.'

'Bell Gorge?' Beef says, leaning between the seats. 'Wowee.'

'That's what I said, mate.'

She's shaking, she grips the sides of the chair. 'I thought,' she says, 'you said you were ...'

Ham peers at her; she sees her own pink face in his glasses. His face cracks into a grin. He turns around to Beef, slaps him on the arm.

'She thought you were a woman,' he says.

'Me?' Beef says.

'Look at ya, you stunned mullet. *Me?*' He laughs again, deep, then accelerates and they're shuddering down the track. 'This here is me road wife, me business partner. Makes me my dinner, don't ya, mate?'

'If I ate your food I'd be shittin' meself all the way to Kununurra.'

'Makes me dinner, sets up camp—'

'Oh fuck off, ya cunt, yer embarrassin' her.'

'I'm not, am I? Don't mind him, he's not used to seein' girlies like you. Should see his missus, got a face like a bush pig.'

Beef leans back, then he's laughing too. 'He's right. She does.'

'So what tour you on? Can't think of any of the local ones that go past Bell Gorge.'

'How on earth did you wander off so far?' Beef asks. 'Bloody lucky you ran into us.'

'Into me, mate. You was out pissfartin' round with them traps.'

'Do you need some water?' Beef is eyeing at her backpack, at the two almost empty water bottles. From this angle, she can see the faint outlines of his eyes through the polarising shine. Creased up. Worried.

Ham hasn't noticed. 'Got a coupla tankards in the back. Need it out here, bloody dry as a nun's nasty.'

'Are you alright?' Beef asks.

Now Ham is looking at her too. Eyeing her hands, the red dirt stuck to her skin by juice, thick in the crevices, etched in her finger joints.

'I'm fine.'

The car goes silent. She sees them exchange a glance in the rear-vision mirror.

Time ticks on. She clutches her backpack to her chest. Ham taps the wheel in time to the music. Beef watches her through the rear-vision mirror. She presses her forehead against the window, it bumps against it.

'So where's your group? I can't see any vans?' Beef says.

The gleam of water, up high near the top of the trees. The falls. She's made it.

'You can just let me out here.'

'What if they've left to go find ya?'

'It's okay,' she says.

'Nah, mate, it's not.' Ham slows, then pulls the handbrake and turns to her. 'I can't leave you on your own out here.'

Her stomach twists again. She points towards the trees. 'Over there.'

'I don't see anyone.'

'They're there, I saw them.'

Beef leans forward and says, voice low, 'This ain't right. Somethin's goin' on. Do you need help?'

She sets her face to smiling. 'Thank you so much for the lift,' and gets out of the car.

'Hey, hang on a sec!' Ham calls.

But she's running into the trees, the empty bottles clacking behind her.

'Wait!'

She keeps going. Pushing through the scrub towards the shimmering water. A car door slams.

'You gonna follow her?'

'We can't leave her, mate.'

She flattens herself against the warm earth, peers between the spindly trunks. Beef is standing outside the car, looking around.

'She don't want you to follow her, mate. She said she was alright.'

Beef keeps scanning the trees. She presses her belly flat, doesn't shift, doesn't crick or crack or break a twig.

'Alright, alright.' Beef pulls himself into the car and they fly away.

She watches. Waiting, checking it isn't a ruse. When the dust from their wheels has settled, she stays on her belly, slithers towards the glimmer. The scrub turns to rock, she gets into a squat, stays low.

She can barely swallow now. She needs to refill her bottles.

The waterfall is three cut rocks, the water slopping from one to the next to the next and down into the thick river.

West is on the other side, straight across, through the water.

She reaches the blue glisten, puts her hands in, careful first. Takes a sip, then another, then she's bending low, drinking straight from the splashing river, water hot.

The bottles fill, pack heavy again. She takes off her t-shirt, it's hot, too hot, rinses it with water and wraps it around her neck. Lets the drips slip down her as she steps, boots wobbling, numb feet, into the water. It pushes at her. Tugs at her ankles. Tries to unsteady her, but she can't be thrown over.

West is so close now.

Steady step after steady step, water past her knees now, and a tug, dark grass wrapped around her calf. She stops. It's not grass. No, it's hair. The woman's hair. She's floating, face down, blood turning the water pink. Jo screams, jerks her leg away and pushes on, eyes closed. Can't look.

Her foot hits something solid. A rock. She knows it must be a rock. Not him. Not her baby. Not Jamie either. Not those little cheeks, that gummy smile. Her fault. Her fault.

She won't look. She won't open her eyes. She steps over him. The water laps at her calves. Then her ankles. She's almost through now.

West. West. She has to go west.

CHAPTER 16

Everything has turned to desert-shimmer. She has eaten the final mango in her bag and her gut is twisting. Her mind bounces around trivia questions.

Which Williams sister has won more Grand Slams? Serena.

What does HTTP stand for? Hyper … hyper text …

Who discovered penicillin?

She bends over. The vomit comes quicker this time. Just water, no solids. It tastes sweet.

She spits, then keeps walking.

*

The sun is fading. She's lying on the ground. Her skin has turned numb. She hears sounds around her. Animals. Sticks crackling. Leaves shifting overhead. Soon as she closes her eyes the woman is there, bleeding from the head. Elias is

161

there, bleeding too. And Jamie. The images twist together. Sorcha sneers and Gabe is angry. Ally tells her to go home. Hyper text transfer protocol. Alexander Fleming.

*

The sun is back, burning hot already. What is the hottest planet in the solar system? At what temperature does water boil?

She can hear something, a low vibration in the ground. Hoofs it sounds like. She sits, head spinning.

West. Away from the sun. The trees are gone. There's nothing to shield her from the heat. She pushes forward. Just never-ending flatness.

Movement. Horses. She's sure. A group of horses, grazing on the yellow grass. She wanders towards them. There's a small one with them, a foal. They're wild, she can tell. Brumbies.

And then, far on the other side, a little girl, watching the horses as well. She has dark eyes and hair, is wearing dirty, faded clothes. It's the girl from the missing posters, come to life.

'Hey,' Jo tries to call. Her throat clicks. She coughs. 'Hey!'

Her voice works this time. The brumbies glance at her, then run off. Their footfalls are loud, thrumming red dust into the air. The girl stares at her. She keeps going, stumbling towards the girl.

'Please,' she whispers. She's not sure whether the girl hears her, but she comes towards her and takes Jo's hand.

Then the girl starts walking the other way, tugging on her arm so she'll keep up.

Jo's legs aren't connected to her body. They must be moving. Her feet must be connecting with the earth, but she can't feel it. She can only see the little girl's head as she walks half a pace in front. The ends of her hair are so dry they're fluffy. Jo sees her staccato blink as she turns to Jo.

First, she feels the cool air. She exhales, makes a little sound maybe, because the girl looks back at her again. Then that salty smell. And the sound of it, the rhythmic pull and crash of waves. There are buildings too. A little group of them, like a tiny town, but they don't look right. She turns away, lets herself be pulled, her torso floating forward, her eyes on the ground in front.

'Little one.' It's a woman's voice. They stop. Droplets hit the sand, turn it from Burnt Umber to Alizarin Crimson.

'Who is she? Hey, are you alright?'

She sees the woman's feet. Cracked leather sandals. The woman's ankles are slightly hairy, soft blonde hair. A droplet of water passes through the hair and gets caught, hovering inches from the ground.

'Honey?'

A cold hand touches her arm and she winces. The woman's face is right in front of her. Mid-thirties maybe. Her skin a universe of freckles. She wears round glasses that make her eyes even bigger, and there is a tiny hairline crack in one lens right in the corner. Her hair is dark red and wet, dribbling down the white men's shirt she wears. It has turned clingy and see-through. She can see the woman's nipples.

A figure comes out from behind the buildings. Brown hair. Soft body. It's Ally. Jo crumples, hands grabbing at her so she doesn't hit the ground.

PART THREE

CHAPTER 17

ROSSACK, NOVEMBER 2018

When Jo wakes the first time there is a woman sitting at the end of her bed.

'Shh,' the woman says. It's Ally. 'It's okay, baby. It's alright. You're here now. We're going to look after you.'

Jo starts to shake, her skin freezing cold.

Ally puts a hand on her ankle and her fingers are like ice. 'You've got heatstroke, but you're going to be okay. Dolly is making up a mixture for you, something for your burns.'

'Burns?'

'Just try to rest. Healing takes time. Don't we all know that.' Ally smiles at her and pats her again, ever so softly, on the ankle. 'Do you want me to sit here with you while you fall back to sleep?'

Jo nods. Then she closes her eyes and sleep is right there awaiting her.

She dips in and out of searing dreams. All of them end with Elias's scream, the woman's scream. Under the blood she sees the woman is her mother.

She wakes with a gasp.

'Whoops! I was trying not to wake you.'

It takes Jo a few seconds to recognise the woman that now sits on the edge of her bed. It's the woman she saw when she first arrived. Jo remembers her round, cracked glasses first. She flinches when the woman presses something wet against her arm.

'It's all good, I'm not trying to hurt you.' She laughs, a honking sound. 'So you're J?'

The woman has a silver bowl resting on her knees. She must be Dolly. Her legs are bare. She's got long thin thighs and knobbly knees. She has on the same oversized white shirt as before. Jo can't tell if she's wearing underwear or shorts, the shadows are too deep in here.

Jo looks around. She is in a single wrought-iron bed against a brick wall. The floor is chipped and dinted wooden floorboards. There is a window, high above the door, covered with tarpaulin. The only light comes from its edges, where the black plastic wrinkles against the glass, and from the outline of a small rectangle on the wall above her feet. Her sheets are sticky.

Dolly stirs a bandage into the bowl on her knees. The bowl is filled with a creamy white liquid.

'It's milk,' she says, 'Ally says it should help. We haven't got any aloe vera cream, I'm sorry to say. Just milk, but it's not pasteurised or anything. Do you know they boil milk before it makes it to the supermarket?'

Dolly wrings out the bandage then plasters it to Jo's arm. Almost straight away it's soothing. Jo stretches her arm up so the liquid doesn't drip onto the sheets. The woman makes an involuntary noise in her throat and exhales through her nose.

Jo can smell it too. A horrible rotting sweetness, from the mangoes, she supposes. She is sweating more than she ever has before, her skin rubbery with it, like she's been in the bath too long.

'I'm sorry,' she says.

Dolly snorts. 'I used to be the worst with that. I'd apologise for existing and then apologise for apologising. We don't do that here.'

'Still—'

'Actually, I was pretty impressed. Thought I'd jumped through hoops to get here, but not compared to you.'

She continues plastering the milk-soaked bandages on Jo's skin, beginning to hum something slow and rhythmic. It takes a moment for Jo to place it, remembering the lyrics about being a lonely painter and living in a box of paints, then she realises it's a Joni Mitchell song. Dolly is a little out of tune, but still it makes Jo's eyelids heavy.

She listens to the humming, feels the soothing touches on her arms. Then on her legs, but by then she barely feels them at all. She just breathes and listens.

Jo sees a woman, her narrow shoulders hunched over. Shoulder blades two wings pressed against her knitted jumper. Her hair is long and dark. She is leaning against the sink, her arms deep in the sudsy water. The tap is running and steam rises above the woman, evaporating into the air. She's singing the song, singing about bitterness and sweetness, about holy wine. It's a small kitchen, the cabinets are a pale familiar green. The floor is shiny linoleum. Water sloshes over the edge, trickles down the cabinet onto the floor.

Mum?

'It's okay, baby.'

Jo jolts. She's in the dark room in Rossack. Dolly has gone from the end of the bed, replaced by Ally. She's wiping a warm cloth down Jo's legs. The smell hits her. The milk has solidified on her skin, mixing with the rotting smell of her sweat. Her sunburn has curdled it.

'It's alright,' Ally says, 'you're starting to blister now, that's good. You'll blister, then you'll dry out and you can wriggle out of your skin like a snake and you'll be all better and new.'

Ally wipes again, even softer this time.

'Thank you.'

Ally's smile is warm, but she doesn't look up. She focuses on Jo's legs, wiping the last of the milk paste away.

'Where's Gabe?' Jo asks.

'He knows you're safe, knows we are the right ones to be caring for you.'

Ally moves up the bed and Jo holds out her arm. Ally doesn't react to the smell and Jo is happy for it. As Ally wipes at her arm, the breath catches in Jo's throat. Her eyes fill. Ally is gentle as she removes the bandages from where the blisters are, but the pain is sharp.

The blisters are yellow. They bubble at the crook of her elbows, on the backs of her arms. They must be on her legs too, but she doesn't want to see.

'You're lucky you had your hair down. If it had been a few inches shorter, you would have a blister on the back of your neck big enough to play golf with. Still, these ones on the backs of your shoulders aren't much fun. Can you turn over?'

Ally slides a hand under Jo's back, helps her roll onto her side. The sheet scrapes against the burns on her arms.

Ally strokes her hair. 'Let it out, baby. It's okay. Let it out.'

It hurts to cry: her throat aches, the shudders of her body grate at her skin. But when it's over, when her breathing is beginning to return to normal, the pain doesn't feel quite so bad.

Ally kisses her hair. 'I know you're hurting,' she whispers.

Jo expects her to say more, say that it will all be okay, that it'll get better, that she needs to grit her teeth and just get through. But she doesn't.

She must have fallen asleep again, because she is woken by a metal creak. Yellow light spills into the room. Jo is lying on her stomach. She pushes herself up with her palm, shuffles around so she is sitting. Her butt and the tops of her thighs aren't burnt at all, and it's a relief to take the pressure off the top part of her body.

The sunlight is coming from that small rectangle she'd noticed just above her feet. It's a metal flap like the letter slot on the front door of her dad's house.

She shifts forward so she can see through the flap. On the other side is a pair of dark brown eyes. She hears a gasp, then the flap snaps shut.

Jo scoots forward, pushes the metal flap the other way. The light is too bright for a moment, but she blinks until she can see. The little girl, the one who had found her, is walking away, her shoulders high and tight.

'It's okay,' Jo calls and the girl pauses, looks over her shoulder to meet Jo's eye. Then she hurries out of sight behind another one of the buildings. Jo imagines how she must appear. Maybe she's scared the girl.

No one else is around, but she can hear voices. There is laughter coming from one of the other buildings, but she isn't sure which one. The ground is dirt and the buildings are strange and old-fashioned. Limestone, with wide roofs held up by wooden poles. The overextension of the roofs gives each building a square of shadow around it.

Her eyes begin to throb, so she pulls back. Lets go of the flap. She is back in darkness again and can barely see. The darkness has a pinkness to it, the sun trapped in her eyes.

She shuffles down the bed, dropping to an elbow then her back. The pillow is soft under her cheek. She closes her eyes. The pinkness throbs in front of her, begins shrinking, becomes a globe.

The little girl and her mother standing in their driveway by the silver car. The picture had been on the front page of the paper in the café, she'd folded it and put it back with the magazines multiple times throughout the day. Briena had shown the photo to her on her phone screen that day in the bathroom at the pub when she'd been gripping the cool porcelain sink with clammy hands. The image again at the bus stop in Broome the day she'd first arrived.

It's the same girl, she's sure of it. She looked different without the cheesy smile she'd been flashing to the camera, but it's her: Nika Makos. The little girl had saved her, brought her here. But why was she here herself, when there were so many people searching for her and her mother?

Jo presses her face into the pillow. It's too much to think about now.

Soon the pink flashing shrinks down to nothing and everything is dim and grey again.

CHAPTER 18

'It's healing,' Ally says, 'you're coming good.'

She's inspecting Jo's back, her hands soft and gentle. Most of Jo's blisters have burst. Yesterday she'd woken with the back of her t-shirt drenched, not with sweat this time. When she'd tried to pull it off it had tugged at her skin. The pus had fused to the cotton.

Now, Jo wears her underwear. Only Ally sees her most of the time anyway.

When Ally isn't around, Jo has been watching people come and go through the slot. Late one afternoon she saw a young woman, maybe twenty-one or -two, walking with Dolly from the direction Jo imagined was the ocean. Both had wet hair dripping down their backs. She'd seen a man walking around shirtless, two other women laughing and talking in Italian. But people only ever seemed to be around when the sun was cast low, either dusk or dawn. During the night she could hear laughter and music, but wherever the group congregated wasn't visible from her slot.

She'd seen the girl a few times, Nika, but she never came close. She looked out for Larissa, the mother from the photograph, but the girl was always alone.

'You know people are searching for her? That little girl,' she says to Ally. 'There were pictures of her in the paper for a while.'

'Seems like they aren't searching very hard,' Ally says, putting down the cloth she'd been using to clean Jo's skin. Jo doesn't look at it; she doesn't want to see its colour.

'Where's her mum?'

'This place isn't for everyone. She left a bad situation and she wanted to make a better one. This was just a pit stop.'

'So she left her daughter behind? That's so sad.'

'I'm sure she'll be back.' Ally sticks a fresh bandage over the remnants of the blister on Jo's shoulder.

Outside, it is silent. The sun is high; she can feel it beating down on the stone around her.

'What do you all do during the day?' Jo asks. She wants to keep Ally talking. Once Ally leaves she'll be alone again. Although now sleeping is coming as easy as breathing. Thanks to Ally.

She ruffles Jo's hair then pats it smooth. Her weight lifts from the bed. Jo props herself up to look at Ally as she lays a fresh sheet over her, the cotton clean and smelling of heat and salt.

'We rest, stay in the shade, recharge. Our rhythms match our place. The sun can be hostile, as you've discovered. Better not to fight it.'

She picks up the plastic container with the lid that Jo has been using as a toilet.

'Sorry,' Jo says, though Ally never seems bothered. Looking after Jo, cleaning her body, soothing her panic, it seems so natural to Ally.

'Maybe it's time for the little mole to come out of its hole, you can't hibernate forever,' she says now, one hand on the brass door handle. 'You should come to dinner tonight, meet everyone.'

'Actually, moles don't hibernate,' Jo says, 'they hunt all year. They use the burrows to bring their prey in to eat.'

Ally laughs. 'You're always full of quaint little facts, aren't you?'

She walks out the door but leaves it ajar, wide enough for someone to put their foot in.

The heat begins to slither in through the gap. Along with the heat comes the smell. The ocean, the sand, the world outside. There wasn't a coastline in Chesterfield or London, and in Sydney she never seemed to make it out to Bondi Beach. Eric said it was all trust-fund hippies and spray-tan-fucktards. But now, the smell of the sea has a tug to it. She wants to follow it. She hasn't seen it since that brief glimpse through the bus window.

Her head spins when she sits up. She leans against the wall and waits for it to subside, then waits a little longer. She tries to count how many nights she's been inside this building. Four? Maybe five. It's been punctuated with visits. Ally, mostly. Dolly a few times. A guy came in. Ho-jin. He couldn't have been much older than eighteen or nineteen, puppy fat still puffing out his cheeks. He'd lingered in the doorway, asked her so quietly if she was okay that she'd had to ask him to repeat himself. He'd come back the next day; she'd woken to him placing a tin cup half full of pulpy-sweet orange juice by her bedside. She'd flinched and he'd apologised, so quietly again, his hand covering his mouth. She'd thanked him as he backed out the door.

Gabe never came. She hoped he would to start with. Then she was glad when he didn't. Her skin. Her smell. She would have hated for him to see her like that.

The sun sinks a little. The shadows shift around her. She can see her silhouette on the brick wall. Her profile is in her periphery, but if she turns to look at it, it disappears. A long way off, she hears talking. People walking in the clearing between the buildings. The sun must be low enough now. She wants to get out before everyone else. She's not sure if she wants to be seen yet, but she wants to see the ocean. Find that perfect aquamarine. Plus Ally told her it was time and, after all Ally has done for her, Jo doesn't want to disappoint her.

She shuffles to the edge of the mattress, then stands. Her feet are pink and sore, her toenails cracked and broken. She won't put those boots back on.

Her backpack is there, unopened since she arrived, the two empty water bottles attached to the sides. She unclips the silver buckle, then flips the top flap off. Her wallet. Her dead phone. She moves them aside. Takes out a t-shirt, the biggest of the two she brought. She pulls it gingerly over her head. Her shorts are crumpled on the floor. She steps into them. She'll just have a look around, then she'll come back to her safe little burrow. Her mole hole, like Ally had said. Jo takes a breath, opens the door and steps out.

The sky is so high. It domes around her. Through the slot, the buildings had seemed bigger. Now she sees they are a third smaller than regular buildings. The roofs lower, the doorways narrow. They're like the beds that real estate agents put into open houses, that little bit smaller so that the room looks bigger. Instead they always have that uncanny effect, that twist in your perception where your eyes know that something isn't quite right but your brain can't quite compute.

No one is out there, although she can hear the yips and laughter of people not far away. She takes another step out, then another. Soft dirt sticks to her feet. Crickets chirp.

Jo turns to see her own building, the place where she had felt so safe. Moves a step backwards to take it in. It's just like the other buildings. Huge slabs of stone, the steel roof halo-ing it. Along the brickwork are painted letters, faded from time but legible: *Post Office and Bonds.*

This whole place could almost be the set for a western film. Except there are details that don't fit. A faded red beach towel and grey-blue t-shirt hang from a tree. A green wooden table with a paperback left open and turned over to hold a page. The gold lettering catching the light: *Parable of The Sower.* Then, of course, there is the car. The green lorry, parked over to the far edge, peeping out from behind one of the bigger buildings.

So he is here.

Jo walks into the breeze. Lets it fill her up, salt and heat and that faint fetid musk of seaweed. She can hear the waves crashing now, calm and rhythmic, and the sounds of voices.

The horizon appears out of nowhere. The division between sky and water only the tiniest of gradients of colour. The ocean has a dab more green. And it glitters. You could never recreate that sparkle with paint, a million winks and teeth flashing. Getting closer, she sees the edge is cut out like a bite, a sharp cliff that looks straight out to nothing. Beneath it, water laps at the rocky shore and a few large boulders and then it's straight ocean. She turns her head to each side. The cliff swoops around and down. On each side the scrabble of shrubs and spindly bushes runs down the steep slope.

There are heads bobbing in the water. A few more on the rocks. Ally sits on a boulder, she wears a one-piece and her shoulders sparkle with water drops. She turns and her smile is huge when she sees Jo. She raises her arm in a wave and the others look up too. Jo wants to rush from the edge, but she stands her ground, hoping she doesn't look strange, too conspicuous, this black dot of t-shirt and flapping hair standing and watching them. The ones on the sand cheer when they see her, waving too and smiling. She imagines the ones in the ocean are too far away to see. She waves back and sits cross-legged on the edge.

They turn back to the ocean. A few heads bob in the water on either side of the bite, some treading water, others gripping on to the jagged orange rocks.

Someone must say something, she's not sure who, but she sees all heads turn to one figure. It's the boy, she thinks, Ho-jin. He's holding onto a rock on the right. They stare at him, and she can hear chattering; can see their arms beckoning him. It's too far for her to see his expression. Is it panic? Excitement? He holds his nose and she sees his mouth open, a huge breath, then he's under. She sees the bobble of his bum, his feet splashing the surface. Then nothing. Silence.

Jo finds she is holding her own breath. After a few seconds, she lets it out. Ho-jin doesn't come up. She scans the water, looking at the heads, the people sitting on the sand bed. No one is moving. She notices the sky has darkened, just in the few minutes she has been sitting here. It's turned grey-blue, but the water is sparkling. Ho-jin hasn't come up. It must have been at least a minute. Is it possible to hold your breath that long? Underwater as well. No one appears concerned. She hears a small laugh. Two women have their heads bent together on the rocks, their shoulders touching.

The breeze lessens, then dies away entirely, like it too is holding its breath.

Jo looks around. Could she get there in time if she ran down and around the incline, could she jump in and try to find him in all that blue water? But then Ally turns again and smiles in that calm way that says it's okay. She knows Jo is worried, but it's okay. And while her eyes are locked with Ally's, Jo hears the applause.

She searches the water where Ho-jin went under. She can't see him. She follows Ally's gaze to the other side. The opposite edge of the bite, so far away the people are miniature. She sees him. His limbs glistening as he pulls himself onto a rock, breathing deep. Another figure clambers onto the rock, and they're so far away but Jo can still see. She can recognise the broad shoulders, the dark hair on the chest. It's Gabe.

He goes to Ho-jin, seems to check him, one hand on his cheek, the other on his arm. He says something, then he pulls him into a hug. When he lets go, Ho-jin stands and throws his arms in the air and everyone is on their feet and cheering. Gabe is standing next to him on the rock. Jo is sure that he is looking at her.

Now that the breeze has lifted, the air is wet and hot once more. She smells something terrible, like fruit that rotted so long it's leaking. It's her. She hasn't washed since the night before she left Denny's. Her hair is stiff with dried-out sweat. She hasn't even changed her underwear.

She gets up from her seat and rushes back to her building. Ally will come, she's sure of it, she'll come and tell her where she can wash. Maybe she'll even help her.

Jo closes the door of the bonds office and then, rethinking, opens it a little again. The way Ally had left it. She sits on the bed and the space is even darker than before, more airless.

She waits. The light outside begins to dim. Ally isn't coming, and Jo starts to wonder if she made a mistake running off. Maybe she was meant to run down into the ocean. That would have washed her, for sure.

Something squirms around in the shadows. An idea, unfurling and ugly. Maybe they don't want her to be here. Maybe she's been a horrible imposition. They've helped her to get well and now they want her to leave. She was never invited. She never was asked to come. She'd thought Gabe had wanted her, but if he did he would have checked in by now.

She shifts, and sees her feet have mucked the bedding. She's brought the orange dirt inside and left red smears on the fresh sheets Ally just laid for her.

Outside, she hears a laugh. She peers out through her slot. It's Dolly, walking with the young woman she'd seen her with before. They are beautiful. Dolly's hair looking crimson against the other girl's dark curls; Dolly's skin even more pale and freckled in contrast to the other girl's spotless brown skin. Jo realises she's been watching them for days, seen them half dressed. She's like a voyeur.

'Hey, Dolly!' she calls, and Dolly's head jerks up.

She grins at Jo and begins walking over. 'Playing peek-a-boo?'

Jo feels stupid. She could have talked to Dolly through the doorway, but she's ashamed of her appearance. And her smell.

'Do you know where I can, erm … have a shower? Or just a wash somewhere?'

Dolly bends over so she's face to face with Jo and cocks her head.

'I stink,' Jo says. 'I want to meet everyone, but I … I really smell bad.'

'Does Ally think you're well enough?'

Jo nods.

Dolly straightens, chin tilting up, eyes squinting behind her flashing glasses. 'If we go now, we can be back in time for dinner. About time you met everyone.'

Jo snaps the metal flap shut. And, just for a second, she wishes she could stay here, where it is safe, where Ally has cared for her, where there is no sun and no one she has to convince to like her. But Dolly is waiting.

'Sorry,' she says, opening the door to the light and air once again.

Dolly looks at her. 'If I could raise one eyebrow, I would be doing it right now. Stop with the apologies.' Then she grins. 'You do look better! Way better. But also, yes, you do smell. I didn't want to say anything before.'

Behind Dolly, the other girl is standing there staring at Jo.

Dolly follows her gaze, turns. 'J stinks. I'll take her to the rock pool,' she says to the girl.

Jo stares at her feet, her face colouring. This isn't how she wanted to be introduced.

'That's Lia,' Dolly says. 'Come on.' She puts her hand on Jo's arm, steers her towards the coastline.

They walk in silence, Jo staring at Dolly's cracked sandals.

'You must be so happy to be out of the bonds office,' Dolly says. 'I mean, the idea of being in there by myself seems awful to me now. Although you were pretty out of it. You were saying all sorts of stuff in your sleep.'

Jo doesn't want to ask what. 'What is this place?' she says instead. 'Like, the buildings look so old. It's like a little western town.'

'Pretty old, yeah. Like mid eighteen hundreds, I think? Then the whole pearling industry moved over to Broome, so everyone left this place.'

'So, what? It became a ghost town?'

Dolly smiles. 'Don't think there're any ghosts. But yeah, it's hardly prime real estate so it was abandoned and they never bothered knocking it down or anything. There's a bunch of these little forgotten places around here.'

They reach the peak that Jo had sat on earlier. Dolly points towards it, but keeps on walking. 'That's Butcher's Inlet. The shore is that side, but if you go to the right down here instead there're some little rock pools. It'll be a good place for you to wash. We don't really do showers, since we're always in the water. For some reason the Irukandji don't come into the inlet. We've never seen any real marine life actually. Not sharks, or dolphins or whales. I guess they know it's our place.'

Jo wants to ask Dolly how she ended up here, what her story is, but she only says, 'I know you don't like it when I apologise. But I … I hope I'm not getting in the way. Being a burden.'

Dolly stops, clutches Jo's arms and whispers, 'Never think of yourself like that. It's such an awful way to think. You're one of us now. We're excited for you to be here, however long you decide you want to stay. Okay?'

'Okay,' Jo says, wanting to believe it.

Dolly's eyes are fixed on hers and Jo looks away. There are marks on the crooks of Dolly's inner elbows. Little bumps of healed scar tissue.

'We've all got pasts,' Dolly says. She lets go and grabs Jo's hand instead. 'Down here.' She pulls her along the slope.

The rock pool is crystal clear. Jo wades into it, holding one arm over her breasts, embarrassed to show her nipples, and the other over her pubic hair. Since puberty, only lovers have seen her naked and she's always made sure her body was ready to be looked at. Now, she is ashamed of her raw nakedness.

'You're so shy,' Dolly calls from where she's lying, stretched out across the rocks. She pulls her white shirt up, reveals small breasts and dark nipples. 'Does this make you feel more comfortable?' She leaves her shirt like that, bunched over her sternum, and rests her hands behind her head again.

Jo takes a tentative step in. The salt water gets into the welts on her feet. She winces. She hadn't thought of that, how much the salt would hurt.

'Keep going,' Dolly calls.

Jo takes another step. Tiny black fish dart around her. She bites her lip and takes another step, then another. Then she sits on the rocks, the water reaching almost to her belly button. The sting is exquisite, making her eyes tear up, more salt water slipping down her cheeks. She cups some of the water from the rock pool in her hands, gasping from the pain as it gets into the cracks in her burnt fingers. She rubs the water under her arms, into the soft hair that's growing there. She's not burnt there, and she grins as the sweat drips off her.

'Do you need help?'

She looks up.

Lia is standing by the pool. She holds a floral cotton dress with thin straps. 'I thought you might want to wear this instead. Your t-shirt is pressing against your sunburn. You should let it breathe.'

'Thanks,' Jo says, crossing her arms over her breasts again. The salt water on her hands prickles against the burns on her upper arms.

Lia pulls her own skirt up around her thighs and wades in. She stands behind Jo.

'Wow, ouch.' Her voice is gentle. 'Your back is going to hurt. You might want to wait, ay?'

'It's my hair. It feels so gross.'

Dolly gets up and stretches out her freckled limbs. 'Alright, let's sort it properly.' She pushes off the rock and wades into the water. 'Lean your head forward, onto your knees.'

Jo puts her forehead onto her knees. Dolly leans over her, heaping cupped hands of water onto Jo's hair, until it's drenched and dripping. She digs her fingers into Jo's scalp and rubs.

More hot tears come to Jo's eyes now, and they aren't from the sting, though a few droplets have dribbled down her back. She sniffs, her forehead pressed onto her knees, tries to hide the sounds of it, tries to stop her shoulders from jerking. But Lia hears. She tucks her skirt into her swimmers and sits in the water next to her. Lia laces her arms around Jo's knees, pressing her warm arms on top of Jo's ruined skin. Dolly rests her cheek on top of Jo's head.

'It's okay,' Lia whispers. 'Whatever's happened, things will be different now.'

*

At dinner, Jo is introduced to everyone in quick succession. There is Zay, a French Canadian man in his late twenties. He's all dark skin and black stubble and clipped-short hair. He's filling the table she'd seen earlier with bowls of food, but stops to clasp her hand quickly between both of his. 'So glad you are better,' he says, his accent rich and his smile wide and gentle.

As they move on, Dolly whispers, 'His boyfriend died back in Quebec, sideswiped by a car when he was cycling to work. Zay was travelling around Australia when he found us.'

The two girls she'd seen sitting shoulder to shoulder on the rocky shore turn out to be Greta and Valentine. Greta has inch-long hair and creamy white skin interrupted by blue and black sleeves of tattoos on each arm. Valentine has brown skin, her dark hair wrapped over one shoulder. She has holes all the way up her ears from earrings she no longer wears.

Greta kisses her cheeks. Valentine says, 'Hello,' in an Italian accent.

'They're from Siena. Been here about two years now.'

Ho-jin comes over and talks with his hand covering his mouth. 'I'm glad you feel better.'

'He's shy,' Dolly says as Ho-jin goes inside to grab something from the kitchen. 'He's from Seoul, he's the most recent here aside from you. He's only been here with us for six months or so. Was doing the farm work like you.'

'What about you?' Jo asks. 'And Lia?'

'Lia? She's local actually, she's Yawuru-Japanese. She's been here a couple of years.'

'Yawuru?'

'Yeah, they're the Indigenous people around here.'

'And you?' Jo asks.

'Perth,' is all she says, but her hand crosses over to her elbow, wrapping around the scars.

'And Ally?' In Jo's mind, Ally should be in the suburbs somewhere, going on power walks and cooking pies. It's all clichés, she knows, but that's what she sees. Ally has brought a bowl of food over to Nika, who is sitting under a tree by herself. She's whispering to the girl, who is nodding in response, her eyes on the ground.

A man's voice comes from behind her. 'There she is.'

She doesn't want to turn around. She knows that voice.

A big palm cups her head. She looks up, annoyed at herself for grinning.

'So I hear you're on the mend?' His smile seems genuine, just like it was before, except he's not quite looking at her. Something has shifted.

'Yes, I'm coming good.' But now her smile feels fake.

'Good. Knew you were a trouper. Wait until you've had Zay's cooking, it's better than anything you've ever tasted.' And he smiles at her again.

It's different this time, but before she can see exactly how, he's turned away and walked over to Zay, so she can only see his back.

CHAPTER 19

Jo wakes to the sound of breathing. They are all around her, filling the space with the rhythm. It isn't like the breathing in the shed on Denny's farm. These breaths sound deep, free. The breath of the breeze is in the room as well, carrying the salt of the ocean. She can hear the waves.

The first fingers of dawn creep through the barred windows. They have been hung with white mosquito netting, since there is no glass. There are layers of netting everywhere, over the windows, around beds and across the open doorways in the cells. Jo's bed is a thick mattress on the warm wooden floorboards.

Last night after dinner she'd walked into the old courthouse with Lia and seen where she slept.

'That bed's free if you want,' Lia had said, tapping the mattress next to hers with her ankle, 'or you can stay where you are if you prefer to have some space. Up to you.'

Jo had gone to the bonds office to grab her bag and the stink of it had turned her stomach. Now she is surrounded by people, in the light and fresh air, those hot fetid days alone feel like a stomach-buckling fever dream.

She sits in her new bed, wraps her arms around her knees. Her sunburn didn't keep her awake last night. The pain is all but gone. She'd let the thought enter her mind for a moment, that she'd be awake in this space all night, her back throbbing. But it seems she really is cured. As soon as she lay down the tiredness was right there to tug her under.

She rubs the sleep out of the corner of her eye. The space is recognisable as a courthouse, though they have taken out the audience seating. Between the haphazardly placed mattresses she can see the shadows of where it would have been on the floorboards. Next to her is Lia and on Lia's other side was Ho-jin, though his bed is empty. From here she can only see the slab of mahogany of the judge's dock. Nika sleeps behind it. Jo had peered over last night and seen the nest the girl had made for herself with a foam mattress and blankets, a few bits of mother of pearl shell she must have found by the water propped against the walls.

Jo slips out of bed. She wants to see what the sea looks like in the pastels of dawn.

Lia stirs next to her. She blinks her eyes open and smiles softly when she sees Jo. 'Morning.' Her voice is croaky. She props her head on her hand. 'Bad night's sleep?'

'No,' Jo whispers back, 'really good. Brilliant. I feel so much better.'

Lia flops onto her pillow. 'Good,' she mouths, then closes her eyes again.

Jo pads across the hall with bare feet, careful to be quiet as she slips between the mattresses of the two Italian girls. She looks down the corridor that used to house the holding cells. The bars are so covered in netting you can barely see them and the doors have been taken off at the hinges. Dolly, Zay and Gabe have a cell each. There is an empty one too, but she's happy sleeping in the room with everyone else. She doesn't like the idea of being surrounded by bars, even if they are covered.

She leaves the courthouse and makes her way to the shore. The sky is a vast little-girl pink above her. The air isn't hot yet. It's not cold, but leaves the tiniest prickles of goose flesh on her bare legs and arms. Her sunburn is too dry to keep her warm now. She's still wearing Lia's thin cotton dress. She slept in it. The dress doesn't feel like her. Too feminine. But it's soft, the material so thin and worn it's threadbare at the seams.

Her feet slip in the sand as she makes her way down the hill. She uses the tufts of dry grass poking out of the sand as footholds. The ocean unfolds in front of her, glistening pink. At the bottom of the hill, she stares out at the endless horizon, her hand unconsciously going to the skin of her shoulders. She's beginning to peel and it's addictive to pull at her skin, bring off the thinnest layers and feel the new skin underneath.

Out of the corner of her eye she senses movement. She looks around, hoping maybe Ally will have awoken early as well. She didn't get to talk to her at dinner last night and she doesn't sleep in the courthouse. She's not sure where Ally sleeps. The others were around her, explaining how things work, when they do things and how. She hasn't needed Ally to take care of her. But already she misses her. She misses telling her what hurts, misses her gentle hands checking her body.

But it isn't Ally sitting on one of the sharp rock faces. It's Gabe. He raises a hand to her. She could just wave back, then walk away, go back up and get in bed again. Instead she walks towards him, conscious now of how much skin this dress shows, of how scaly her sunburn is becoming. Apart from their brief conversation yesterday, he hasn't even looked at her. She climbs onto the rock next to him.

'Hi,' she says.

'Didn't pick you as an early riser too.'

He talks to her like everything is normal, like he hasn't been avoiding her since she got here, pretending they barely know one another.

She wants to be the kind of person who would call him on it. Ask him what the problem is. She's always been bad at relationships with men. Always so afraid that they are going to reject her if she tells them when she's annoyed or angry, or if she lets them in too deep. In the end, she leaves them before they get a chance to leave her, because she knows they will.

'I've never seen the sea this colour,' she says.

'I know. I always thought of it as blue, but here it seems like it can be more than that.'

'It's mostly green, but it looks grey sometimes too. Or last night it was black. In England it was brown. And the sand was pebbles and broken shell.'

'Did you go to the beach a lot back home? Family trips?'

'No.' She resists the urge to elaborate. She feels stupid. Foolish. Like she followed him here, some lovesick teenager obsessed with the boy she likes. He didn't even visit her in the bonds office. But now she's so glad she's come, and it's not about him any more.

'Did something happen,' he says, 'at Denny's? Or did you just get sick of it or was it—'

'Something happened.'

She stares out at the pink rippling water and tries to tell him about it in as few words as possible. She doesn't tell him that it was her that missed the mango, that she was the reason Elias leant down. She tries to not think about the sound, that horrible wet slap of scalp.

'Wow,' he says, when she's finished. 'I'm sorry. So sorry. That's … poor Elias.'

'Yeah.' She pulls her knees into her chest and hugs them. She should get in touch. She should find out if there are any updates. And she left so abruptly. Sorcha and Yan may have asked if Denny gave her a lift and found out he didn't. They might be worried. She stands up. If she stays she'll keep talking, keep telling him things, and she doesn't want that.

He looks at her, brow furrowed. So earnest she wants to laugh.

'Just so you know, I wasn't …' he swallows, 'I wasn't trying to give you directions when I told you about it here. I never ever thought you'd try to walk it. I wouldn't have—'

'I know. I hadn't slept. I wasn't thinking straight. I thought it was a test.'

'It wasn't.'

'But you wouldn't have just driven me if I said I wanted to come, would you?'

He doesn't answer quick enough, so she jumps off the rock. She wants to have this conversation, but the earnestness is unbearable. It's that same expression as when she leant through the window, kissed him. The memory of it is right there, his lips on hers. His hands in her hair. His smell.

She makes her way back the way she came, careful with her footing.

'Bet you don't miss the Britney,' he calls after her.

She turns. 'Poor Denny. His loneliness is killing him.'

He laughs. 'He shouldn't have let you go.'

She forces a smile, then turns back and keeps going.

It's all a little false, but they are back to jokes and the earnestness is gone and that's enough for now.

She glances at the ocean as she climbs to the settlement. It's mirroring the sky still, the pink turning to burning peach.

She can hear quiet singing as she reaches the clearing. She follows it towards the kitchen. Zay is standing by the door, but when he sees her he puts a finger to his lips. Ho-jin is inside. He's peeling the skin from some kiwi fruits and singing to himself. She doesn't recognise the song and realises the words are not in English. An old Korean song, maybe. Even without lyrics, she can hear the emotion of it. Zay looks at her and his eyes are alight. She can't believe Ho-jin, who always covers his mouth when he speaks so that she can barely hear him, has such a beautiful voice. His fingers are delicate as he removes the skin, like he is singing to the piece of fruit. His voice fills the space. Then, though neither of them have moved, he turns. He sees them standing in the doorway. He puts a juice-slicked hand to his mouth again.

Jo is about to rush an apology, but Zay passes her and puts a hand on Ho-jin's shoulder. 'You know I love it when you sing, Ho. It's one of my favourite things in the world.'

Ho-jin stares at the ground, but he's smiling.

'You're happy about yesterday?' Zay asks.

Ho-jin nods. 'I didn't think I'd ever be able to do it.'

'I knew you could. Once you make the doorway, it's easy.'

'What's the doorway?' Jo asks.

Ho-jin turns back to the kiwi fruit.

Zay puts his hands out. 'It's just one part of something big.'

The sadness she saw in Zay's face is back now. He opens the fridge door, begins pulling out fruit.

'You want to help with breakfast, J?'

They've been calling her that since she arrived. She wants to tell them that it's not her name, it had never even been a nickname, just what Gabe seems to call her. But it seems rude to correct them.

'Sure.' She goes to the wooden box of utensils and rummages until she finds a knife. She looks at the fruit. Grapes, passionfruit and mangoes. Some of the grapes are brown and the passionfruit is split. The mango is bruised, one of the ones she would have taken off the belt.

'We call them the uglies,' Zay tells her, reading her expression. 'Instead of throwing them out, the farmers let us have them. They still taste great, just avoid the busted bits.'

'Okay,' she says, taking a passionfruit. She doesn't ever want to touch a mango again for the rest of her life. She begins chopping, scooping out the seeds from the middle of the fruit. The tropical smell fills the small room.

'How did you do it?' Jo asks Ho-jin quietly. 'I've never seen anyone go underwater that long unless they had an oxygen tank.'

'We can all do it,' he says.

'What? They can all hold their breath for that long?'

'Longer,' he says.

She watches him chop, not sure what to say. He's quick with his hands. Graceful.

'So you came from a farm?' he asks. 'You were doing the days?'

'Yeah,' she says.

'So did I.'

She knows there's a story, doesn't ask. 'Did you finish it?'

'No.'

'Wait, but what about your visa? You didn't get an extension?'

He laughs, but doesn't look up. 'None of us did. They're hardly going to check our paperwork out here. Greta and Valentine have been here ages. Zay for longer than them.'

*

They sit under the tree, waiting out the sun. Zay is lying on his back, a hand over his eyes. Lia is reading *Parable of the Sower*. The Italian girls are sitting cross-legged facing each other, weaving some sort of net. She knew they looked familiar. She has seen them before. Greta and Valentine, arm in arm in black and white. And Zay's face, under *Felix Debonair, Last Seen*.

'You're all missing,' she says, to no one in particular.

Zay laughs, but doesn't open his eyes. 'We're not. We're right here.'

'I've seen your posters. Near the airport. I swear it said your name was Felix.' Then she looks at the little girl. She is sitting under a tree by herself, her fruit bowl in front of her. 'Nika and her mum have been in the paper too.'

Nika doesn't look up. She sits staring into her bowl, licking at the skins of the fruit, crunching on the passionfruit seeds.

'Bet my poster wasn't there, ay?' Lia says, eyes on her book.

Jo thinks. She can't remember seeing it.

Zay's jaw is set. 'We're happy here. And we aren't hurting anyone.'

'Shouldn't you tell your families? They must be worried.'

'We have,' he says, 'but they hear what they want to hear. I sent them a letter, they know I'm okay. They just want me back with them, probably.'

She thinks about that for a moment. 'You don't feel homesick or anything? Or miss the city?'

'Do you?'

She laughs, shakes her head. She's not missing England. Or Sydney.

They go back to silence, but the comfortable kind, punctuated with the occasional rustle as Lia turns a page of her book. Jo leans against the tree, tenderly letting her shoulders rest against the smooth trunk.

Gabe appears. He's shirtless and Jo can't help but avert her eyes. He sinks to the ground near Zay and lays down as well.

'Harvest tonight,' she hears him mutter.

'Cool,' Zay says.

From this angle, Jo can see Gabe's eyes underneath his sunglasses. His eyes flick to her. She looks away. When she looks back, his eyes are closed.

They are beautiful, laying side by side. Both of them shirtless, Gabe in shorts and Zay in low-slung jeans. Gabe rests one foot over the ankle of the other, puts one arm behind his head so his underarm hair is visible, sparse and soft-looking. The sun coming through the branches dapples their bare skin with speckles of light and shade. If she were to paint them, it would be in the Pre-Raphaelite style. She'd use golds and glowing sienna. She'd paint every abundant detail, every beautiful prickle of grass, every glint of light on their skin.

After a while she sees Dolly emerging from a building marked *Galbraith & Co.* Her head is bowed, and Jo can see she's wiping her cheeks.

'Are you okay?' Lia asks, when she reaches them.

'Yeah. You know how it is.'

Zay pulls Dolly down next to him, rubbing her arm. She leans her head onto his stomach.

'J wants to see the doorway,' Zay says.

Dolly looks around at her. 'You do?'

'Yeah.'

CHAPTER 20

Jo holds tight to the rocks as she clambers out around the edge of the inlet. If she weren't gripping hard her hands might be shaking. She's wearing someone's brown one-piece; she didn't ask whose. It's too big for her. It sags around the waist and the straps slip down her shoulders, scrape against the pink scales there.

Dolly and Lia sit on the rocks ahead. They're quicker than her. They know where to put their feet. Jo's own feet are throbbing, the already sensitive skin scraping against the jagged rock edges. Dolly grins and throws up a hand in a wave towards the shore. Jo looks over her shoulder. Ally is sitting by the water. She's far away, but she's sure Ally is smiling at her. She's glad she's come to watch over her.

She makes it to where they are sitting and steadies herself against the rock. She's out of breath and lightheaded. She pushes herself onto the rock. Dolly in her white shirt, Lia in an oversized t-shirt. Both are nude underneath.

'So where is it?' she asks, panting.

'What?'

'The doorway.'

Lia grins and points towards the water.

'What?' Jo looks at Dolly, whose eyes are on the shore, on Ally. She's squashing her lips together, like she is biting them on the inside, and she is pinching at the skin of her other arm. It's turning pink.

She turns back to them. 'I'll go first.'

Dolly pulls her shirt off over her head. Jo averts her eyes when she sees her bare breasts.

'God, you're so British,' Dolly says.

'I'm not. I'm just not an exhibitionist.'

Lia laughs 'It's more natural this way. There's nothing between us and the water. It's how the Ama used to do it.'

'The what?'

'Japanese divers. They pass it down from mother to daughter.'

Dolly slips from the rock into the water. She splashes a little water on her face, then takes a very slow breath in. Then she bobs down. Jo watches the water close above her. Not even one air bubble breaks the surface. Just like Ho-jin, Dolly seems to disappear.

Jo lets herself imagine it. A little wooden trapdoor on the sandy seabed, Dolly, mermaid-haired, reaching for its handle.

'So, wait, there is a door under the ocean?'

'No.' Lia laughs. 'You're so literal. It's not a real door.'

Jo cringes, tries not to show it. 'Okay. So it's, what, something spiritual or something?'

'You aren't watching,' Lia says.

'I am.'

'You've missed it.'

Across the inlet Dolly reappears. The afternoon light shimmers from the water in her hair. Dolly slicks her hair back, then she turns to them. Lia puts her hand out, palm flat, to Dolly. *Wait.*

'You won't see anything from up here.'

'What? You want me to watch from under the water?'

'Yeah, of course.'

'Well, do you have some goggles or something?'

'We don't need them.'

Jo looks from Lia to the water. 'It'll hurt my eyes.'

'It's salt water that comes from your eyes when you cry, right? It stings for a second, then it's fine.' She looks at Jo. 'Trust me.'

And Jo has to trust her, since all she's given her is kindness. Jo lowers herself into the water. Legs first, knees, thighs and then she slips the rest of the way, bobs down to her neck and then back up. Her burns are healing, but still, the pain from the salt water going into the blisters on her back is like a slap.

The current is throwing her around. She places her palms against the rock, kicks with her feet to stay afloat.

Now she is in the water, the other side of the inlet seems even further away.

'Okay, ready?' Lia says to her, and she nods. She waves and Dolly takes a breath then dives under the water again.

Jo takes a breath too and sinks down, her palms against the rock, trying to get a grip to keep herself under. She tries to blink her eyes open, but the water burns. She pulls herself up, rubs her eyes with the heels of her hands.

'Quick! You're going to miss it!'

She takes a slow breath, then dives. There was mild irritation in Lia's voice. She forces her eyes open, tries to keep them that way despite the burn. It takes a second, then things come into focus. The light beaming through the water, the fogginess making it look even more like a dream.

And there is Dolly. She's dived right down low, near the seabed. But the water is so clear that Jo can see her. Dolly isn't swimming. She is walking, arms outstretched, face serene. It takes a moment, then Jo sees what she is walking on. There is a rope underwater, stretched from one side of the inlet to the other. Dolly is tightrope walking.

Jo splashes to the surface, spluttering. She rubs her eyes again, which feel stingy and dry.

'Did you see?'

'Yep.' Jo coughs a little, tries to take an even breath. 'How is she doing that?'

Lia grins at her. 'The doorway! You get to a certain point underwater and the pressure starts pulling you down rather than pushing you up. It opens its arms to you and pulls you in. *The doorway to the deep*, that's what it's called.'

Dolly surfaces and slowly breathes in and out, then smiles at Jo. 'Just wait until you can do it, J, it's honestly the best feeling.'

Lia leans down and touches her cheek. 'Don't be scared. It's not magic, mate. It's just untapped potential.'

'You want me to do that?'

'Not the first time, it takes practice to get it,' Dolly says, pulling herself onto the rock, breathing deep with that small smile on her lips. Jo looks back at the shore, but it is empty. Ally is gone.

She tries to grip onto the rock, but the current is pulling at her and her head is starting to spin.

'Here.' Dolly takes Jo's hand. Her arms shake as she clambers onto the rocky edge.

'Do you want to have a try?' Lia says. 'Or watch me do it?'

The sun is low, but the glare of it is starting to bore into Jo's eyes. The clouds around it are grey, like it's going to rain.

'I actually think maybe I pushed it a bit hard today.'

'Alright.' Dolly checks the sky. 'Should we go back? We probably shouldn't stay out too long anyway.'

A look passes between Dolly and Lia, but Jo doesn't try to understand it. The stinging was slipping away now, but her fingertips were prickling and her arms felt numb.

'You okay?' Lia asks.

'Yeah.'

'Maybe too much too soon,' Dolly says. She wraps an arm around Jo's shoulders. 'It was only yesterday you were bedridden. We got excited to show you, but maybe we should have waited another day or so.'

'No, I'm okay,' Jo says, 'That was …' She scrunches her face, trying to fight the floaty feeling and think of the word.

'Come on.' Lia squeezes her wrist then pulls her t-shirt on over her head and starts to climb the slope.

Jo follows, keeping her eyes focused either on her hands on the rock in front of her or the creases at the backs of Lia's knees. Her head is hot again and she knows she is sweating. Her throat is constricted.

When she gets onto the sand, she finds she is stumbling a little. The sky is high and dizzying above her. A few speckles of rain hit her skin.

'Almost there, mate,' Lia says, taking her hand as they walk up the sandy incline. When they reach the buildings, Jo can hear the sounds of talking and laughing coming from the kitchen, but Lia leads her right past.

Lia takes Jo into the courthouse, and pulls the door shut behind them. Jo's eyes feel better instantly.

'That was incredible, you know, so crazy incredible.' Jo sinks into the bed. 'She was like a mermaid.'

'We're all mermaids,' Lia says, 'you'll be one too. But now, just sleep.'

Jo laughs and dreams of Gabe with a fish tail and a huge golden trident.

CHAPTER 21

When she wakes, she's shivering. She's still wearing the too-big swimmers and the room is black. It's late, very late, she knows that instinctively. She twitches, then rolls towards Lia. Expecting to see her there, head on the pillow. Asleep, the moonlight glinting from her eyelashes. But there's just crinkled sheets. Lia's bed is empty. Jo sits. The moonlight coming from the windows is dim, but it's enough to see the other bare mattresses around the room. There's no one else here. It's silent except for the whirr of the crickets and, faintly, something else. A bird maybe.

She stands up. Something isn't right. Why would they all be out there, not talking, or making any sound at all? She pushes the door open, the clunk of the wood loud.

Out in the darkness, she still can't hear them. Just the crash of the waves, the hum of the crickets and that distant warble. She walks towards the cliff, thinking they'll be by the water. The sound of them must be carrying out towards the horizon on the breeze, but there is no breeze. The dirt under her feet is damp, it has rained while she was sleeping. The air is still and hushed, and when she reaches the cliff she sees that the ocean is slick black, rolling and empty. There's no one.

The green lorry. She turns back. Doesn't run, she won't run, just walks towards the other side of the tiny town. She can't see it, peeping out from behind the Galbraith & Co building like usual, so she looks at her ruined feet and keeps walking, until she is on the other side of the courthouse and she has to look up. There is empty space where the lorry has always been parked, and heavy tyre tracks in the dirt.

She wraps her arms around herself. The space is huge and open. The warbling sound comes again. It's closer here. It's not a bird, she realises. It's human. It's the sound of someone crying.

Lia's book lays abandoned under the tree, the white shirt Dolly was wearing earlier swinging from a branch like a hung ghost. The crying sound again. A mewling that only a human can make. Jo pulls the straps of the swimsuit onto her shoulders and walks towards the sound.

In the dark the land is flat and empty. There is a scramble of shrubs no higher than her waist catching the light of the moon, and further on a huge boab tree. She'd thought of them as the nightmare trees, with their broken arms and bottle-shaped bodies. She pushes through spear grass, trying to remember if snakes are nocturnal. It doesn't matter, because her imagination is already filling in the shadows with whips of tails and the dark shine of black eyes. Something sharp on her heel and she jumps. But it's just a stick. A shrill, hysterical urge to giggle rises in her throat. To die out here, alone in the bush in a swimsuit. Briena was right.

The cry again, breathier now, more stifled, and the urge to laugh dies. She's closer now, to whatever it is. Whoever.

She stops, not sure whether to trust her eyes.

It isn't the moon shining from the leaves. The small gully of low, twisted black shrubs is glowing. The tiniest of lights coming from inside. Aliens. Sobbing aliens in the outback.

She walks on, no hesitation now, and at the sound of her footsteps the light is extinguished.

'Hello?' she asks. 'Are you alright?'

A shuffle and a sniff. She can hear it properly now, the timbre of the breath. She knows who it is.

'Nika?'

The shuffle stops and Jo kneels at the edge of the trees. 'You okay?' she asks.

The light flicks back on. Nika is there, dirt on her face. She scrambles out and comes to sit next to Jo, wrapping her arms around Jo's waist.

Jo presses a hand on the little girl's head. 'It's okay.' She tries to sound soothing.

'It's not.'

Jo stiffens. She's never heard Nika speak before. She pulls back, but the girl's red-rimmed eyes are cast down.

'Do you know where everyone is?' she asks.

Nika blinks. 'They do this sometimes.'

'So why'd you go out by yourself? Were you trying to find them?'

'No, not them.' And she juts her lip out and Jo isn't afraid any more.

She stands and takes Nika's hand. They'll be back, they just didn't tell her because she was sleeping. Everything is okay.

'Come on, let's go to bed.'

'I was looking for Mum,' the girl says, staring at the ground. Jo kneels again and pulls Nika in for a hug, wanting to coo in her ear, tell her everything is going to be okay. She brushes her hand over Nika's hair. It's so knotted. She wonders if Nika would let her brush it sometime. She could even braid it, if she wanted.

'Why don't you use that torch to light our way back?' she says.

'You scared?' Nika asks.

'Yeah! Do you know how many snakes there are in this country?'

The torchlight flicks on. It's not a proper torch, like Jo had assumed, it's a tiny LED light set in rubber attached to a string around her neck.

Nika takes Jo's hand. 'I haven't seen even one snake around here yet,' she says.

She keeps asking Nika questions, but the closer they get to the settlement, the quieter Nika gets. At the door of the courthouse, the child is silent once again.

'Tired?' Jo asks, pulling open the heavy wooden door and standing back to let Nika walk in first. As she passes, she notices there is dirt on Nika's neck. Rough, like it's gotten into the pores of her skin, like you'd have to scrub it pink to get it out. Nika's feet are dirty too, the skin between her toes scaly with it.

She watches the girl go to the judge's dock. How could her mother have just left her here alone? She feels a flash of anger, but tries to keep it out of her voice.

'I know a good place to wash, why don't I take you there tomorrow?'

Nika looks back. 'Alright.'

She disappears behind the wood panel and Jo closes the courtroom door.

'You okay back there on your own?' she calls. No answer.

She goes to her own bed, pulls the straps off her shoulders and rolls the swimsuit off. She stands for a moment, naked in the empty space. It's a relief. She needs to give Lia's dress back, probably give it a bit of a wash somewhere first. She squats naked next to her backpack and pulls out her last clean pair of underpants and a black t-shirt.

She lays in the bed and waits for them to return.

It's okay, now, to wait. Now she knows they've done this before. That they are definitely coming back. She doesn't mind being awake in here. She knows they'll bring sleep back with them.

It takes a few hours until she hears the sound of the lorry. The crunch of tyres gets louder and louder, until the crunching stops and the engine is cut. Voices, too far away to recognise, but she can hear the tenor of them. Fast talking, giddy giggles, everyone speaking on top of each other.

After a few minutes there is the crunch of wood, the door being opened, and silence as they make their way to their beds. Next to her, the floorboards creak and she hears the whisper of sheets as Lia settles. The air is shifting around her. Salty, hot and wet. They smell like the ocean.

CHAPTER 22

In the morning, Jo wakes before the rest. Lia has her back to her, black hair spread out on the pillow, bare shoulders curved inwards. She goes to look over the judge's dock, and sees Nika's eyes are open. She reaches her hand out and Nika takes it. Jo finds a towel near the door, which she takes with them. As they go down the slope, she looks for Gabe on the shore, but he's not there.

Nika lets go of her hand. 'I don't want to go in the sea.' She's doing that rapid staccato blinking again as she looks out at it. The girl must be afraid of the ocean. That must be why she never comes swimming with them.

'You don't have to. Come on.'

She shows the rock pools to Nika, hands her the towel. 'Wash behind your ears, okay? And scrub your neck. I can help you if you want?'

Nika looks at her, deadpan, making Jo laugh.

'Alright. I'll sit over there, keep my back to you. But call out if you need anything.'

She sits up on the rocks. The pink sea and sky are hers this morning. Listening to Nika's soft splashes behind her, she makes a promise to herself. Next time, wherever they went, she won't be left behind. This is it, the home she's been searching for. Giddy plans begin to lay themselves out in front of her. Her toes curl. She'll need to contact Sorcha and Yan. Perhaps it would be good to call Briena too. If Jo's not back exactly eighty-eight days after she left, Briena will be calling the papers. She tries to work out how long she's been gone for. It's impossible. She's lost count of the days.

Nika comes and sits next to her on the rock. She's redressed herself in damp clothes and her hair is dripping wet, but the day will dry her soon. She'll take care of this girl, like Ally took care of her. She'll pay it forward.

'Don't you want to go home?' Nika asks.

'No,' Jo says, 'no, I want to stay.'

They head back up the slope together, then Nika ducks back into the courthouse. Jo keeps going. The tree is adorned in coloured fabrics this morning, swimmers. The table underneath is filled with plastic buckets, greys and blues. It's like a bizarre Christmas tree: the swimmers the decorations, the buckets wrapped presents. One bucket must have a leak. At the edge of the table water drips onto the red dirt.

When she reaches the table and peers in, she's not sure what she expected to see. But it's not this. The buckets are filled with oysters. Seven or eight large oysters at the base of each one, the water shimmery around them. They're huge, as big as her hands, the shells like the clams the little mermaid wears as a bra in the Disney film. Jo touches one of the shells, then flinches. They are slick with slime. Next to them, a bunch more LED torch necklaces like Nika had worn.

'Morning.'

Gabe is walking towards her, jeans slung low. She averts her eyes. 'Hi.'

'Hope we didn't wake you last night.' He comes up to her, still with that special grin. 'Lia said you still aren't feeling great?'

'I'm okay.' She wraps her arms across herself. 'I did wake up, and you were all gone. Thought you left me to have this place all to myself.'

He sees right through it, laughs and pulls her into his chest. 'You were worried? Thought we'd abandoned you, left you here alone? Course not.'

It's dizzying, being pressed against his bare skin. Maybe he feels it too—he takes his arm away, shoves both hands into his back pockets.

'I was thinking,' she says, 'I want to stay on, you know, if that's okay. I'll do everything I can to help and all that.'

He nods, and she's sure that there is real pleasure there, flashing excitement.

'And if that is okay, I also think I probably should tell everyone that I'm going to be away for a while. You know, so they don't worry or anything.'

'Yeah, I see what you mean. But also we've got to be cautious. If people hear how good we have it here we might have a great invasion. Not just a small sunburnt invasion like yours.'

She laughs. 'I don't need to tell them where I am. You know, just that I'm fine. I'm happy.'

'Yeah, you probably should. But maybe talk to Ally about staying on first.'

He sees her reaction before she masks it.

'I'm sure you'd be welcome. But things aren't simple. Best to check.'

'Okay,' she says. 'I want to talk to her anyway, haven't had much of a chance since I left the bonds office.'

'She's always in high demand.' And if she thought his eyes shone when he looked at her, they shine brighter now.

'So you found all these down at the inlet?' she asks, going over to the buckets. She doesn't want to see it if he lies.

'Nah,' he says, 'can't find oysters like this down there.'

He plucks one out of the water and the sun shimmers on its wet surface. It's large, with ribbing like waves across its shell.

'We're going to have a real feast tonight,' she says, 'and probably tomorrow too.'

He drops the oyster back. It cracks against the others in the bottom of the bucket. He pats her on the shoulder as he walks past her to the kitchen. 'Ally's in Galbraith's Store if you want to see her.'

A drip of water hovers on the corner of the table. It vibrates as it fattens with liquid then, when it's too heavy, drops from the wood and onto the new mud underneath.

Jo walks to the far side of the settlement. Galbraith's Store was constructed with mottled brown and black bricks, and faded white paint borders its door and roof. Under the roof, the lettering of its sign is legible.

She stands by the door, unsure whether to knock or just walk in. The writhing, burnt, naked thing that Ally had cleansed and coddled doesn't feel like her any more. She knocks.

'J?'

She pushes the door open. Inside, it shines blue. It takes her a moment to figure out why, until she looks up. A large section of the roof is missing, and the hole has been covered with blue tarpaulin, not unlike the black tarp covering the window in the bonds office where she had slept. The effect was different here. Where the black tarp had blocked out all light, this tarp washed everything in its blue glow.

'Thought it was you.' Ally sits on the soft, squishy armchair near a couch. It's comfy in here, the single bed made up with patterned sheets. The chair and couch are frayed but full of stuffing. There is an old wooden chest of drawers in the back—it might have been an old, battered Ikea—and a chipped coffee table with some mugs, papers and an esky. If she were to paint it she'd highlight how suburban it all looked, but she'd mix a dab of blue with every colour.

'How'd you know it was me?'

'I've been expecting you,' Ally says. Then, smiling, 'And no one else knocks. Don't look so awkward, you can sit down.'

Jo pulls the door closed behind her and crosses the room to sit on the couch. She grabs a cushion. It's lumpy, not very comfortable, but she hugs it to her body. 'Did you just wake up?' she asks.

Ally leans her head into the headrest. 'I'm the oldest person here, if you haven't noticed. When nights are long, days are long as well.'

'Okay,' Jo says, 'so why did you all go out fishing or whatever in the middle of the night? Isn't it easier during the day?'

Ally doesn't answer, just watches Jo without expression until Jo averts her eyes. 'Is that really what you came to ask me?' she says finally.

Jo cheeks heat. This woman had nursed her back to health, cleaned her body, even dealt with her waste, and Jo is in here demanding more again.

'Sorry!' Her voice sounds breathless and shrill, but she continues, 'Sorry, I'm being so rude. I came in here to thank you. To say how much I appreciate you helping me get better after it was completely my own fault that I was so unwell. Honestly, you really are incredibly kind.'

Ally nods. 'I'm glad you're feeling better,' is all she says.

'I am. I'm feeling so much better. Lia and Dolly have been showing me around. What you've created here is so special. It's—god—I've not been a part of anything, anything like this before.'

'Why do you think that is?'

Jo's smile falters. 'What?'

'You said you've never been a part of anything.'

'Oh. No. I mean I've not been part of anything that's as interesting as this. Everyone is so nice.'

Ally tilts her head.

Jo looks at the ground and suddenly feels an urge to cry. Like a little kid glugging big ugly tears. She wants to ask Ally what has happened, why she doesn't like her any more.

'Have I done something to make you angry?'

'No, baby.' Ally's voice is soft like it was before but Jo can't meet her eyes. 'But you're still being a little mole hiding away in safety and politeness. I don't need you to tell me that we're all kind here, I know that and I know why. I want you to tell me why you knocked on my door. The real reason.'

Jo swallows. She doesn't want her voice to crack. 'I want to stay.'

'I can't make you leave.'

'I want you to want me to stay. I want to be part of it.'

'You barely know what *it* is.'

'I know.'

Jo knows that Ally is considering her and she forces herself to look up, to meet her gaze. But Ally rises from her seat and goes over to the esky and takes out a brown bottle. She pours the contents into a chipped mug and Jo can smell the lemon and honey from where she sits.

'This isn't a holiday. What you're saying. It's a big commitment.' Her back is still to Jo.

'I know!'

'We've chosen to separate ourselves, to disconnect in order to really connect.'

'That's what I want.'

Ally makes her way back to the chair with her mug. There's a heaviness in the way she moves. She really is tired. She sits on the chair, shifts her weight to a comfortable position. 'Why?' she says and takes a sip from her mug.

'Well, erm …' It's hard to put this feeling, this *want*, into words. 'Everyone seems so free here, so happy. I care about all of you already. Being here feels right.'

Ally nods and Jo feels herself lift up. She's finally said something right.

'Things have felt wrong for a while?' Ally asks.

Jo nods back, because she's right. Now she's said it there is nothing that is more true. Sydney with Eric, the farm. Long before that.

'I can see so much fear in you. Are you aware of it? Or have you swallowed it all down?'

'I, erm … I guess I'm aware.' Her voice sounds strained, but Ally is nodding.

'Good. It's easier if you aren't hiding it, you haven't let it curdle in your belly yet, turn into anger. Nothing is worse than anger born from fear. Tell me, baby, what is your first memory of feeling afraid? The first time of feeling pure fear? Can you tell me?'

'My first memory?' she asks, but she can already see it. The woman, her mother. Face crumpled in anger, a silvery scar shiny on her forehead. Screaming *Your fault, your fault.* The dream of the woman screaming and bleeding. They go together, but she doesn't know quite how. She doesn't like to think about this.

'You saw something already, didn't you? I felt that flash, the fear was worse for a moment.'

She swallows. 'Erm. My mum. She used to kick me out of the house sometimes at night.'

'But what did you see?'

'Her face. She was so angry.'

Jo, back when she was Josephine, would sit outside in the dark, watching through the windows. So cold, the light in her house toasty yellow. She'd shiver, waiting, waiting, waiting, until her mum would settle somewhere, turn still enough so that she could sneak back inside. This, she remembers. This, she's sure of.

'You know, you wouldn't recognise Dolly from the girl I first met.'

And Jo grins, because they are talking about someone else, together.

'She was in so much pain and was doling that pain back to herself in double measure. She couldn't be happy; she never even knew where to start. Because she didn't know where the pain started either. Once we figured that out, she could finally transform.'

Jo is nodding, even though she's not totally sure she understands.

'You've felt very lonely.'

And Jo keeps nodding, the lump in her throat back again now but something beautiful has mixed into the pain because Ally sees her.

Ally puts down her mug and she comes over to Jo. Puts her arms around her. Jo sinks into her softness and the lump in her throat burns.

'You won't feel that any more. It's going to take work, but I'll help you. You'll be happy here, my little mole.'

*

Back at the clearing, everyone is standing around the table. Their laughs carry on the breeze.

Everything feels scattered. Jo's not sure she understands what Ally was saying, but she knows that she's been invited to stay.

Gabe sees her, concern all over his face, and the others turn. She expects awkwardness, maybe a pat on the shoulder. But Lia hurries to her and flings her arms around her.

'How did you go? I know it's hard and weird at first but it will be so worth it, trust me.'

'It went … fine. She said I could stay.'

Lia pulls back and squeals in delight. Then everyone is hugging her. Dolly gripping her tight, Ho-jin gently. Zay kisses her on the cheek, Greta and Valentine grip her hands. And finally it's Gabe and he wraps both arms around her and everything was worth it for this.

'So what are you all doing?' she asks when he releases her. They are fully dressed for once, t-shirts with damp patches at the front.

'We're opening these oysters,' Lia says. 'Do you want to help? Or do you need another rest?'

'I want to help.'

She goes to the table and Gabe walks alongside her. He's standing next to her like something has changed now, and maybe it has.

'I'll show you,' he says. He takes a bucket and two kitchen knives from the table and goes to the dirt under the tree. The rest go back to chatting and working on the shells with their knives. Gabe sits cross-legged and Jo mimics him, her knee touching his, the bucket between them.

'Okay,' he says, picking up an oyster with one hand and the silver knife with the broken blade with the other. She takes another oyster out of the bucket. It's slimy and cold in her hand and heavier than she'd thought.

Gabe leans in close. 'You're meant to follow what I'm doing,' he whispers.

'Oh.' She laughs. 'Yes. Sorry.'

She grabs the other knife.

'So you shove the knife in where the two shells clamp together and keep twisting until it opens.'

'Easy,' she says. 'You know, I've never eaten an oyster before.'

He smiles. 'Zay will fix that.'

'What do they taste like?'

'Like the ocean.'

She grins and feels for the ledge where the shells meet. The mollusc is big, bigger than her hand, and perfectly curved.

She holds the ridge with her thumb and then pushes the knife onto it. She beats it with her palm until it begins to slide, tries to push it down, to cut the two sides apart from one another. It's harder than she thinks. She rubs the slime from her hands onto her t-shirt.

'Hey, so I'll probably be going out in the truck in the next few days,' Gabe says, twisting his knife in his own oyster.

She remembers he said it would be over a month before he went out again. He looks at her, like he knows what's passing through her mind.

'It's earlier than Ally and I had planned, I know. But you can come if you want? We can swing past Denny's so you can sort that out, and maybe go past the payphone too if there is anyone else you need to talk to.'

'Amazing. Thank you.' She remembers the last time they drove around together, how long ago that seems, how much she wants to do it again.

Her clam won't open. She tries twisting the knife like Gabe is doing, and that helps. The two sides crackle and begin to open. She sees a glimmer from inside, a sparkle.

'So what happens now? How do I transform into a mermaid like you?'

He twists at the shell. 'It's not like there's any rule book. But I guess you'll learn how to dive, if that's what you want. And you'll have to go and see Ally, talk about what it is in your past that's been holding you back.'

'Was there something for you?' She keeps cutting downwards and prising the shell to unclamp it.

'Of course. It's hard, but it's worth it, trust me. All that anxiety, all that sadness that you thought was a part of you? It's not. Once you figure out the root of it, everything changes.'

She twists the knife again as hard as she can and the shells crack apart. Inside glistens with mother of pearl, orange, yellow and blue.

'Wow, this is so pretty. I should give it to Nika.'

'If we haven't broken them we keep them. But if you break the shell too much, then yeah, sure.'

She's about to ask what they'd keep them for, when she notices something within the wet glob inside. A bump, like some kind of strange fish egg. She rubs her forefinger over it and, like a knot in a spine, it's hard underneath the soft flesh. She pushes into the oyster with her fingernail and it breaks apart. She squeezes out a shiny white bead. A pearl.

'Bloody hell!' She holds it up to show Gabe. 'Look at this!'

He smiles at her, but not with excitement. She looks into his wide palm, shiny with slime and grit. He is holding a pearl too, a golden one.

'What?' she says.

He winks at her and gets up. She follows him over to the table, eyes on the pearl in her hand. It's a beautiful creamy silver colour. It catches the glitters of sunlight around them and glistens in the subtlest of pastels. She'd love to paint this.

Gabe holds out a bucket for her. It's a quarter of the way full with pearls, perfect glowing balls.

'How is that possible?' she asks. 'How could they all have pearls in them? I thought it was rare.'

'Not if you know where to look,' Dolly tells her.

She almost wants to keep the one she's found. But that's not how it works here, she knows that. She doesn't have to live just for herself. So she takes one last look at her pearl and drops it into the bucket with the others.

CHAPTER 23

'You want to talk about my father?'

She's sitting on the sofa that faces Ally's chair. Ally is warmer today. The pink is back in her cheeks and she is smiling again. Jo knows she was being brattish yesterday, but that Ally has let it go. In fact, Ally's face was bright when Jo knocked on her door half an hour ago. She's poured some of her lemony tonic into a tin for Jo. She's happy Jo's here.

'You don't want to talk about him?'

She doesn't. She's let the past go, doesn't see the point of dredging all that stuff up. She takes a sip of the tonic.

'He did right by me,' she says. 'He was a good man. We weren't really ever close.'

'Three very evasive comments in their own right. What was he doing when your mother kicked you out of the house?'

Jo rubs the scab on her thumb. They'd spent all day yesterday opening oysters, squeezing out the pearls. They'd almost filled a bucket. Nika had come and sat across from her, and they'd slid their hands into the bucket, enjoying the feel of the cold, heavy beads.

And again, last night she'd slept. It had come to pull her under like magic barely an hour after dinner.

'You are somewhere else.'

'No, no, it's not that. It's just not something I like to talk about.'

'It's hard to cut through. That's okay, we can talk about whatever you want.'

Jo smiles at her, relieved. But a little of the warmth has gone out of Ally's face. She's disappointed.

'Lia checked my back last night,' Jo offers. 'She says it's almost back to normal.'

'Great,' Ally says, 'I'm glad to hear that.'

Jo leans her head on the top of the couch, her throat long and open. The light shows all the textures of the blue tarp. Every filament of the plastic material. The wind is a little higher today, and the fabric shifts. But it feels safe in here.

She doesn't see the point in this. How will telling Ally about her childhood make her feel more free? She'll do it, because Ally asked her to, but it's unnatural. Still, if this is what she has to do to stay here, it's not the worst thing. Maybe it makes Ally feel more comfortable to know more about her, to know where she has come from.

'We lived in a little two-storey terrace. The stairs were so steep, and the carpet made them slippery. I used to climb them on all fours most of the time, even when I got older. I was scared that I'd slip down them.'

'Okay good, good.' Ally's voice is crooning. 'So you're climbing the stairs like a little cat, what colour is the carpet you see below you?'

'Cream. It might have been white once though.'

'And what does it feel like under your hands?'

'Coarse. Wiry.'

'Where are you going?'

'Upstairs, to my room, probably.'

'Okay, keep climbing, go up to your room.'

Jo wants to cringe. This is stupid. She stares at the shifting blue and tries to see it. She tries to relax and somehow, she can. Her breathing slows. She can see her old house. The block is starting to fall away.

Up the steep stairs to the second storey. Standing on the third step from the top. Hand on the railing, thumbing that segment where the white paint has chipped away to show the sky blue paint of whoever lived there long before they did.

'What's your room like?'

Her room is on the left, her dad's is at the end of the corridor, white-blue light coming from under the door.

'My room has posters on the walls, always. They'd change as I was growing up. Bikini Kill and The Clash, and then Monet art prints later on.'

'Lie on the bed.'

The sheets would have been unmade, her duvet cover wrestling around her duvet. They'd be clean though. Her dad was keen on laundry, thought it was foul if she left it any longer than a week. He'd bulk buy packs of laundry capsules from Tesco and he'd use at least two for every wash. Everything in their house smelt of discount Tesco-brand frangipani.

'Are you lying on the bed?'

'Yes,' Jo says. She wishes she were under the tree with the others, watching Lia read her book, or in the courthouse, or napping in the shade somewhere. Or maybe seeing where Gabe was, talking to Gabe.

'Do you feel safe, lying in that bed?'

'Sure. I was probably just bored. Dreaming of moving to London.'

'What about your mum, where is she in the house? Is she there?'

'Downstairs, I guess. Doing the dishes.'

'Where's your dad?'

'He'd be downstairs with her, talking about her day.'

'Get up and go into the hallway again. Is your parents' room right there?'

The hallway is silent. The house was always quiet. She didn't like to invite friends around; the silence was too thick.

'Can you go towards your parents' room?'

The light under the door, the silence, especially thick from that room.

'You don't want to, do you?'

'No.'

'Why?'

'I'm not allowed in his room.'

'In their room?'

Her head snaps down, away from the wavering blue tarp. She looks at Ally. She's caught her out. She expects that disappointment, that distance from yesterday. But Ally's face is open. She leans forward, puts her warm hands on Jo's bare knees.

'It's a lot all at once, isn't it?'

'A bit.'

'You know, I can see the most beautiful power in you, J-baby. You are going to be magnificent when you are ready for it.'

'Really?'

'Absolutely.'

'But I'm not ready for it yet?'

'That's up to you, my darling.'

'Should we keep going?'

'It's enough for now, I think.'

So she did catch it, the lies. Of course she did.

CHAPTER 24

Out in the heat, Jo squints into the day. The sun is high, bleaching out the buildings around her as she makes her way to the courthouse. It's too bright, her head is muzzy from the warmth and dark. Later, she'll be going out into the ocean. But she won't think of that now.

Lia is lying under a tree, reading her book. Jo settles in next to her. She lies back, covers her eyes with her arm.

'You go okay?'

'Yeah.'

'You're amazing.' Lia grips Jo's hand in hers for a second, then goes back to her book.

'What's that book about anyway?' Jo asks.

'It's about this girl who kind of creates her own religion. She starts her own community. It was written in the nineties and meant to be dystopian but it's kind of scarily accurate to the way things are going. It's pretty violent, but it's hopeful too.'

'Maybe I'll read it when you're finished.'

'You should.' Lia's eyes stay on the page, continuing to read, face calm.

Jo tries to settle, tries to be like Lia. Calm. Serene. England couldn't be further away from her now. It would be morning there. Her dad would be getting up in the dark. He would only turn on the kitchen light and sit eating his Special K and staring out into the black windows. Back then, when she'd come down the stairs onto the darkened landing, school bag heavy on her back, he'd seem like a flat image. His white t-shirt stark, his workman's dungarees undone and the top half tied around his waist. His beige steel-capped boots set evenly on the lino. His hair, never more than a centimetre long, the overhead light catching the threads of silver that were multiplying. As he crunched the cereal she'd see the tight ligaments in his jaw. She'd always wondered what he was thinking about.

*

Later, when they are holding her underwater, her father in the kitchen is one of the images that flashes in her mind. It's like her mind is holding on to things because her hands cannot.

She tries to clear her head, to relax. But she starts thrashing, stinging eyes wide. Zay and Dolly hold her arms, Ho-jin and Lia press down on her knees. She can see them through the two inches of water above her face. Her limbs flail out at the others paddling around her. She finds Dolly's arm, tries to pull herself up. Dolly's grasp is rigid. She tries to kick. She can't breathe. They need to let her up. Her chest convulses. Her mouth opens. Clawing sea water fills her throat.

Her arms are tugged and she's released above the surface now, choking. They pull her onto a rock. She splutters, tries to breathe, but the water is still there. She heaves, her stomach cramps and she vomits water onto the rock, head spinning.

'Sorry,' she coughs out as Zay moves to one side to avoid the puke dripping from the rock. Dolly pushes her glasses up her nose but doesn't say anything.

'You just have to trust yourself,' Lia says, that lightness in her eyes again. 'It won't work unless you do.'

'It's natural,' Ho-jin adds.

Jo coughs again. 'How could not breathing be natural?'

'When you are inside your mother, you know, the gestational fluid?' Dolly asks. 'It's three per cent salt. The water of the ocean is three point five per cent salt.'

'Being inside the belly of the ocean is like you're a baby again. Your body remembers.'

'Okay,' Jo says. She turns back to shore. Gabe is there, looking out at her. He doesn't come to give his own instructions, to push her under and pull her back up. She remembers her thrashing. Looks at Dolly's wrist. There are scratches.

'Sorry,' she says again.

Dolly touches her finger to the scratches. 'It's normal. But maybe us holding you isn't helping.'

'Apparently when someone is drowning you are meant to hold out a stick or something to them,' Zay says, 'otherwise some instinct kicks in and they'll pull you under with them, half the time the rescuers drown too.'

Dolly takes Zay's thin t-shirt from the rock, begins twisting it round in her hands to make a rope. 'Do you trust us?'

Jo's eyes are sore. She blinks, tries to steady herself. 'Yes.'

'You're safe.' Lia strokes her shoulder. Dolly ties the t-shirt around Jo's wrists. 'Nothing bad is going to happen here.' Dolly squeezes the cotton tight so her arms are pinned against her back. 'Again?' she asks.

'Give her a minute to recover,' Zay says. His eyes are scrunched up when he looks at her, like he isn't sure she can do it.

'Again,' Jo says.

They help her off the rock, wade into the water with her. Ho-jin is holding her forearm, Dolly grips around her waist on one side and Zay on the other, Lia swims behind her, rubbing her hands. Jo's arms flex involuntarily, and Lia squeezes her hand in between Jo's.

'Okay, deep breath,' Dolly says. 'Deep and even.'

Lia squeezes her hands again, then lets go. They push her onto her back so she's floating on the surface. Past Dolly's and Zay's faces is the sky, blue and clear and solid.

She breathes in as slowly as she can and stops when her lungs are full. They push down and she wants to scream out, call for them to stop, but it's too fast. She's underwater again.

She closes her eyes. Her ears plug. She can just hear the deep rumbling. A bubble escapes her nose and she can hear the tinkle of it as it rises from her and hits the surface. She wants to twitch and struggle but she clamps her muscles tight. Holds every muscle rigid.

She can do this.

Her heart starts beating faster. Her chest burns. More bubbles tinkle free of her. Her stomach contracts, her throat feels strange, empty. She wants to swallow.

Her shoulders twitch. She can't help it. Her legs buck.

The images come. Her dad sitting at the table. Ally's disappointed face. Her father's room. A black desktop computer. Her mother, face screwed up in anger. Jamie's big eyes staring at her.

She bucks again. Her arms pull against the bind. She needs to breathe. Her stomach clamps. Her chest convulses.

Something clamps across her shoulders and she's pulled from the water. She gasps in air, eyes still scrunched closed. She coughs, tries to breathe, coughs again.

'You're pushing her too hard.'

'Of course we aren't, this is the only way to learn.'

'It's too much all at once.'

It's Gabe's voice, right at her ear. She tries to open her eyes, but they sting and the bright is too bright. She closes them again.

'This is how we all did it.'

She twists against him and his fingers pull at the roped t-shirt around her wrists. It tightens, cutting into her flesh, then loosens, and her arms drop free. She chokes on the air as she breathes. Her throat constricting, the ligaments in her neck clenching. She puts her arms around him, clasping her legs around his waist so she isn't swimming. Coughs again.

'You can't let your personal feelings get mixed up in this,' Dolly says, and Jo can hear that note of irritation in her voice.

'I'm not.'

Jo opens her eyes again. They sting but she keeps them open, squinting. Gabe's shoulder is right under her. She sees the droplets dribble down it as he bobs above the surface.

'Are you okay, J?' Ho-jin whispers.

'Yep,' she croaks out.

Gabe pulls her upper arms off his shoulders. 'I'm going to swim into shore, okay? You can hold onto my back.'

He doesn't wait for a response, just flips himself around then pulls her back onto him. She holds his shoulders as he pulls her along, turning back, wanting to say sorry. But they aren't even looking at her.

She grips his shoulder tighter, tries to kick with her legs too, but only gets in his way. So she holds on and lets herself be pulled to shore. Once it's shallow enough to stand, he pulls her from his back and holds her up in the water.

'Gabe.' Her voice is a little hoarse.

He looks at her and she could reach up now, she could kiss him.

'I can walk,' she says.

'Oh.' He stops, sets her legs down, but keeps her hands in his as they wade to the shore. And she's glad, because without him she knows she would sway. Her head is thumping.

'Are you alright?' he asks.

'Yeah. It was just—' She swallows, trying to moisten her throat. 'It was a lot.'

'I know. It was too much.'

'But if you all did it ...' She stops, the tide at her ankles. 'Maybe I should go back. I want to stay here, I really do, and I want to learn.'

The thought of going back makes her throat constrict again. She closes her eyes, breathes, opens them again. Gabe is staring at her. He's smiling.

'You're so stubborn.'

'So are you.'

'How do you know?'

'I can tell.'

'Alright,' he says, dropping her hand. 'But how about we have a go in a different way for a bit? We try on dry land so you feel more comfortable before you attempt it in the water again.'

She looks over the ocean, rising and falling in swells, at the group on the rocks. Lia and Zay are in the water, Ho-jin is on the rock and Dolly is nowhere to be seen. She must be underneath.

'Just us?' she asks.

He raises his eyebrows. 'You don't feel like you can control yourself with me?'

She whacks his arm and starts walking up the incline, shivering in the heat. Her breathing still doesn't feel right.

They walk in silence towards the courthouse. Once they get inside, he turns to the cells.

'In your room?' she asks.

He raises an eyebrow at her again, and so she follows him before he can say anything. She hasn't been in his room before.

The boards creak under her feet. She pulls her wet hair over her shoulder. It's dried a little around her part, that's how hot the sun is, but the ends are still drenched and dripping. She's got the too-big brown one-piece on and wishes she'd brought a t-shirt or something to put over herself. It's too late now.

Gabe goes into his room and sits on the bed. He's made it nice in here, despite the wrought iron bars all around. There's a high window, a stack of books and a notebook lying on the pillow of the mattress on the floor.

'Your journal?' she asks.

He takes the notebook off the pillow and puts it on the stack of books. 'Old habits.'

She approaches him and stumbles as a floorboard moves under her weight.

'Careful,' he says. 'Some of them are rotted.'

She watches her feet, standing on only the solid-looking boards, and sits next to him on the mattress. She stretches her legs out in front of her. 'So how exactly do we do this in here?'

'Just lie down.'

She laughs, can't help it, then lies on his mattress. She stares at the high ceiling. 'Does it ever make you feel weird, sleeping in a cell?'

'No,' he says. 'I don't think of it like that.'

His sheets smell like him.

'Is it okay that I brought you here? I know you can make your own decisions, it just felt like—'

'I wouldn't have come if I didn't want to.'

She breathes again, feeling more like herself. Her throat isn't hurting so bad now; the nausea is passing. 'It's just, I dunno, now that I'm here, now that I've found you all, I don't want to have to go. I want to stay, and if you all think that talking to Ally and diving will make me happy like you all are, then I should do it. Right?' She shifts her head on the pillow to see him better.

He leans his chin onto his hand. 'How is it going with Ally?'

She groans and rolls onto her stomach.

'You know,' he says, 'I feel like it might be connected. You're scared of letting go. You aren't trusting yourself underwater, you aren't trusting Ally in your subconscious.'

'My subconscious?'

'Yeah. I mean, that's kind of what she does. She used to be a psychiatrist, you know.'

'Really?'

'Yeah. But I think she got sick of it. You know, medicating them instead of actually helping people who needed her.'

'Needed them to trust her in their subconscious?'

'Well.' He chuckles. 'Yeah. It might sound hokey or something.'

'Hokey,' she repeats, smiling at him.

'Yeah, I mean, Ally can see it before even you can. Just by looking at you she can see through it all, find the root hurt. Sometimes you aren't even aware of it yourself, but when she helps you see it, god, it's the best thing ever. It makes sense of everything.'

She looks at him through her drying hair. 'I know what my root hurt is. I don't think talking about it is going to help it. My baby brother died when I was a kid.'

He touches her arm, brushes his thumb over the soft underside. 'What happened?'

'My dad said it was an accident. I don't know, I wasn't there. My earliest memories aren't until after that. I can't even picture my brother except in my dreams.'

'When I was a kid, my babysitter abused me,' Gabe says.

It's so blunt it makes her start. It's the last thing she expected him to say. But he keeps going.

'I didn't even remember it until Ally helped me. I just remember the fear, the humiliation. But now I have the memories too. She'd take my clothes off and put me in the washing basket, then she'd sit and watch as I tried to get out. Pennsylvania winters would be freezing cold, but she'd turn the heating off. And she did worse stuff too.'

He hasn't broken eye contact since he started talking and she is scared to look away.

'That's horrible,' she whispers.

'It was. But the thing is, all that time when I thought I was living, I was carrying that around with me. Holding it in, all that fear and humiliation, took so much energy. Moving to New York, trying to make it, even just pushing through the streets to get anywhere. It all felt so hard all the time. I had this weight on me. My heart would beat too fast—I had arrhythmia, the doctors said I'd live with it. Anxiety and depression too; the counsellor said that it was just a part of me. But then I came here. And ever since I faced it, figured out the root of it, all that weight has gone away. My heart doesn't beat too fast any more. If the doctors could see it, they'd say it was a miracle.'

She takes his hand in hers. 'I guess it sort of is.'

He shakes his head. 'The only miracle is that I managed to find my way here. The rest is just Ally.'

'Thank you for telling me,' she says.

'I've wanted to for a while, just so you can see what's possible for you. Although I really did bring you here to help you with the breathing.'

'Do you think it's as simple as letting go? Then I'll be able to do it? It's just, in the water before, it didn't seem possible.'

'It's possible if you give yourself to it completely, mind and body. You can't be scared, you have to relax. If you're relaxed you'll be fine.'

'And if I panic?'

'Don't think about panicking?'

'Why? Because then I'm more likely to.'

He grinned at her. 'You know, my grandad used to do free diving as a kid. He grew up in Symi, one of the Greek islands. He'd go out with his dad, who used to collect sponge from the sea floor.'

'I didn't know people did it in Greece.'

'People have done it all over the place. Scandinavia and Japan and South Korea. Even here in the Kimberley, colonists blackbirded the Yawuru people, made them dive to get pearl shell to make buttons.'

'That's horrible.'

'It is.'

She thinks of the buttons on the vintage shirt she used to wear all the time in London, how she'd loved the way they'd shine rainbows. Now the idea of wearing them makes her feel sick.

'So can you speak Greek?' she asks.

'Nah. I don't see myself as Greek at all. My grandad came to the US when he was a teenager and got a job at the Ford factory. He did everything he could to drop the accent, married an American girl. He died when I was really young so I never got to ask him about it. But my dad liked to talk like he was the descendant of some Greek free-diving god, like it was in his blood somehow. He would always talk about this annual championship in Kalamata, as if he could just turn up one day.'

'Did he ever go?'

'He was an accountant at a chemical plant. He had a drinking problem. He never even left the state. It was all talk. That's what I'm saying. You can't half-ass this. You've got to commit completely, trust completely.' He lets go of her hand. 'Turn over.'

She does. 'I just don't understand how you can do it. Like, it's not possible to not breathe. Don't you need oxygen to live?'

He puts a hand over her chest, his fingers damp with sweat. 'It's like a trick in your body. When you stop breathing, your chest starts convulsing—did you feel that?'

She nods. Her sternum pushes against him with every inhalation.

'If you can get past that, trust your body enough to hold on, then you can stop the convulsions.' He moves his hand to below her rib cage on the left. 'Your spleen here, it lets out oxygen-rich blood, that's how you get the extra time. It goes to your brain and it feels ... I can't really describe it.'

He moves his hand to above her left breast. 'And being underwater like that ... it changes your body too so you don't need so much air. Your heartbeat goes to just twenty beats per minute or lower.'

His face is so close to hers that her eyes flick to his mouth.

He moves his hands so one is above her ribs, the other under, making her arch her back. 'And your chest compresses. It squeezes closer in.' He pushes his hands tight against her rib cage.

'You know a lot about this,' she whispers.

He winks, doesn't move his hands. 'Because I've felt it. It's amazing. Better than any high you've ever had. Do you want to try it? We aren't underwater, so you won't get the full effects. But we can try and get through the fear right now if you want.'

She nods, wondering if he can feel how quick her heartbeat is.

'Do you trust me?'

She nods again. She takes a slow breath in and closes her mouth. His eyes don't leave hers. There is a fleck of gold in the brown of his left iris. He has the faintest lines around his eyes, she'd noticed that first time they met when he'd pulled over in his car. She strokes his eyebrow with her thumb. His gaze doesn't break from hers. Then her throat makes a noise, a strangled gargle she can't control. Her stomach braces.

Her sternum twitches between his hands, her heart beats harder. She can't do it. The room twists.

Her throat unclenches to take a breath.

His hand clamps over her mouth, squeezes her nose shut between his thumb and forefinger. She pulls deeper into the pillow, but his hand follows.

His eyes are tender. He isn't trying to hurt her.

Trust me, he's saying.

If she dies, she dies. She stops fighting.

Her body shifts and revolts against the mattress without her permission. Her diaphragm convulses four times, then stills.

Little dots between his eyes and hers. And peace. Arching waves of peace.

His hand lifts from her face and she slowly exhales, then inhales again. The new air is so fresh, like cold water.

'That was definitely over a minute,' he says, 'you did it. You got past the convulsions. In the water it will be even easier. Are you alright?'

She breathes in again, then out. But the lovely peace is still there. She laughs. 'Yeah.'

He laughs too. 'It's something, isn't it?'

And his face is still so close. She leans forward, kisses him lightly on the mouth. He pulls away and she has a moment to lean back onto the pillow, about to apologise, before he is pushing into her. His hands move under her skull, pulls her in closer. His mouth is just as she remembers, but better. Rough stubble and soft lips. She wraps her legs around his bare waist and he grips her thigh. There is sweat on his back as she runs her hands down it.

His hand slots inside the loose swimsuit, gripping her arse. She licks his neck and tastes the salt and she doesn't know if it's sweat or the ocean or both. His hand slides around under the loose swimmers between her legs where it's hot and wet and she can't help but groan it is already so good. Her nails dig into his back and he's pulling at his belt buckle but then he looks at her and stops.

'What?' she says, panting. 'What's wrong?'

He moves to the edge of the bed and sits with his back to her.

'Are you okay?' she asks, her body thrumming.

'Yeah,' he says. 'Yeah, it's just—I haven't done this since I found out about what happened to me, you know?'

'Oh,' she says and sits up. 'Sorry. I didn't think about that. Was it … was it weird for you?'

'No. Not at all, actually. I was worried it would be, but it wasn't. Isn't … I mean so many things, I don't want to put too much on you before you're ready, and I feel like you need to figure things out with yourself first, you know? Also …'

'Also, what?'

'I mean, it's not like it's not allowed. We can do what we want. It's just, no one here has ever been together. It might change the balance, you know?'

She leans into him, wraps her arms around him. He turns to her and kisses her again.

'But, Jesus, I do want this so much,' he says, breath hot.

He kisses her deeper and her fingers touch his neck, the gentle skin there.

The grating sound of the main door opening.

She jumps away from him.

'J?' It's Ho-jin's voice.

She pulls her swimmers straight, takes a breath, then gets off the mattress and walks around the rotten floor to the hallway.

'You okay?' Ho-jin asks, looking at her from the main room.

She grins and nods. 'I think I'm getting it,' she says.

CHAPTER 25

That night, as they are finishing dinner, Jo touches Ally's elbow.

'Can I come visit?' she asks. 'Once I've helped clear up?'

Ally smiles. 'Of course, baby.'

And as she clears the dishes with Nika like they do every night, as she rinses them in the plastic tub they use instead of a sink, hands each one to Nika to towel dry, it's going around and around in her head. All the lies she can tell to keep Ally at bay, but at the same time she knows she must tell the truth, that she wants the weight to drop off her shoulders.

Ally's room is different in the dark. The blue glow has gone and she's lit candles, little flickering flames dancing orange light onto the walls.

Jo is sitting in the corner of the couch, her feet wrapped underneath her, a tin of Ally's tonic in her hands.

'Thanks for letting me come again. Twice in one day, you're probably sick of me.'

Ally looks at her, head tilted. 'Don't feel like this is some chore for me. Being here, with you, helping you, it's nothing but joy.'

'Don't you feel like everyone is heaping their problems on you, though? Doesn't it make you feel, I don't know, put upon or something?'

'That isn't how I see it. I'm just one part of what makes our community work.'

'No,' Jo says, 'you are the heart of it. I don't think anyone would be here without you, I can already see that. You're the reason it works.'

Ally smiles and shakes her head. 'We're all the reason. There is no separation here. The world you've been brought up in teaches you to think as an individual. You experience your pain in your little box while the women above you and below you feel the same in their own little boxes. We don't do that here. If one of us is in pain, we all are.'

Already, she feels good here. Being around Ally makes her feel warm and relaxed. 'I'm not in pain though. I feel great to be here, I'm excited.'

'You don't feel anxious? Worried that we're going to leave you, that we don't want you? Worried that you don't fit in?'

Jo pulls out a cushion from behind her and wraps her arms around it, sinking deeper into the couch.

'Do you wonder where that comes from? That fear?' Ally sips from her tonic. 'It feels to me like you are running, screaming, from something. I can see it in you, that blind panic. You ran to London, then you ran to Australia.'

She remembers the night she'd booked her flight. Alone and drunk on a bottle of Australian pinot noir and feeling like she couldn't stand one more minute by herself in London, that there had to be something better for her.

'Then you ran out to that farm and you ran away from there. Now you are here, but will you run away from us? If you don't face that thing that has you so scared, won't you just keep on running when this is hard too?'

Jo can't speak. She's never heard her whole life summed up like that, so effortlessly and simply. She'd always thought she was running to something, a better life for herself, but maybe Ally is right.

'I can see her, that afraid little girl, wanting to run again. What is she so afraid of?'

Jo can't look at Ally, so she gazes at the candle in front of her instead. All her excitement, the thrumming energy from her encounter with Gabe, it's dripping away. Ally is right, she does want to escape. She wants to get out of this room, with its thick, stifling air, she wants to run down to the sharp rock face, jump into the water, anything to get away from this woman and her searching eyes.

'Did your mum really live in that little house with its steep, steep stairs?'

'No. I haven't seen her since I was little. I was taken off her.'

'And your dad? He raised you?'

'Raised.' She smiles a bitter smile, the fear hot in her. 'I guess so.'

'He didn't?'

'No, it was just … he did everything he was meant to. Got me a school uniform, gave me an allowance, made sure I brushed my hair and my teeth. But he didn't …'

'Love you?'

'No, no, I'm sure he did in his own way.'

'Nurture you?'

She swallows.

'I want you to go back to your room, J, you're standing at the door and looking down the corridor. Are you afraid to go into his room?'

'No.'

'Well, picture it for me. You're standing at your door. Behind you is your unmade bed, your posters on the walls. The cream carpet is prickly under your feet. Is your dad's door open or closed?'

'It would have been closed. He always kept it closed.'

It had been a good day. She'd walked home from school through the village, hood up, headphones in. It wasn't raining, but it was cold. The nice kind of cold, where the chill is fresh, wakes you up a bit. She'd stopped by the bakery, jingled the change from her pocket and bought herself a Chelsea bun. The sweet bread sticky with glaze, the sultanas popping in her mouth. She only had a few months left at school. It made everything that was shit about where she lived, everything that she'd hated, not quite so bad. She'd be out of here soon enough, one way or another. Breaking up her bun with her fingers as she walked, she could have grinned at that crooked spire, she could have nodded hello to the gang of toughies in their Tesco two stripes, she—

'Tesco two stripes?'

'Like the Adidas pants, except from Tesco, so they only had two stripes instead of three.'

'I see. Continue.'

She hadn't been expecting the letter until next week. Still, it was the first thing she'd do when she opened the front door. Look at the mail that had come in through the slot and landed on the mat. She didn't need to sort through them this time. It was there. Right on top of the bills and the ad for the new Chinese restaurant down the street. A letter with her full name typed on it. And stamped in the corner: *Slade School of Fine Art.*

She'd thought maybe she'd be the type to hold onto it. To call one of her friends who might care, to sleep with it under her pillow, to follow some sort of superstition. But she hadn't. She'd sat on the carpet by the front door and slid her thumb into the opening, telling herself it didn't matter as she ripped the envelope, that she'd move to London either way, even though she knew it absolutely mattered. It mattered more than anything.

After she read it she'd stood straight up. She'd run up the stairs, those steep stairs, taking them two at a time.

Dad?

His door was closed, but he might be in there. He was usually home from work before her.

Dad?

She walked down the hallway towards the door to his room.

'Go on. Don't stop now, J. Go on.'

She would normally have knocked, and if there was no response, she would have let it be. But she was so excited. She was so eager to tell someone. She'd opened the door.

'And what did you see? He was in there, in his room, doing something?'

The room was empty. Just his bed, neatly made, his desk, his computer. She might have turned around then if she hadn't seen the screen was on. That blue light she'd see under his door emanating from it.

'So you walked over, you looked at his screen.'

She walked over. She sat in his chair.

'What you saw, it upset you. It was awful, what you saw. Was it a picture?'

It wasn't a picture.

'Are you sure? You can tell me the truth. However painful, the truth will make you feel better. I promise.'

A forum page was open. A group of men, pouring out their hearts to one another. One of them, Steanny51, her father. But he wasn't that kind of man. She knew that. He couldn't talk about his feelings, it just wasn't who he was. She'd tried when she was younger, to hug him, to tell him about the other kids at school. But he'd always turn away. She'd figured it out eventually—he couldn't do it. He wasn't able to show her warmth. He just wasn't the kind of guy to talk about emotions.

'But he was.'

He was. She scrolled. Scrolled through his crush on a woman from work, to nightmares he had from his time at a children's home, to her. His daughter. *I know its bad to say, I feel bad saying it. But Im just not meant to be a Dad. Im counting the days til she be going, if Im honest. Shes a good kid, but thats the truth.*

Ally gripped her, pulled her in close. 'We care for you, J. We want you here.'

She realised that she was crying, the big thick sobs of a child.

'You're safe here, J. Always. We will always want you, always need you to be here. You're part of something bigger now. Out there, it's different. This man, he wasn't taught how to love so he didn't know how. He was blocking himself away, like so many do, hiding. You don't have to hide here, we will love you completely and absolutely. It's safe here. We won't judge you like they do out there. We won't break your heart. You're with us now, baby. We love you absolutely.'

*

The silvery sea dances as Jo wades towards the black silhouettes, the laughter coming from the rocks. The water is chilly against her legs, but she keeps going. Her skin is gooey hot from Ally's airless room and the candles.

The water reaches her waist and she slips into it, dives under and pushes forward. She forces her eyes open under the surface, looks towards the splashes, the legs treading water. The sting is there but she knows it will pass. It does. Her chest begins to cramp, but she keeps swimming towards the splashes, feels the first buckle in her lungs, her head heavy, but she's almost there now. Just a little more, a few seconds. Then she breaks the surface, not far away from them at all.

Lia is watching her, grinning. 'That was actually pretty awesome, J. Way longer than this morning, and we weren't even holding you.'

She smiles back, breathless, reaches for the rocks, tries not to splutter. Dolly is there too, her legs crossed in front of her, and Gabe. She looks away from him.

'So Ally helped?' Dolly asks.

'Yeah.' She pulls herself up on the rock, her head heavy. She notices Dolly's fingers touching the scratches on her wrist.

'Sorry, again,' Jo says.

'It's fine,' Dolly tells her, 'honestly, you're making such quick progress. I'm proud of you.' She kisses Jo on the shoulder and pushes off, falling into the ocean feet first. When she surfaces, she slicks her fiery hair flat over her skull.

'We all are,' Gabe says from next to her, and she feels his eyes on her.

Lia interlocks her fingers with Jo's against the rock. She can feel the warmth coming from Lia on her wet hands, but also from the stone underneath her, a deep heat that radiates into her.

'I'm going tomorrow,' he says.

She looks over. 'What?'

'I'm going out in the car, to sell the pearls. You wanted to come, right? Zay is coming too. We have to go to Denny's anyway, so it'll work out well.'

It's like the wind has turned cold. She lets go of Lia's hand and wraps her arms around her legs. Sorcha will have so many questions. Briena too. They'll probably tell her she's making a mistake, and she doesn't want to hear it. She can almost see the look of disdain on Sorcha's face, the unimpressed expression on Yan's. She can hear Briena tell her she's going to be killed out here. That somehow Sydney, with its crime and loneliness and apathy, is safer.

She doesn't need all that judgement again, the negative voices telling her she's wrong but never helping her to figure out how to be right. And if she calls her dad … No, she doesn't even want to think about talking to him.

'You don't have to,' Lia says, 'don't feel pushed.'

'Yeah, of course,' Gabe tells her, 'you can write a note or something for me to pass on if you like. I'll post one to England too, and Sydney, so no one's worried.'

'Yeah,' she says. It's dark, but she can just make out the shape of Dolly at the other end of the inlet now, hoisting herself onto the rock with Greta and Valentine. 'Yeah, actually that would be great, if it's okay.'

'Of course,' Gabe says, and he wraps an arm around her shoulders, squeezes for a moment, then pulls away and slides into the water himself.

CHAPTER 26

It's like when an aeroplane descends too fast. Stomach lifting. Pressure building in her ears until there is the edge of panic.

Jo tries to swim deeper, kicking her legs with every bit of strength she has, reaching down. She can see the rope, she isn't far. But the fear is still there. Her brain cannot quiet. She is worried about later, what she'll say to Ally. It's been two weeks of diving and talking and talking and diving, and she can't quiet that doubting voice.

The pressure thrums in her ears. Her chest cramps.

She's gone backwards and forwards with Ally over the last few weeks. When she first came to live with her dad, her time in London. Eric. She'd cried for two days about the miscarriage, told Ally all about that tiny baby-like silhouette she'd seen on the ultrasound monitor. It was barely bigger than a fig, but she could see its big head, its little curved body. A half-fish, half-child floating in her belly.

And then they'd gotten to Jamie.

The clamping on her ears is like a vice, it's too much. Her stomach is cramping, the chest convulsions unbearable. She's still kicking, but not strongly enough, she's rising, back to the surface.

She gives into it, pushes upwards, her head thumping so much that she has to squeeze her eyes closed just to bear it. The pressure weakens in her ears as her head breaks the water and she forces herself to exhale first, then slowly, unbearably slowly, pull in a new breath when all she wants to do is gasp and gulp it in. The new air is delicious and fresh and new. The thumping lessens and the relief is stronger than the disappointment. She exhales again, then breathes in.

'You were pretty close that time,' Lia says. She's lounging on a rock, letting the morning sun dry her hair. Jo paddles to her, tries to pull herself up on the rock, but her swimmers have fallen off her shoulders again, taping her arms against her body.

'It still seems impossible.' She yanks the straps back up, clambers onto the rock. She puts her head between her knees until the headache eases.

'Try not to get frustrated, it only makes it harder.'

She's about to snap back, but seeing Lia's smile makes her want to smile back. Her swimmers slip off her shoulder again.

She stands, slips the straps off, rolls the wet swimmers to her ankles and kicks them off to one side.

'Finally,' Lia says.

Jo lays on the rock, feels its heat against her stomach and breasts. The breeze strokes her bare back and bum. After a few minutes, it soothes her head, relaxes her muscles.

'Is there something going on between you and Gabe?' Lia asks.

Jo props herself on her elbow, trying not to give anything away. 'Why do you ask that?'

Lia's eyes are closed. 'I've just felt something. You look at each other in this way, and he seems a little less at ease around you. He's usually hugging everyone, but with you he's a bit cautious, almost like he wants to touch you so much that he's monitoring himself.'

Gabe and Zay had gotten back a few days ago. They'd been driving all around the Kimberley, selling the pearls they had found to farmers in the area. They were so spread out it had been a long trip. The same trip that he'd been doing when she'd first met him. They'd had trays of fruit as well, boxes of the damaged ones that the farmers gave them for free because they would otherwise be thrown out. They'd bought grain, kegs of petrol for the generator, candles and matches. Jo had been able to cover her excitement at his return with enthusiasm for the new supplies. Things had been getting tight while they were away. On the last night they'd had to just eat bulgar left out to soak in the sun for the day.

'You know, I feel like I'm back at school,' Jo says now, 'gossiping about whether a boy likes me.'

'Is that what school was like for you?'

Jo thinks about it. 'Yeah, sort of. We'd take these big plastic bottles of five-pound cider to the park on a Friday. Sit around drinking ourselves warm, then the boys would come and if you were lucky, the crush you'd been talking about all week would be there. You'd go off into the bushes and have a drunken, slobbery pash.' She can still remember the icy-cold hands pushing under her layers of clothes. 'It was the talking about it that was the fun bit.'

Lia smiles, her eyes closed. 'I can't imagine you like that.'

Jo settles her cheek against her hands. 'What were you like in high school?'

'I hated it,' Lia says. 'I didn't fit in.'

'Why not?'

'My stepdad sent me to boarding school in Perth when he married my mum. I think he just wanted her to himself. I hated living there, sharing a room with other girls who didn't like me. The only class I liked was photography. I was obsessed with Tracey Moffatt. I'd sit in the library and go through this big book of her pictures just so I didn't have to be in my room. I had this whole dream for myself that I'd come back here and become a photographer.'

'But it didn't work out?'

'No. Maybe I'd been away too long. Things were different to the way I remembered. I didn't fit in here any more either.'

'That sounds awful. I'm sorry.'

'It doesn't matter, because now I'm here.'

'Yeah,' Jo says. She shifts to her other cheek so she's looking away from Lia, out to the endless horizon.

After a while, Lia speaks again. 'It's just that we all love each other unexclusively here, you know? If we started coupling up it would make these individual units. This way we are one unit, all together, all even.'

'So you've never …? With anyone here?'

'No.'

It's obvious now, Jo should have noticed it. All these young people and no one sharing a bed.

'And I don't want to, anyway,' Lia continues. 'Sex … it's not worth it. Don't you feel like it can be so tied to violence? To pain and heartache and control?'

Jo tries to think about it, but her head is bleary now. The adrenalin has drained out and left her body mushy.

'What we have with each other here is on a different plane. It's still passionate, but it has so much more real, pure, free love.'

'Yeah,' Jo says, because she has to say something. It seems silly to her, to draw these lines in the sand. She doesn't want to disrupt the group, to do anything that might mess with the magic that keeps them floating in this unity. But she wants to touch Gabe again, she can't pretend she doesn't. Her body is different when he's close.

'Do you think—' she starts, but there is a splash in the water as Ho-jin surfaces in front of them. She watches him exhale then inhale and grin at them. That docile smile they all seemed to get after walking the rope. She didn't know how they could look so serene when all she felt when she surfaced was panicked and headachy.

Ho-jin climbs onto the rock as Dolly breaks through the water behind him. Ho-jin's body looks almost childlike, his skin soft, the slightest dimple in one cheek of his bum and a few pimples on his shoulders. Dolly's body tells a whole story. She has beautiful freckles all over her calves and arms, and her torso has barely a sprinkle. She's skinny up top, ribs visible under her breasts, but her bum and thighs wobble.

There's track marks on her feet as well, and pink self-harm scars on the tops of her thighs.

Dolly and Ho-jin lay back on the rock too. They don't say anything, but Jo can hear the way they breathe—deep and full.

She notices Nika. She's sitting on the cliff where Jo had watched the ocean that first time. Nika has her chin on her knees, staring out at them. Jo puts a hand up, a wave, but Nika must not notice. She doesn't wave back. Maybe the glare is in her eyes, or it's her fear of the ocean. Jo should take her out sometime. Show her how magical it is. Teach her to swim.

Jo rests her head on her hand. It'll be time soon to slip into the water, paddle to shore and go and see Ally. She'll try to take this feeling with her, this looseness that's radiating from the others. She wants to be more like them, open to the moment, not daydreaming about Gabe or blocking the hard things away. Now, when she looks back at her life, she can see she was always one step removed. All the pain and negativity and loneliness has made her shut off. Ally says it's like when you turn a tap off so tightly even getting a drip of water out feels impossible. She says that once Jo gets a dribble it will become easier, that soon things will be flowing and the future will be easy and bright.

Jo wants to be like the others, to not be scared. To trust her body enough to reach the rope, to feel the doorway of the ocean opening for her.

*

She hangs the brown swimmers on the tree, not sure if she's going to wear them again. It had been like being in the women's changing room when she'd had a short-lived membership at the gym in London. All those bodies, the older women not covering their wrinkled bottoms, the little kids running around nude and gleeful. It had been nice, just bodies together.

A shuffle behind her. She turns. Gabe is there, but he's walking away, head to his feet. The day is too hot suddenly, and she grabs Dolly's shirt from the line and throws it over herself, aware of her nipples pressing against the fabric, wondering how her arse looked. But she shouldn't think about it. No point in thinking about it.

She wanders towards Galbraith's Store, imagining how she must have looked, standing there stark naked. It felt like she'd been walked in on in the shower or like she was parading around when she wasn't meant to be.

A yell, guttural and long. A man, she is sure, deep and horrified. It echoes around the empty space. She looks around, then takes another step towards Galbraith's. It came from there, she was sure of it.

'It's okay.'

She jumps. Gabe is coming out from behind the kitchen, holding some of the empty petrol cans.

'What was that?' she asks, wrapping her arms around herself. The wet droplets from her hair slithering down her back make her shiver.

'It's fine. It's just Zay. He's in with Ally. You should come back later.'

'Is he okay?'

'Yeah. Well … he will be. When we were away, something happened between him and one of the farmers that we crashed with. It must have brought back some stuff.'

'Okay. Are you sure we shouldn't check?'

'Yeah. He's inside a memory right now—interrupting would be the worst thing we could do.'

'But ... I thought he was done with that. I thought all of you were.'

He lifts and drops his shoulders. 'That's the danger of going into the outside world again, I guess. It's safer to stay here. I wouldn't go if I didn't have to.'

'So you didn't have a good time?'

'It was fine. It makes me appreciate being here.'

'How was it at Denny's?'

'It was fine. You don't need to worry. Sorcha and Yan were happy to get your note.'

'So they were still there? I was worried maybe they'd already left.'

'No, they were there.'

'Did they say anything about Elias?'

'They said that he was doing really well, but they were working so we didn't talk much. Denny had two new guys from Malaysia too.'

'Oh,' she says. 'I guess the other guy didn't last.'

'Yeah, Denny mentioned him. Skipped out after a week—his uncle was sick or something.' He laughs. 'Denny was pretty annoyed, said it was bullcrap. He says he's only going to hire Asian workers from now on, kept going on about them having a better work ethic. Although his harvest is basically finished now.'

He puts one of the empty barrels of petrol under his arm, runs his hands through his sweaty hair, staring at his feet. 'So, um, sorry, you know, about just before.'

'No,' she says, 'no, it's—'

Then he looks up and catches her eye, and she can't help but smile. He smiles back and they are both laughing, a little awkwardly.

She thinks about asking if she can help him. She wants nothing more than to spend time with him, even if it's lugging petrol cans around in the heat.

She watches him walk away, lifting the jerry can to rest on his bare shoulder.

When she used to paint with oils, she was taught to never layer on top of drying paint. Different pigments dried at different times and if you put white over black before it was dry, it would crackle and peel. Maybe Lia is right. She needs to focus on Ally right now. She's so close, she can feel it just out of her reach, the end to the doubting and worrying and guilt.

CHAPTER 27

'Is Zay alright?'

'He will be,' Ally says, leaning back in her chair. She looks tired.

'Are you?'

'Of course.'

The air is heavy, like Zay has left behind something from his memory. An uneasiness.

She'd waited for hours. Eventually, she'd seen Zay crossing the clearing, sniffing, eyes swollen like the emotional violence he'd felt had given him a literal beating. She'd hesitated after that, told herself it was to give Ally some breathing space, though she knew it was just fear again.

'Today we go deeper.' Ally folds one leg over the other. 'We're going to push through.'

There's an edge, like she's irritated. Maybe Zay's setback has affected Ally more than she wants to admit.

'I want you to lie down,' Ally says, 'and close your eyes.'

Jo moves the lumpy cushions aside and lies flat. The old leather of the couch sticks to her sweating skin. She closes her eyes. She's going to try this time, really try.

'I want to know more about your brother.'

She'd known this was coming. She shifts her weight on the couch and it squeaks underneath her. She takes another sip of the tonic. She doesn't want to talk about this.

'What about him?'

'You've told me that you barely remember him.'

'That's right. I was only six when he died. My mum kind of went off the deep end after that. She couldn't look after me properly.'

'Are you still in contact?'

'No. She used to call me sometimes in Chesterfield. But it was always sporadic. Sometimes she was drunk.'

Jo had hated those phone calls. She'd shake her head desperately when her dad held out the receiver to her. When she got older, she'd just refuse to take the phone at all, and he'd make some excuse that she was in the shower or had ducked out. She'd never given her mum her mobile number, and told her dad not to either. Once she'd moved to London they weren't in touch at all. Every so often she'd get an email and she'd delete them without opening them.

'How did he die?'

'My dad said it was a boating accident. My mum used to love going out on her boat.'

'Your dad said that? But you don't remember?'

'I don't know. It was a long time ago.'

'Did you and Jamie share a father?'

She laughs. 'No. I guess it was a one-night-stand sort of situation.'

'Did she have a lot of boyfriends?'

'I can't really remember. I don't think so. I can barely remember that time.'

'What about that memory you told me about the first time you felt fear? I want to go back to that.'

'Okay.'

'Close your eyes.'

But Jo doesn't, she turns to Ally instead. 'Did you used to do this a lot with patients and stuff?'

'What do you mean, baby?'

'When you were a psychiatrist. Is this something you would do with patients? I can't imagine you as a psychiatrist, to be honest. I always kind of imagine you as a mum.'

Ally is staring at her, a strange expression on her face. 'Who told you that?'

'What?'

'That I was a doctor before I came here?'

Something about Ally's expression makes her be cautious. 'I don't know,' she says. 'I thought someone said it at dinner, didn't they? Or maybe I was guessing because you seem to know so much about this kind of thing.'

Ally doesn't say anything, just keeps staring. Then she smiles. 'Are you trying to talk about my past so you don't have to think about your own?'

Jo looks away, back at the ceiling, 'I don't know. Maybe.'

'I think you should close your eyes.'

Jo does as she is told. But still, that block is there. Like a brick wall between herself and those memories.

'I want to find it, don't you? That thing you are running screaming from. Do you want to be unburdened? Do you want to not feel fear any more? No more nervousness and worrying?'

'I want that so much.'

'So imagine it, honey. That first moment of fear. Even if the memory isn't forthcoming, we need to call it up. Think of your little angel self, standing at your house. Your mother is screaming. How are you feeling?'

'Afraid,' she says, because surely that is right. She must have been afraid. She would have been so scared.

'Can you see her? Yelling at you?'

'Yes,' she says. Every time she thought of her mother, every time her dad dangled the phone in front of her, she'd see it. Her mother's face, all crumpled with rage.

'She was a cruel woman; I can see that. She would hurt you.'

Would she? Jo can't remember that. She can't remember her mother ever hitting her, although that doesn't mean it didn't happen. Did it happen?

'Where are you standing?'

'On the cement steps going into the backyard. There were two of them and I was on the second one. My mum is standing there, her hand on the doorknob. Her knuckles are white, she's gripping it so hard.'

'And you?'

'I've got my arms wrapped around myself.'

'You're cold?'

Jo nods. Hungry too, but she doesn't say that. Her mum had stopped going grocery shopping. She didn't give her money for the canteen at school either. But sometimes her friend Gracie let her share her lunch.

'And then?'

'Then the door bangs shut. It's not locked, but I know I can't go back inside. I go and sit by the garden fence. It's far enough away from the window that she can't see me. Our grass is patchy and unmowed. I've got to be … I'm crying but I've got to be quiet, the neighbours might hear and I don't want them to. Our neighbour has a little girl a few years older than me and I don't want her to see me cry.

'I sit near the fence where it's dark. There's gaps between the palings and I can almost see down to the bay. The water is black and oily.'

'Look back to the house, baby. What can you see in the house?'

The leather is sticking to her. She's sweating. She can feel the beads dripping down her skin. But she isn't hot. She's cold, freezing cold, wrapping her arms around her knees. Moving them every few seconds to give each bit of her arm a turn to be warmer. She can see her jacket through the window, her little red jacket on the hook next to the back door.

'What's your mum doing?'

That old guilt twists in her belly. 'She's walking around the house. She's drinking out of a water glass. But it's not water. It's clear, but it's not water. It makes her breath stink and her eyes go funny. It's my fault. It's my fault she's drinking.'

The rooms in the house were toasty yellow. Everything outside was grey and black, the colours sapped out, but inside was yellows and colours. Her red jacket hanging on the hook. The blue couch. The television on, but no one in the living room to watch it.

'It's not your fault, baby. What is your mother doing?'

'She's gone into Jamie's room and she's just standing there.'

'Is she looking at the cot, Jamie's little baby cot?'

'Yes.'

'She's going towards it.'

'Yes, she's crying. She's staring into the cot.'

'She's angry. I can feel her anger.'

And her mother's face twists from anguish to anger. The tears dry up. She's angry and standing in Jamie's old room.

'Jamie's in there too, isn't he? He's in there and he's sleeping. I can feel his little baby dreams.'

Jamie is inside the cot. He's not solid, but she can see him in his blue onesie.

'I have already seen it. I already know what happens next. But you have to see it, J. You have to know.'

'What happens?'

'You tell me. What can you see? Can you see her looking at him? Seeing how that sweet little cherub is sucking her dry? Looking at him and knowing how much easier life would be without him? She's tired, so tired. And she's angry.'

She can see it. That glazed-over anger. The tiredness.

'She's putting her glass down. She's putting it on his drawers and leaning into his cot. She's not thinking clearly. She just knows that he's causing her misery.'

'No.' Jo can't bear that. 'No. It's my fault.'

But she can already see it, she already has it in her mind. Those yellow lights. Jamie's blue onesie. Her mother is leaning into the cot, her face twisted. She's picking up a pillow.

'I look away,' Jo says. 'I hide my head in my knees. I don't want to see it.'

'But you know, don't you? You know what is going to happen next.'

'Why don't I go in? Why don't I stop it?'

'You're just a little cherub yourself. Tiny and innocent and scared. What happens next?'

'I don't know. She takes him and puts him in her car?'

'Yes, of course. And you, what do you do now she's gone?'

'I go back inside. I go inside and hide in my bed until the sun comes up and then I go to school and pretend I don't know.'

'And you pretend and pretend until you believe it too.'

'I do.'

'But you feel guilty? Like you could have said something? Like you could have stopped it.'

'Yes.'

'But you couldn't. None of it was your fault. None of it.'

'Really?'

'Poor little Josephine. Running from that guilt that wasn't yours to bear. You're still running. From that moment on you're screaming and running from what you know, you're burying your little head away and hiding every chance you get. But not now.'

'No?'

'No. You've faced it now. You aren't running any more. I can feel it. You're home now. You're safe now, for the first time since that night, you're safe. You're not scared. You've faced the scariest thing imaginable and you've been scared ever since, but you're not scared now. You were put out into the cold, and ever since you've been afraid to be sent out there again. But we'll never do that. You'll always be inside with us, inside in the warm.'

Ally sits in front of the couch and clasps Jo's hand in hers. 'You did it, J. You found your root hurt.'

Jo opens her eyes. Ally is in front of her, her face so tender, her hand so lovely and soft.

'I'm so proud of you,' Ally says. 'Sit up now, baby. Come on.'

Jo pushes herself into sitting. Things don't seem quite real.

'You're different now, can you feel it? Can you feel that you've healed? That you're finally whole.' Ally puts a hand to Jo's chest. 'Can you feel it, baby?'

And she can. That brokenness is gone. There is heat inside her now, and strength. She doesn't need to be scared; she isn't going to be scared.

'You've accepted the worst thing. You've come from so much pain. But that's over now, you're home. Can you feel it?'

'Yeah,' she says, 'I can.'

And though her cheeks are soaked from sweat and tears, she's smiling. She's not going to be afraid any more.

*

Outside, Jo leans against the tree. The others are in the water, she can hear them splashing and calling to one another. She wants to go to them, but she needs a moment to process, to catch her breath. It seems insane that she's been carrying this memory around, all this time, without realising it. But the more it swims around in her head, the more sense it makes. The revelation has her split; on one side she is repulsed, stunned, by what her mother did. She has so many questions, so many gaps that aren't filled. But on the other side there is a strange relief. For if this is right, it explains so much. Every bad relationship, every bad choice. It gives a reason for why she's never felt right in the world. Most of all, this guilt, this awful twist that somehow she is bad inside, this feeling she's always had that she'd done something awful, finally has a source. And Ally is right. It wasn't her fault. The guilt is seedless.

The light has dimmed while she's been with Ally. She rights herself and heads towards the inlet. The sky is glowing low, the rocks jellied purples and blues. Jo looks over the others in the ocean. If she accepts what she has learnt, then she can let it go. She can accept the root reason of everything bad she has experienced since, and start over. Ally has told her she is rid of her fear, of her guilt and anxiety. And, as she walks to join the others, Jo knows that Ally is right, it all lifts off of her. Now that she's accepted the past, she never has to think about it again. She can be free.

*

It's easy now, to keep going down. To not let the pressure in her ears panic her. There is no fear, that's done with. She trusts now, trusts herself and the others with her whole heart. She can do this. It's unwavering.

She strokes with her arms against the cooling water. She kicks out, muscles working. The rope is there. Five metres ahead. Then four. The others are waiting. But she doesn't feel pressure from them, doesn't feel afraid of disappointing. Because she won't disappoint. They love her, she's certain, and she'll do this.

Her chest is hot and bursting, her ears thrumming, skull buoyed. Deeper. It's right there, a body's length away. She's doing it. She's going to do it this time.

Then she feels it.

A tug.

The pressure eases, changes. She's being pulled down. The ocean is accepting her, bringing her in, welcoming her feet to land onto the rope, feeling its soft give.

She steps forward, arms outstretched.

Seconds slow. The water wraps around her. Everything glitters, the sun slipping through the surface in beams.

Nothing could ever make her scared again.

The rope is coming to its end. She's on the other side. Things are dimming around her, but she's not worried.

She could stay here forever if she wanted.

She kicks off, pushes against the doorway for a few seconds, then the pressure changes and she is being helped to the surface instead. The ocean with its lapping hands helps her up.

Her head breaks the surface, out into the sweet air of dusk. She breathes out, slow and even, and relishes the new air as she breathes back in. There are sounds around her. Sounds of joy. Cries of delight, applause.

An arm is held out and she reaches her hand up. Someone grips it, strong and gentle all at once. It's Gabe, his face lit with pleasure. He pulls her onto the rock and they all crowd around her. Lia and Dolly and Ho-jin. On the other side are Greta and Valentine and Zay. And there, between the bodies pulling her into hugs, is Ally. She's sitting on her rock near the shore and she's smiling at Jo. She's happy and she's proud. Jo is aglow inside. The world is solidifying.

'You did it!' Gabe is yelling. 'I knew you could!'

'How do you feel?' Dolly says, holding onto Jo's forearms to look at her.

'Amazing,' Jo says, 'it's better than anything.'

'*You're* amazing,' Ho-jin says, and he's not covering his mouth. She can see all his teeth when he smiles.

'So I can come next time?' Jo asks. 'Next time you go out to get oysters, I can come?'

Dolly looks over her head to Gabe and he must nod or something because she looks back to Jo with the biggest grin. 'Of course. Next time we go, you'll come with us.'

CHAPTER 28

Jo is dreaming sweet dreams of sunbeams glinting through the ocean when she's stroked awake. A soft caress on her bare shoulder.

'J?'

'Mmm?'

The beams flicker, then go out. She opens her eyes. Gabe is smiling at her.

'Hi,' she whispers. It's dark outside. 'Is everything alright?'

'Yeah, I was hoping you'd go on a drive with me.'

'A drive?' She blinks, then turns and looks around. Everyone is asleep around her. Ho-jin on his front, his arms stretched out around his pillow. Lia shifts under her sheet.

'I think we'll all be going out again soon. There are things I need to explain before that. Easiest if I show you.'

'Alright.' She rubs the sleep out of her eyes, sits. His hand is still on her shoulder. The smile lines around his eyes are caught in the silver moonlight.

'You get ready and I'll go wait in the truck, alright?'

'Wait,' Lia says from next to her, voice croaky. 'I'll come.'

Gabe stops rubbing Jo's shoulder, removes his hand. 'You want to?'

'Yeah, I'll explain it better than you can.'

Gabe nods once, then gets up and heads out, feet padding between the mattresses. Jo starts pulling on clothes, dimly aware that Lia is looking at her. She stops, turns to her, but Lia looks away, sitting up and yawning wide.

'Why do we have to go so early?' Jo asks.

'It's a bit of a drive. We don't want to have to stay overnight.'

Lia's not looking at her now, she's shuffling to get ready herself. Pulling on shorts and a singlet. She grabs a brush from her mess of things and runs it through her hair. She's never seen Lia brush her hair before. She yanks it through almost violently, until her ringlets bounce out soft and gravity defying.

'Hey, can I borrow that later?' Jo whispers.

'Sure.'

Jo tucks her hair behind her ears, pulls on the t-shirt she's been wearing for days. Its fabric smells of sweat and the ocean.

Outside, the chirps of crickets are thunderous. There is something else singing with them too. A throbbing sound, deeper. She looks at Lia, eyebrows knotted.

'Frogs,' Lia says, not looking at her. She's worried, maybe, or just distracted. Her arms are wrapped around herself, but it isn't cold. The opposite. The air is heavier than yesterday, swollen with heat and moisture.

'When did you last leave Rossack?'

Lia only shrugs in response, tight and guarded. 'During the day? A while ago.'

The darkness is milky near the horizon; dawn isn't far away. But the headlights of Gabe's lorry are stark, though the rumble of the engine falls under the crickets' and frogs' duet.

Lia slides into the front seat and slams the door shut. The croaking and chirping falls silent for a second. Jo pulls the back door open and, as she steps up, a solitary frog croaks and then the rest start again.

Gabe pulls off the handbrake and starts the drive. There's no road here, or no trace of it at least. If there was once some kind of dirt track it has long been reclaimed by nature. The wheels bump over the clumps of spear grass and she's thrown around against the side door. She clicks on her seatbelt.

'So where are we going?' she asks.

'Into Broome,' Gabe replies.

'Oh, okay, awesome. I got the bus through there when I first arrived. Looked so different to any town I'd seen before.'

Neither of them reply.

'It'll be cool to check it out,' she adds. Still nothing.

In truth, the idea of the town makes her stomach twist. It's not big, tiny in fact. When she'd first driven through she had been expecting there to be so much more to it, had been surprised when it had disappeared behind them so fast. But now other people in general seem like a concept. She's gotten so used to it being just them.

The headlights light up the tufts of grass in front of them, the bramble to the side. It's too dark to see much else. She closes her eyes. The heave and throw of the back seat is making her head spin. She clutches the handle of the door, tries to steady herself. Focuses on breathing. She doesn't want to ask them to pull over. Nothing would be more embarrassing than retching on the side of the road.

But she doesn't need to think like that. Imagine worst-case scenarios. Picture humiliations. She's noticed this a few times since she recovered her truth. Every time she has to remind herself: her fear is gone. It's easy for her mind to wander there again, a habit, like twisting your hair or cracking your knuckles.

Once the jerks and bumps ease she peers through her eye-lashes. Yes, they have made it onto a real dirt track. It's still rough, but the suspension on the lorry is good enough that she knows she can look around without nausea. She releases her grip on the doorhandle, tries to relax into the cushioned seat. She can see the edge of both their faces now. Dawn rims their cheeks in gold.

'So what did you want to show me anyway?'

She sees a look pass between them, so quick she could have missed it if she hadn't been watching.

'If we told you now there would be no point driving all the way to show you,' Gabe says, eyes smiling from the rear-vision mirror. But they are hiding something. Or perhaps they're just nervous. She can't tell.

She leans her head onto the glass. The sun shifts and they pass boab trees, the coast coming in and out of view. Sorcha and Yan would probably be getting up for work. Now she's out of Rossack, their existence is more real.

Eventually, they pull onto the empty highway, real bitu-men now. The road she started on. The landscape slides past, red rocky hills and tangled mounds in the distance.

Her eyelids are slipping closed. The glass window is broiling from the hot air outside.

She remembers her mother driving their tiny old white car. She'd be squeezed in the back, her red jacket wet and squeaking against the seats. Her mum grinning at her, singing along to the Spice Girls together, 'Viva Forever', the heat beating through the vents wonderful and snug, She felt bad for all the people in the cold wet grey outside. Her mother, smelling of jasmine. Charlotte's face is clear and bright and she has one hand on her round belly and that angry, twisted scarred woman seems impossible.

'What do you think, Josephine, my love? Beck's for tea?'

Jo sits straight. She's done with looking back now that she's found the root hurt, accepted the truth. But it's like Ally had said about turning on the tap. Memories she thought were long gone keep sneaking up on her.

She keeps her eyes on the front windows. After a few hours, houses begin to pop up. Then little clusters of communities off the road. Hooded roofs and big driveways and bright steel reflecting the sun. They reach sprawling streets of new buildings, cheap looking and set close together. But there are no cars around. Not even in the driveways.

'It feels empty,' she says, realising she's breaking a silence that's been held for hours.

'Yeah,' Lia says, arms crossed in front of her. 'All these new developments run on tourists and tourist money. It can be pretty dead in the off-season.'

'Off-season?'

'Tourists won't come because it's too humid and stormy. It's well into Man-gala now. We might even get a cyclone.'

'Have you had a cyclone at Rossack before? Is it, erm …
you know. Safe?'

'Those buildings have been standing for longer than any
of us have been alive,' Gabe says.

Lia smiles at her. 'You should see the way the ocean looks
during a cyclone. It's amazing. The storms here aren't like
anything you've seen anywhere else. It's like the sky is ripping open.'

Jo tries to smile back.

'The tourists come in Marrul or Wirralburu, when it
changes and cools a little. You should see it then. It's like a
different place, completely packed.'

They drive past the day spas Jo remembers from when she
first arrived. A lot of them Japanese themed with Buddha
statues and elaborate fountains out front. The sky is over-
cast, giving everything a strange, unreal quality.

They pass the bigger buildings, red brick double storey
and corrugated iron roofs. On a nature strip in the middle,
a group of people sit under a tree. Yawuru, she remembers
Dolly saying. Jo had always been fascinated by the Indigenous peoples of Australia, their artwork and iconography
everywhere in tourist shops in Sydney. She remembers the
Aboriginal art section of the Art Gallery of NSW. She went
in the first month she'd been in Sydney, unmoored but
still in awe of the heat and accents and space of Australia.
She remembers the huge echoing gallery, with its polished
concrete floors reflecting the paintings on the walls. She
had stood in front of a work by Gloria Petyarre, struck by
the sunny yellows and greens and dark brick reds cascad-
ing across the canvas like a thousand leaves caught in the
wind. She'd stared at a newer painting, by Daniel Boyd.

Tiny dots coming together to create a dark image, like trying to see the colour of the shore at midnight. When she was in London she used to take close-up photos of work she liked on her phone to analyse later. She'd zoom in on passages of brushwork, try to work out their technique. But now that she was no longer an artist herself she could just stand and look, and not have to pick apart how the magic was made.

Lia slides down in her seat and pushes her face into her shoulder. It's strange to imagine that she'd grown up so close by. For everyone else, this was a refuge away from their usual lives.

'You okay?' Jo asks her.

'Yep,' Lia says, 'it's just … everyone knows everyone around here.'

They pass to the other side of the town and she relaxes.

*

Finally, they can see the ocean again. It's a relief for Jo, like a sentinel force, watching out for her. It makes her feel safer to know that now she can run into it, disappear under it until it holds her down.

They approach the shoreline and drive alongside it. There are a few people around. An old guy fishing. A couple of middle-aged white women standing in the shallows, talking. Two young Yawuru boys and a Chinese-looking kid, probably eight or nine, shirts off, laughing and mucking about. Lia sees them too.

'Oh, pull over,' she says, and winds her window down. She sticks her head and shoulders out.

'Billy!' she calls. 'Jim! Oscar!'

They look up, stricken, like they might be in trouble, then they jump up and down, grinning, when they see her.

'Dani!'

Lia pulls back into the car. 'Hey, do you mind if I catch up with you guys in half an hour or so? I just want to say hi.'

'Why did they call you Dani?' Jo asks.

But Lia is looking at Gabe, who says, 'Do you think that's okay?'

'Yep,' Lia says, as she pulls off her seatbelt and jumps out of the car and towards the boys. 'I'll meet you at Roebuck,' she calls over her shoulder.

Gabe keeps driving.

'Should Lia not have gone?' Jo asks after a while. 'Do you think it'll regress her? Like with Zay.'

'Maybe,' is all Gabe says.

Privately, she thinks Lia is taking a risk talking to those kids. People won't understand the choices they've made, they'll judge them. Plus, there is always that risk of unwelcome visitors. If others knew what a haven they'd made, they'd surely come. Ruin it.

But she's glad Lia is gone for a while. She watches Gabe's hands on the wheel. Even the hair prickling up his arms is desirable. There's so much for them to say to each other, so much she wants to say, but something is overriding everything else. She clamps one thigh over the other. It's been building for a while, but now her bladder feels fit to burst.

She catches a glimmer of something out the window. A golden statue of a woman, pregnant belly protruding, hands outstretched. But it disappears behind a motel before she has time to see it clearly.

It's less than ten minutes before they pull into a parking lot. It's almost empty. Just a beat-up old Kombi van that looks like it's permanent and a sleek silver BMW. She jumps out of the lorry.

'God, I need to wee so bad,' she says, jiggling on the spot and scrutinising the spindly shrubs for somewhere with decent coverage from the road.

'Wow, you've turned wild quick,' he says. He takes her by the shoulders and moves her body to face a grey brick toilet block.

'Oh,' she says, laughing. Now she's standing, the pressure of her bladder is even worse. She tries not to rush on her way to the block. Inside, it smells of sand but also mildew and old urine. The doors are cracked and the floor is dirty with shoe prints. She hurries over to one of the stalls and pulls the door shut, locking it. The plastic seat feels strange underneath her. He's right. She's turned wild already.

Once she's done she rinses her hands but keeps her head down. It's been nice not seeing her reflection. Liberating. Plus she's worried the sunburn might have changed her.

Coming out, she sees he's waiting for her, leaning against the lorry, a silver flask dangling from a string in his hand.

'Didn't you need to go? That was a long drive.'

'I went in the bushes.'

She shoves him. 'I forgot we were back in the patriarchy. I piss in the bush and I might be arrested. You do it and you're just being a guy.'

'Actually I went around to the men's. I was just quicker than you.'

She elbows him, laughing. 'Hey!'

He wraps an arm around her and pulls her in. 'Sorry!'

She's never been so turned on by someone's sweat before. But now, god. She could happily drown in it.

They head down to the water. It's not like their ocean. This is a huge, flat expanse of sand with bins every few metres, signs with instructions about when to swim. She has to hop over a dog turd.

He passes her the flask and she takes three gulps of water. The bottle has kept it cool and it's a relief. She passes it back to him and he drinks from it. The sun is high now, not when they'd usually be out. The air still is thick, her clothes damp. Her thighs stick to each other as she walks.

He squeezes her a little tighter and stops by a wooden blockade. He kisses her shoulder through the cotton of her t-shirt and leans against the edge of the wood. Further on from them is a jetty, where a few boats have pulled in.

She smiles at him, waiting to hear why she's been brought here. But he pulls her in and kisses her instead, running his hands up the sides of her body.

'Shit,' he says, pulling away. 'Told myself I wouldn't do that.'

His hand doesn't leave her, tracing the line of her waist.

'It's a bad idea, isn't it? It might change things.'

'Yeah,' he says, and his hand drops away.

She runs her fingertips down his face. Feels his stubble, the line of his jaw, his soft hair. She rubs her nose against his. Brushes her fingers lightly along his neck.

Then they are kissing again and time falls away. It's so hot her skin is boiling underneath his hands and she can barely breathe. He squeezes her arse and she wants to undress him right there. Make love to him in the sand where the man is playing fetch with his dog a kilometre away.

She takes a breath, leans her forehead on his chin. 'Lia might see.'

'Yeah,' he says, wrapping his arms tightly around her.

'Plus we're meant to be here for you to tell me this secret of yours.'

'Yeah,' he says again then sways them both from foot to foot. 'I'm just afraid you're not going to like it.'

'What is it?' She's worried now, but not enough to want his hands to leave her.

'Shit,' he says. 'Okay. I have to tell you now otherwise you're going to think something worse. I haven't been trying to be mysterious, it's just … I don't know. Maybe Lia should be here, actually. She grew up around here, she'll explain it better.'

She pulls back further. 'Okay, no. Tell me now. You aren't killing people or something, are you?'

He shakes his head, and that smile is back. She can imagine him breaking hearts with that smile, can picture so many girls in that little town in Pennsylvania who must have cried over him. It's not what she should be thinking about.

'Just tell me.'

'Okay,' he groans, then moves to stand beside her, a hand resting on his shoulder. 'See them?'

She looks out. There is a boat in the water.

'This is where we found all those oysters.'

'Here?' She'd been imagining some secluded spot, phosphorescence and sea caves.

'Yeah. Well, fifteen minutes or so down that way.'

She follows where he's pointing, sees rows of buoys floating in the water in the distance.

'But isn't that a pearl farm?'

He looks at her.

'Oh,' she says.

She watches the boat. The people on board are pulling ropes with trays on the end. The trays are thick with barnacles. Workers begin chipping them off with flat blades.

'So you didn't *find* those oysters. You stole them.'

'I guess so. Yeah. I'm not going to lie to you. We go when it's raining, when visibility is poor. Then we shuck them and sell the pearls on to a couple of the farmers who we know need the money. They sell them online, I think.'

She crosses her arms, shifts further away from him. 'So, wait. Is this why we learn to dive? To steal?'

'No!' he says, looking at her straight now. 'No way. We do this because we can. And it means we can live the way we do. We couldn't survive without some form of income.'

She doesn't say anything. This wasn't what she was expecting.

'This whole industry,' he says, 'it's got decades of nasty history and now they take tourists on champagne cruises at sunset.'

'I don't think you can really be taking a moral high ground.'

She watches the men on deck in the distance, putting the trays down and moving onto the next. She still can't think. It's too hot. A fly lands on her cheek. She swipes it away.

'Can I have some more of that water?'

He hands it to her. She takes a gulp; the water is lukewarm in her throat. The sun has bounced off the silver flask, heated it. He rubs a hand down her arm but she shifts away.

'Just … I need a second.'

The sand is blinding now. It's too white. The fly lands on her again, just inside her nostril. She shakes her head to get rid of it.

'So what if I don't want to do it? I mean, is it obligatory?'

'No! I mean, we all do it, but I'm sure … Yeah, I'm sure we could figure something out.'

'You don't sound sure.'

The fly lands on her again. Right on her eye this time. She shakes her head, blinking her eyes. 'Bloody hell!'

'I'm feeling like this is not going well,' he says.

Lia is striding over to them. She's smiling again, the weariness from earlier gone. Lia lied to her too.

The smile slips off her face as she gets closer. 'Wow, so you told her?'

'He did.'

'I know how it seems. And I feel like you're mad at me too, which is fair, I suppose.'

Jo looks out at the pearl luggers. The fly lands on her again. 'Can we go? I don't want to be here any more.'

They head to the car in silence. She shivers as the cold air of the air conditioning touches her syrupy skin.

Once Broome is behind them, Lia and Gabe talk a bit. Lia mostly. She tells him about the kids she saw, how she used to look after them all the time. How Jim's learning to surf, how Oscar looked like he was coming down with something—she'd told him to go home—how Billy told her he'd heard all sorts of crazy rumours about her.

Her stories peter out and she falls silent and stares out the window. As they drive on and on in silence, Jo tries to bring it all into alignment. The diving isn't a means to an end. It can't be. Stealing the pearls is a happy by-product, a way of ensuring their survival. It was naive of her to think that they could live without any kind of money.

If she doesn't agree to be part of it, what will happen? She can't even think of it without panic swirling through her mind. She tries to steady her breathing, tries to remember what she's learnt. Fear is behind her now. She's strong. Her life with them makes her solid.

'Hey—look at that!' Lia says. 'That's got to be the cutest thing I've ever seen.'

Jo looks up. Her stomach drops. Denny's farm. She hadn't thought they might pass it. That dirt driveway, the hill, those lines of mango trees. All so hideously familiar.

She squeezes her eyes shut.

'Did you see it? There was this boy riding around on a bike with a goat running alongside him! It was gorgeous, like they were real mates.'

Her stomach stops rolling. She opens her eyes. The landscape has turned back to thistle and trees.

*

Jo sits on the wooden bench with Nika between her knees. She's brushed out her hair, smoothed out those tangled ends. Now, she is braiding it softly, revealing Nika's neck, bent over and thin.

Nika has the brush in her hands and she's pulling out clumps of hair from between its bristles. Dolly has been lying on her back next to them. She gets up, brushing the leaves from her back, and wanders towards the kitchen.

'Do you think if I put this hair out by those silver gums, the birds will use it for their nests?'

Nika's voice is quiet. Jo has to bend over her to hear.

'That's a really nice idea.'

Jo holds a section of hair between her index and middle finger, another between her middle and ring finger, and one in the other hand. She weaves them together, keeping the shiny hair tight. From the kitchen she can hear Dolly and Ho-jin chatting and laughing and the clunks of them beginning to prepare for dinner.

'Is Lia alright?' Nika asks.

Lia had gone to bed early when they came back yesterday. This morning she'd seemed distracted, then she'd gone back to bed, rubbing her arms like they hurt. When Jo had gone in to retrieve her brush, she'd been fast asleep.

'Yeah, I think so.'

A drip of water lands on Nika's head. It slips down the notches of the braid and then soaks into the hair. She looks up at the grey clouds. Jo holds on so the braid doesn't undo.

Another drip lands on Jo's arm.

'They'll be going out tonight,' Nika says.

Jo ties the end of the braid with the rubber band she found in the dirt near the kitchen.

'Are you going with them, Jo?' Nika says, turning to look at her.

'Yeah,' Jo says, smiling. 'Of course I'm going.'

CHAPTER 29

Jo sits in the tray of the lorry with Greta and Valentine and Lia. The night sky is breaking above them. Orange lines of lightning cut the dark into pieces. The thunder growls.

Valentine and Greta hold hands and squeal. 'Allucinante!' Valentine calls to the sky.

Jo lifts her chin, opens her mouth and catches the water drops on her tongue. This is freedom, like nothing else.

Zay is out the side window, arms raised and eyes closed.

Jo wraps an arm around Lia's shoulders. 'This is incredible,' she whispers.

Lia pushes into her shoulder. Her skin is sticky, fever-hot. She'd caught whatever sickness the kid on the beach was coming down with. She'd been in bed all day, barely moving, as the rain rapped its fingers on the courthouse roof. Ally was furious. She's worried the whole group might catch it. All feel Lia's punishment for mixing with outsiders.

'Maybe you should have stayed with Nika?'

Lia shakes her head.

'You'll be okay,' Jo says, squeezing her tight, feeling the tremors sliding through her.

Another slice of lightning cuts the blackness above them. The Italian girls squeal again, giggling, the water dribbling down their cheeks.

*

When they get close, Gabe turns the headlights off. The Italians quieten. Everything is silent.

He pulls in by a tree and they pile out of the back. Jo helps Lia down, trying to conceal how much of her weight she is carrying. Gabe drives further under the tree. The lorry is barely visible beneath the branches.

Dolly, Ho-jin and Zay slip out from the back seat, Ally and Gabe from the front. They close their doors softly.

Ally steps forward, looks out to the sea. It's loud and dark, the raindrops prickling its surface. There's a slope and then a red cliff a few metres up. Jo can barely see. It's like that Daniel Boyd painting come to life. She wraps her arms around herself.

'J.' Ally points to a set of black buoys bobbing atop the undulating water, a huge grid of them. 'That's the longline system. Under the surface there are trays attached by ropes. Just slip the oysters out of their cubbyholes and fill your bag. We'll jump from the cliff at next thunder, then swim back to the beach when you're finished.' She traces a finger from the buoys across to the sand at least a kilometre away on the right. 'Follow Lia, alright? She'll lead you.'

Jo looks to Lia. Her nose is running and she's sniffing, watery eyes on the ground. She's going to be even worse tomorrow.

'Alright.' Ally grins at them, at Jo in particular, and leads the way to the cliff. Far off, Jo can see a boat with a spotlight attached. But it's so distant that the light is a white smudge.

She walks to the cliff holding Lia's hand in hers, trying to stop Lia from falling as well as not stumbling herself. The wind rages against her, pushing her back, spinning her hair into the sky. Her clothes sop from her skin. The torch on the string around her neck is heavy, pulling.

Once they reach the cliff everyone starts to undress. She lets Lia's hand go, pulls her t-shirt off her over her head, tugs off her shorts. Her torch is off, all of them are. They aren't going to turn them on until they are under the surface.

'Why do we have to wait until thunder?' she asks Dolly, who is already naked and stretching next to her.

'So they don't hear the splash.'

Lia isn't undressing. She's staring at the water. She goes over to Ally; Jo follows a few steps behind.

Lia tugs on Ally's sleeve. 'I don't think I should. J can follow Dolly instead. Or Gabe.'

Ally doesn't look at her. 'No, she'll follow you.'

Jo is about to butt in, say it's okay, she's happy to follow one of the others.

'I'm sick.'

'I've noticed that.'

Ally's voice sounds different. In the dim light, her face is just a shadow. She steps closer.

'It's dangerous.'

'We came here for a purpose. Now it's time to accomplish our purpose.'

Lia folds her arms in front of her body. 'You're telling me I have to do it?'

A crack of lightning, orange veins across the sky.

'Yes,' Ally says.

Lia's arms are still crossed. Jo doesn't want her to dive if she doesn't want to. She goes and stands next to Dolly, grabs a string bag from the pile, jiggles on the spot.

She only hears the first second of the roar before Dolly has disappeared. She launches off to follow. The worst thing would be to be left behind.

The water slams against her like a brick wall. She's under. Deep black. Pushing her back up. Her mind was on diving, not breathing. She darts to the surface. Air. She looks around. No heads bobbing up, just hers. On the cliff, two shadows looking down on her. She's meant to be following Dolly.

Inhale, slow and even.

She's under again.

She sees the twinkles of their dim torches. She pushes towards them. Fumbles with the torch around her neck, fingers slipping on the hard plastic. The button. She squeezes and a little glow surrounds her too.

She goes lower, lungs clasping, chest stuttering. Up close the others are black silhouettes, anglerfishes, creatures of the deep.

There, the pull.

The doorway welcomes her in. She reaches out for a tray. Black-brown pockets, oysters inside. Six, she sees.

Her bag opens, slow motion in the water. Floating upwards. She moves jelly-slow, tugs one oyster out. Another. They slip in her fingers and she could laugh. She's almost there, she tugs the next, one more.

Soda fizz around her.

They are kicking up, bags full. Another oyster. Last one.

Her torch is dimming, the water blackening. Up. Up. She hooks the bag on her arm, sees one of the others surfacing ahead of her.

But no. Long dark hair webbing out. Red spilling from her head. She pushes further. Closer. Her torch isn't working. It's just blackness and the woman.

Then, coolness.

'Breathe!'

Dolly's face in hers. Whisper-scream.

'Breathe!'

She tugs in a breath, slow. Then out. The bag is heavy now.

'Come on.' Dolly tugs her hand. 'And turn your light off. Quick!'

She looks down, her torch is glowing still. She fumbles. Drops it. Picks it up, presses the button. Dolly pulls on her hand.

'There's someone still under,' Jo says.

'No, you're the last one. Hurry.'

Her eyes adjust and she can see Dolly. Her hair sticking to her neck, face white, blinking against the rain.

'Come on.'

Her feet touch the sand, the bag weighing on her wrist. She drags herself onto the beach. Gabe throws his arms around her.

They run to the tree. She gets onto the tray. Lia is already there, waiting in the corner, a ball of wet clothes.

When they are back on the road, Jo counts and counts again. Dolly, Greta and Valentine. Lia didn't dive. Ally is in the front, the driest of them all.

'I was so sure I saw someone, a woman, down there,' she says to Lia.

'I've seen things too,' Lia whispers, head on knees. 'Not enough air to your brain. It happens.'

'But I'm so sure. She was floating, bleeding. I thought it was Dolly but she was fine.'

She saw this woman before, she remembers vaguely, during her walk to Rossack. It was her mother, a spectre from her past life. But now that she's accepted her root hurt, she'd thought she wouldn't see her again like that, wet and bleeding.

Lia rubs under Jo's nose with a bent finger. It comes back darker. Blood.

Jo licks her top lip. Tinny-tang. She wipes the blood away.

'Are you alright?' she asks Lia.

Lia nods. 'Just want to get dry.'

Jo squeezes her arm, then looks into her bag. Six large, slimy oysters are inside. Valentine grins at her. Jo looks to the sky, raises her face to the rain.

CHAPTER 30

They put their oysters into buckets of seawater, all laughing. Giddy, still whispering, eyes alight. Ally heads to Galbraith's, head bowed. The others trickle away as Jo watches Gabe smearing his wet hair back, water droplets hanging from his eyelashes.

'Did you enjoy it?' he says.

She nods. 'My moral compass was more easily tampered with than I thought.'

'Good,' he says, string bags empty now. They look at each other across the table in the dark. His hand inches across the wood towards hers, fingertips brushing against fingertips.

A rustle from the bushes. Dolly approaches. 'You did good, J,' she says.

'Thanks.'

They follow Dolly to the courthouse. They go through the doorway, and Gabe pulls it shut behind them.

'Well,' Jo whispers, 'goodnight.'

'Goodnight,' Gabe says.

'See you in the morning,' Dolly says

Inside, the beating on the iron roof is thunderous. It's hot, clammy from sweat and excitement and nerves. She sits on her bed, watches Gabe and Dolly's backs disappear down the hallway.

It's loud enough. No one would hear.

Greta and Valentine whisper in bed. Ho-jin is face down, his back bare and beautiful. Lia lies still, eyes closed, probably asleep.

It's hard to stay motionless. She doesn't want to sleep. She's not ready for the night to end. She'll wait ten minutes. She counts them in her head until the numbers are jumbled, but it's nothing like tiredness.

Once the others have silenced, she sits. Lia has rolled to her side, sweat dripping down her forehead. Ho-jin hasn't moved. Valentine and Greta sleep facing one another, Greta's lips slightly parted like she slipped into dreams halfway through a word.

Jo tries to stand without making a sound. Slips down the corridor. She hasn't been there since he taught her how not to breathe.

She shouldn't, she knows she shouldn't.

She gets to his cell, peers through the mesh. He's awake. The door is open, but then it's probably always open. She ducks under the mesh, comes in and then, no—a squeaked groan—she looks down. The rotting board. He stares at her. They're both frozen. But there isn't a sound from either side.

Her skin quivers. He may tell her to go.

He reaches a hand out and she takes it and climbs into the bed next to him. He's naked under his sheet, skin still damp from sweat and rain and the ocean. She pulls her t-shirt off and throws it on the floor and now she is naked too. His arms wrap around her bare skin, pull her close against his chest. Their flesh sticks together with sweat and her stomach fizzes. She can feel the hard heat of him pressing against her stomach. Her body is pulsing, ready, and she kisses his warm mouth, desperate to close the space between them. He smooths the wet hair from her neck, licks the salt from her skin. A whimper escapes her.

She pushes him onto his back, straddles him.

'Okay?' she breathes.

'Hell, yes.'

She licks the bead that's appeared at the tip of his cock. His head tilts back, throat long, and he groans loud.

She freezes. They look at each other. Listen for movement. It's just the thrum of the storm on the roof.

His hands grip her hips, then one brushes between her legs where she's humming, wet and swollen, like one of their molluscs. Unbearable heat rises through her body as his fingers move on her. She's panting from it, her skin on fire. She takes his other hand, puts his fingers into her mouth. They're salty. She can't wait any more. She slides onto his cock and it's already what she wants.

They move together and it's unlike anything she's felt before. It's like the ocean is here with them, hot and wet and sharing its rhythm. And she wants to gasp, she wants to scream, so she holds her breath.

*

The knife slips between the two shells. Jo twists it, hears the crackle, bits of grit flake off. She digs her fingers between the two halves, pulls, then saws lower and twists the knife again. This shell has a bit of give to it. She pushes her finger into it again. It's spongy.

Nika sits in front of her, playing with pearls on the ground. She is laying them into patterns. The rest of the group crowd around the table, all except Lia, of course.

Gabe is there and it's like he senses her. He looks over the bowed heads of the others. Grins at her. She grins back, returns to her work.

The shell cracks open. Inside, it doesn't look the same as the others. The oyster is misformed: teeth-like barbs and twisted spines. She digs her fingers in, rubbing for the hard lumps. There's only one, and when she squeezes it she sees it isn't right either. It's asymmetrical, undersized. So it can happen to oysters too.

She hands the pearl over to Nika, who holds it up to the light then places it into her pattern, right in the middle, the crowning glory.

'I went looking for Mum again last night.' She doesn't look up.

'Oh, pet.' Jo leans closer. 'I'm sure she'll come back eventually.'

Nika twitches, looks at her, blinking fast again. 'What?'

'Even if she doesn't, we're here for you. We'll look after you.'

Ally approaches and Jo holds the soft shell up to her.

'This one didn't form quite right,' she says.

Ally takes it from her hand, runs her fingers across it.

'Poor thing. The ocean's turning to acid, they can't get strong. Every time we go out there are more like this. A few years back it was just one.'

She rests a hand on Nika's shoulder, who is wrapped up in a ball, then goes over to the group, speaks to Dolly in a low voice. Jo looks away before she catches Gabe's eye again. If Ally sees, she will know straight away.

Nika scoops the pearls in her hands, goes over and pours them into the bucket. Jo begins on the next oyster, watching as Nika shuffles away. She makes a silent promise to herself: if Nika's mother doesn't come back in the next few weeks she'll talk to Ally about lessons. They could do it between them. Surely each of them knows a bit of something: grammar, math, sciences?

The next oyster in her hands is a little spongy too, but not as bad as the one before. When she cracks it open, she sees the bulge straight away. It isn't the right shape. She digs her fingers in and pinches out the pearl. It's two pearls, conjoined. It's the shape of a heart. She looks around. No one is watching her. She slips it into her pocket. They won't be able to sell it anyway. She'll sneak into Gabe's room, leave it on his pillow. He'll be going away again soon, tomorrow maybe, to sell these pearls. Maybe he could take it with him, feel it in his pocket. It's corny, she knows. She's not sure if she's ever been with someone who made her want to be so corny.

*

At dinner, Gabe comes to sit by her. He doesn't talk to her. He talks to Ho-jin while she talks to Dolly. But he lets his knee lean against hers. Casually, like it's nothing. His skin touching hers is like fire.

'Hey,' she says to Dolly, 'who's going along with Gabe this time?'

'Not me,' Dolly says. 'The last time was enough for me. If I could I'd never leave here, even for harvest.'

'Should I?' Jo asks, voice level and even. 'I mean, it might be nice to help. It feels like it's my turn.'

'Hey, Gabe, you want to take J with you? She's volunteering.'

He turns. 'Yeah, alright. If you want? Zay isn't allowed and you're not too keen, are you, Ho?'

Ho-jin shakes his head.

'Alright, cool. We'll probably go tomorrow,' he says to Jo and turns to Ho-jin, but his hand comes down, just for an instant, and strokes underneath her knee.

She eats half her food, then pulls back from the table. She can't concentrate on what Dolly is saying. She's already there, feet on the dash, talking about everything, teasing him, being teased. They'll have sex in the back seat. Sleep together in beds at the farmer's houses. She'll hide in the lorry at Denny's, that's a definite, but apart from that, it will be golden.

Jo walks out of the patch of light into the dark towards the bonds office, holding the bowl in front of her.

'Is that for Lia?'

She sees Nika has followed her. The girl is so quiet sometimes she doesn't even realise she's there.

'Yeah.'

Nika stares at the dark bonds office. 'Is she okay?'

'She's fine.' Jo looks around. She doesn't want anyone to see her slipping in—Ally told them Lia needed space.

'I'll come back and do the dishes with you in a bit, alright?'

Nika just stands there. 'I went out looking for Mum last night. I think I found her.'

The poor kid. Jo feels for her, she does, but she really can't stand here by the door holding this food for anyone to see.

'She'll come back soon, I'm sure she will. Let's talk about it later, okay?'

She knocks gently on the bonds office door, she doesn't want to wake Lia if she's sleeping.

'Yeah?'

'It's me.'

There's a long pause. Jo's about to say she can come back later but then, a shuffle.

'Come in.'

'Do you want to come in too?' she asks Nika, but she's already walking away.

Jo opens the door. Lia is sitting in the bed. From the light spilling through the door Jo can see her face is glimmering with sweat. It's hot in here, hotter than outside. Stuffy too—it smells like sickness.

She leaves the door open, sits on the end of the bed.

'Here,' she says, passing over the bowl, 'you should eat something.'

Lia takes it from her, begins wolfing down the food.

'Ally said you shouldn't eat. That you were too sick. But I thought …'

Lia looks at her, eyebrows creased, then keeps going. Soon the ceramic is shining clean. She places the bowl on the sheet covering her, looks into it like she can will it to refill.

'How are you feeling?'

'I'm not contagious any more,' Lia says. There're deep shadows under her eyes, which glint in a strange way.

'You still look pretty sick.'

'It's a punishment, because I didn't dive.'

Jo shakes her head. 'No way. You just need—'

'No, Jo,' Lia says. 'I know what this is.'

Maybe Lia is still feverish. Maybe she shouldn't have come. Ally might be disappointed if someone has seen her. She told everyone to leave Lia.

'You know what I was thinking today?' Lia says, voice quieter. 'If I wanted to leave, I couldn't.'

'You want to leave?'

'That's not what I'm saying. I'm saying, I can't. We can't. None of us. I mean, even getting to the main road would take a few days as long as you were sure you were going in the right direction. But I don't even know the right way— do you? Everything looks the same out there.'

'But everything here is so beautiful, so perfect.'

Lia doesn't look at her.

'The world is sick. The world is what hurt all of us.'

'You sound just like Ally.'

Jo doesn't know what to say to that. Lia is making it seem like sounding like Ally is a bad thing.

'Are you angry at her for trying to make you dive?'

'You don't get it. How could you possibly get it.' Lia still doesn't look at her. Jo wishes she could see her better, read her expression.

'Are you saying you want to leave?' Jo asks.

Lia's eyes shift back to Jo and sharpen.

'No!' She smiles and it's strange, quivering. She looks scared. 'You know I'm talking crap, right? I'm not saying I want to leave. Not at all.'

Jo takes her hand. 'I know. It's okay. I won't tell her. I know you don't mean it. In a few days you'll feel better. Do you want me to get your book or something?'

She follows Lia's eyes to the window. The tarp is still there.

'Maybe you can come and visit me again in the morning?'

'I'm going to go out with Gabe to the farms. But I'll try to come in before that, okay? Bring you some breakfast.'

'Okay. Yeah, just … okay, cool.'

Jo picks up the bowl. 'I think you'll be out of here tomorrow afternoon. The rest is doing you good. You look better than yesterday.'

Lia looks away, but nods.

Instead of heading back to the light and laughter, Jo cuts behind the kitchen. She places the bowl in the tub and goes to the courthouse. Slipping her hands into her pocket, she skims her fingertips over the heart-shaped pearl.

The courthouse is empty, but she'll have to be quick. Everyone is tired from last night, some of them might be early to bed. She sneaks down the hallway and under the gauze curtain. He'll know it was her. He'll know what she's trying to say. They'll laugh about it tomorrow on the road, joke about how goofy she is.

She's reaching into her pocket when something cracks beneath her. She trips. Falls hard on the floor, kneecaps on timber. She looks back. The rotten floorboard has broken off. Fallen into the gap beneath. Her toe is pounding. Big toenail bent up. A right-angle pointing towards her. Stupid. She touches it, winces. Then puts her fingers underneath, takes a breath, pushes it down with her thumb. She screams silently, mouth wide, eyes closed. If anyone else were around she wouldn't make a big deal, but she's alone so she can be melodramatic. She rubs her foot gingerly.

Gabe's floor, on the other hand, doesn't look great. She crawls over to the hole. This was meant to be a sweet, nice gesture. Now it feels foolish. Embarrassing. She reaches into the hole. If she can pull the board out, maybe she can put it back the way it was. Maybe it won't be too obvious.

She feels around, but her hands don't touch wood. They touch thin plastic. She grips it between two fingers, pulls it out. It's a ziplock sandwich bag. There's a strange little gadget inside. It looks like a remote control, though it's half the size, with a small screen and two silver knobs sticking out from the top. It doesn't belong here, she knows that.

In the moonlight through the window, the borrowed light from the kitchen area, she sees the silver bits aren't knobs. She can see the lines on them, the mesh beneath. They're microphones. There's a button with a red circle on it under the screen. It's a recorder.

She doesn't want to look. To check. To listen. But she has to now. She can't just put it back. She prays for the battery to be depleted. Surely it will be. The ziplock unclasps. The switch is there, on the side. On/Off. She switches it on. The screen lights up. Fake grey-blue.

She scrolls to recordings. A whole list in date order. But from over a year ago. She goes down the list, not knowing what she's looking for. Then she stops, takes a breath, presses play at random.

'Hey, so I've been here about two weeks now—' his voice, whispered, '—God, you would have no idea how hard it was to get this thing charged. So I had my first session with Ally, who seems like she's some kind of leader here. It was super strange, as in really whack—'

She presses pause. It's him. But it's not him. She goes to the next one. Hits play.

A swishing sound, like a pocket-call, and then—

'Hi, come in.' Ally's voice.

'Thanks, is it an okay time?'

'Of course it is, baby.'

She stops it. She can't listen to that. Not to Ally being betrayed, no. She scrolls further, until she is near the beginning of them all.

'Hey, so, it's me.' He sounds more awkward, like he's going to start laughing. 'So I made it here to Broome. This article better be fucking worth it, I'll tell you that. The heat, the flies. This place—Jesus Christ. I want a book deal, alright? I know, *Vice* doesn't publish books, but this will be your first. So … yeah, so I'm meeting up with this guy tomorrow, Matty, the one that Jim told me about. He says he knows where they are. I'll try to record it if I can. So Broome … I should describe it, shouldn't I? Broome is like—'

She stops it. She's heard something. The door. Wood on clunking wood. She flicks the recorder off. The grey-blue light vanishes. Her eyes are dim now, they can't adjust. She feels for the hole, throws the recorder down, reaches in.

She can hear someone coming. It could be one of the others. Valentine or Greta, or maybe Ho-jin. They might not come down here. They might just get into bed and she can sneak past them.

She searches for the board. If she can put it back the way it was, he needn't know. Her fingertips touch soft wood. She grabs it, tries to angle it out of the hole.

The creak of boards. They aren't stopping in the main room. They're turning down the corridor.

She pulls the wood half out, then her sweating hands slip and she drops it onto the dirt underneath. A dull thud. The footsteps don't pause. She clasps her hands tight. They are covered in red dirt. He'll see. He'll know.

But they continue past the room. She can see the shape move past the gauze. Dolly. If she had turned to look she'd have seen Jo, squatting next to a hole in Gabe's floor. But she doesn't. She hears Dolly go into the room next door, the creak of the mattress. A sigh.

Jo reaches down again. Silent. She grips the wood. It comes out of the hole. She holds it with both hands. It's split, almost completely, but if she places it just right, it won't be visible.

She holds the wood tight. Puts it into the gap. It fits, almost. The edge sticks up above the corner of the board next to it. She pushes her fingers into it. If she lets go, it might break in half. She pushes harder and, with a squeak, it falls into place.

'Gabe?' Dolly calls. 'What are you doing?'

Jo jumps up and walks down the corridor. She rushes to her bed and dives into it. As she does, something clatters to the floor. She grabs it, holds it tight in her palm. The heart-shaped pearl. She pulls the sheet over her head, pretends to sleep.

CHAPTER 31

Jo watches Gabe load the lorry. The empty petrol canisters, his bag, the pearls—cleaned to sparkling with sea water. His muscles clench under his singlet. She still wants him, even though he has turned alien, monstrous. The man who has looked to her three times now, his secret smiles changing, growing concerned. She doesn't know this man. She knows the magazine he works for. Smug. It's all 'Meet the Midget Strippers of Burma' or 'I Lived on the Streets of San Jose for Six Months and Here's What Happened'. How will he turn what they've built here into a freak show? 'There's a Group of Free-Diving, Pearl-Thieving Outcasts in Outback Australia and I Became One of Them'.

He's opened the passenger door, put his water bottle inside. The one they shared on the beach last week. He opens the glove box, snaps it closed, looks over his shoulder at her. A darting glance, like he's been caught out.

Like there's something he didn't want her to see. She might not have noticed it yesterday, but now, everything he does looks suspicious. Strange. He throws his bag on the tray, rubs his hands together and comes towards her: it's exaggerated, overblown, to make her smile. It's an act. This man is an actor. She wonders if there is another microphone on him, if he's recorded any of their conversations. If he is recording her now. There are no lumps in his pockets.

'Got your stuff?' His eyes are searching, looking for a bag.

Will she be part of the story: 'How I Joined an Off-The-Grid Community and Got Lucky'?

'I don't think I'm going to come.'

She watches his reaction. The crease between the eyebrows doesn't seem fake. The hurt.

'I'm sorry,' she says, unable to stop the warmth creeping into her voice, 'I want to. It's just …'

There is a crescent of red underneath each fingernail. She balls her fists. Presses them between her calves and the wooden seat.

'I don't feel right. My throat is all closed up. My head feels too full.' Three truths. 'I think I've caught what Lia has.' One lie.

He looks around, then bends, kisses her on the top of the head. She flinches.

'Don't.' Her fists clench tighter. 'You'll catch it too.'

'That's a pity,' he says. 'Honestly, it's all I've been thinking about since yesterday.'

Looking at him, it plays out again for her: endless hours of driving and talking, sex in the back seat. Time alone. She wants to take it back, say she'll come.

'I'm going to go say bye to Ally, alright? Have a think about it. If you don't feel that bad you can just sleep in the car or something? Up to you.' His smile is self-conscious. 'I don't want to let it go.'

She waits until he is out of sight before she approaches the car. She's not sure what it could be in the glove department that he doesn't want her to see. Another microphone? A notepad? A phone?

The plastic of the catch is hot as she hooks her fingers in. If there's nothing, maybe she can pretend that there's nothing under his floor either.

She opens the glove box. There's no microphone, or phone, or anything. Just some papers. The beat-up user manual for the lorry. Letters.

The handwriting on the front is shockingly familiar. It's her own.

Briena's name and address on one, her dad's on another, and *Sorcha + Yan* written on the third. He's kept them. Ready to reprint for his article. She snaps the glove box closed.

*

She doesn't watch him drive away. Instead, she goes out to where she found Nika that night, where no one seems to go. She sits by the spindly undergrowth, where she can feel alone. She wishes she could go to the water, disappear under the surface. Everything would be clearer there. But she can't go. The others are at the water. His secret is now hers. Pretending everything is okay, even just for a few hours, even just in the moments of surfacing, would be lying. Part of her wants to go back to his room, take the recorder out. She wants to listen to every word. Hear the real Gabe, the one with the nervous laugh, the self-conscious inflection. Then, she could throw it out into the ocean, let the sea swallow it. But that wouldn't solve the problem.

The spindly plants bite. The sun is getting high. Heat drips from her skin.

She knows what she has to do. She forces herself to sit. To stand. Then she heads back towards Rossack, knocks on the door to Galbraith's Store.

CHAPTER 32

'Where were you this morning?' Jo asks Lia. They are lying under the tree as usual. The sky is a congealed white. There'll be rain tonight.

It's been a week since Gabe left, since her talk with Ally, and things have taken on a new normal. She knows he won't be back for a while and so she lets herself believe he'll never be back.

Yesterday, Lia came out of the bonds office. That strange glinting presence that Jo had seen, the doubter, the questioner, must have been the fever. When she came to dinner last night, Lia had shadows under her eyes, her cheeks were hollowed, but she was smiling.

She hadn't come diving this morning. Instead she'd sat fully dressed on one of the rocks, her eyes cast down, not even watching. The last time Jo had surfaced, giddy with wonder-love, the rock had been deserted.

'I went for a walk,' Lia says.

'A walk?'

'I need to get strong again to dive.'

Jo props herself on her elbow. 'I'm sorry I didn't visit more. Ally said it was better for you to be alone.'

'If Ally didn't want you to come it's best that you didn't. It was what I deserved. I was lucky. A week isn't long really.'

'It is. I think I was only in the bonds office a week and it felt like a lifetime.'

Lia shakes her head. 'Nah. Dolly was in there for two weeks apparently. Zay for almost three.'

'What? Why?'

'Everyone goes there when they first arrive.'

'Were they sick?'

'I guess so. Dolly was withdrawing, I think.'

'And Zay?'

'He's lucky she didn't make him go back there after the farmer.'

There it is again. That flicker. She's talking about Ally like she is doling out punishments, rather than helping. When Jo was in the bonds office, it was like Ally was bringing her back to life. Ally had doted on her, bombarded her with more love and affection than Jo could ever remember experiencing before. How could that be a bad thing?

But then Lia looks at Jo with such tenderness. Touches her arm. 'Are you missing him?' she asks.

'No,' she says, because she's not.

Ally had been surprised. Jo's voice had been breathless as she told her everything. The attraction. The sex. What she'd found. Ally's face had turned white. Bloodless. Jo had been sure Ally could see everything, but not this.

She'd shown Ally the place and Ally had taken the recorder. She'd gone back to Galbraith's Store. When Jo had tried to follow, Ally had stopped near the doorway. She'd turned stiffly to look at Jo, clasping the microphone in its little plastic bag. Jo held out her hand, expecting Ally's face to be folded up with pain and betrayal. It wasn't. Jo's hand hovered between them. The way Ally had looked at her. Her expression was totally smooth. Unreadable.

'That will be him,' Lia says now.

'Who?' Jo asks. But then she hears it too. The faintest rumble. A car. The lorry.

'But doesn't he usually go for longer? Last time it was two weeks.'

Lia lifts her shoulders from the earth. 'Depends.'

Jo tucks her knees under her and watches as he pulls up. Watches him get out of the lorry, the others coming forth to greet him, hugs and grins and whacks on the back. Lia doesn't move, so she doesn't either. As long as she's around others, they won't need to talk. She'll wait for Ally to see him first.

Her hurt has scabbed over, turned brittle.

She watches as Ally emerges, waits for the still anger, for loud words. But instead she sees Ally's face lighting up with warmth, her arms outstretched and opening. They hug, then they chat. Gabe gives her a grey backpack from the tray. Jo looks closer. Nothing in Ally's movements looks angry or hurt. The opposite.

*

All day, Ally is still pretending. Jo watches her smile, looks for hints, but there are none. Maybe she's not pretending. Maybe all is forgiven.

At dinner, Gabe glances over the table, trying to catch Jo's eye, but she keeps him only in her periphery. She's not sure she can look at him without the betrayal sticky and burning in her throat. Instead, she keeps her eyes glued on Ally. After the meal she is the first to her feet, to take dishes, to begin clearing. If she stays busy, stays around people, maybe she can avoid this storm. Something has to happen. She's sure of it. He betrayed them. He can't stay here, keeping on pretending.

When she leans over to take his bowl, Gabe continues his story to Zay about someone named Mark and Joan, but his hand caresses the back of her knee. The touch sends cold bristles through her, brings back the sticky burning. She stiffens. His hand drops. She moves on to the next bowl.

*

The next day the wind lifts, fills the air orange with dust. She stays in the courthouse, close to Lia, so there is no moment for a secret touch or a question. She watches Lia read.

On rainy days, Josephine and her mum would read. They would lay on the couch, her cheek pressed onto her mother's soft woollen jumper. Their gas heater would tick on and off, making the room smell like burnt dust. Her mum would read Harry Potter out aloud, a different voice for Hagrid and for Dumbledore and for Dobby the House Elf. Josephine would try to follow the words along, but she'd get muddled and just close her eyes and listen and she'd be able to see the worlds come to life in her mind.

Lia gets to the final page, closes her eyes, then turns the book back to the beginning and starts over.

'You're going to read it again straight away?' she asks.

Lia doesn't look up. 'It's the only book I brought with me. I've read it five or six times already.'

'That doesn't bother you?'

Lia doesn't reply. The wind beats at the windows.

'You know, I think Gabe has other books.'

'I like this one. It's mine.'

There is a wooden clunk and Jo holds her breath. She turns away. If he were to catch her eye, nod his head to his room, what would she do? Lia looks up, puts the book down. Straightens.

'Hi, babies.' It's Ally.

Jo turns around. At last, she's come to tell her what the plan is. How they are going to make everything better again.

'Hi.' Lia grin-grimaces.

'J,' Ally says, 'Gabe and I are going to go out tonight. Rain's coming.'

'Harvest?'

'No,' Ally says.

'You're returning?' Lia asks.

Ally nods. 'Do you want to come, J? We don't need everyone.'

Jo is nodding though she doesn't know what returning means, she just needs an end to all this.

'I'd love to come as well, if that's okay,' Lia says. Ally considers her.

'To make up for last time,' Lia says.

'Alright, as long as you're feeling strong enough, baby. Don't feel pressure.'

'I'm better now.'

When Ally leaves, Jo asks Lia what returning is.

'We have to do it sometimes, so the pearlers don't clue onto what we're doing. It's why we keep the shells. They only open them every two years, and so we try and get in at least a few months before that. Then we put them back, slot them in, so that when they open them later they just think they are defunct, pearl-less.'

Jo hadn't thought of that. 'But isn't it obvious they've been opened? The knife marks and stuff.'

'Dunno,' Lia says, 'I think they are so covered in algae and barnacles by the time they hoist them out it's not super obvious. It's been working for us so far.'

Lia goes back to her book. Chapter one, beginning again. But Jo can see her eyes aren't moving, they are just resting on the first page.

Jo lies down again, closes her eyes and listens to the beating hammer of the wind thumping louder and louder.

CHAPTER 33

That night, when they set off, the wind is so high she can barely hear. The sky is a slow-motion mushroom cloud. The rain hasn't erupted yet but the wind is drenched.

Jo huddles next to Lia on the tray. Lia is gripping her torch in her hand, not speaking, eyes darting at the sky. Jo can see inside the lorry through the back window, where Ally is driving and Gabe is sipping a can of tonic. They're laughing, smiling, like everything is normal.

'Is it going to be safe? This doesn't feel safe,' Jo says.

'I don't know … I wouldn't want to dive tonight.'

Every bump in the road and the bags of gutted oysters clack together.

'But you will, right?' Jo asks. 'If we go together we'll be okay.'

'Did you tell her?' Lia's staring at her now, voice loud from her lips but reaching Jo in a whisper.

'About?'

'Did you tell her about you and Gabe?'

'No, we aren't—'

'I was awake that night you went into his room.'

Jo looks into the lorry. There's no way they can hear them. She can barely even hear herself. Lia grips her hand, speaks close.

'Be careful, okay? Promise me you'll be careful. Don't tell her about you and Gabe. Don't trust her.'

'Ally? But how could I not? What do you mean?'

They're getting closer now, passing houses, with storm window shutters sealed tight.

'You're smart, Jo.'

J, she wants to correct her.

'If it's working for you, fine,' Lia goes on. 'If you can't be where you belong, then fine. But don't lie to yourself. Don't let her lies be yours.'

It's too loud for Ally to hear, but Jo is sure she will. She will hear someone saying something like this about her.

'It's him that's lying,' Jo says. 'Gabe has been lying. He's trying to ruin it for all of us. We made utopia and he's—'

Lia is shaking her head, holding her tighter. 'Where do you think it all goes, the money from the pearls? Where do you think it goes? Just be smart and be careful, alright?'

'Alright,' she says, because what else can she say with Lia's eyes such glinting strobes? It's not right, she can feel it. Nothing about tonight is right.

Ally is slowing the lorry and Jo's fingers are pins and needles and Lia's flashing grin has come back and she's jumping down from the tray and she's pushing something into her pocket.

'You girls alright?' Ally shouts, coming around to them. And it's still her, warmth and softness, and Lia is standing straight and ready next to her like what she said was just the storm and Jo never heard any of it.

'We're ready.' Lia holds a hand out to Jo and she jumps down from the tray.

'We'll have to go the back way, alright? It's further but safer. That guy could have got us last time.'

Gabe joins them and they each take a bucket and begin the walk. Gabe falls into step next to Jo, Lia ahead of them and Ally leading the way up front. He's watching her as they walk and she can't help but slip looks back at him.

'Are you okay?' he asks. 'Is something wrong?'

'Nervous,' she says.

Gabe squeezes her hand, his fingers hot and wet. 'Let's talk tomorrow, okay? Meet early on the shore?'

'Alright,' she says. She'll tell him. If Ally won't, she has to. She's looking forward to being under the water, letting this confusion fade.

'Good.' He laughs and it sounds strange, almost drunken.

Ally takes them to a low cliff further up the beach. They can see two boats now, two guards, with spotlights on their boats. The bobbing grid of buoys is so far away it's barely visible. It's too far, and if they surface the guards will see them.

Lia pats her chest. 'My torch. I must have left it in the tray. Sorry, guys, I'll just run back, I'll be two secs, alright?'

'Okay.' Ally is looking at the guards.

Jo watches Lia as she runs off. She was sure she saw her wearing the torch. In the shadows, Lia stops, turns to look at Jo, then runs on.

'It's too far out here. Let's go to the other cliff,' Gabe calls against the wind. His eyes look glazed. He rubs his hands together like he's trying to get the feeling back in them.

'We can do it.' Ally gives him one of the bags and pulls her dress over her head. 'Quick,' she yells. 'I'm coming too this time, babies. It's so loud we don't even need to wait for thunder.'

Jo pulls her shorts off, tugs her t-shirt over her head. The wind catches it and it soars off, a black bat.

'I feel strange,' Gabe says, but Ally must not hear him in the wind.

'Ready?' she yells, hair flapping from her face. Gabe picks up the bag, looks at it like he's forgotten what it's for.

'Wait, Lia will be back in a minute,' Jo yells.

'She can follow. One!' Ally steps to the edge, Gabe stands next to her, Jo takes a deep slow breath. 'Two! Three!'

Jo's muscles flex to jump, but something seizes her arm. She hovers, stumbles, watches Gabe jump. She barely hears the splash.

Ally is gripping her arm, fingers digging into flesh.

'What?' Jo yells.

Ally doesn't let go. Her fingers hold tight. The sky flashes around her but her face is stony.

Jo looks into the water. She can't see anything. Not the tiniest glimmer of light underneath. 'What's happening?' she asks. 'Why aren't we jumping?'

'Just wait. We will in a second, baby.'

Jo looks out at the water, at the distant torchlights gliding around. There is no light under the sea, no little anglerfish under the surface. Gabe's torch isn't on.

'You're hurting me,' she says, and Ally's grip loosens and lets go.

'He's not coming up,' Jo says, eyes searching the water. There's nothing. Something is wrong. Something is wrong. Something is wrong.

'Wait,' Ally says, and Jo can barely hear her. 'He knows what he's doing. Just wait.'

Jo takes a breath. Ally reaches for her again but Jo is too quick. She jumps.

Brick wall water slap. She's ready for it this time. She lets the momentum pull her down. Pushes the torch on. There he is. A black shape. Writhing thrash. Big bubbles rising. She goes deeper, kicks down. Her heart a drum-roll thud, too fast.

She reaches him. His eyes are white slits. His nose is shooting red lines upwards.

Her lungs shudder, chest jerks.

Arms around his middle, he's not fighting, he's slack weight. Heavy. She kicks.

Pushes.

Hands gripping fabric, legs kicking. Through the red water towards the surface. She can see it. The surface. Where the black is grey and wink-flashing. Each time the flashes get darker. Everything gets darker. He is so heavy. The light is turning shadow. The surface is there, she knows. But it's only black.

*

Josephine plopped to the surface, taking a gulp of breath.

'I told you!' she screamed. 'I told you I'd jump!'

Her mother's face clenched with exasperation. 'I can't come in and get you, Josephine! You know I can't with Jamie on me.'

It was icy in the water, seaweed slicking against her toes.

'I want Hobnobs!'

'Good choices, Josephine. Remember? You're a big sister now. Get back on board.'

'No!'

Her mother took a breath, then turned away from her. The silent treatment. Josephine knew this trick.

'Mum!'

Her mother didn't look up, her eye to the viewfinder of her camera. One hand on the focus, the other on the baby carrier, patting a soft rhythm on Jamie's back.

'Mum!'

A distant growl. Thunder. Jamie's chin wrinkles grew deeper. Her mum looked at the clouds.

'You need to come up now, my love. A storm's coming.'

'No!'

It was cold and wet and she'd jumped off the boat like she'd said she would and her mum didn't even care.

Her mum started loosening the ropes to adjust the sail, ignoring her again. She loved Jamie more. Ever since he'd come, her mum always ignored her.

Josephine gripped her fists tight and screamed. Then two things happened so fast it took a second for her mind to untangle. Her mother straightened, gasping, looking around at her, and the wind gusted fierce, smacking the loosened sail into her mum's forehead. Charlotte fell with a slap into the water, Jamie in the carrier on her chest.

Josephine looked at the sail whipping back and forth. The boat was empty. The thunder growled again. She dived after her mother. She saw her sinking in her woollen coat, her dark hair spidering around her, the bundle still attached to her chest, blood floating from her forehead.

She dived deeper. Her hands were gripping fabric, her legs were kicking.

Through the red water.

*

'Breathe.' Something soft on her mouth. Twinkling stars in her eyes.

She pulled. She kept pulling the dead weight.

'J, breathe.' Lungs puffed, chest full. She coughs, chokes, rolls to her side and coughs again. Cutting salt water unplugs and runs from her mouth, down her chin.

A warm hand on her back, rubbing. 'It's okay, baby, you're okay.'

Gabe. Where is Gabe?

She heaves in a breath, looks around. There he is near the shore, a crumpled thing. She crawl-drags towards him.

'It's okay, baby,' Ally coos.

Up close she can see the blood. It's dripping from his nose, from his ears and from his eyes. She grips his shoulders, pulls him onto his back. She pushes on his chest, remembers the way they were taught at school. His head to the side, pink water dribbles out. She puts her mouth to his, tastes blood, squeezes his nose, puffs deep. One, gasp, two, gasp, three, gasp, four. Nothing.

'It's okay, baby.'

Again—one, two, three, four. Then he splutters and she turns his head to the side and it's a pink fountain of spray coming out.

'Gabe?' she screams. 'Gabe?'

His hand comes up, clutches her arm.

'Are you okay?'

'Yeah,' he croaks, and coughs again, splutters the pink water.

They can't stay. Gabe manages to stand and he stumbles between Jo and Ally as they walk to the lorry. Lia isn't there. Ally looks around for her, but Jo knew she wouldn't be.

They pull Gabe into the back seat and Ally drives and it's silent inside the cab. Jo has Gabe's face in her lap and she stares at his chest and watches it move and remembers. She remembers her mother, floating in the water. It isn't a glimmer memory like the ones she found with Ally. It's solid.

When they pull off the road onto the dirt track, Ally says, 'The others will be so upset.'

'Yeah, they will,' Jo says.

'I'll talk to them. Explain it.'

'Good.'

When they pull in, Jo tries to lift Gabe and his eyes roll around under the lids then slide open.

'Gabe?'

'I'm okay,' he says, then shudders. 'I can walk.'

He manages to sit up, but as he steps out from the lorry he stumbles and falls on top of her. His weight lifts. Ally is taking his other arm.

'Hush, angel,' she says to him. 'It's alright, put your weight on us. We'll take care of you.'

It's like he thinks he's walking on a boat, leaning from side to side to try to make up for the tides. They stagger him into the courthouse. Jo looks over, half-expecting Lia to be there, in her bed. But it's empty. Her book is on her pillow. Not left open to a page like normal, but closed.

'Go back to sleep,' Ally says. She's talking to Ho-jin, who has sat up in bed, wide-eyed.

They get Gabe around the corner and walk him to his cell. This time, they side-step the busted board and lay him on the mattress.

'Maybe we should have taken him to a hospital or something?' Jo says. She hadn't even thought about it until now. She'd forgotten about hospitals.

'He'll be okay tomorrow. Won't you?' she asks.

Gabe nods, then stops like it hurts him. 'I'm fine,' he says.

'Come and see me for a session tomorrow, J, alright?' Ally says.

'Alright,' Jo says.

Ally turns and leaves them alone.

Jo slips into bed next to Gabe, wrapping her arms around him.

'Are you sure you're okay?' she asks.

'Mmm,' he says and everything is still and she has so much to think about, but all that fear is pumping out of her and she can barely think of anything but being glad for his warmth next to her.

CHAPTER 34

Jo wakes up to Gabe's open eyes, the bars of light from the window reflected in his irises.

'You okay?' she asks.

'Yeah. Last night was something, wasn't it?'

'I'm so relieved you're alright.'

He squeezes her closer. 'My little saviour.'

She breathes him in, rests her cheek on the rasping hair of his chest. It sticks with sweat, but she doesn't care.

'I can't believe I panicked though. I didn't think I would, after all that time.'

She sits up. 'No,' she says. 'Gabe, you didn't panic. There was something wrong with you.'

'What?'

'I don't know,' she whispers. 'But it was her. Ally. She did it on purpose.'

He smiles at her like she's kidding, then his brow creases. 'I think you swallowed too much sea water as well.'

'No, Gabe. I'm telling you. She did something.'

'Why would she do that?' He puts his hand to his head, goes to sit up too but sways a little. 'She has no reason to do that.'

'Here, lie down,' she says. 'I think you need to rest a bit longer.'

'Yeah,' he says and lies back. She takes a drink from the water bottle next to his bed. Her throat is still aching-dry. She passes the bottle to him.

He takes it, strokes her arm. 'You should go, someone might see you in here. Maybe they already have.'

She nods. 'I'll come and check on you, alright?'

*

Everything outside feels artificial. Like she's on a film set. Or in a dream. She can hear them laughing, out in the ocean. She heads towards them. Up to the point and then down the slope to the water. Valentine and Greta are on the far side, Ho-jin and Dolly are on the closer rock, and Zay's head is bobbing above the surface. Without Lia, it feels like there are too few of them.

She wades into the water, intending to swim out to them, but the tide pulls at her knees and the smell of it makes her stop, clench tight. She doesn't want to disappear into the ocean now. The water is not a safe place.

What she saw is the truth. She is sure of that. The memory was right there, barely hidden. She'd looked away from it for so long it was easy to believe she'd forgotten. She can remember her mother in the water, remember trying to pull her out, but she was too heavy. That still little bundle pressed to her mother's chest and Josephine only strong enough to pull her mother's chin above the water. She remembers the tourist boat that fished them out.

The guilt of it settles on her shoulders. She was throwing a tantrum because she was jealous of Jamie. She delayed them heading home when the storm started. She'd screamed, that's why her mum had looked around, missed seeing the sail catching the wind. Her fault.

The other memory, of her mother locking her out of the house. That was true too, but it came after. Her mother blamed her, *your fault*, she'd say when she was drunk. That night, standing outside in the cold while her mother cried into the cot, that was real. What came next was confusing. Ally's memories were there. The glowy ones, where her mother was a monster, did monstrous things. Among them were other murky memories. Flashes of torches, close faces, someone's warm arms picking her up from the back fence, drying the cold tears from her cheeks. The feelings are easier to remember: embarrassment, shame. Ally told her a story, told her it was truth. But her mother was never a murderer. That memory was false, implanted by Ally and her soft low voice. It was Jo who caused Jamie's death, and her mother had blamed her for it. No wonder her father had lied, told her she wasn't there during the accident. He was trying to shield her from what she had done. But part of her always knew.

'J.' Zay is walking up from the water, his face glossed with dive-bliss. 'Are you alright?'

'I'm okay,' she says. 'Last night was ... yeah. Not great.'

'I know.' He comes to stand next to her, his body glimmering with sliding droplets. 'I can't believe she did that.'

'Ally told you?'

He nods, rubbing a hand over his hair. 'We all spoke about it this morning. It's a pity. I'm angry with her, yes, but I'll miss her.'

'Miss her?'

'Of course.'

'You mean Lia?'

'Yeah.'

'Why are you angry with Lia?'

Zay wraps an arm around her and pulls her in. 'You are so kind, J. You never want to see the bad in people.'

'Why are you angry?' she says again. She doesn't want to play.

'We all are. She abandoned you, ran off, and poor Gabe pushed his body too far to make up for it and got hurt.'

She takes a step away from Zay.

'Are you coming in?' he asks.

'No,' she says.

'Okay, I will see you later.' He wades towards the others.

The sun is out, like the storm never happened. The day is mild. She needs to think. She needs to be alone.

*

Jo goes to the only place she can think of: the spindly bushes where she'd found Nika crying that night. She sits and wraps her arms around her legs, digs her forehead into her kneecaps.

Ally is a liar.

Lia is gone.

But not just gone. She ran. She was afraid. She knew she couldn't get away unless she faked it, came along with them.

Ally tried to hurt Gabe. There's no denying that. Even if she did it for them, to save them from what he might do, it didn't matter. She's not sure how, but Ally tried to hurt Gabe. Maybe more than hurt.

Ally is a liar.

Gabe is a liar too.

Everything divine from these past months has twisted sour.

She hears a snap from the bushes and jumps, afraid it is Ally, suddenly worse than a snake or spider. But no, she remembers the Ally from the bonds office, washing her skin. But then there was Lia in the bonds office, eyes scared when she looked at Jo. Lia's hand gripping hers, talking about the money from the pearls.

Grain. Petrol. Fruit and vegetables. But no, she remembers now, the fruit and vegetables are the castoffs, removed from the conveyer belts. They were given those for free. So just the grain. And enough petrol for the generator, which only powers the fridge, and for the lorry.

Ally, when she first saw Gabe after Jo had told her. Smiling, wrapping her arms around him, taking that bag. It was grey, a backpack, with a red zipper.

Another rustle. She starts. There is definitely someone in there. Or something. She peers into the undergrowth. A shape moves towards her. Small and thin limbed. Nika.

'So is this where you go during the day?' Jo asks.

'Sometimes.' Nika pulls herself out from the bushes, bats at her hair to get the leaves out. She scoots over to sit cross-legged in front of Jo.

'You okay?' she asks.

'Yeah.'

'Did Lia leave?'

Jo nods.

'She just ran off?'

'Yeah.'

'Okay.'

Nika fiddles with a stick, brushing patterns into the dirt. The pattern she is making is like the one she made when they shucked the pearls that day, before everything went so badly wrong. She'd said something about her mother, and then Ally had come and Nika had left. Jo would have thought Ally would play mother for her. Ally would be teaching her things, caring for her. But she remembers her hand on Nika's shoulder. The way the girl had shrunk into herself, a terrified insect. She thinks about how Nika only ever speaks to her when they are alone. When anyone else is around, she goes silent.

'Why do you look for your mum when we go out?'

Nika's stick keeps brushing. 'I wanted to find her.'

'But Ally said—' She stops. Ally said that Nika's mother had left. But Ally is a liar. 'The other day, you said you found her. What did you mean?'

The stick stops.

'I thought she'd left. That she was going to come back for you. But if you found her … then, I mean, well … where is she?'

Nika looks at her. She's blinking rapidly again, like her mind is whirring. 'She wanted to leave. She realised it was a mistake, that we should keep going, get to Yia Yia's.'

'Yia Yia?'

'My grandma. We were meant to go to my grandparents' house.'

'But she didn't go?'

Nika stands, takes her hand. They walk away from the settlement. The glare stings Jo's eyes. She remembers the photo of Larissa. Dark arched eyebrows, strands of hair escaping from her ponytail, that maternal look of pride as she stood next to her daughter.

'I woke up and she wasn't there,' Nika says. 'Dolly and the others were meant to be keeping an eye on me. But I snuck away. Mum never left me alone. Something bad was happening. I snuck down to the water. Mum didn't like the diving. It scared her. Ally said she had to but she said no. Ally was with her. She was holding her under. Mum wasn't fighting back but I don't know why.'

'Her hands were tied,' Jo says.

'They took me away when I started screaming. They made me stay in that bonds office room and locked the door. They made me stay there for so long in the dark. Ally tried to convince me she was a bad mum, that she'd hurt me. But it wasn't true. None of those things she was saying was true.'

They've stopped near the boab tree. Jo looks up. It's huge, maybe the biggest one she's seen. It's got a ridge running down its trunk and for one horrible moment Jo thinks maybe Nika means her mother is inside the tree. It's large enough for a person to stand in.

But then she looks down.

The sun winks from the pattern of pearl shell. Organised in sizes and shapes to make a mosaic of flowers on top of the grave.

CHAPTER 35

Jo goes through the courthouse door, the mattress room, around and down the hallways, to Gabe's room. He looks pale. The skin in the corners of his mouth has the slightest tint of blue.

'Are you alright?' she asks.

'Yeah,' he says, but his eyes aren't right. They are grey, watery.

'We need to go.' The panic makes it easy to say it.

He smiles. 'Huh?'

'Gabe, I found your recorder. I know why you're really here. Ally does too. That's why she did it. It's okay, I'm not angry now. But we need to go. It's not safe.'

He pales even more. 'Shit.'

'It's fine.'

He puts his hands over his face, muffled. 'I should have gotten rid of it.'

'It doesn't matter. I promise, it's all good. I'm not mad.' She looks around. There's no shadows in Dolly's or Zay's rooms, but she whispers, 'You were right. This place is crazy. I can see it now.'

He turns to her, shakes his head. 'No, no. J, you don't need to say that. I wanted you to know. Ally too. It's been so horrible, this lie on my shoulders. I've been wanting to tell you both, but I was too chickenshit. I'm surprised you can even look at me.'

She takes his hand, it's clammy. Cold.

'I was awful. Everything was always half a joke. I thought I was smarter than everyone. It's so lonely thinking like that, taking nothing seriously except for your own ambition. But I need you to know, what I told you wasn't a lie. That stuff with my babysitter, it's true. Feeling so lonely and anxious in New York. None of it was a lie.'

'It's okay, it doesn't matter. We can talk about this later. Right now we need to go. It's not safe here.'

He winces. At first she thinks it's in response to what she said, but he balls his fist, presses it to his shoulder.

'Are you okay? What's wrong?'

'Nothing.' He swallows the words, puffs his breath in and out, eyes squeezed shut. Hand squeezing on his left shoulder.

'Is it your heart? Oh god, we really should have taken you to a hospital.'

'No,' he says. 'I'll be fine by tomorrow. My heart is strong now, Ally fixed it. That's how I realised that I was so wrong about everything, that somehow my smug asshole self had stumbled onto this—'

'She's a fraud! That's why you came here, right?'

'No, no. That's what I'm telling you. I was wrong. She showed me the truth.'

Jo sits back on her heels. His last recording was over a year ago. She should have realised.

'We have to go,' she whispers. 'It's not safe here. I know what happened to Nika's mum.'

Gabe shakes his head. 'That was an accident. Ally told us Larissa panicked. Ally was trying to help her. But she gave in to fear. Ally tried to pull her up, but she attacked her. If Larissa had trusted, not given into fear, she wouldn't have drowned.'

She'll just take him. Load him in the car against his will if she has to. They have to get out of here.

'Can you come with me?' she asks. 'I want to show you something.'

'I don't feel great.'

'You'll feel better soon.' She wraps an arm underneath him, pulls. He tries to sit. His eyes loll. She pulls him with all the strength she can muster, hands slipping on skin. He is too heavy; the mattress is too low to the ground.

'I just need to rest for a bit longer, okay?' he says.

She lets go and he slumps onto the mattress, a dead weight. She's sweating, skin prickly, forehead slick.

Nika is waiting out in the hallway, her legs crossed and head down.

'Can you help?'

Together, they manage to get him to his feet. Nika squats on the mattress, pushing, while Jo pulls him up from under his arms. But he writhes against them.

'I want to stay here, I need to lie down.'

'Come on,' she tries to say it gently, but it comes out as a grunt.

He wobbles again, then he's being sick, stomach lurching against them, breathing heavily. Only water comes up.

'Sorry,' he says, and he's shaking.

'This isn't going to work,' Nika says.

She's right. They hold him and try to soften the collapse as much as possible. They roll him onto the mattress. Jo pulls her t-shirt off; it's wet with his sick. Nika follows her as she goes to her bed, replaces it with one Lia left behind.

'What now?'

'We'll have to get someone to help us. Zay will be able to take his weight. Even with just Dolly I think we'd be able to do it. We'll find a way to distract Ally—'

'Are you stupid?'

'What?'

'They won't help you. They're all under her spell. You're the only one who wasn't here when they hurt Mum. That's why you're the only one I can trust. I try to pretend I don't exist in front of the others, but you're different.'

Is she? She's been falling under Ally's spell too, and Nika's had to watch.

'I'm sorry,' she says. 'You've been ... I should have realised. I've had everything confused.'

'Just please don't tell them. They'll tell her and then ...' Nika clenches her eyes shut. Her mouth is tight, but her chin wobbles. No child her age should have to hold in that much panic.

Nika is right. If they believed Ally about Lia, about Larissa. After all she's done, they've just stood by. Jo needs to show them. They need to find a way to show them who she really is, then they can all get out. They can all leave.

'How's the patient?'

It's Ally's voice. She's there, standing at the doorway, her face that calm reflective blank. Jo puts a hand on Nika's shoulder. She can feel a tremble ripple through the girl.

'He's asleep.' Jo keeps her voice even, normal. 'He was actually just sick on me. Before he fell asleep.'

'That's no good.' A mother's coo. Her face twisting concern, but that blankness underneath. Cold. How had she not seen it before?

'I've been waiting for you, baby,' Ally says, 'you were going to come and talk with me, remember? I've been waiting all morning.'

Jangle-twists all through Jo's veins. She keeps her body still.

'Oh, I'm sorry, I got distracted. Erm …' She looks at Nika, but the girl's face only reflects the panic in Jo's blood. She looks away. 'Okay, well, I'll come in just a second, alright? Nika's helping me to pick a new top to put on, and she's got a bit of sick on her too. So we'll sort out that, and then I'll come straight over, alright?'

Ally smiles. 'Of course.' She clicks shut the door.

They stand. Listen. There is no shuffle of feet.

'Oh, did it get in your ear, that's so gross.'

Nika can't speak.

'It's alright, okay? I know it's gross but we'll go to the water, just quickly, and get you cleaned up, okay? But just quickly.'

Shuffles in the dirt. She's going. They stare at each other.

'We have to go now,' Nika whispers, 'right now.'

'How? We can't just wander off—even if we get a kilometre away she'll see us. There's nowhere to hide.'

'The bushes.'

'They'll look there!'

'We have to go.'

'We need the lorry. And we need Gabe.'

Nika's shaking her head, her whisper pitchy. 'We have to go now. She's not stupid.'

'Neither are we.' And the fake calm works. They need to show the others who Ally is. Then they can get the lorry, get Gabe. Everything.

'Look, I would bet you anything that she is hoarding money,' Jo says. 'That's what Lia thought too. It will be in Galbraith's. In that backpack. We just need to show them.'

'How?'

She tries to breathe, tries to think. 'I don't know. I guess ... shit, alright, I go in and we wait, what? Five minutes, ten tops. Then you call out for her, say you have to show her something, something bad has happened or something, distract her, even if it's just for like two minutes. I'll find the money, show the others. Then they'll have to believe it. We'll get the lorry, get out of here, call an ambulance. We'll call your grandma, your yia yia. They've been looking for you; you've been in the papers. We can get out of here. It will be okay.'

Nika looks at her, and for once her gaze is steady.

CHAPTER 36

Josephine Ainsley is knocking on the door to Galbraith's Store. She is going to keep her shit together. She isn't going to forget who she is.

'J-baby? Is that you?'

'It's me.'

She tries to keep her movements normal, casual, as she walks into the room. Sits on the sofa. She can't look at Ally.

'You're not looking at me, J.'

She fidgets with her hair. 'Last night was weird.'

'It was. It was a lot to take in, wasn't it? Gabe's betrayal, then Lia's betrayal. It's been a tough time, hasn't it?'

'Lia didn't betray us.'

'She did. She left. What else do you call that?'

She forces herself to look at Ally. She has to seem normal, like she hasn't figured it out.

'I guess you're right,' she says. Jo glances past Ally to the chest of drawers behind her. That'll be where the bag is. And all the money from the other harvests too. It's probably crammed with cash.

'But it's not Lia that we need to talk about. She made her choice.'

'Then what do you want to talk to me about?'

Ally's eyes are locked on hers and she tells herself not to look at the drawers again.

'We need to talk about Gabe,' Ally says.

She holds Ally's gaze. 'What about him?'

'Your relationship. His treachery. I imagine it's brought up some awful things for you. I can see it, baby. You don't need to hide it.'

'See what?'

'Your fear. It's back.'

Jo tries not blink.

'That's why you swallowed water in your dive last night. I tried to stop you going in because I could already see it all over you. How can you give in to the water when you have so much fear?'

Jo wants to object, her skin growing hot with anger.

'I can see it. And I don't blame you, it's alright. He fooled all of us, but none more than you. How does it make you feel to know it was a game to him? That he never really cared about you?'

He did. He does. 'It feels shit.'

Ally nods. 'Let's go back, baby. To the first time you were betrayed by a man.'

She thinks of Richard, her tutor at art school. That smug expression on his face every time he touched her. The way he'd treated her during sex. At first she'd liked it, being so objectified. Then she didn't but he did and they couldn't go back.

'How did he make you feel?'

It had made her feel so empty.

'Was it your daddy who didn't want you? Who saw you just as an obligation? We want you, J.'

But no, she can't do this. She can't let Ally get in her head again.

'I don't want to talk about this,' she says, her eyes locked on Ally's.

'Gabe is a leech. He's a liar. He lied to you right from the start. He's been laughing at you.'

A knock on the door. Ally doesn't break eye contact.

'Ally? Can you help?' Nika's voice.

Ally's eyes flick away to the door. 'You know, I haven't heard that poor child's voice since she was abandoned here.' She stands. Goes over to the door. Opens it.

'Ally, can you come? Something's happened at the water. Please, can you come?'

'Wait there, J.' Ally looks around the wooden door at Jo, who nods. Ally surveys her. Then she turns away, pulls the door closed, and Jo is left in Ally's room. Alone.

She takes a breath. She doesn't have much time. Not enough to sit. Not enough to take a breath. But still, she breathes. Then she crosses the room and opens the first drawer.

Clothes. That's all that's in there. Clothes. Folded neatly.

She pushes it, it sticks, but then slots back into the dresser. The second drawer. Inside are some books. Some stacked papers and the backpack. Grey with the red zipper. This is it. She'll take it out. Show the money to everyone. They'll see, they have to see. Or at least there will be so much confusion that she'll be able to get someone to help her with Gabe, no one will stop her when she takes him. When she and Nika drive him away from here.

She pulls the zip. Straight away, she can feel it. There's too much give in the fabric. She pulls open the zip and hopes that the answer will be in there. But the bag is empty.

Underneath the bag are white plastic bottles of prescription pills. She picks one up, reads the label: Valium.

That sticky, gooey feeling she'd get when she was in here talking to Ally. She'd drink her tonic and she'd feel so relaxed. She'd thought it was Ally.

No wonder she's been sleeping like a baby.

Shuffles at the door.

'Don't grab my sleeve like that. What are you doing?' Ally's voice.

'No, but one other thing. I just want to show you one other thing.' Nika.

Jo remembers Gabe's glazed eyes last night. And Ally had been driving. It was always Gabe who drove the lorry. She saw him drinking from Ally's silver tin in the car. It must have been a huge dose.

The last drawer. The money has got to be in the last drawer. This is her last chance. Last drawer. Last chance.

She pushes the second drawer closed as the door opens.

Ally stands there, Nika at her side. Her face isn't calm now. Her jaw sets. She's angry.

There's no point in pretending. Jo grabs the handle of the bottom drawer.

'What are you doing?'

She pulls.

'J, stop it.'

The drawer opens with a squeak. There are packets of chips inside. Chocolate wrappers, hundreds of them. The silver foil catching the light. But no money.

'Get out,' Ally says.

Jo jumps to her feet.

'Zay!' Ally calls. 'Dolly!'

'Jo, come out!' Nika yells.

Jo realises it. They will lock her in. Like they did Nika. They'll lock her in the bonds office until she is J again.

She comes up to Ally, stares her right in the eye. Ally's face is all soft maternal concern again.

'Move,' she says.

'Baby—'

'Move!'

Ally's face resets. Cold. She steps aside.

Jo grabs Nika's hand, walks backwards, away from Ally and her stare.

'What's going on?' Zay is there, rubbing his eyes. Ho-jin is behind him. And Dolly from the other side, arms crossed over her chest. Her eyes dart between them.

'Why are you looking at us like that?' she says to Jo.

Valentine and Greta are in the distance too, emerging from the courthouse. Jo pulls Nika a step back.

'She's crazy!' There's no hiding her terror now, her voice is a pitchy quiver.

'What?'

'Ally! She tried to kill Gabe! She's been lying to us all! And she's been hoarding money.'

'What money?' Ally says.

'Did you find it?' Nika whispers, hand holding hers so tight.

'That's why you were ransacking my room?' Ally asks. 'Looking for cash?'

'Has something happened, J?' Dolly asks. 'Do you need money for something?'

'No! No, that's not it.'

Ally looks into her room. Jo sees it, her eyes, flicking around, taking stock, then returning to Jo's. Triumphant. The money was there, somewhere. She didn't find it, but it was there.

Ally turns to the others. 'I haven't wanted to upset you all, to put this nastiness on your shoulders. Jo has been having some real troubles. She's been making threats.'

'No, I—'

'She's been saying she is going to tell everyone about us. Tell the police about the pearls. Put signs up in the back-packers about where we are. She wants to ruin us. She was blackmailing me, asking for cash.'

'Stop lying,' Jo says, her eyes not leaving Ally's face.

'She wants to ruin everything we've built.'

Jo keeps staring at Ally, looking for a crack.

Nika jerks her arm. Jo breaks her gaze from Ally and looks around.

The wild anger in their faces makes her stumble as she takes another step back and they step closer.

'Run,' Nika whispers. 'Run!'

Then Nika's hand unclamps from hers and she runs at Ally, shoulders bent forward, bull like, and shoves her in the middle. Ally slams backwards onto the ground and Nika is running again. Jo springs after her. They run behind Galbraith's.

'Ally, are you okay?'

'Oh my god!'

'Let me help you.'

'I'll help you.'

Nika and Jo zigzag between the buildings.

They sprint out into the desert. Into the endless, flat nothing.

The lorry. They need the lorry if they are going to get out of here. But it's back there, on the other side. They won't reach it. She's already breathless.

'We need to hide,' Nika wheezes. 'They'll be coming.'

Jo looks around. There's nowhere. The single boab tree. Orange earth. Horizon. Baking sun. It gleams off the mother of pearl mosaic on the mounded earth of the grave.

She can already imagine it. Another two mounds on either side. Three maybe, if Gabe isn't helped.

Hide. They need to hide. Now. Behind the tree? There's nowhere else. She grabs Nika's hand, pulls her towards it.

The slit in the trunk. That vertical black mouth. Wide enough for a person to slip through.

'Go.' She pushes Nika in first, through the gap, hopes like hell that it isn't some animal's home. Still. They'd have more of a chance with something wild.

She wriggles after Nika. Takes a step up, foot wobbling. Slots her body in sideways. Flesh squeezing against the opening. Her head to the side, skull scraping. Nika grips her arm, yanks her inside. She falls onto the girl, thwacking into the inner wall of the trunk.

She finds her balance. It's dark in here. A line of light comes through the seam, but aside from that there is only grey shade. Nika is against her chest, her hands gripping Jo's t-shirt.

It's like they are inside the tree's belly. Bumps and ligaments twisting and coagulating around them.

She can't see insects, but she can hear them. Legs brushing together. Clicks. She wraps her arms around Nika, holds her tight until they both get their breath back.

Voices.

'Keep going!'

'They'll be in the bushes!'

'No ... look!'

The sounds of them. The beat of their footsteps. The rumble of their voices. They're getting closer.

Soon, someone is right by them, circling the tree. Jo presses her cheek to the top of Nika's head, looks out into the strip of light. The flash of a red t-shirt. Ho-jin. He was wearing red. The steps circle the tree again and—

His face. Staring into the slit. Sun bouncing from the sweat on his forehead. Unfocused eyes.

He's looking away. She can't tell if he saw them. If from his side it is just a black shadow. Or if he's going back now to tell them.

She hears the crunch of his footsteps slowly grow quieter. The outside is silent. Then, the rev of the engine. The lorry. So he didn't tell.

For the next hour they hear its engine. Getting louder and softer, louder and softer as they hunt for them. Once it is so close she can hear the crunch of its wheels. But it travels away again.

'What are we going to do?' Nika whispers.

'Wait.'

'Wait for what?'

'For them to stop looking for us.'

'And then?'

This little girl is totally dependent on her. She'll do what Jo says. Live or die, both of their lives are on her.

Nika's t-shirt is drenched now. It's hot in the belly of the tree. Airless.

'We need the lorry.'

'They're in it!'

'I know. We'll wait …' She thinks. 'We'll wait for dark. For them to give up, to think we're long gone. Then we'll go and get it.'

'But the keys?'

'They're in the ignition. They never take them out of the ignition.'

'But …'

'I know. But they'll think we're gone. We've got to try.'

'Okay.'

Nika pushes her head into Jo's chest. It's too hot to be holding each other like this. But she won't let the child go. She swallows. If they can't get the lorry they'll be out in the dark again, walking until they find something. Even Lia didn't do that, and she knows this land. What chance would Jo have with this little girl to look after?

Her throat is dry. She had that gulp of water this morning and nothing since. There was water all around her. Next to Gabe's bed, at the kitchen, in Ally's room. And she didn't take it. She swallows again. Gabe. He's alone with them. Something's wrong with him. His heart maybe. They'll just leave him there, in that little cell. They should be going now, running to get help. But she can still hear the engine of the lorry in the distance.

'What's your mum like?' Nika asks.

'What?'

'I was thinking that, even though my mum's dead, I feel like we are so close to her here that she'll protect us. You know?'

'Yeah. I mean—'

'Is that silly?'

'No.'

She squeezes Nika tighter, but then shifts back as much as she can. It's too hot in here to be so close. Something slips between her shoulder blades. She jumps. Bats at it with her hand. It slips down, onto the shadowed ground under them.

'What are you doing?'

'A bug, I think. It went down my back.'

They hear voices. In the distance. Too far away to hear what they are saying. The engine keeps going. Hours pass. They lean into the sides of the tree, feet thrumming numb from their weight. They jiggle from foot to foot. The engine gets softer for a while. And then returns.

'She loved pop music,' Jo says, 'my mum. She loved really cheesy pop music.'

'Like Ariana Grande?'

Jo laughs. 'Yeah. She probably does like Ariana Grande now.'

She sees her mother, laughing in the front seat. Singing in the kitchen. 'She was creative. Really creative. She'd get in these strange moods sometimes where she was so focused on what she was making it was like she was in another world.'

She remembers watching her mum in the darkroom she went to every Saturday. Her mother consumed by her work, the room all pretty and dark with the red lights. Every time she'd pass Jo she'd still pat her on the shoulder, kiss her on the head.

'She loved me,' she said, 'even though I did something terrible.'

'What did you do?'

Jo doesn't want to talk about it, doesn't want to burden this child with something beyond her comprehension.

'Tell me.'

'I … when I was a kid I was jealous of my little brother. It was just my mum and me for so long, I felt like he was taking her away from me.'

'You hurt him?'

'No, no, nothing like that. We used to go out on the boat in the mornings. A storm came and my mum was so distracted by me and my stupid tantrum she got thrown off the boat with Jamie in the carrier … He died.'

'That's horrible.'

'Yeah.'

She expects Nika to recoil from her but instead she wraps her arms around her.

'How old were you?'

'Six, I guess. I went to live with my dad about six months later, when I was seven.'

'You were just a little girl,' Nika says. 'You didn't do it. It was an accident.'

Jo is about to argue, but she stops herself. Just a little girl. Nika herself is so small, and Jo had been years younger that day. She's been carrying the guilt for so long, never understanding it well enough to know whether it was justified. Nika's arms are fragile around her. Jo would never blame her for anything, she's just a little girl.

'I bet your mum still loves you. My yia yia loves me. My papu too. My yia yia always made a halva when we came to visit, even though my mum said I'd never sleep from the sugar. It'd be syrupy and hot, with walnuts on top.'

'We'll call her. First thing when we get out of here. We'll call her.'

'They aren't even that far, they live in Port Hedland. My mum said that we were only five hours' drive away. That's where I was trying to go. When I found you that day you arrived. I thought maybe I'd be able to walk there, but then I saw you and knew I couldn't.'

'Five hours is nothing. With the petrol in the back as well we can make that.'

'We'll go to Yia Yia's house. You can call your mum from there.'

'Yeah,' says Jo.

The line of light changes colour. Turns golden, then grey.

The crickets start. The constant drone. Then the frogs' warbles.

They wait.

'I'm so thirsty,' Nika says.

'I know. Me too. Not long now. It's getting cooler at least.'

She watches Nika. She can see her hair sticking to her neck, to her forehead. The smears of dirt and black dust. She couldn't let anything happen to this kid. She had to get her back, get her to her grandma's house, eating halva. Her heart beating fast only from sugar. Not fear. Having a clean neck and wearing shoes.

The line of light glows on her arm. Her skin used to be fair, now her forearms are covered in freckles and a few pale sun spots. Her English skin doesn't belong here.

She doesn't belong here. Maybe none of them do, except Lia. All these people from other places, outsiders, staking claim to this relic from a past they don't know, stealing from the industry of a town they don't even understand. The wrongness of it hits her. But not just that—the arrogance of it.

Soon the slice of light is gone completely and she can no longer see her skin. They are in darkness, the sounds of insects shifting and clicking around them.

Steadily, she hears the lorry again. Getting closer. Pulling in at Rossack. The engine cuts. The doors open, slam closed.

They've stopped looking. They've given up for the night. Nika's hand finds hers and they clasp them together. Wait some more. The sounds of voices die out as well.

'How much longer?'

'We'll only get one chance, may as well wait until they are definitely asleep.'

'And if the keys aren't there?'

If the keys aren't there they don't stand a chance.

'We'll run. Try to get some water, and then run.'

'Okay.'

After a while, a bird starts singing, its low tune woeful, repetitive.

'I'm scared,' Nika says.

There's no point in lying. 'Me too.'

'What if it's a trap?'

She hadn't even thought of that.

'No. I don't think so. They think we've run off somewhere far away.'

'But if it is?'

The bird keeps singing. Jo is wobbly on her feet, like she might faint. Her tongue is getting stuck on the inside of her mouth.

Another half-hour passes. Or maybe longer. She wonders if her mum does like Ariana Grande. If she is there, somewhere, in St Ives, driving through the rain and humming along to one of her songs. The image creates such aching tenderness, such need, she starts breathing heavily.

'You okay?'

'Yeah. I think we are going to have to do this. Like, now. We can't stay here.'

'Okay.'

'But, god, I kind of do just want to stay here.'

She breathes in again. She can't fall apart now. Nika can't be the one to comfort her.

'Alright. I'm going to go out first. Look for any movement. Okay?'

She can't see Nika's face, but she can imagine what she's thinking. If Jo is taken, Nika may as well be taken too. She won't survive on her own.

'Okay,' she says. So maybe that wasn't what she was thinking.

'Okay.'

Jo holds the gap on either side, steps up to it, then slips into the open. The bird keeps singing. The crickets keep chirping. There's no one around. Rossack is dark.

She puts her hand in and Nika grasps it. She pulls the little girl out next to her. The lorry is there. They can see it.

They start walking, trying to drop their feet as evenly as possible. They are in full sight now. If anyone looks up, they'd see them. If anyone hears their footfalls they're done for, so they can't run. The bird stops singing. They stop too, looking for it. Wherever it is, it's probably looking back. It doesn't start again.

They keep moving, ducked down low, the darkness of Rossack getting closer and closer. At least out here there's nowhere for anyone to spring out from.

The lorry. The moonlight glows from its windscreen. They're close. She's already picturing it: the ignition. Empty. No keys.

They reach Galbraith's. Sidle past. The courthouse. Windows dark. Their feet are crunching, no matter how soft they drop them.

The lorry. She crosses around to the driver's side door. Looks in through the window. There they are. The keys sparkle in the ignition.

She turns to Nika, shoots her a thumbs up. Nika rushes around the other side. They open the car doors, metal-click.

'Don't close it,' she mouths to Nika across the inside of the car. Nika nods. Jo steps inside. Nika steps in on her side. Sits in the passenger seat.

Jo puts her hands on the wheel, fingers humming. She puts her foot on the clutch. The other on the brake. She turns the key. The engine starts. It's a monstrous growl in the silence. She forces the clutch and hits the accelerator.

'Hey!' Zay yells, loud and angry.

She doesn't turn to look, just pushes down, spins the wheel.

'Stop!' Dolly, her voice high and pitchy. 'Get the hell back here, J!'

They fly forward, the doors swinging. She changes gear. Pushes down harder.

'What the fuck are you doing? Come back!' Dolly screeches.

They speed ahead and the doors slam shut with the force of it, blocking out the yells from behind them. They traverse out onto the flat, past the boab tree, across the plains. Forward, quickly forward.

'Is anyone chasing us?'

Nika looks back. 'Yes!'

Jo's eyes flick to the rear-vision mirror. Dolly, Zay, Valentine, Greta and Ho-jin are running after the car, bathed in the red glow of the tail lights. Zay is the fastest, running full pelt, Greta only metres behind him.

'Seatbelt! Quick!'

She waits for the click of Nika's belt then floors it. The engine revs. She shifts gears. She prays they won't stall. They are going too fast for the bumpy track. It's throwing them around in their seats. She hasn't got her belt on but she can't pause. Forward, forward, forward. *Don't stall*, she prays. She can feel the engine under her feet. Feel the droning in her hands. *Don't stall, please don't stall.*

'Still?'

They bound over a dip, keep on going.

'No,' Nika says. 'No! They're gone.'

Jo lets herself exhale but doesn't slow. Her eyes flick to the rear-vision mirror. There is nothing behind them, nothing but the tail lights glowing red on red dirt. There's nothing ahead either, just wide stretches of space.

Then, finally, like a mirage she sees it. A dirt road. The tyres crunch as they slide onto the flat earth. She slows but doesn't stop. They don't talk. Her gaze keeps going to the mirror, but it's only darkness.

Up ahead, at last, a clearing. She turns, and the head-lights bounce off black bitumen now. Black sky and black road. Back where it started on that drive with Denny, driving through blackness into the unknown.

They see something ahead. Buildings. Getting closer, she recognises them. The little general store. She'd biked there. Called Briena from the phone booth.

She slows down.

'Don't stop! There's no one there.'

'The phone booth.'

'We don't have money.'

'You don't need money for emergency calls.'

'You said we'd go to Yia Yia's!'

She swerves into the kerb right by the phone box. Opens her door and jumps onto the road. There's a tap near the wall, made for hoses. She goes over to it, turns it on with a squeak.

'Come on,' she says to Nika, who rushes over to it, puts her head underneath and drinks. Once Nika has gulped some down, Jo puts her head underneath as well, lets the warm water absorb into her throat, feels her headache weaken.

'I want to keep going,' Nika says. 'I don't want to stay so close to her. Please.'

Her face is dirty. She looks like she is going to cry.

'We'll call and then we'll get straight in the car and keep going, alright? But we have to call. For Gabe. And for your mum.'

Nika sniffs, then nods. She puts her head back under the tap.

There are still missing posters stuck to the glass of the phone box. The wet weather has wrinkled them all, blurred the pictures beyond recognition. But there is one paper that's new, white with sharp edges. When Jo picks up the receiver she sees that she recognises the face on it. Blunt fringe, sideways smile. *Josephine Ainsley, missing two months, please help.*

PART FOUR

CHAPTER 37

ST IVES, JANUARY 2019

Charlotte Ainsley used to be a mother. Now she is only mother to a small grave in St Ives cemetery and to a young woman whose face she might not recognise if she passed her in the street.

But something twitches and awakens in her chest when he says it.

'It's Josephine. She's missing.'

'Missing?' she repeats.

'They say they'll find her. That we shouldn't panic.'

The battery sound on her phone bleats at her. The sodding thing didn't last a full hour any more. She goes to stand by the kitchen counter, plugs it into the charger.

'Start from the beginning, Sam. Please. Josephine is missing? In Sydney?

'No, no. She were in some rural place, on a farm.'

'A farm? What on earth was she doing on a farm?'

'Working. Fruit picking.'

'Why?' Charlotte shouts. She knows she shouldn't shout. She wraps the charger cord around her hand and makes a fist. Inside, the maternal instinct wants to lash out, scream and lunge and fight.

'I don't know,' he says.

She swallows. 'How long has she been gone for? What are the police doing about it? Should we be going down there?'

'To Australia?' He laughs. Actually laughs. 'No, no. I don't think so. They say they have it all under control.'

In that laugh she hears the fractured wrist he didn't mention until a year later, the painting that won a school prize that he'd never sent a picture of. She hears that he didn't visit Josephine once when she moved to London.

'Why aren't you worried?' she says. 'Why aren't you panicking?'

An exasperated silence. In it, she hears the man who raised their daughter even though he'd never wanted a child.

He gives her the number for the Broome Police Station. Tells her nothing is stopping her following it up, nothing is stopping her from going to Australia herself if she thinks it's so necessary. As usual, he hangs up first.

Charlotte relies on Sam, who was never meant to be more than a one-night stand, to tell her about their daughter. For the first years, she wasn't allowed to call. And then when she did, she wasn't in a good state. *I'm her mother*, she would slur and he would hang up.

Now, she calls every few months for updates. Josephine had moved to London to go to art school. Josephine loved art school. Josephine was having trouble with art school. Josephine had dropped out and was working at a pub.

For a long time Charlotte had thought about going to the pub. She just wanted to be able to look at her daughter, see what kind of woman she had become. But in the end she'd decided against it. It wasn't fair, not after what she'd done.

And then it was too late. Sam told her that Josephine had moved to Australia, of all places.

Charlotte pulls out the little stepladder she uses for the high shelves and sits fast. It squeaks on the linoleum. She rubs her hands over her face. They stink of developer fluid. Ten minutes ago she'd been in her darkroom watching a photograph of the bay swim into focus. She'd heard the phone ring through the wall. Considered not even answering it.

Maybe she used to be a mother, maybe she wasn't any more. But she can call. The twisting, desperate instinct inside her won't let her do anything else.

She keys in the number for Broome Police.

The phone clicks in confusion a few times, beeps, then starts ringing with a dial tone she has never heard before. A desk sergeant answers, his accent so Australian she's too stunned to speak for a moment. She asks to talk to the contact Sam gave her.

'Oh, nah, he's not here now. I'll tell him to call ya back when he comes in.'

'This is urgent. It's about Josephine Ainsley.' Even in this situation, it feels so good to say, 'I'm her mother.'

'Yeah, but it's three in the mornin'. He'll be asleep.'

'Oh. I see. Alright.'

She leaves her number, asks him to read it back to her twice, and hangs up the phone.

While she's waiting, Charlotte turns on her computer. It's an old brick of a thing, an IBM, she only uses to check her email on Wednesdays. She types *Broome Australia* into the search engine. Red dirt. Orange cliffs. Long, endless horizons. This isn't just rural, it's the Australian outback.

Images come into sharp focus. Josephine, thumb out, on a long stretch of road. A man in hunting gear pulling in to pick her up. Josephine, running, screaming, through peeling gum trees, the man chasing her with a pistol.

Josephine, face white, hobbling through the dirt. A bulging snake bite on her ankle, her veins showing black through her skin.

Josephine, lips cracking, endless space around her. Brain so warped by the sun that she's calling out to her. Calling out for her mother.

The thing inside gnashes its teeth, pulls at its hair.

Broome Australia missing person she types in. She finds the page on the police website. She expects to see Josephine's face straight away and finds herself staring at the black keyboard with its blue light shining through. She hasn't seen her daughter's face in a very long time. She last saw her in person when she was seven years old, although those last months are hard to remember. Sam sent her a picture from the day Josephine had finished primary school. She'd have been twelve and she looked so uncertain in the photograph, so in need of a big tight cuddle, that Charlotte still can't look at it for too long.

Josephine is now twenty-seven.

She looks at the screen. But it isn't Josephine she sees. It's other young faces. An American man in his thirties. A Korean boy, still a teenager. Two Italian women, smiling with their cheeks pressed together. A French-Canadian man in his twenties. All of them young and international and missing within the last few years.

And then, there she is. Josephine Ainsley. And she shouldn't have worried, of course she'd know her face, no matter how much time had passed. Her little Josephine. Those same eyes looking out from under a blunt fringe.

The mother inside her stops screaming. Just stares, awe-struck, at this beautiful young woman. At her own flesh and blood.

The phone rings. She jumps in her seat and runs to catch it, her fingers tingling on the black plastic.

'Hello?' she says. 'This is Charlotte Ainsley.'

A delay and then another Australian accent starts talking. Introducing himself, saying they were doing what they can, that they could keep her number down for updates if she'd like.

'How long has it been since she was last seen?' she asks, cutting him off.

There is a pause, longer than for the delay.

'Other workers on the farm say she left middle of November. Said she was going to go and get the bus. The driver doesn't remember her, but that—'

'Sorry,' she says, 'sorry, did you say November?'

The pause. 'Yes.'

Out through the kitchen window she can see the tree where the Christmas lights had been.

'But …' She is so stunned she can barely speak. 'But it's January.'

He doesn't reply.

'Are you saying no one has seen my little girl in months? That she's been gone all this time and no one has told me?'

He clears his throat. 'Yeah, well, seems like it took a while for anyone to notice. If it weren't for a particularly … persistent friend of hers in Sydney it may not have been discovered at all. Usually we have parents calling in here soon as their kid hasn't checked in.'

'I see.'

'When was the last time you heard from her?'

'It's been …' But then the instinct inside her surfaces, takes control. It's strong, even after all this time. She is still a mother, always was. Her little girl needs her and this time she will step up. 'I'm coming,' she says. 'I'm booking a flight to Australia, I'm going to come and help you find her.'

'Can if you want. Truth is, people round here wander off sometimes. Usually they don't want to be found. But do as you like.'

He tells her that he will keep her informed. To let him know when she's going to arrive. She is barely able to say goodbye. He's hung up and she sits on the stepladder, her phone on her lap, too afraid to even stand.

*

In the week since Charlotte first talked to Broome police she has been busy. She went out and bought a new mobile phone with a long-life battery. She kept it with her everywhere she went. She was like one of the teenagers, checking it every few minutes in case Australia had called.

She'd been in touch with the British Embassy too, tried to get the bureaucrats to stop twiddling their thumbs and do something. She'd gone online and set up a Facebook page. She'd booked her flight to Australia, had Tina's daughter down at the travel agent sort it for her. She'd not left Cornwall before in her life, but she'd do it. For Josephine, she'd do anything. She had an emergency passport ordered.

If there was ever a time she'd go back to the bottle it was then, but she didn't. She wasn't even tempted. She was getting her daughter back.

The day before her flight she got a message on her Facebook from a Marie Debonair. A woman from Quebec. She said her son, Felix, was missing from the same area. They messaged back and forth for a while, and Marie told her all about her son. About how miserable he was after his partner had died, how consumed with worry she had been for him. She told Charlotte about how he'd thought seeing the world might help. A fresh start, a jolt to the system. That was over two years ago now. He'd sent her an email from Kununurra. He'd sounded lonely and alienated. And that was it. She'd never heard from him again.

She'd asked Charlotte when she'd last spoken to her daughter, and Charlotte had said she was so sorry but she had to go. That she'd keep her updated if there was any news. Messaging with Marie had only made her more determined. This wouldn't be her. She would find her girl.

Running on coffee and no sleep, Charlotte had gone to do her final errands before her flight. She was afraid of flying, afraid of those red dirt roads, but she was trying not to think of that. She pulled her magenta puffy jacket on, zipped it up to her chin and went out in the cold. She didn't want to drive. She would do no good to Josephine if she was dead from falling asleep on an icy road. She walked down her porch stairs and the windy road to town. Over the hill she could see the bay, that sparkling water that had taken her son's life. But she had no anger towards it, she hadn't for a long time. Deep sadness that would be there forever, but no anger.

She'd just passed the travel agent when the mobile phone rang. She'd almost dropped it pulling it out of her jacket pocket, her fingers numb from the morning chill.

'Hello?'

'Mrs Ainsley? Hi.'

She recognised the accent straight away, 'My passport's come and I have my tickets. I know you think I should hold tight but—'

'We might have some news,' he said.

She stopped on the pavement. Jeremy, the butcher, bumped into her from behind. 'Sorry, love,' he said and then winked and kept walking.

'We had a phone call. Thought it might have been a prank, if I'm honest. But Mark and Sim went out there and, wowee.'

She takes a steadying breath. 'Have you found her?'

'Well, we aren't sure yet. We found a group living off the grid in one of them old pearlers' towns. They were weird, I'll tell you that. One of them was barely alive but he was pleading with them not to take him to the hospital.'

'Was my daughter there?'

'Dunno yet. The boys had a pretty good look at them all, but they said they wanted to stay and no one else was hurt so they left them be. They are going to take a look at her photo when they get back here.' He paused. 'And there was another thing.'

'Yes?'

'Well, caller said there was a body.'

'What?'

'But they didn't find anything. There was a woman out there, strange, sure, but helpful too, apparently. Told them there'd never been any deaths.'

'Okay. Well.' She's not sure what to say.

'But the boys will be back soon. There were three women around your daughter's age, chances are she's one of them.'

'Call me as soon as you know something, alright?'

'Will do.'

It sounded bizarre, not something that her Josephine would get mixed up with. But then again, how was she to know? She'd go by the church, that's what she would do. She still had seven hours until her flight. She'd go by the church and light a candle that he would call back and Josephine would be one of the ones he had found. She wouldn't think about what he'd said about a body. They hadn't found anything, so that must have been a mix-up.

She pushed her hands into her pockets, her left clamped tight around the phone, and made her way up the footpath to Sacred Heart. She usually only went into the hall for her AA meetings. But now she went into the church, dimly lit and solemn. She slotted a pound coin into the wooden box and lit one of the tea candles. She closed her eyes and said a prayer. That Josephine would be one of those people they found. That the Australian sergeant would call back and say she was safe. They'd found her and she was safe.

Head bowed, Charlotte made her way home. There were other errands she should do before she left. Bills to pay, people to tell, numbers to leave. But she couldn't think of anything.

As she walked up her stairs to her front door, the neighbour's ginger cat wove between her legs. Usually she'd stop to pat him, but she could hear the trill of her landline through the door. She stepped over him and hurried to get her keys out, dropped them, picked them up and ran to the phone, leaving the keys hanging from the keyhole. A second before she reached for it she knew she'd missed it, but she grasped it anyway.

'Hello?'

It was just the dial tone.

She retrieved her keys, closed the door against the aching January chill and called Australia.

'Did you call me?' she asked the sergeant when he picked up. 'I just missed it, sorry.'

'Nah,' he said, 'wasn't me.'

'Oh. Well, is there any news?'

'Yeah.' He paused. It was the most hideous of pauses. 'I was going to call you anyway. She wasn't there. Mark and Sim are sure. I'm sorry, I shouldn'ta got your hopes up.'

She couldn't speak.

'I'm sorry,' he said again.

'It's okay. I'll see you soon,' she said and hung up the phone.

Charlotte stood in the kitchen. It was like she was being punished. Always, she was being punished.

The phone started ringing again. The Australian sergeant calling probably, telling her not to come. To sit tight. As if that was even an option. She answered it.

'Hello?'

There was just silence. Long, crackling silence.

'Hello? This is Charlotte Ainsley speaking.'

A breath, and already she knew. She could tell, just in that breath.

'Mum?'

'Josephine?'

'Mum. Erm ... yeah. It's me. I ... I'm in Port Hedland. In Australia. I ... erm ...'

She could hear another little breath. Her daughter was trying not to cry.

'You just wait there, my love. Wait there, my darling. I'm coming. I'm going to come and get you and bring you home, okay?'

A long pause and then, 'Okay.'

CHAPTER 38

JUNE 2019

The boat creaks in the warm June breeze. A seagull squawks overhead. It is dawn, the sky of the bay peachy-warm. Her mother snaps a photo.

'That's a winner,' Jo says.

'We'll see.'

Jo pulls her knitted jumper around herself and continues sketching. The lines of the cove, the little changing boxes, the inn where her mother used to work. It is mid-summer in St Ives, but there is still that English chill to the air.

Her mother looks into the lens of her camera, adjusting the focus.

'You know today is the due date. Or it would have been,' Jo says. She hadn't meant to bring it up. She will mention it to her counsellor, that's why she'd booked the appointment for today. But she hadn't intended to bring it up to her mum. Especially not here.

Her mum pulls away from the lens to look at her. It is still strange to see her. Jo has been living with her in St Ives for four months now, but still isn't used to her. When Charlotte had pulled up in the taxi at Nika's grandparents' house in Port Hedland, she and Nika had peered at her through a gap in the curtain in Nika's bedroom.

'That's your mum?' Nika had said.

'Yep,' Jo had answered. It was her mum, not dressed at all for the weather in a jumper, jeans and boots. Her hair still dark, but now cut shorter, with grey shot through it. Charlotte had put her suitcase on the footpath and glanced at the window, right at them. Jo had been shocked at how old she'd become. She'd been thinking she would look the same as she had when they'd last seen each other.

Nika said, 'She looks like you.'

Now, Charlotte squeezes her shoulder. She was still hesitant in the way she touched Jo, careful, like Jo might break. Or pull away.

'Today might be a hard day,' she says.

'Maybe,' Jo says, and goes back to her drawing. Charlotte goes back to her camera. She turns it around, onto Jo, and snaps her photo.

'I wasn't ready,' Jo says, looking up.

But her mother just smiles at the image she's captured.

Coming out on the water at dawn has become one of their traditions. When Jo first came back, her insomnia returned. She would lay awake playing what happened over and over in her head. She would hear the soft tinkle of her mother's alarm, the sounds of her getting out of bed, shuffling around, trying to be quiet. Jo would clamber out of bed, dress quickly. She didn't want her mother to leave without her. She was scared to be alone in the house. Now, she manages to sleep at least four or five hours a night. Sometimes more. Now, she comes because she likes it out there. This quiet time when it's just the two of them and the ocean.

When people begin to come out for work, they pull the boat in. Charlotte packs her equipment and ties the boat up while Jo calls Nika. She calls her at least twice a week. It used to be more, almost every day.

'Morning,' she says.

'Goodnight,' Nika says.

'How are you?'

A shuffle of sheets, and then, whispered, 'They've been having talks. Quiet ones they don't think I can hear, but Papu is deaf so he's not great at whispering.'

'About you going back to school?'

'No. I heard … her name.'

Ally. Nika never liked to say it. 'What did they say?'

'Nothing that made any sense.'

Jo and Nika had spoken to the police many times in Port Hedland, but they'd never found Larissa's body. Ally must have moved it. It's horrible to think of them digging up that grave under the boab tree.

Ally had sweet-talked the police, it seemed. Told them that same story, that Nika had been abandoned, they weren't doing anything illegal living off the grid. The police didn't find any money either, or any pearls.

'Well—' Jo thinks, '—it's natural they might talk about her. Maybe they are going to the cops again. Trying to get them to do another search.'

'Maybe,' Nika breathes, then in her normal voice she says, 'Countdown time. Only two weeks.'

Nika has been dreading going back to school. Jo encourages her, but she worries too. She's missed so much, but doesn't want to have to repeat a year.

'Really?'

'Yeah.'

'Still scared?'

Nika thinks about it. 'I guess so. But also ... maybe back to normal will be good.'

'Maybe,' Jo says.

'I've read every book in the house and they are terrified of me going out alone but it takes both of them about a million years to walk to the library.'

'And other kids? That's good, right?'

'Dunno.'

'Don't know?'

'What if no one likes me?'

'I like you.'

'Yeah, but maybe that's weird. You're my best friend and you are like thirty and live on the other side of the world.'

'I'm not thirty!' Jo says. 'Not quite yet.'

They chat for a while until she can hear in Nika's voice that she is sleepy and then she says good morning again and Nika says goodnight, and she promises she will call again in a few days.

She meets her mum at the little coffee shop up the hill. It's tiny, a few chairs squashed inside, and every so often they'll have to move out of the way so the kayakers can retrieve the oar on the wall that she'd first thought was décor.

'Morning, Josephine,' Kyle says, and starts making her coffee.

'Morning.' She smiles and slots in next to her mum. Everyone knows her mother in St Ives and so everyone knows her as well. People she would never have recognised have come up to hug her in the street, tell her with teary eyes how grown up she is.

'You've got class this afternoon, right?' her mother asks.

She nods. She's started teaching art classes at the nursing home. It was voluntary to begin with, once a week, something to distract her. But she got on so well with everyone that they asked her if she could be permanent. Turns out old ladies like still life and realism as much as she does.

She's going to start her trivia nights again as well. Her mother's put in a good word for her at the Sloop Inn. Between the two things it's not a lot of work, not a lot of money, but it's enough to live on. She finds she'll walk down the street now and nod hello to the people she passes and she'll get into a chat with someone at the grocery store and she'll realise she hasn't even thought of any of it for hours. Or she'll be teaching a class, and watching the way a woman in her eighties sees light in such a different way to her, and a whole afternoon will go by.

'Here you go,' Kyle says, putting down the mug of steaming coffee.

Her mum holds up her own mug. It's got a thick brown glaze on the outside and glossed clear inside so you can see the grain of the clay.

'You know, George's daughter makes these, just around on Higher Stennack. She does courses too, shows people how to throw, get their hands dirty, make things.'

Jo smiles. 'I'm fine. You don't need to keep finding things for me to do.'

Charlotte puts the mug down. 'Just think it might be good for you.'

Jo puts her hand on top of her mum's soft wrinkled one. 'Honestly, Mum. I'm okay.'

Charlotte's eyes gloss and she looks away. 'Okay.'

*

'You don't have to be okay,' the counsellor tells her later.

Jo has found she likes the counsellor's office. At first its seaside kitsch jarred her. The starfishes above the coat hooks, the shell-adorned tissue boxes, the big painting of dolphins swimming above the counsellor's chair. It wasn't just that. Sitting in the chair with someone trying to pry into her brain felt all too familiar. Although her counsellor, Diti, is nothing like Ally. She is a straight-talking Pakistani woman. There are no mind games. She'll call Jo out straight away if she thinks she isn't being honest.

'I know,' Jo says now, 'but maybe I am okay, you know? I've somehow managed to build a life here.'

'How are you sleeping this week?'

'I'm doing what you said. Not staying in bed if I can't sleep. I've been getting up. Reading. Painting too. I've been painting Mum's old candlesticks, the dried flowers in the kitchen. Whatever I can get my hands on.'

She'd thought maybe she wouldn't remember how, but by the time she'd poured out the linseed oil and solvent into little jars her hands automatically began mixing the colours she needed. She was playing, not attempting to get things exact. Last night she'd tried putting white over black before it was dried. By this morning, the paint was drying into cracks and speckles, but she liked the way it looked.

'Are you enjoying it?'

Jo shrugs, although the answer is yes. 'When I do sleep I don't have nightmares much. And for once in my life I feel … centred. I don't feel like I'm looking for something.'

Diti nods. 'Do you still think about them?'

She does, of course, but less so. For a long time, she worried about them. About how they'd survive without the lorry. About Gabe. She knew he'd go back as soon as the hospital released him. Worse, when things were hard here, she'd sometimes think of it to calm her. How it felt to be inside the ocean. The warm rocks pressed against her skin. Some wretched part of her wishes she'd never left.

'Don't you think it's time to move on?' Jo says now. 'Put all of it in the past?'

Diti leans forward. 'You know what I think. You keep trying to push a football under water. No matter how much energy you put in—'

'I know.' Jo's heard her say this before. 'It'll just keep bobbing back to the surface and you only tire yourself out. But what do you mean? That I should keep going over it all again and again?'

'I mean you need to take the air out. I wouldn't say it's time to move on. I think it's time to heal.'

'Sit around and wait to feel better?'

Diti smiles and looks at her. 'What do you think?'

Jo looks out the window at the undulating ocean in the distance. How different it is under the mild English sun.

'You know, there was one thing Ally said that kind of haunted me more than anything, because she was so right. She said that I've spent my whole life running away.'

'Do you think that's true?'

'I guess so.'

'From what you've told me, you had solid reasons to leave the places you left.'

'Maybe. I don't know.'

'Running is one way to see it. But another is searching ... seeking. It seemed like you were looking for something.'

Jo hadn't thought of it that way. There was a big difference between running away and looking forward.

'All this time ... I've just been looking to find a home and now ... I don't know, now that I'm back with Mum here, it sort of feels better. It feels right in a really deep, core way, but also ... I have so many questions, you know? So many things that I thought I could live without knowing the answers to.'

'But now you're not so sure?'

For once Jo lets the question hover, unanswered. And they stare out the window in silence until the time is up.

*

Later, as Jo is holding a woman's hand that is shaking with Parkinson's, helping her hold her brush steady as she applies Winsor Green across the canvas on her easel, she starts to wonder what the time is in Australia.

*

Jo is in her mum's backyard. She's too nervous to sit on the step. The light of the day is fast dimming. She takes a breath, then makes the first call.

'Hello?' Eric's voice sounds just the same.

'Hi. It's, erm ... it's Jo.'

'Oh. Oh, wow. Okay, hi. How are you?'

Jo laughs. 'This is weird, I know. I was going to text you first, organise a time to call. You know, get in touch in order to get in touch. You know what I mean?'

'Yeah, yeah. I sent five emails yesterday organising a time to do a ten-minute call with someone at Melbourne Uni, it was just stupid. We aren't even in different time zones.'

'Melbourne Uni? Are you moving?'

'Yeah,' he breathes. 'Yeah, well, we'll see. They might be offering me a senior lecturer role, so ...'

'So you finished your PhD? You're a doctor now?'

'Yeah.'

'That's fantastic. Congratulations.'

'Yeah, well. Doctor of *The X-Files*, not sure if that means much. But ...'

'Maybe you'll get upgrades now. When you fly.'

'That's the plan.'

'It's about eight am there, right?'

'Yeah,' he says, and she can picture him. Sitting on their tiny balcony, drinking a black coffee and rolling his first cigarette. That slight hunch to his thin shoulders.

She can't imagine that she'd ever sat there by him, a world away.

'I'm glad you called, actually,' Eric says. 'Briena went crazy when they couldn't find you. I have to say she spooked me a bit. I was worried.'

'Yeah. I'm going to call her too. I feel pretty terrible for making her freak out so much.'

'Are you okay now?'

'I'm, well, you know, getting there.'

'I was worried it was because of what happened with us. You know, not getting married and stuff.'

'No,' she says. 'No, it wasn't that.'

'Thank god.'

'Yeah,' she says and sits on the step.

They talk for a little longer, about his new job mostly, and she finds that by the end of the call she's just bored.

*

'Hi, it's Jo,' she says, 'Jo from the farm.'

'Jo? Oh shit.' Sorcha starts laughing and Jo can't help but laugh too. She'd looked for Elias's number first, then Yan's. But it was only Sorcha's she could find, through her LinkedIn profile.

'I'm still in bed, got absolutely blootered last night, and now you call. Jesus.' Jo hears a shuffle, then, 'So I take it from the area code you're back in England?'

'Few months now. And you're still in Australia?'

'Worked hard enough for it, we thought we should stay the rest of our time. Then we're going to Dublin. Yan's going to come with me.'

'You're still together?'

'She left for work about half an hour ago. If you'd called a bit earlier you could have caught her.'

'Did you keep travelling in the end?'

'For a bit. Went down the coast of WA. Ended up in Fremantle. We like it here.'

'That's nice. Something good to come out of that place.'

Sorcha laughs again, dry this time. 'Crazy to think they're still there, isn't it? That psycho kid. What was his name? I can't even remember.'

'Tyson.'

'Oh, yeah. That snake, when it reared up like that? Just about pissed myself.'

Sorcha laughs, but Jo doesn't. She remembers the way Tyson had tried so hard not to cry that night, how his face had looked in the moonlight.

'Have you heard from Elias?' she asks.

Sorcha stops laughing. 'We're in touch here and there. He's okay. Back in Germany now, doing long distance with Emma. She's talking about moving over there but I don't know.'

'And his … you know, his hair?'

'Reattached it. His hair doesn't grow quite as thick there and he's got a fecker of a scar. Now he can tell his own scar story, unlike Denny's bollocks.'

'That's amazing.'

'Sure is.'

Jo tries to think of what else there is to say. It was Elias that she really wanted to know about.

'You know, when you disappeared and the cops called us later, god, both me and Yan felt so guilty. We should never have let you walk off like that. We should have made sure you were okay.'

'It's okay,' she says. 'Let me know if you're even in this part of the world. We'll have a beer.'

'Oh gawd, don't mention alcohol,' Sorcha says. 'But yes. That would be quite a night.'

When Jo hangs up she stares at the phone until the screen goes black.

She wishes she could find out about the others at Rossack. She knows Lia would have never gone back. She'd be in Broome, and Jo imagines her at the beach with those boys they'd seen from the car that day. Maybe surfing, a wetsuit on.

The rest of them would still be at Rossack. Dolly, Zay, Ho-jin. Gabe. They'd still be there. Doing what they always did, living by the rhythms of the sun.

She only has Briena left to call. She steels herself. She should have called months ago. When Briena answers, Jo launches into it, explaining how messed up she was but that it's no excuse, she should never have gone off without getting in touch. She doesn't mention Rossack.

'It's okay,' Briena says, 'seriously, I was just happy when you turned up alright.'

'Well, I am sorry. You were a great friend. Thank you.'

'You're right, I am a great friend. And it was interesting actually, getting a different perspective on the police process. Victim advocacy and all that. I've been writing an essay on it. My professor thinks I could probably get it published in the law review, so really I should be thanking you.'

Jo snorts a laugh. 'So, how is school going? You've got, what, a year or so left, right?'

'Semester break now,' she says, 'only six months in the classroom after that, so that's pretty exciting. And I'm head and shoulders above all these twenty-two-year-old trust-fund kids who seem to cry every time we get an assignment. I mean, what? They thought law school would be easy?'

'So you're on holiday now?'

'Yep, if you call full time at the café a holiday. I'm just on break, sitting in the alley around the back. Got my head-phones in and about to attempt to eat a stale panini. It's bliss, really, you're missing out.'

'Still listening to your true crime podcasts?'

'Oh my god, yes, you interrupted a juicy one.'

'Yeah?'

'It's called *Lustre*, something to do with the way some people reflect light back at you or whatever, and pearls.'

Jo stops. 'Pearls?'

'Yeah. It's not as bloody as I usually go for—you'd be proud of me.'

'How is it crime, if it's about pearls?'

'You should listen to it, it's a really good one. This journalist, American guy, he goes undercover at this weird cult, and he gets completely indoctrinated. He totally falls for it, gets completely sucked in. They're stealing pearls from this fancy-as-shit pearl farm, that's how they live. They do all this diving stuff, which seems kind of crazy to me. I had to google it.'

'Google what?'

'Free diving. Anyway, so you're in England now? How is that going?'

Jo stands, starts pacing the backyard. 'It's fine. Good. What's the name of the guy who made the podcast?'

'His name? It's on the tip of my tongue. I know that as soon as I stop thinking about it I'll remember.'

'Gabe? Gabriel?'

'Um … nah, I don't think that was it. His voice sounds like he'd be hot though. He's searching for this girl, called Jay or something, who was there with him and basically saved his life. Pretty romantic. He's, like, trying to get justice or something. They've arrested the leader now as well. This woman who was this rich psychiatrist but lost all her money in malpractice suits. The cops got pressured into doing this raid and they found, like, hundreds of thousands of dollars in her couch cushions, isn't that crazy?'

'Crazy.'

'Apparently there's a body buried there too but they can't find it, even though the cops were told about it months back but ... Hang on, Jo. Yeah?' Briena starts talking to some-one, then she says, 'Sorry, I've got to go. Table of ten has just walked in. Talk soon, alright?'

'Yes, definitely.'

The line goes dead and Jo tucks the phone into her pocket. It's starting to get dark now. Inside the house her mother is making dinner. She stands out in the yard watching the warm golden rooms. Then her mum looks up. Their eyes meet. She puts down the spoon. Comes over and opens the back door.

'Did it go okay?' she asks, looking at her from the step.

'Yes,' Jo says, 'yes, it went great.'

'You're smiling.'

'Am I?' she says, but she knows she was.

They grin at one another, then Jo follows her mum inside their house.

ACKNOWLEDGEMENTS

This book is both the hardest and most rewarding novel I've written. Thank you so much to all the people who helped me persist. Stephanie Rostan, my wonderful agent, I feel like the luckiest author alive to have you in my corner. You made this novel what it is. Thank you.

To HQ Head of Publishing and editor extraordinaire Jo Mackay, thank you so much for helping me wrangle this story into shape. Thank you to Annabel Blay and Kylie Mason for being able to see the trees when I couldn't even see the forest any more. Thank you to Christine Armstrong for this stunner of a cover, and Natika Palka and Jo Munroe for advocating for me.

The first spark of this book came when I was visiting Rubibi/Broome, the land and waters of the Yawuru people. I was fortunate enough to be able to return to this beautiful place again four years later to finish the book. I met some incredible people there. Thank you to Allegra Mee for inviting me in the first place. Thank you to Julie Weguelin for showing me your mango farm and answering all my highly specific harvest questions. Thank you to Wade at the Malcolm Douglas Crocodile Park for walking me through a death roll. Thank you to Rachel Bin Salleh from Magabala Books for being so generous with your time and making me feel so welcome.

Thank you to all the eighty-eight day agricultural workers who told me your stories.

So many people gave me such wonderful feedback on the early stages of this book. Thank you to Alison Hutton, to Georgia Frances King, to Laura Elizabeth Woollett, to Katherine Brabon, to Claire Stone and Jemma van Loenen and Rebecca Miller. Thank you to my muse Lucy Roleff— watching your paintings come to life every day is magic.

Most of all, I owe a huge debt to my friends and family who listened to me talk for years about pearls and mangoes and false memories and the mammalian dive reflex. To my beautiful friends Lou James, Phoebe Baker, Tegan Crowley and Beth Wilkinson, you nourish my heart and soul. Especially to Roz Campbell, Jacqui Shelton and Isobel Hutton who also read the full manuscript in different stages and encouraged me to continue. Martina Hoffman, in particular, who gave me unending support as well as a few kicks in the butt when I needed them. Thank you to David and Tess for cheering me on from the other side of the globe.

Thank you to the endless (really endless!) support of my mum and dad, and my sister Amy. I am beyond lucky to belong to a family full of such kindness, generosity and creativity.

And, of course, to the two loves of my life: Ryan and Sadie.

Connect with Anna on Instagram @snoekstra

talk about it

Let's talk about books.

Join the conversation:

 facebook.com/harlequinaustralia

 @harlequinaus

 @harlequinaus

harpercollins.com.au/hq

If you love reading and want to know about our
authors and titles, then let's talk about it.